Praise for *Traveling*

"Thalasinos's sophomore novel beautifu... ....
resonances of broken hearts and disappointed dreams."
                                              —*Kirkus Reviews*

"Thalasinos's unerring interpretation of the importance of the
human-animal connection makes this a solid addition to the 'follow your heart and finally set yourself free' category of feel-good
fiction."   —*Booklist*

Praise for *An Echo Through the Snow*

"Destined to become a classic."
                    —Susan Wilson, *New York Times* bestselling
                                     author of *One Good Dog*

"Powerful debut . . . stark, gorgeous prose and a timeless story of
love realized, lessons learned, and paths taken."
                                      —*Booklist* (starred review)

"Beautifully drawn and emotionally resonant." —*Kirkus Reviews*

"A historic, inspiring, and uplifting race to the finish."
                                              —*Modern Dog*

"Delicate and vivid . . . an elaborate weaving of past and present."
                —Michelle Diener, author of *In a Treacherous Court*

"Compelling and evocative."
                    —Patricia McConnell, Ph.D., author of
                                 The Other End of the Leash

FORGE BOOKS BY ANDREA THALASINOS

An Echo Through the Snow

Traveling Light

TRAVELING LIGHT

Andrea Thalasinos

A TOM DOHERTY ASSOCIATES BOOK
NEW YORK

TRAVELING LIGHT

A Forge Book
Published by Tom Doherty Associates, LLC
175 Fifth Avenue
New York, NY 10010

www.tor-forge.com

Forge® is a registered trademark of Tom Doherty Associates, LLC.

The Library of Congress Cataloging-in-Publication Data is available upon request

ISBN 978-0-7653-3302-5 (hardcover)
ISBN 978-0-7653-3778-8 (trade paperback)
ISBN 978-1-4299-6655-9 (e-book)

Forge books may be purchased for educational, business,
or promotional use. For information on bulk purchases, please contact
Macmillan Corporate and Premium Sales Department at 1-800-221-7945,
extension 5442, or write specialmarkets@macmillan.com.

First Edition: July 2013
First Trade Paperback Edition: February 2014

Printed in the United States of America

0 9 8 7 6 5 4 3 2 1

For Marge Gibson, director of Raptor Education Group, Inc.,
and to wildlife rehabilitators everywhere, who tirelessly
and with untold devotion strive to make
this world a softer, better place

TRAVELING LIGHT

IN THE BEGINNING

You can never step in the same river twice.
—HERACLITUS OF EPHESUS, 535–475 BC

As a baby Paula Makaikis had trouble digesting milk products. She'd scream and double up with stomach cramps, kicking and drawing up her little fat-ringed legs in agony.

"Nothing stayed in this one for long." Eleni pointed her chin toward her daughter, launching into the story for the millionth time—usually on someone or another's Name Day. Paula and her two younger balding cousins (more hair on their chests than heads, clashing colognes) were trapped behind the dinner table against the wall. One cousin walked with a slight limp after having had his legs broken years ago by the mob; the other had served time as a juvenile for holding up a liquor store at gunpoint. A photograph of their three dead fathers hung overhead.

The two baldies traded insults, showing off to the blond *kseni,* or outsider, girlfriends, who sat on either side of Eleni across the table. Each cousin was the spitting image of his father and seemingly oblivious that only a few years separated him from the age of their passings, thirty-five years ago, when a New York City clerk typed the names of Alex and Demos on the Certificates of Death.

Eleni paused and her two nephews nodded attentively. A cue they were with her. Both were too afraid of the older woman not to pretend they weren't hearing the story for the first time.

"Uchooooo." Eleni turned to Paula before she proceeded. "Too bad your husband's not here to listen." She then explained to the cousins, "Roger's a scientist; always busy doing experiments," her eyebrows closed in on her hairline as she nodded her head slowly before continuing on with her story.

"All the way from the subway steps on Union Turnpike," Eleni continued, "*my husband* could hear that girl crying." Eleni always spoke of Paula's father that way, as if no one remembered him or she was especially proud of having been someone's wife.

She clicked her tongue and shook her head, fanning her décolleté with a white paper napkin blotched with lamb juice, folded accordion-style into a fan. The memory is too much. Her dyed red hair, though at one time chic, makes her skin seem sallow; nappy and thin, it smells of cheap hair spray and old-lady sweat. Though to her credit, at eighty, Eleni's cleavage—though crepey from sun damage—is still ample enough to cloister a thick gold chain jangling with Vassili's wedding ring, a tiny blue evil eye, an Eastern Cross, and a round gold image of the Parthenon.

"*My husband*"—she paused to look up at the family portrait like it's an icon of Jesus—"complains, when he leaves, Paula's crying, he comes home that girl's *still* crying." Eleni mimics his facial expressions.

So different were those three brothers. In the old photograph, Vassili's expression was defiant and cocky as ever. Demos looked frightened, as if a ghost was standing behind the camera. Alexandros the youngest brother's face was blank. Perhaps his hope had the good sense to evaporate the day he stepped off their ancestral island in the eastern Aegean and headed toward the New World.

"'*Po, po, po, po, po*—that's it!' he'd holler," the elderly woman went on. "'I'm going back to work another shift with Demos.' Then *my husband* would turn around to walk back to the subway."

Eleni's bird eyes pecked at Paula, who listened, fingering the fold-over clasp on her antique Victorian bracelet with the pink topaz stones. There was always something hanging around her wrist to monkey with. Her mother recognizes it as a ploy to avoid eye contact, though Eleni never lets on that she knows.

And after hearing the same story for fifty years, Paula's learned. Patience borne from the understanding that her mother needs to tell it more than anyone wants to hear it. With each successive telling new wrinkles and sags devolve Paula's mother's face, though Eleni's still a handsome woman. Vassili's bride—now a widow for more than forty years, who never gives the slightest inkling of being sad.

"No amount of singing or rocking soothed that girl." Eleni dipped her chin, her eyes looking across the table at her daughter. "Only loading her up on the front seat of the 1962 red and white Oldsmobile we co-owned with both your fathers, remember that car?"

Eleni waits. They all nod.

Vassili and Demos had been waiters; Alexandros was a janitor. Sixty years later Eleni still works for the same furrier, hand-sewing raw fur pelts together into coats and jackets. A slight hump has formed between her shoulders after decades of stooping over a wooden worktable nine hours a day creating garments she neither wants nor can afford.

For Vassili and Demos, twenty years of running up and down cement steps shouldering heavy trays of food from a basement kitchen blew out their knees. Their hearts quit by forty-two. Alexandros, after decades of sweeping and tending to a taciturn boiler in a large office building, made it to forty-six. For all of Vassili's swaggering, his *xhethia* too big for underwear Eleni would allege after a few glass of Metaxa, often replete with a demonstration, "youda thought a man like that would live forever."

"You know what calmed that girl down?" Paula's mother asked.

Their eyes widen.

"Driving up and down Union Turnpike." She looked at them, excited as if seeing the whole scene unfolding once again.

"And *boom!*" Eleni clapped her hands, startling the *kseni* who hadn't seen it coming. "That girl was out like a light." As her eyes rested on Paula, Eleni leaned back, causing the rickety wooden chair to squeak. "And then that girl's face was the most peaceful little thing in the world." The old woman's black eyes gleamed.

Paula looked up at her mother.

And so it was when Paula's ten-year marriage dissolved, boom. Ten years. The last bloom of her youth spent sleeping on the downstairs couch. Clutching the cool flesh of her arms, confused and ashamed that Roger, her husband, didn't long for her in the way she did for him. Too embarrassed to let anyone know that he slept upstairs alone—ears plugged, door dead-bolted, the bedroom filled from floor to ceiling with boxes. Piles covered the side of a bed that by marital right should have been hers. But no marriage was perfect, she'd reasoned.

Excuses had peppered their life together until one quiet morning a phone call from Celeste, Paula's best friend, changed things forever. *Boom*—just like Eleni crashing her hands together. Paula woke up.

She would awaken from a decade-long slumber along the banks of the river Lethe, the river of forgetfulness, one of five rivers of the underworld in Greek mythology. Whoever drank of the river's irresistibly pure, blue crystal waters would grow drowsy and forget who they were.

And maybe that's why, even today, Eleni speculates that perhaps her daughter's early cocktail for tranquility was what triggered Paula to embark on the longest drive of her life.

CHAPTER 1

It had started out as one of the last quiet days of August. Down on West 4th Street overlooking Washington Square Park, Paula Makaikis worked as director of the Center for Immigrant Studies at NYU. The maples were beginning to singe red and orange; it was the twilight in between seasons right before the start of the new semester, when autumn surprises everyone with the first few mornings of chilly, fresh air.

Paula was struggling to relax by sneaking a cigarette. She stared out the office window, blowing smoke out the sullied bluish-black edge of the window screen.

While relieved the staff was gone for an early birthday lunch, the sting of their backhanded invitation still lingered. They'd gone to the Thai place everyone raved about. Paula likened the food to the detritus one clears from a kitchen sink.

"Paula?" Guillermo, the associate director, had asked. "You will join us, no?" He'd smirked and stepped back, folding his arms and shaking his sandy-colored pin curls. This was the man she'd called in every favor to hire, despite allegations he was a prima donna and intellectual lightweight. They'd believed he was banking on the legacy of his great-granddad who'd been assassinated, a leftist president from some Latin American country. The associate director's smirk also triggered a dimple that he knew to strategically turn toward the young grad assistants, through whom Paula guessed he was working his way. A shaft of sunlight had broken through autumn's early rain cloud, backlighting Guillermo's hair as if he stood center stage in *Jesus Christ Superstar*.

"Paula-a-a?" Guillermo drew out her name.

The staff cringed, hoping she'd say no. She felt it. No one thinks the boss has feelings. Her chest ached for a cigarette; and while she hated smoking, the road to destruction was paved with comfort.

"Thanks but . . ." She'd gestured toward her computer screen. A half-written copy block for the Web page announced the daily schedule for October's Conference on the Seven Stages of Immigrant Adaptation. "I'm hoping to tie up more loose ends." *Yeah, right, keep hoping,* she thought.

Several of her staff harbored resentment over last month's trip to Greece. This was the first time Paula had accompanied her mother on the annual weeklong trip. At eighty, traveling alone had become too difficult for Eleni; and, at the last minute, Paula agreed to help. Though she'd been back nearly a month, the staff still avoided eye contact—like she'd been hobnobbing on Scorpios with Onassis instead of cooped up in the mothball-smelling apartments of Eleni's ninety-year-old first cousins. "*Christos kai Panayia,* may that be it," Eleni had pronounced in the cab on the way back to the Athens airport. "What pushy people, eh?" She'd looked to her daughter for confirmation, but Paula was watching a handsome young man cup his girlfriend's ass. Paula sighed; were it possible to die of aggravation, she'd have been riding back to JFK in cargo.

The conference schedule should have been finalized in April. Complaints were streaming into the Dean's office. People carped to Christoff about mismanagement and having to make last-minute hotel and airline reservations. Yet despite the hullabaloo, Paula was preoccupied with the male cardinal that had landed on her window ledge.

Paula sighed, her cigarette a long line of white ash. She was sharp-tongued and sad eyed, with wild dark hair that no amount of expensive hair product would tame. Her eyes were light amber, a color that no one could recall having seen in either side of the family, that clashed with her drab olive complexion.

Three narrow silver Victorian bangles pinged together quietly like little bells as she pressed her stomach with her hand. Her gut churned. Early that morning she'd polished off yesterday's half-eaten Egg McMuffin she'd tucked behind the computer monitor. Though its crinkly wrapper smelled of her cigarettes, the muffin felt fresh. As for the egg and Canadian bacon, in an office kept so frigid they wore sweaters year-round, she took her chances. The birds had scarfed up the crumbled bits of muffin she'd placed out onto the stone ledge. At one time she'd kept a bag of birdseed tucked beneath her desk, but the janitor left a note about it being a rat magnet.

Every day she set something out. Usually sparrows and chickadees gathered, with an occasional visit from an overly empowered blue jay. Pigeons avoided the ledge for some reason, and she was grateful to be spared the criticism of feeding "flying rats." Birds would swoon as they'd land and peck at one another before looking questioningly at her through the glass. Their tan and brown feathers wove into perfect herringbone patterns where their wings met. Then they'd burst off in unison, like they'd been summoned.

Her window ledge was a regular stop on the circuit. It was relaxing to watch, reminding her of the years she spent between high school and college working in a pet store on Union Turnpike in Queens. Those were the most meaningful years she'd spent working anywhere, explaining to people how to care for their pets, finding homes for the animals—an event always tinged with sadness, but also happiness. Despite all the personal turbulence of her early years, days spent handling birds, guinea pigs, snakes and a mean-spirited chinchilla named Chilly were some of her most enjoyable ones.

During long staff meetings she'd excuse herself to dash downstairs to the basement vending machines. Repeatedly inserting a wrinkled dollar bill, she'd impose her will onto the electronic sensor until it caved. She'd get a Pop-Tart to crumble into small pieces for the birds, lest they think she'd abandoned them.

Guillermo would sometimes glance from his desk, watching as

Paula spread crumbs. She could feel him watching. "Ella poula-kia," she'd murmur to them in Greek. How pathetic she looked. The whole staff found the devotion odd, yet glimpses of their boss's loneliness were too raw to make fun of. Everything else was fair game—the bird-feeding, brilliant, dowdy director who had donned princess jewels and was obsessed with hair-straightening product. She'd given them a lot of material.

So far she'd frittered away the entire morning bird-watching, stalking and swatting flies instead of returning her e-mail. Then the Dean called.

"Paula. What the hell is up?" Christoff slowly enunciated each word. "For God sakes people are calling; they need to know if they're presenting; you haven't returned e-mails in weeks." It was a mouthful and she heard him pausing to lick his lips, as they typically dried out during confrontation. "Is . . . everything all right . . . at home?"

It took her by surprise. She'd anticipated a collegial nudge but not a probing. There'd always been special warmth between them since it was twelve Junes ago in Christoff's living room that she'd been introduced to Roger.

"Take the work home—get a bottle of wine," Christoff instructed. "Go through the papers and decide. There you can smoke yourself to death." Six months ago she'd have eaten her own entrails to avoid this conversation.

Funny how no one complained about smoking at department parties when everyone was drunk and puffing away, trading sly looks, being so clandestinely dangerous. Cool like Che Guevara. Paula had grown up to Eleni walking around, lips pursed, gripping a cigarette, farting as she explained how smoking helped her move her bowels. Vassili never *wasn't* smoking. Even in the shower, an ashtray was balanced on the windowsill. He and Demos would have smoked as they delivered food had it been allowed. Paula would have bet a paycheck Alexandros had smoked as he'd checked for gas leaks. Smoking was their way to give life the finger.

Paula tugged on her dark bangs, a habit from childhood. Humidity was springing them into corkscrew coils. "Shit," she sighed deeply. One thing was clear; though her work and home life were on the verge of collapse, they also threatened to grind on forever. The boss doesn't walk away with grant money sprouting on trees. And with a third marriage you force yourself into acceptance.

Life was easier when she alone comprised the Center for Immigrant Studies. But after ten years of meteoric success, grant money pouring in, people begged her for a chance to hop onto the gravy train. The Center had taken on a life of its own; it had reared its quantitative wings and turned on her, confronting her like an alien creature out of her control. Her staff regarded her as an artifact—by their sighs, silences and expressions, she knew. And in the quiet, still moments she believed it, too.

And if the staff elbowed her aside she let them. For better or worse, Guillermo was the hungry one, the ascending boss. She felt it, knew it, and he was better at it anyway. Sometimes gaining footsteps in the stairwell prompted a glance over her shoulder, wondering if he would just as soon shove her down the stairs like some nut-job in late-night reruns of *Murder She Wrote*.

Turning fifty last month hadn't helped. She'd been unexpectedly rattled. Music from the Weather Channel made her tear up. While standing behind a broad-shouldered, heavily tattooed Polynesian-looking man in McDonald's on her birthday she'd fought the urge to rest her head against his back. It looked so nice and comfortable.

But all hating aside, Guillermo *was* right. A delegator she wasn't. He was the stronger one. She had neither the heart nor the backbone to tell her staff what to do. It seemed bossy and mean, and she'd gotten enough of that in childhood. And while Greece is long credited with being the Birthplace of Democracy, the Greek family couldn't have been credited with its conception. She'd more "suggest" to the staff than issue directives. At first they were elated by their good fortune at getting the "cool boss." But within weeks she'd get the stink-eye when asking them to do something that interfered with their coffee breaks.

Roger was stronger, too. So were the flies she couldn't kill and the recurring plantar wart on the bottom of her heel for which she lacked the endurance to follow through with the directions on the package and tend to every night.

She smoothed back her hair and sighed. "Dendron," Eleni likened her hair to the tree-like seaweed that washed ashore on their ancestral island within view of the Turkish coast. Her relatives had hopped from one tiny island to another only to then be stranded with eight million people between two rivers on the other side of the world. Such was her inspiration for creation of the Center—to gain understanding and perspective and maybe even to bridge the gap between grandparents who'd been shepherds on a remote island with no running water and a granddaughter with a Ph.D., who taught at a college, was married to *kseni* and lived in Manhattan.

Paula's stylist had promised transmutation through a new hair-straightening product. But product isn't alchemy. Not the miracle tears allegedly cried from an icon of Panayia, witnessed by an old widow living on the sun-bleached island of Kos, where some still hang out the bloody sheet after a wedding night. Paula wound back her hair and clipped it even though it exposed the gray roots. Damn, there were so many things to worry about. Her bangs had spiraled like bedsprings to her hairline; it looked like her grandmother's 1920 immigrant passport photo.

Roger didn't mind Paula's hair. Curly, frizzy, straight, he didn't care. Neither did he care if she was fat or thin or wore makeup. For months they'd avoided eye contact, and she wondered if he could pick her out of a police lineup. Sometimes comfort is born of neglect—a fine line between acceptance and not caring at all.

Roger was the strongest yet most fragile man she'd every known. He'd take a bullet for her yet wouldn't move the piles of crap off his bed to clear space for her. Shoulder-high stacks of astro- and particle physics journals served as his foot- and head-boards; piles of clothes draped over chairs to form haystacks. The closets were packed and rendered useless long before Paula'd arrived. Yet she'd doggedly believed that the magic of those first months of courtship (along with a Greek church wedding) had formed a sacred union. Her commitment was such that she'd never once doubted that someday one of them would bury the other.

Her first glimpse of Roger in Christoff's living room years ago had left her thinking that he looked "humanoid." His shiny pink head and sharp-ridged cheekbones made the skin look newly stretched—dewy, like he'd just stepped out of a pod where he'd been spawned. But, except for Heavenly and Tony, Roger was the only person with whom she didn't have to fake a laugh.

She was enthralled by his electric blue eyes—alight from years of peering deep within the recesses of the universe, into the spaces between particles—and even more by how his penetrating gaze sought that which bound her together. From that first meeting on, his unusually intense stare made her knees relax and part ever so slightly. "The urge to merge," he used to joke.

Roger's eyes were framed by white eyebrows, those you'd expect to see on Santa. After they'd make love Paula would run a finger over one and then the other in wonderment at their silky fur. She'd marveled at the tenderness in her heart. This was the shard that pierced—that he cherished her in a way her parents hadn't, in a way no one had. She'd kneel on the couch on the lookout for Roger after he phoned from his office at Columbia saying he was on his way. Like a joy-struck, besotted dog at the window, twitching with anticipation for the first signs of her master. Even the sounds of Roger rummaging upstairs at all hours of the night in his vampire way were comforting. It was a landing spot she'd fought long and hard to find. And while she was prepared to do battle to make this one work, little had Paula known that Roger would require full surrender and retreat.

And so it would be until the day she left for lunch and never came back.

The first time she stepped into the foyer of Roger's brownstone she'd caught a whiff of musty basement odor. As Roger unlocked the door and stepped inside, he must have had second thoughts, and then turned, using his large frame to block Paula's view.

"Hey—what are you doing?" She'd chuckled and turned it into a game by poking him where she knew he was ticklish. As he ducked and grabbed his sides, she glanced past his shoulder, eager to see what he didn't want her to. The cardboard boxes.

"You moving?" It was an innocent enough question.

"No."

She'd squinted in dim light to get a better look. "Looks like you are."

"Ummm . . . I'm just reorganizing—ignore all of this," he issued the disclaimer, and seemed edgy. She'd never seen him unsure or tense.

As her eyes adjusted to the darkness, she panned the foyer. There was a lot to ignore. Boxes piled several high, stacks of academic journals, some to the top of her head.

"Most of this was my parents'."

Peeking around the corner, she spotted a pile of folded Oriental rugs stacked on top of a piano (she could see the legs) so high they grazed the white plaster ceiling medallion. It looked like a madman's warehouse.

"I'm sorting," he'd explained. "Cleaning—I hadn't planned on company."

She looked at him. The comment stung. She was on the verge of saying, *Hey, bucko,* you *invited* me *here,* but didn't. A self-imposed gag order set into motion with a silent agreement.

"'Pay no attention to that man behind the curtain,'" Roger deflected her with a joke. It worked; she laughed. "And don't worry," he said, looking deep into her with those eyes of his, "If we get married we'll sort this all out and make it *our* place." He'd lowered his face, his breath tickling her skin.

"Marriage?" she joked, play-shoving him back. She then stepped onto the tops of his boat-like shoes, facing him as he began walking her out the door. She'd slipped her arms around his neck and drew him closer. "Who said anything about marriage?"

And so she'd laughed along with her witty beau. Who keeps a tower of three-legged broken chairs, tangled and intertwined like a strand of DNA? A thick layer of frost-like dust like that doesn't accumulate overnight? But like many women hopelessly mired in the throes of early hormonal love, Paula turned a deaf ear, instead hearing only refrains of "love will find a way" whirling about in her poor love-starved heart.

The next ten years played out so bizarrely that she couldn't have explained it with a gun held to her head. One can only explain what they understand. It had been an out-of-the-blue-freak-thing-that-she'd-never-in-a-million-years-seen-coming. But what bride gets married thinking a cardboard box filled with two hundred can openers (saved just in case the one in the kitchen drawer breaks) would be more important than her?

Even after all these years she'd still bump into people who'd swear, "God, Paula, that wedding of yours was the most lovely, heartfelt one I've ever been to." Then her heart would rush with hope. Their words were sincere enough, but chilling. As if the wicked fairy of Sleeping Beauty had been in attendance; perhaps Paula had pricked her finger on the spinning wheel. But she hadn't felt a thing that afternoon and instead marveled at how she could be so lucky and that finally, finally, her time had come.

But like the fairy tale, it didn't take long for Paula to sink into a silent sleep.

The cell phone buzzed in her black leather purse. "Fuck." Paula turned away from the window, cigarette burned clear down to her knuckles. What now? She'd just started to unwind after Christoff's warning. She looked back out the window, resting her forehead in her hand. Ignore it. Maybe it was Roger calling about the

NSF grant. Even so, he wouldn't call. He was too calculatingly cheap about wasting cell-phone minutes. "What's the fuss? I'll see you later," he'd dismiss. "Go ahead; waste your minutes." They'd always kept their money separate.

Thank God the phone finally stopped. She sighed and watched as birds gathered, chased each other, and then flew off. Did they ever lose their way? She watched one flapping its wings in a puddle next to the bench. Were they ever afraid of getting lost? Did they make friends? If they did, how did they ever find each other again in the vastness of the sky?

A voice from down on the sidewalk made her look. A middle-aged blond woman chatted and strolled arm in arm with a much taller man who was smiling shyly. How she liked men with shy smiles. Roger's smile had been like that. The woman sported a yellow plastic tote bag she swung seemingly without a care in the world. What must their lives be like, the stuff nobody sees? Who would suspect how she and Roger lived?

Without thinking, she shoved up the double-hung window farther and switched elbows. Thick air collided with the bone-dry air-conditioned room. The din of street noise was calming, horns from everywhere blended into one long complaint. Bus exhaust and urine, aromas of week-old garbage in alleys across the street, rushed in like a humid belch.

Her desk phone rang and it startled her. No one ever called.

"Shit." Maybe it was Christoff again, newly baptized as Mr. Micromanager.

Mashing the cigarette butt, she waved away the smell and shut the window. Her tight black cotton skirt bunched up around her hips; it was roomier a month ago in the fitting room at Bloomingdale's. She yanked it back down to the tops of her knees. Her underwear felt like a girdle; a new roll of fat hung over the top elastic.

Paula picked up. "Queens County DHSS." It was Celeste.

"Who died?" Paula's pitch lowered on the last word.

"No one yet," Celeste mimicked.

Paula's best friend was nicknamed Heavenly by fifth-grade boys after a science class on astronomy, as she was the only girl with fully developed breasts—heavenly bodies. The name stuck, even with her parents and eventually Tony, her husband, too.

"You busy?" Heavenly asked.

Paula gave a nasty laugh. She glanced at the seventy unopened e-mails on the computer screen. "I should be."

"Hey—take a long lunch," Celeste coaxed. "I'm at the hospital. Sounds like you need a break anyway."

Paula snorted. "Yeah, something like that."

"They just brought in an elderly man speaking Greek," Heavenly said. "Looks indigent, probably homeless."

"Greek? Who?" Paula's mind ticked off all of the old people in Eleni's neighborhood in the vicinity of the hospital.

"Never seen him," Heavenly said. "No ID. Can you come translate?"

Paula thought of all the old Greeks. She'd never once heard of anyone being homeless. Even if a Greek managed to get everyone to hate them over the course of a lifetime, someone still took them in. It was more shameful to leave them to the *kseni* than to face down a lifelong grudge. Surely she would have heard about it from Eleni.

Heavenly explained that the man had been walking with a large black dog before he'd collapsed. A Korean grocer on Northern Boulevard reported seeing him listing to the left as he walked the dog on a rope leash and carried several plastic grocery bags. The man first sat and then lay down on the sidewalk just under the storefront window. Thinking it bad for business, the owner called the police. Squad cars arrived. Next paramedics and Animal Control were on the scene. There was a commotion before they whisked him off to Queens County Hospital. He'd become agitated, calling to the dog as they struggled to lift him onto the gurney. The dog had bitten one of the officers and fought like a wild animal against the grab leash until Animal Control could subdue him. "How fast can you get here?" Celeste asked.

Paula hesitated. Curiously, her stomach burned with the old sickness, as she called it. An unease not felt in years, normally elicited by tense childhood family dinners and hurt feelings she'd have to hide or risk getting slapped. "Stop with the long face, *katsika* [goat face]." Vassili and Demos would sit elbow to elbow in white shirts so freshly starched they smelled like rice. Humid house aromas of lamb cooked with garlic and the oily cinnamon fragrance of moussaka. The brothers brooding as they shoveled down mouthfuls of *yemisis,* the rice mixture falling in flakes off their spoons. "Smile, goddamn it, for once. Fake it," Vassili would come up for air to bark between mouthfuls. Paula's stomach would fall to her knees. "Sit up straight," Eleni would then correct. All forks would halt, eyes focusing on young Paula's slouch. Once she inadvertently knocked over her milk, which loosed a flood of curses as to how she'd ruined yet another dinner, as if by that one mistake, a shaky little hand, their entire lives had become so miserably hard.

The unease emanated from somewhere. Perhaps a muscle she'd not used for millennia. "You there?" Heavenly asked. "He won't make sundown." she whispered. "I need a name—a relative."

"Yeah." Unease tickled inside Paula's chest cavity.

"Time is critical, *miksa mou,*" Celeste said, calling her my little snot face in Greek, an old nickname from childhood.

"I'll get a cab," Paula said in a quiet voice.

"Thanks, kiddo. I owe you." Celeste paused. "You okay with this?" Heavenly was surprised by Paula's reluctance.

"I'll call from the bridge."

For months she'd dodged Heavenly's "you look sad" observations.

Well, who the hell isn't? Paula had wanted to carp back.

"You know—it wouldn't kill you to go talk to someone, Paula."

No, but it wouldn't help either. Nothing could help. Speaking of it would be disloyal to Roger. She'd felt sworn to secrecy; no one knew, not even Celeste, though Paula could tell she'd found something odd about how Paula and Roger lived. Celeste and Tony had always figured Roger for an oddball.

"Hey," her husband, Tony, always the detective even when off duty, would break Roger's balls on their way to dinner, "you guys got illegals up there, meth cooking in the bathtub?" to which Celeste would shoot him a *don't spoil dinner again or I'll kill you* face.

At dinner Paula and Roger would each pay separately. So many times they'd swing by the brownstone to pick up the couple for an evening of seafood out on the Island, and it would be Paula, standing alone out on the front stoop. "Hey, Roger can't make it, so I'm your date." There was Paula alone again. Even when Roger would join them, Paula looked alone.

Over time Paula had become masterful at hiding. "Roger prefers to meet people out for dinner," she'd explain. "How about *we* take you guys out since you had *us* over last time?"

But Paula's composure had begun to unravel three weeks ago in the ladies' room. She looked into the mirror to enjoy the reflection of her beloved and most precious of cameo pins, the carving of Psyche, the Greek goddess of the soul. To Paula's horror, there was an empty oval in the gold setting where the cameo had been. Her jaw dropped. She'd stood staring under the unflattering fluorescent bathroom lighting, which makes even eighteen-year-olds look like hags. The emptiness bore past her collarbone and deep into soft tissue. She'd not been able to move, her mouth open, lips slack, like a stretched-out piece of elastic.

She'd dashed into action, searching around the toilet area behind sweaty metal pipes. Flinging open doors, she retraced her steps, asking at the Welcome to NYU Center if anyone had turned in a cameo. An elderly white-haired woman patted Paula's hand, saying, "Relax, dearie. Give it time. It'll probably turn up."

She ventured out to McDonald's on Fifth and then back to their brownstone—as if anything could be found there. The cameo had probably fallen down a sidewalk grate or been crushed un-ceremoniously under the wheels of a city bus. As Paula bent over, scouring the pavement, her insides gnawed, like she'd lost a finger. And though she'd unpinned the empty frame of the brooch and tucked it into her purse, she felt Psyche's absence on her chest.

Passersby paused at her posture, looking on the ground, too. "Lose something?" they asked, but she was too stricken to an-swer. Such was the fate of the carved piece of Italian helmet shell complete with the classic butterfly hovering just atop Psyche's head—which had survived innumerable births, deaths, not to mention wars. The first piece of antique jewelry Paula had ever purchased. It had been on a six-month layaway in a junk shop in Berkeley, her reward for finishing the set of twelve-hour Ph.D. prelims. And while not her most expensive piece, it was the only one she'd have grabbed in the event of a house fire.

She hung up the phone with Celeste. With newfound purpose Paula stuffed twenty-three conference submission papers into her bag, vowing that later she'd find a quiet bench in one of Manhat-tan's hidden Victorian parks to review them. They'd been printed months ago and hauled around until their edges were bent and ratty. The shoulder strap rocked into its familiar groove as she rushed downstairs. She kept an eye peeled for Psyche on the gray cement stairs. Her bag tapped against her hip as if to hasten her along.

Pushing open the front door of the building, Paula clutched her torso as she looked up to the sky. Explosive bursts of wind signaled an incoming rainstorm. It had gotten so gloomy that the park lights flipped on, twinkling through maple branches that seemed to bow toward their breaking point. Their leafy arms waved like lantern-carrying roadmen advising travelers to seek shelter.

A red dragon-shaped kite swirled in arcs against the slate clouds just above one of the taller oaks in Washington Square. Its long tail streamed a flight path. Paula traced the string. It stopped at the higher branches. No desperate kid dancing to untangle or scramble up the tree trunk to get a leg up on the lower limbs. No telling how long the kite had lain in the upper branches of the oak's canopy, waiting for the arrival of a storm front to trigger its flight.

CHAPTER 2

In bumper-to-bumper traffic, it took the cab almost an hour to reach the hospital. Paula lowered her head and scooted through the entrance of revolving doors, thinking she could sneak past a young security cop and a heavyset woman attendant encased in a bulletproof Plexiglas cube.

"Ma'am," the attendant called.

Paula rushed toward the double doors in the ward where Celeste had an office.

"Ma'am." The woman rose from her chair, signaling the cop.

By his unsure, modulated swagger Paula guessed he was new to playing cop, relegated to patting down chubby, frizzy-haired middle-aged women in a hurry. She darted a furtive *you gotta be kidding me* glance, feigning the well-practiced disdain that longtime NYU faculty use when asked to produce university ID in the entry lobby.

"Ma'am." The boyish cop caught up and positioned himself in front so as to body-block in case she made a move.

Okay. She stopped and massaged her forehead as an act of surrender. Turning back, she approached the security desk.

"I dare you to say you missed these *huge* signs about checking in," the woman quizzed without looking up, making circling motions with a blue plastic Bic pen to direct Paula's attention.

To save face, though God only knows why, Paula craned her head as if she were shocked.

"How can I help you?" There was nothing helpful in her tone.

Paula held up her phone like a bidder at an auction.

"Celeste de la Rosa. It's urgent. I've got her on the line," though Heavenly's voice mail had kicked in.

"I don't care if Obama's on the line." The woman glared over the top of her reading glasses, pointing at Paula like she was a car going the wrong way down a street. "You're required to check in."

"Photo ID in the divot please." The woman tapped the metal tray with her pen. "Tell Barack Angie says 'hi,'" she said without changing her tone.

Paula wrangled out her driver's license and checked the expiration date before complying. She rarely drove, except out to a Long Island beach in Roger's car. He housed it in a private garage over on Lexington Avenue that cost more than most people paid in six months for rent. The attendant snatched up the license, examined it briefly and without looking up tucked it into a slot behind her.

"You get it back when you surrender this." She held up a temporary ID pass in a clear plastic holder on a long string.

"Great," Paula muttered. She glanced around for Celeste.

"Spell the name." Fingers poised on the keyboard, the woman waited and sighed.

Paula sighed, too. Each for reasons that had nothing to do with the other.

She spelled her name twice. This time she hadn't changed it; Roger hadn't cared. His Polish "eye-chart name" would have been worse anyway. As she studied the pink jeweled butterfly appliqué positioned near the outside corner of the woman's eye, it looked out of character. Something belonging more on a twelve-year-old, though it matched the color and sparkle of the woman's nails.

"Wait here for your escort." The woman rolled her chair toward the printer and snatched a temporary ID card. "Wear it with the front side out at all times," she said in scripted cadence. "Check in at this desk after your business has concluded. Now step off to the side."

Paula slipped the string over her head as if it were some sort of perverse lobster bib and waited for Celeste. Her tote weighed a ton. When she nudged off the shoulder strap, it dropped like a boat anchor. She rotated her shoulder joint and watched the attendant tangle with the next person in line.

"Photo ID. Your picture," the attendant annunciated to a couple. The man smiled and shrugged. As the attendant pantomimed, pointing to her face with the pen, the couple kept shaking their heads, waving their hands with that universal gesture of "no speakie."

"Picture," the woman said louder, still pointing at her face.

Paula ran her hand over the crown of her head, massaging it with her fingers. Everything was such a struggle. Suddenly her purse felt heavy, too, and she lowered it on top of the tote. What she'd give for a cigarette, but the cop would probably use his Taser.

"Paula." Heavenly waved in the doorway and mouthed, *Hurry up*. Tucked under Celeste's arm was a file.

"Sorry." Paula slung the bag of papers back over her shoulder along with her purse. "Traffic was murder." They hurried down the polished green granite floor toward the elevators, their heels clacking as they rushed.

The hallway lights made the diamonds in Paula's platinum pendant shimmer.

"Hey, ni-i-ice." Celeste pointed. "Another new one, huh?"

Paula touched it, embarrassed she'd not thought to tuck it under her neckline or, better yet, take it off and stuff it into the coin part of her wallet. Unhappiness buying. It was elating but made her feel foolish and indulgent. Aware of a salesperson's eyes, Paula would chat on lightheartedly, making up this or that about a birthday or Christmas present, how her husband hates to go shopping. She'd cringe at the hollow sound of her fabrications, yet she persisted. Her Visa card would beep in approval, signaling a quick end to the pretense and the sweat that triggered the scent of her deodorant.

The initial rush from each purchase wore off quickly. Even when she forced herself to wear a piece, the underlying sadness was amplified. Because all she'd wanted was Roger and not a collection of metal and rocks. And while no substitute for affection, necklaces, bracelets and rings were all she had to show for ten years of sleeping on a couch. It was only by pretending to be encircled in the arms of an imaginary lover that she could fall asleep. The whole thing was insane: a grown woman living in this fantasy world, sleeping alone while her husband lay snoring upstairs in a locked bedroom. How pathetic, and how grateful she was that no one knew.

Aside from her beloved Psyche, there were days Paula wanted to gather up the entire collection and stuff it down the drop chute at the Salvation Army. It was a constant reminder of what she didn't have. There was no answer. No solution. It wasn't some hypothesis where running a different regression equation could yield valid results. Her husband didn't want her. In the hard light of day, that was the bottom line—the one variable she couldn't change.

Heavenly would purposely go scab picking to trigger Paula's anger. Only a week earlier, during their standing Thursday lunch date, the sparkle of diamonds in a bracelet caught Celeste's eye.

"God, doesn't Roger care you're buying stuff like this?" Celeste had asked. "Tony'd kill me." Heavenly's eyes punctuated the sentence for good measure.

There'd been a brief pause, as if Paula was gathering her forces.

"Roger doesn't care what I do as long as I don't ask him to be a real husband." Her words flew like buckshot, knocking the wind out of them both. The bitterness made Paula cough. She'd looked down at her half-eaten shrimp; her stomach clenched.

Heavenly reached to touch Paula's hand on the table. "Yeah, but you care," Celeste said softly. 'I know you do, *miksa mou*." The silence was painful.

Paula had fished out a twenty and tucked it under the salt and pepper set, muttering, "I gotta get back for a meeting."

Roger had more money than God yet refused to throw out a pair of pants until the crotch would split open. "I guess it's time

for a new pair," he'd say, calling Paula upstairs to view the hilarity
of his white thighs bulging through a split in the fabric. His income from Columbia was mid–six figures; proceeds from national and international patents more than matched it. This,
combined with the sizable inheritance from his parents, including their brownstone, set him up for life. Yet in ten years he and
Paula had not bought or owned one single thing in common.

The only time Eleni ever spoke ill of Roger was five years earlier
when he and Paula had taken her out to dinner for her seventy-
fifth birthday at the Four Seasons. At the end of the meal Roger
had casually requested a separate check. Paula grabbed it, hoping her mother hadn't seen, but Eleni missed nothing. Her sharp
eyes pecked at Paula before she said in Greek, "I'm surprised he
doesn't shove a cork up your ass to make sure you don't waste a
thing."

Heavenly pushed the elevator button as they waited. "He probably spoke English at one time," she explained. "Often in ad-
vanced old age people default to their first language."

They looked up at the display, waiting for a car. Heavenly
jabbed it several more times.

"You know that doesn't make it come faster," Paula said.

"Eat shit." Heavenly grinned. "Get a name, next of kin," she
said as the door opened and they stepped inside.

Heavenly shrugged as the elevator doors closed. "All he says
is . . ." She looked at the chart. " 'Fotis. *F-o-t-i-s* moo.' Maybe
that's his name or something."

"Fotis? *Fos* means 'light,' " Paula said. "Like light." She pointed
at the overhead fluorescent slabs. "*Fotis mou* means 'my light.' "

Heavenly pressed the ninth-floor button. "Maybe he's hallucinating."

They walked swiftly past elderly patients in wheelchairs, their
bruised, blotchy skin looking as delicate as tissue paper. "I love
you, honey," one called out in grandmotherly tones as they passed.
Wheelchairs were parked amid gray metal supply carts piled
high with bedsheets, others with bins jammed full of syringes

and glass tubes. Stands of IV machines wound up in their own wires, hooked to no one, lined up like a regimen in marching formation.

Paula held her breath as they passed through intermittent scent clouds of urine and rubbing alcohol. Heavenly slowed at a door marked only with a patient number. Celeste took out the chart, looked at her watch, marked something and then softly knocked.

"Come in," a nurse's voice.

Celeste slowly pushed the door open, gesturing for Paula to follow.

"Hell-o-o?" Heavenly said in a singsong voice.

A nurse was rearranging a white waffle thermal blanket around the emaciated frame of an elderly man, tossing him around in a robust way as if he were nothing but a bundle of sticks.

"There," the nurse chirped to the patient. "Now isn't that better," she affirmed, seemingly pleased with her work.

"Stamata," a soft but raspy voice complained, "enough already" in Greek.

The woman smiled at Heavenly and peeled off purple latex gloves, tossing them into the biohazard disposal bin. Gathering a digital thermometer pack, the nurse looped her stethoscope around her neck and raised her eyebrows as if to say, *He's all yours.*

The room had darkened from the storm, making it seem later than it was. Raindrops pattered against the window. The two of them approached the foot of the bed.

"Kalimera," Paula bid him good afternoon.

Bedsheets rustled at the sound of her voice. The old man turned his head.

"Ella," he called her closer.

Paula took a step.

He squinted. "Paula?"

Celeste turned to look at her.

The voice was familiar, though Paula couldn't pinpoint it. Like recognizing words in a language spoken in a dream.

"Ella tho," he asked her to come closer. His voice was weak. "I knew you'd come, Paula," he said in Greek.

She peered at his face in the dim light, blinking several times as she thought.

"They said you wouldn't." He choked up and pointed to the ceiling so convincingly that Paula looked up, too, fully expecting to see people. "But I knew you would; I told them."

She looked at him.

"Paula with the yellow eyes—Athena's owl."

She was stunned. Recognition rushed her all at once and she had to sit down, covering her mouth with her hand for a moment. He was still alive? She looked at her bare knees peeking out past the hem of her skirt. He'd seemed like such an old man some forty-odd years ago. Yet he'd probably been younger than she was now.

"Theo," she said, calling him Uncle as he'd instructed her all those years ago.

He smiled. She hadn't remembered his eyes being so ghostly pale. Wisps of white hair patched his head.

"Ella," he called her closer, his voice almost a whisper. "Come closer so I can see you—I want to see you all grown up."

She stood and stepped closer, touching the side of the bed.

His arm shuffled under the blanket as his hand struggled to get free. The nurse had wrapped him as tight as a mummy.

Paula searched for the end of the blanket.

"Wait for the nurse," Heavenly said, reaching across the bed to press the call button.

Paula frowned. She found the corner of the blanket and began to unravel him.

"Look how pretty the curls around your face," he said.

She freed his arm. His hand reached for hers. It was as light as paper. He let go and reached toward her face. She bent closer and he touched her curls. No one had touched her hair in a million years.

"Such sad eyes," he said. "Like when you were little. Remember when you used to play with my Fotis then?"

An uncomfortable burning sensation ached in her throat. Pain pulsed in her chest and upper back. The muscles beneath her collarbones began to throb. She didn't know what was happening until her tear ducts stung, until she remembered the feeling of tears as they make their way up from the place inside. Leaning forward, she braced against the side of the bed.

Heavenly stepped up and touched her between the shoulder blades. "*Miksa,* are you okay?"

Paula couldn't answer.

"My Paula." His voice was definitive. "You're such a good girl."

A few quiet moments passed. The burning in her chest wouldn't subside; she tried to breathe without sobbing.

"They took my Fotis," he said. His face contorted and then broke into a child's sob, but his eyes were dry. He was out of tears.

"Ksero, Theo," she told him she knew.

"Fotis bit them."

"I know."

His body wobbled. "He didn't mean to."

Their eyes met.

"I know."

"He's my Fotis, Paula. You remember. My protector, my *palikari.*" His voice became a whisper. "My Fotis never bite anyone." His hand trembled, fingers fluttering like the wings of a bird. His pale eyes were sunken and shadowed with grief. His legs feverishly rubbed against each other as if trying to ignite the energy to run. He tried to sit up. "They're gonna kill him, Paula."

He wrestled with the swaddled blanket, feet swishing against each shin in a bid to find comfort. "That's what they do."

"He's getting upset," Heavenly said, pulling on the back of Paula's blouse.

"Voithise ton, Paula," he said.

"I'll help," she promised. She couldn't keep a dog, didn't even want one.

He tried to rise on one elbow but fell back on the stack of pillows.

"Look, Paula, he's getting too upset." Heavenly tapped her arm again. "Maybe we should go."

"Theo." Paula had to get a name. "Ti eni to onoma sous?" she asked respectfully.

He seemed confused.

"To onoma sous?" She pointed to him. "Paula"—she touched her sternum—"to ononma mou," and then touched his. "To onoma sous?"

He looked as if he didn't understand.

The familiar raspy timbre of his voice had been his name. When she was a girl he'd walked the neighborhood, wearing a long black overcoat, even in summer, a hat, carrying a plastic tote bag lined with a brown paper grocery bag and always accompanied by a dog. He'd smelled like the ocean and the beach after a long day in the sun. For weeks she'd see him every day and then for months not at all.

Theo's grasp relaxed. His fingers slowly opened, eyelids twitched, mouth went slack as he drifted off.

Paula touched Theo's shoulder through the blanket as he slept. She looked at Celeste.

"You get a name?" she asked, but Paula said nothing.

Instead she bent over, rummaging through her purse to get her phone. As she straightened, Heavenly looked more closely at her.

"What?" Paula pulled back. "Why are you looking at me like that?" Paula returned the look. "No, I didn't get a name." She gestured with her head for Heavenly to follow her out into the hall.

She dialed Eleni and put her on speaker.

"Hi, Ma."

"Oh, Paula, it's you." Her mother sounded surprised. "You never call on Wednesday."

"Ma, remember the old man with the dog who used to walk around the neighborhood when I was a kid?" She waited.

"Ma—the one in the long black wool coat?" she went on. "The one I called 'Theo'?"

There was a long silence before her mother answered.

"I'm busy taking up a hem," Eleni said.

At first Paula thought her mother was giving her the bum's rush except for the edge of impatience in Eleni's voice.

Heavenly leaned against the wall and made a face. What a pain in the ass Eleni could be. Despite the gravity of the moment, it made Paula laugh.

"Ma, I know you remember—"

"What *theo*?" Eleni blurted out. "Everyone was 'Theo.'"

"The one you said not to call 'Theo' because he wasn't my *theo*. And when I asked you what to call him, you said, 'Call him *tipota*,' meaning 'nothing.'"

Eleni was silent.

"He's dying, Ma."

Celeste took the phone. "Mrs. Makaikis, we need to contact a relative," Celeste spoke in her official-capacity voice.

Paula's mother was silent, which was odd. Ordinarily Eleni would have made accusations about selfish children who move off to places like Arizona and California, leaving their parents behind to languish.

Celeste handed back the phone. Paula tipped it up to check the bars; she looked up and shrugged.

"Mitera?" Paula asked in Greek. "Eleni," she called her mother by name, which she'd never done, hoping to snap her out of whatever had silenced her.

"Ti?" Eleni's "What?" sounded curt in Greek.

"Remember the man who wore the black topcoat even in summer, who always carried a tote with him and had a dog on a rope?" Paula asked.

"Dthen ksero tipota."

They only spoke Greek when there was something they didn't want others to hear.

"That's not true," Paula answered. "Speak English, Ma—I know you remember him."

An uncomfortable shuffling came through the line. Eleni was never known to falter; it was always the other party who sat on tacks.

Paula broke first. "Ma, you used to scold me, telling me his dog was filthy and had disease."

Celeste's eyes narrowed.

"He'd sneak into the back of the church at Easter," Paula said. "Everyone would whisper. He'd tie his dog to the outside railing. I'd sneak out to sit with the dog and you'd scold me."

Celeste grinned, slowly shaking her head.

"Did he have any kids, Ma?"

"Only a nephew. Peter Fanourakis from Staten Island," Eleni said in a quiet voice. "Probably lives in Jersey now—I'll call Rania; maybe she knows."

"Weren't we from the same village—"

"This village, that village!" Eleni hollered. "What's the hell's the difference at this point?"

Paula's mouth fell open. Heavenly's eyes widened, her eyebrows arching so high they almost touched her hairline.

"Crazy young man, crazy old man, so what?" Eleni's voice sounded about to break.

"I'm handing you back to Celeste."

"Thanks, Mrs. Makaikis." Celeste took the phone and began scribbling notes.

Paula stepped back into the room to sit with Theo. She touched his relaxed hand as the nurse checked in, monitoring his vitals. After a brief conversation with Heavenly, the nurse looked at Paula and smiled. Heavenly then sat back in a La-Z-Boy chair in the corner of the room.

Within the hour Theo could no longer respond. The room fell silent. It was a different kind of stillness, a quiet Paula had never heard. Heavenly stood and walked over to take his pulse. She looked at Paula and then reached to press the call button.

Paula took in his sunken eyes, slightly parted lips, open palm. She didn't know what to feel.

"Yia sou, palikari [bless you, brave one]," she'd said, and leaned over him, resting her cheek on his shoulder near his face. "Eonia I mnimi," she said, the haunting chant of eternal memory. I'll remember your name forever. "Eonia I mnimi," she whispered. "Yia sas, filos mou [good-bye, my friend]." Her eyes burned.

The nurse walked in to confirm the time.

"Take as long as you need," Heavenly said.

Soft conversations bustled on behind Paula about the business of death. Theo was gone. She looked around the darkened room. There was his dog, her promise.

Looking at her watch, she stood and lifted her purse. It was just after two. She walked toward the door and peeked out for signs of Celeste. She glanced back at the empty body, the chant of "Eonia I mnimi" still with her. Every hair on her body prickled. Paula wobbled out into the hall, bracing her hand against the wall.

"You okay?" Celeste asked, steadying her with both arms.

"I'm not sure."

"You look like you're gonna faint."

Paula stood, purse dangling on her forearm, her thoughts whirling.

"I gotta go." Celeste turned to the attending physician. They stepped back into the room to begin making arrangements for the body.

"Hey, Heav." Paula turned and quickly followed back in, tapping Celeste's arm. "Heav, where's the dog?"

Celeste held up a finger as she scribbled down what the physician was saying.

"Heav," Paula interrupted. "Where's the dog? Where'd they take it?"

Heavenly turned and mouthed, *Wait.*

The doctor gave Paula a stern look.

"I need to know."

"Excuse me," Celeste said in her velvety voice. "I do apologize." She turned to Paula. "Jesus Christ," she growled, rifling through the intake report. "Animal Control on Queens Boulevard."

"What's the address?"

"Uhh—Ninety-Two Twenty-Nine."

Paula turned and rushed, tracing her way back through the halls. She spotted the red "Down" on the elevator arrows and ran.

In the lobby she flew past Obama's buddy, the string from the hospital ID swinging from side to side as Paula dashed out the revolving doors and into the traffic circle, before making eye contact with a cabbie.

"Ninety-Two Twenty-Nine Queens Boulevard." She pulled the door shut.

"Jesus, you gotta slam the fucking door?"

She looked at the back of the driver's head. In the rearview mirror she saw the Mets insignia. She had one foot in another world.

"Sorry," she mumbled.

"I'm heading back to the City," he said.

"So am I."

"That ain't the City."

She looked at her watch. "I have one stop."

"Everyone says that."

Leaning up to the grate, she said, "If you'd stop complaining we can be there in ten minutes."

He sighed loudly in disgust. The meter beeped as he set it. "Fine, but it's gonna cost you," he warned. "It'll be running the whole time," he said in a singsong voice.

"Fine."

"How long you gonna take?" he asked.

"You said it'll be running, so what do you care? If it's running in Queens or Midtown you get paid, right?"

"Save it for your boyfriend, lady." He pulled out abruptly; the cab jerked and the tires squealed. She braced herself. Rolling down the window, she lit up and exhaled toward the street.

"No smoking in my cab."

Their eyes met in the rearview mirror.

"Oh really?" She glared at him. "Then how come it smells like an ashtray?"

He chuckled and looked at the road, pulling a cigarette from his shirt pocket.

"Asshole," she muttered. She caught a smirk in the mirror. Thank God he'd put a cork in it.

How long it had been since she'd thought of Theo. It had never occurred to her back then that the street might be his home. Besides, Greeks never talked about such things. There's a different score sheet for Greeks than for the *Amerikani*.

Her memories of him blended together. In those days metal roller skates were always attached to her shoes. Cracked red leather straps. Vibration from the wheels on cement would make her teeth feel as though they were rattling. Fotis would press against her thighs like a cat eager for her touch. She'd chase him, giggling as she'd skate after him. Her earliest memory of Theo was as she sat on the stoop of the apartment building, hunched over, cheeks spilling out into both palms, wild dark hair encircling her head like an angry halo—fuming at Eleni, who'd just massacred her hair with a pair of thinning shears: "You look like a Medusa."

She remembered touching the back of her shorn head; how fragile the back of her skull had felt without hair. Then she'd spotted Theo. He gracefully listed from side to side as he crossed Union Turnpike. His long black overcoat caught the wind like a sail. Dark shoes and pants, tall lambs wool hat with a fold in the middle, he'd always appeared formally dressed, though always wearing the same clothes. Yet she couldn't remember him ever smelling stale. He'd always carried a clear plastic tote bag decorated with faded pink and yellow flowers. Inside stood a crisp brown paper bag that looked starched and ironed. He'd seemed like such an old man at the time, yet he'd probably been in his forties.

Theo had halted right in front of the stoop. "Paula with the yellow eyes of Athena's owl," he'd address her formally, bending at the waist to bow.

"How come you know my name?" she'd asked.

"Ahhh." He'd dismissed her with a wave of his hand. "I know everybody's name." He'd gesture down the block.

He'd whistle, prompting Fotis, a black and white collie-type dog, to come barreling across Union Turnpike, dodging pedestrians and cars to claim his place at Theo's side.

"This is Fotis," he'd proudly introduced the dog. Fotis had plopped down on Theo's shoe, ears perked at the sound of his name as if delighted by the introduction.

"Does he bite?" she'd remembered asking.

"Who?" The man had looked around comically, pretending not to know who she'd meant. "Him? Oh no, no, no, no, no." Theo had shaken his head, seemingly amused by the preposterousness of such a question.

"Fotis never bites anyone. You can bite him and he wouldn't bite you back."

She'd remembered laughing.

"Why do you call him Fotis?" She'd remembered the dog's silky head and his pink scratchy tongue.

"Every dog is my *fos*. My beacon," Theo explained in a quiet voice. "He reminds me to feel." He touched his chest.

"How can a dog teach you to feel?" She'd scrunched up her face and laughed but was instantly sorry. Fotis studied her carefully. She hoped she hadn't hurt his feelings and wondered if it was possible to erase such a thing from the heart of a dog.

"My little one," Theo had said. "Everything you ever need is right here." He'd placed his hand on the buttons of his overcoat. "Just listen." And with that he'd cupped his large, wrinkly hand around his hairy ear.

"Wanna see me skate?" she'd ask.

He'd never decline and would clap as she did, saying, "Bravo, bravo," even when the wheel would catch in a sidewalk crack and she'd fall. "No, wait," she'd said, standing up and brushing off her palms. "I can do it better; wait, I'll show you."

The cab pulled up and double-parked across from Animal Control.

"I'll be right back." She flipped him two twenties through the grate and unlatched the door.

"It's still running." He snatched the bills.

"Good," she congratulated him.

But as soon as he glimpsed the Animal Control sign he declared, "Ah shit."

She climbed out and slammed the door.

"You ain't bringing no animal," he shouted.

Paula laughed but didn't look back as she strode across the street. She threw down what was left of her cigarette, stepping inside and up to the information desk.

"I'm here about a dog that was brought in earlier this morning by Animal Control," she explained. "I'd like to claim it; I don't know what your process is."

"Name?"

"Mine or the dog's?"

The attendant's look said: *Are you serious?* "Yours."

She spelled it.

"Have a seat." The woman gave her a somber look, picked up the receiver and spoke quietly, keeping an eye on Paula. She said, "Someone'll be out with you shortly."

After about ten minutes an animal control officer in uniform walked out.

"Ms. Makaikis?"

Paula stood.

The man sat down in a chair and sighed as if he'd not sat all day.

"Have a seat." He gestured. "Please. Are you a relative?"

"Yes," she said quickly.

"Immediate family, niece—"

"Daughter," the lie slipped right out.

"The dog bit one of the officers."

"Yes, I heard," she said. "He was protecting the ol—my father."

The officer's brows knitted as if he was trying to decipher just what kind of a nut-job she was. She was dressed conventionally, but sometimes those are the most dangerous.

"Fotis was scared," she said.

She could tell the whole thing sounded sketchy.

Looking at his nameplate, she said, "Look, Officer Rodriguez," trying not to sound patronizing. "The dog's all I have left of my father." Unexpected tears for which she couldn't account (and which she couldn't have faked) choked her up. "I haven't seen him for a long time."

"'A dog with a bite history can't be placed,'" he quoted a statute.

"You're not 'placing' him—I'm claiming him," Paula insisted.

"He's in rough shape."

Paula looked at him. "You mean he's gonna die?"

"God no," the officer exhaled with impatience. "He's probably loaded with intestinal parasites," he clarified. "Maybe heartworm positive. As it stands, he's in the euthanasia run. He broke the officer's skin."

"He was scared." Her voice began to rise. "It was an isolated incident."

"We don't know that." The man stared at her as if enjoying seeing her squirm a bit but then looked down, as if disappointed to admit, "He *does* have a valid rabies tag—we just ran a check on it with the vet."

"Is that other stuff treatable?"

The officer looked at her. It was some time before he nodded. His eyes were as black and impenetrable as Eleni's.

"Look, I'll take care of everything," Paula said. "I'll sign a waiver or whatever you want, something to absolve you of all responsibility." The words flew out of her mouth; their urgency surprised her, as if they were someone else's promises. She hadn't yet thought about what she'd do with the dog.

The officer looked her up and down.

"We haven't processed him yet."

"What does that mean?"

"It means he's not in our system."

"Oh, so can I just take him then? You know, off the books."

He gave her a sour look and shifted in his seat.

"Hey—I'll pay all fees."

"How did your 'father,'" he said skeptically, "end up so rough?" It was an accusation.

She looked down into her lap.

"You know the dog's name?" he asked.

"Fotis."

The officer nodded reluctantly, almost disappointed she'd passed the test. He stood and moved toward the reception desk. Paula followed.

"I'll go talk with my supervisor," he said, staring at her. "Have a seat."

She sat down again, wondering what the hell she'd do with a dog anyway. Maybe Celeste and Tony would take him; they loved animals. Someone would take him. People talked in the office about wanting to adopt an animal from a shelter.

She picked up a magazine from a side table. *Dog Fancy.* Too fidgety to read, she paged through it. Ads about fluid that cleaned ear canals, dog crates, no-bark collars—a whole world she'd not been aware of. After a while, the officer walked back out with a uniformed female officer.

"So I understand you're the man's daughter?" The female officer looked Paula up and down.

She nodded.

The woman sighed as if not quite sure. After a brief pause she looked down at Paula's red toenails as if that were the deciding factor.

"All right," the officer said.

Paula relaxed.

"It's like this." The officer tucked a clipboard under her arm and began, "The dog's in okay shape, friendly but reserved. He's a really big boy. Seventy-five pounds. He's thin but nothing some good food won't cure," the woman instructed.

"He's about three or four. Neutered; the rabies tag checked out; vet says he's up to date on all his shots. As down on his luck that your father was"—she looked at Paula sideways—"he did right by his dog."

Paula looked at her.

"He's in bad need of a bath. I don't know what's up with the teeth; they're huge. We don't see teeth like this on a domestic dog. From a cross somewhere, it happens. His size, his undercoat, the teeth."

"What does that mean?" She'd assumed he was a mutt.

The woman continued. "They're pristine, though, not one spot of tartar. He's got matted sections on his shoulders, hips, in desperate need of a good grooming. His double coat might have already shed. Vet claims he was heartworm tested this spring and on meds; get him in next week to get more pills. Probably give him a general wormer, too. You never know what he's been eating."

"Can I get the vet's phone number from you?" Paula figured she'd pass it on to Celeste.

"Not a problem. Like I said, I'll jot it down on the release form. Might be helpful to get the dog's complete history."

"I'll get him in first thing."

"There's a twenty-four-hour clinic just off Queens Boulevard in Forest Hills. I'll give you their number; you might want to go with that."

Celeste had cats and a neurotic dog who couldn't stop humping his bed. She and Tony could bring Fotis to their vet.

Paula nodded again, though she felt overwhelmed. Second thoughts jabbed at her. Where would she take the dog? She'd call Celeste. Maybe they could keep him. Maybe they'd want him. Guillermo had talked about getting a dog. She could put up notices at NYU; the boards were always littered with pictures of puppies. It had been a long time since she'd made such a bold move, since she'd made any move at all.

"He does answer to his name," the officer explained, "but no commands—like 'sit,' 'stay,' 'down'—nothing else. We just fed him." The woman looked at Paula in a meaningful way.

Paula nodded vigorously, though the significance was lost on her. "Okay," she said.

The officer placed a clipboard on the counter and "x-ed" all the places Paula needed to initial.

"I just need to see a picture ID."

Paula reached to get her wallet. *Shit.* Her license was back at the hospital with Obama's buddy. Paula felt for the temporary hospital ID and slipped the string over her head and tucked the badge into her purse, making a mental note to go back to get her license.

"Is my NYU faculty ID okay?"

The woman nodded and extended her hand. "This'll open space," the officer sighed. "Thirty dogs are on their way from a busted fight ring in Brooklyn." The officer wiped her brow.

"We'd appreciate a small donation if possible," the officer said.

"Of course."

The woman looked over her glasses at Paula. "She'll take it." The officer motioned to the receptionist.

Paula stepped up and produced her wallet.

"Thanks," the officer said. "I'll bring your dog right out."

She checked the last donation box, "other" with a blank line, and wrote in "One thousand dollars," handing over her bank card. Money had become a strange thing since she married Roger. All her life Paula had struggled to get by, often having to swipe rolls of toilet paper out of the ladies' room at school. Now she had no idea how much money she had. Every month the money fairy at NYU deposited her professor's salary into her old money-market checking account. After she paid off her student loans, which hadn't taken long after she and Roger were married, her salary had piled up for more than a decade. She'd had no expenses, other than replacement blouses, sweaters, since she wore almost the same thing every day, and, of course, antique jewelry. Since the bank had gone online, they no longer sent out paper statements. She'd never bothered to find her online account.

Paula listened to the barking ruckus behind the metal door that said: "Staff Only." It had to be Fotis. Her stomach squeezed. What the hell was she doing? She kept telling herself, Celeste and Tony would take him. She'd text Guillermo, too.

The door opened and out walked a large wild-eyed black and white dog. The officer spotted her. "Jailbreak," she joked. "They all go nuts when someone gets out."

Paula must have looked bewildered.

"You okay?" the woman asked.

"Oh yeah." Paula stood. There was no resemblance to the Fotis of her childhood, though she could feel Theo's presence. Paula smiled to herself. The old man must have named every dog after *fos*, or light.

"Hi, Fotis." Paula crouched down beside him and held out both hands.

The dog looked excited, as if he'd walked into his own surprise birthday party. His muzzle was white with black freckles, he had one blue eye and one brown and his ears stood akimbo. His fur was haphazardly spiky. He was funny and Paula realized she was smiling.

The shelter worker handed her the rope leash. It felt oily and slippery from grime.

"Sorry. He came in with it. You'll probably want to stop and get a new collar and lead."

Paula nodded. She looked at the rope in her palm.

"Transfer his rabies tag immediately when you get a new collar." The officer waited for Paula to look up. "It just saved his life. And make sure you call the vet and get his information switched to you."

She blinked an acknowledgment; the excited dog jerked her off balance toward the shelter exit.

The officer laughed in relief. "Funny how they all know the way out. Good luck to both of you."

The cab was idling across the street in the same spot. The driver spied her crossing with the dog.

"Oh no, no, no." The driver shook his head and held up both hands to block her out. "Oh my God," he said in disgust. "I should have known."

Paula opened the back door of the cab. "Oh, stop with the melodrama," she muttered.

Fotis cowered on the curb as the door's edge grazed him.

"No animals—it's my policy."

"Oh—like your smoking policy," she said.

She stared at him in the side-view mirror.

"Come on, Fotis," Paula said in a high voice, patting the backseat and ignoring the driver. "Up, come on." She patted it again like she'd seen people doing in the Jones Beach parking lot only a few weeks ago. She then tried to push up the dog's hind end, but he shied back more.

"Shit," she grunted, and stood, placing her hand on her hip. The cabbie watched in the rearview mirror and chuckled.

"Why don't you help?" she sniped.

"Nah—," he said in a reflective way. "It's more fun to watch." Then he lit a cigarette and inhaled deeply as if to savor the moment, alternating between rear and side mirrors to best view the spectacle.

"Come on, Fotis."

She threw her purse into the backseat and scrambled inside, kneeling on the seat, and turned to face the dog. Holding on to the rope, she tried to drag him in. "Fotis, come on," she coaxed. Instead he reared back, his nails scratching on the cement. His rabies tag jingled as he tried to yank out of his collar.

"That dog's never been in a car," the driver announced.

"Brilliant," she sniped. Beads of sweat formed around her hairline, tickling as they trickled down her neck into the collar of her blouse. Except for the animal control truck not more than three hours ago, the driver was probably right.

She climbed out of the back and stood on the sidewalk next to the dog.

"Pick him up; pick him up," the driver's voice rose.

She looked at him.

"Pick his ass up." The cabbie gestured. "Put your arms around his belly," he instructed, "and pick his ass up."

"He's heavy."

Paula circled Fotis' belly with her arms and lifted him, scooting him onto the backseat.

"Christ, whew—finally," the driver muttered. "After that I need a nap."

Fotis sat bent over, his head hanging almost down to his front paws, ears drooped off to the sides.

"Roll down the back windows," the cabbie instructed. "Give him some air."

Paula rolled down one back window, then the other as she reached across the drooping dog. Her blouse had become transparent with sweat, sticking to her back.

"Thanks," her voice softened.

"No, thank you," the driver said, wiping his eyes. "That's the most fun I've had since my wife died."

Paula looked at him, not sure she'd heard right.

"Washington Square," she said. "Anywhere in the vicinity'll do."

Fotis began drooling. The cab was queued bumper to bumper in a line of traffic along Queens Boulevard for the feed on to the Queensboro Bridge. Strings of clear fluid streamed from the dog, collecting in pools on Paula's black skirt.

"Jesus," she mumbled, trying to redirect the dog's mouth over the rubber mats on the back floor of the cab. The interior of a New York City cab was made to be hosed out.

Then the dog's body started rhythmically moving, his head jutting back and forth. A deep burping sound bellowed up from his throat.

"My God," her voice quivered. "He's having a seizure." She looked up at the rearview mirror for help.

The cabbie tilted the mirror down to look. "Nah—," he said reassuringly yet amused. "He's puking on you, hon."

Her eyes met the cabbie's and he laughed himself into a coughing fit.

Paula looked down as the dog produced a pile of partially digested dog food in her lap.

"Lady," the cabbie said, shaking his head as he caught his breath. He opened the grate and tossed back a soft package of Kleenex.

With traffic, it took them until almost four thirty to get down to Washington Square. She'd called Celeste several times and left messages: "Got the dog, need to talk to you, call me." "Call me, got the dog. Need to know what to do, if maybe you could watch him for me."

Paula scanned storefronts as she walked, looking at her phone to see if Heavenly had called. Maybe the place was on Fifth. Fotis walked snugly at her side; his flank had coated the side of her skirt with a swath of grime.

"Goddamn it," she said out loud, and stopped, looking for the pet store she was sure she passed every day.

Fotis looked at her when she spoke, one ear standing up, the other half-drooped. Despite the vomit stain on the front of her skirt, now punctuated with white tufts of tissue fragments, the dog had made a full recovery.

Paula stopped again. The person walking behind them almost crashed into her.

"Oh, sorry." She moved out of the way toward the curb. She could have sworn it was here by the Emilio's Pizza joint.

It had started to sprinkle. Swollen gray clouds looked about to surrender their contents. Motion from across the street caught her attention. Someone was scurrying about. Aha, she spotted empty white marble tables. "Pets du Jour," that was it. A clerk was rolling a clothing rack full of tiny costume-like garments toward the door. Ball gowns and garments covered with sequins, organdy ruffles, accessorized with crowns and magic wands, meant for small dogs.

Paula crossed the street and ducked in with Fotis.

"Are you still open?"

"Yup, we're open till nine."

"Good. Okay if I come in with a dog?" She motioned to Fotis.

"Sure. We don't bite," the woman said as she positioned the rack off to the side and turned to face Paula.

Paula laughed and pointed at her. "Good one."

"Yeah, well—dog humor," the woman said, and held up both hands. "Goes with the territory. Bring . . ."—she bent over to glace at Fotis' crotch—"him, too," the woman said in a singsong voice, designed for animals. It worked. Fotis' tail began wagging.

Paula felt a pang. He'd not wagged for her since the shelter.

The shop door was propped open with a vintage concrete cat. Paula had expected to smell cedar and pine bedding like Pet World, the place she'd worked in Queens after high school. She looked around for birdcages, listened for the chirp of a parakeet, but saw nothing but walls of color-sorted collars and leashes. Inside, another clerk stood arranging the wall of colorful dog jackets and looked up.

"Don't you have any animals here?" Paula asked tentatively, marveling at the colorful merchandise. It looked like an upscale children's boutique.

"No, we only cater to dogs and cats."

Fotis seemed at ease.

"Wow." The salesclerk placed her hands on her hips. She looked the dog over. "You're a big boy, aren't you," she said in a goofy doggie voice. "Looks like someone's hurting for a bath." The woman squatted down eye level and then reached both hands out for Fotis to sniff. "Would you like to have him groomed? I just had a cancellation."

Paula nodded. "Oh my God, yes. It's a bath, isn't it?" She figured it would be good to have him cleaned before dropping him off at Celeste's.

"Absolutely. It'll take me thirty minutes, maybe a bit more." She looked at Paula. "He's pretty rough."

They both looked down at Fotis.

"You in a rush?"

Paula shrugged. "I guess not. A bath sounds perfect," Paula agreed. "But I have to tell you that he bit an animal control officer."

"Which one?"

Paula stared blankly at the groomer.

The dog's ears lay back; his tail began to wiggle as he watched the woman.

"You're kinda dirty," the woman said in her baby voice. The other clerk stepped over and knelt down. "Let me see how it goes. If he gets agitated I can muzzle him. He's got that 'you-just-got-me-at-the-shelter' look,'" the other clerk said, and knelt down, too.

Paula nodded. She checked her phone for messages. Nothing. She began dialing Guillermo's number but then stopped. She should wait until she heard from Heavenly first.

"They usually bathe 'em and get 'em all cleaned up before adopting 'em out," the woman said.

Paula was too exhausted to go through the whole story and just shrugged in response.

"You want a treat?" the woman asked Fotis.

Her intonation made his ears perk up.

The clerk grabbed a biscuit that looked like a miniature hamburger.

"Can you sit?" She raised her hand.

Fotis stared at the biscuit.

"Guess you don't know that one, do ya," she conceded, and handed the biscuit over anyway.

Fotis took the treat gently. It was gone in seconds; he looked at the woman for another.

"He takes it nicely," she remarked to Paula as she nodded. "With some of the guys you could lose a finger."

Paula checked the woman's fingers.

"More dog humor," she said.

Paula nodded. The clerks seemed genuinely caring.

"What's his name?"

"Fotis."

"Cool. Never heard that one before."

"It's Greek for 'light.'" Paula nodded. "I like it," she said, not wanting to explain that Tony or Celeste might change it. Guillermo would probably name him something Spanish. Tony had changed their dog's name from Princeton to Humpty after they'd gotten him from the shelter. They called him the Hump.

The clerk looked back at the dog.

"Makes sense. Look at those bright, happy eyes." She offered Fotis another treat. He took it again nicely, proving the first time wasn't a fluke.

"Fotis needs a collar, too," the other clerk said as she sized up Fotis' neck. "Let's try twenty inches." She began rustling through the racks of hanging collars, all sorted by color and pattern.

"You want a buckle, snap, limited slip collar?" She handed Paula a red and white ruffled polka-dotted shopping basket.

She hadn't the faintest idea.

"Buckles are better," the woman answered her own question.

"Then buckles it is," Paula said.

"Any particular color?"

Paula shrugged. "I don't know, blue for boy?" She had no clue.

"I was thinking maybe red." The woman put the collar on Fotis. It fit.

"It sets off his coat nicely and his one blue eye. Cool. I like it," the woman said. "What do you think?"

Her thinking faculties had shut down. But Paula nodded nonetheless. Fotis looked at her.

"You're such a pretty boy," the woman said. Fotis wagged and wiggled.

There it was again. Apparently Paula didn't speak "dog."

"Looks like a collie and some kind of big husky cross," the woman observed. "Double coat, the shape of his head and set of his tail. He's so dirty it's hard to tell what color he is. What do you think?" She turned and looked at Paula.

Paula thought nothing.

"Here's the matching lead." The clerk tossed it into the shopping basket, too.

The groomer reached to take the rope from Paula.

"Okay, big guy, bath time."

Paula reluctantly handed it over

"What'll she do to him?" Paula asked, watching the dog being marched off to the grooming station in the back room.

"Oh." The clerk smiled. "It's just a bath. A brushing. Not the firing squad—he already dodged that. Blow drying. She'll trim his nails, brush out those matted areas."

"Can I go in there with him?" Paula asked.

"It's better if you don't. They get agitated if they see their doggie mom."

Doggie mom.

"Hey," the woman distracted Paula. "Let's pick out some essentials; is this your first dog?"

Paula nodded.

"Then how 'bout after we shop I make you a complimentary cappuccino or latte to celebrate while you wait?"

"Deal." *Thank God,* Paula thought. "Latte would be great."

"Uhhh—I'd say you need two good brushes." The clerk grabbed one that looked like a garden rake and then a second that looked more like a metal comb. "He seems really good-natured. Be sure to use this one"—she held up the rake—"to get out matted fur." She chucked both into the basket. "What's he been eating?"

Paula shrugged again, questioning her own judgment.

"Here's a small bag of food to try—easy on the stomach." The clerk placed it in the shopping basket. "Pooper-scooper." The woman threw a long plastic-looking spoon into the basket. "Dog bed." The woman snapped her fingers. She lifted a fluffy rectangle from where they'd been stacked.

"Now some toys—"

Toys? Christ.

"You'll need a crate."

The woman directed Paula's attention to wire boxes that looked like prison cells.

"Mmm." Paula shook her head. "Don't think so."

"A lot of dogs like them," the woman advised. "It simulates the den."

"No thanks."

"Makes them feel safe," the woman offered.

Paula shook her head no. The clerk was bordering on pushy.

"It'll help with house training while you're gone," the woman said in a last-bid effort to persuade.

Paula gave her the *Back off* look.

The clerk shrugged. "Okay." Paula had been warned; the clerk was absolved of all responsibility for chewing and "soiling."

House training. Paula had not thought of that.

"Some treats then, bowls for water, food." The clerk snapped her fingers again, mentally checking off the list for start-up homes. She picked up two white ceramic bowls with cobalt calligraphy that said "nourriture pour Chien" and "Chien d' eau."

"This'll get you started." She looked at Paula.

The computer beeped as the merchandise was being tallied.

"Got his shelter papers?"

"What?" The question snapped Paula out of a stupor. "Oh, I'm sorry." She began fishing through her purse.

"Pet adoptions get fifteen percent off." The clerk smiled. "Except for the ceramic bowls, of course. They're French," she said in a somber tone. "Latte's on the house," she said, tilting her head and lifting both hands.

"Thanks." Paula produced the donation receipt from Animal Control she'd stuffed into the front pocket of her purse.

Bewilderment set in as Paula looked at the pile of dog paraphernalia. Still no word from Celeste. Paula watched as the woman carefully rolled each bowl in Bubble Wrap and taped it. The dog bed was rolled and tied with a rough-hewn twine. Probably organic.

"Here you go," the woman's cheery voice followed with a smile. "This'll get you started. Want it delivered to your home?"

Home. Roger. She looked at the time.

"No. That's okay; I'll take it."

Paula took a seat as her latte was being made. She covered her mouth and then rested her chin in her palm. She closed her eyes, needing a cigarette.

Roger had allergies to both dogs and cats. He'd break out in seconds. She hadn't considered that; in fact, she hadn't considered him at all.

Before she knew it the back door opened and Fotis emerged. Shiny, fluffy, his coat gleamed. He kept pausing to shake off before he reached her.

"Oh my God." Paula stood up at the transformation. Her purse fell off her lap onto the floor.

"I can't believe that's the same dog." The clerk paused to stare. "He's got my vote for most improved." She looked at her colleague, who nodded in agreement.

"Boy, he cleaned up well," the groomer said. "No fleas or dermatitis,"she explained. "I thought he was in worse shape, but," she went on to say in a high-pitched baby voice directed to Fotis, "you were just dirty." Fotis wagged.

His coat was darker, almost a rich black, with dappled freckles across his muzzle and along the inside of his front legs from his armpits all the way down to his front paws.

He licked the clerk's face as she tested the new red collar around his neck.

"He's so good-natured," the groomer remarked.

Taking a pair of pliers out from a drawer, she removed the rabies tag from the fraying old collar and transferred it onto the new one.

"There. Now you're all set," she said to the dog, and then looked at Paula.

"Shall we toss these?" The clerk held the old collar and leash between her thumb and index finger, the end of the rope curled and spiraled like a piece of rotini pasta.

"No," Paula said a little too emphatically. "I'll take those."

The clerk's eyebrows arched in surprise. Paula reached for Theo's two earthly remains. Without a word, the woman lowered each into a large ziplock bag, sealed it and handed it over.

Paula added it to the shopping bag.

"Now there," the woman said as Fotis' eyes brightened at the tone of her voice. "Look what a pretty boy you are."

The clerk snapped on the matching lead and handed it to Paula. "Good luck."

CHAPTER 3

Paula brought Fotis to her office because she didn't know what else to do. Though it was going on seven, she hoped Guillermo would still be there. Maybe he'd take the dog to Brooklyn for a day or so until she could figure out what to do, but no such luck.

There were several missed calls from Roger that she hadn't picked up. Unease burned like indigestion under her collarbones each time his incoming call lit the display. It felt like she was cheating. Her sense of obligation pressured her to offer up a full account of Theo and the day's events. She settled down into her office chair and worked up the nerve to call.

Roger answered immediately.

"Where are you? I've been calling."

"Yeah, sorry."

"Why didn't you answer?"

"I was busy."

"With what?"

"I uhh . . . kind of . . . uhh . . . got a dog."

"Yeah, right, and I just signed with the Yankees." He laughed darkly.

"Roger, I'm not kidding."

"We're meeting Arnie and Sophie at seven. Remember? Their place?" He paused. "I suppose you forgot again."

She had. Fotis looked up at her as if sensing the need for moral support. She touched the top of his head. It was so soft; she smiled without realizing it.

"I told you I, eh, I got this dog."

Roger was silent except for the sound of his mind ticking through a litany of theoretical possibilities.

"Paula, what are you up to?" He chuckled with ridicule. She slouched as if ready to guard her midriff.

"I have this dog," she stated as if she couldn't believe it herself. "I'm waiting for Celeste."

There was a long silence.

"I, uhh, I don't know what to say." His snort was incredulous. She didn't answer.

His inflection made her think of Jimmy Baldacci, the kid who broke up with her in seventh grade. How strange to think of Jimmy after all this time. That Friday afternoon when she knew just by his posture as he approached he'd wanted his silver ID bracelet back.

"It's a very long story," she said.

"Why didn't you answer?"

"Like I said, I got this dog."

"You've said that three times."

Her heart sank at the mocking edge of his voice. An even longer silence enveloped them.

"Paula, what are you doing?" He'd asked that exact question during their second week of married life after she'd marched into his bedroom, climbed under the covers and declared, "I'm not leaving. I didn't get married to sleep alone on a couch for the rest of my life," to which he'd asked, "Paula, what are you doing?" with the same quiet, belittling tone. With that she'd dug her nails into her forearm. Her heart sank as she got back up, left the room and headed downstairs.

Paula ignored Roger's question.

"I might have to bring him home for now—"

"My allergies—," he interrupted her.

"Nothing a little prednisone won't fix—," the words shot out before she could soften their meanness, their fodder being eight years doped up on powerful allergy medications to combat the mold and dust of his brownstone. Her allergist once looked questioningly at her, puzzled. "Tell me about how you live; what's your house like?" That simple enough question uncorked a torrent of blubbering, snotty confessions. The doctor had reached to grab tissues from the counter. Slowly shaking his head, he'd watched as she blew her nose, looking directly to catch her eye. "Paula—find a better husband."

"Now's not the time, Paula," Roger said. Maybe the time would be right, as Eleni used to say, when "Aiyia Pote," or St. Never's Day, came .

"My phone's beeping," Roger interrupted. "Just a minute. It's Arnie," he said. "Probably wondering where we are." Roger exhaled with an impatience reserved for those he termed the "lesser gifted."

"I've got the dog."

"So leave it somewhere, Paula," he raised his voice, more aggravated, less suspicious.

"Leave him where?"

"Wherever you found it; I don't care what you do."

"Yeah, you really don't . . . ," she said, meaning something else.

"I'm leaving." His voice became cool. "I trust you'll find your way there." It was a tone he used with disagreeable colleagues.

She had nothing to say. The stone wall of his frustration was like a fist, getting in the last punch.

Fotis settled down to lie on her foot, panting as he looked up at her. Damp warmth from his belly fur felt good.

"I don't know what else to say," Roger concluded.

"Yeah, well, I guess I don't either," she said.

Paula ended the call and set the phone down, leaning back in the desk chair. She'd never mutinied against Roger before, not like this. Though the day was a blur of exhausting emotion, both her hands were relaxed and not clenched into balled fists like usual. It felt like the riddle of the last ten years had come down to one brief conversation.

Fotis' body shook in time with his panting. The conviction that prompted his rescue from the shelter was fresh and true despite the ridicule. But dread flooded through her. The red message light pulsed on her desk phone—probably Christoff with another slew of complaints.

"Well," she sighed, and stood.

The dog stood, too.

"Come on, Fotis."

His ears moved ever so slightly at his name.

"Let's go find a room; I'm beat."

She grabbed the Pets du Jour shopping bags and tucked the dog bed under her arm. Here she was, homeless, armed with shopping bags and a leashed dog, in search of a place to sleep. Tears burned her eyes. With the irony of Theo rose the sticky feel of the ocean's salt air, the scratchiness of his black coat blanketing them. It was eerie but comforting. Maybe love was that simple, could be that simple.

The dog followed her toward the door. The top of his head looked downy and puffy from the bath, like some of the younger birds on her window ledge.

"Let's go." She mimicked the pet shop woman's baby-talk doggie voice.

Fotis stared deadpan at the fraudulent attempt.

"Okay." Paula snickered, respecting his lack of enthusiasm. Setting the packages down, she squatted to look squarely at him.

"Hey, look—I never said I was fun, okay?"

Paula was an adult who'd managed to escape childhood without learning to play. Vassili and Eleni didn't play; they worked. While other kids played in the street, Celeste would try coaxing Paula into a game of either jump rope or potsy—but Paula, perpetually plagued with the fear of being no good, would shy away. "Celeste," voices from the street would beckon. "Forget about her; come and play."

She declined department invitations to "Wednesday Night Scrabble." Roger was always good for a ready-made excuse: "Oh, sorry, but my husband's already made plans," when in fact he spent most nights cloistered on the third floor in a dark room wearing a food-encrusted sweatshirt that looked riddled with bullet holes. The fabric was so thin you could read a newspaper through it. He sat squarely behind a computer screen, his face illuminated by colorful three-dimensional mathematical models of the time-space continuum of black holes.

She walked toward West Broadway with the dog, heading toward a hotel where she'd frequently book rooms for visiting professors and scholars. She remembered the hotel's Pet Friendly signs.

In front of the hotel entrance, Fotis stopped, lifted his leg and drenched the entire side of the metal news box with a long stream of urine. *Shit.* Maybe the pet shop clerk had been right about getting a crate.

The lobby was quiet; business looked slow as Paula approached the front desk.

"Hi, would you happen to have a room for the night?"

"How many?"

"Me and a dog."

"How many nights?" He looked at her.

"Ummm, I'm not sure. One, maybe two."

"I put you in for two nights," the young East Indian–looking man speaking perfect Brooklyn English confirmed. It was a week before the onslaught of parents, before Labor Day and the start of the fall semester.

"Perfect."

"A deposit of one-fifty is required for pets on top of the room charge of three-fifty per night," he explained in an unbroken sentence while reading from a computer monitor.

"Fine." She leaned across the desk to try to peek at the screen.

"If there's no damage upon inspection," he continued, "we'll refund your deposit."

The desk clerk looked at her, shifting his weight onto another foot as he waited.

"Damage?"

He turned back to the screen. "Chewing, soiling, ripping up sofa cushions." He paused as if having lost his place. "You can exercise your dog two blocks down at the dog park furnished by the City near the NYU campus."

They'd just passed it on their way to the hotel. She walked past the park every day.

"Your pet is not to be left unattended in the room at any time."

"What if I'm in the shower?"

He looked at her.

She placed her debit card on the counter.

As the elevator doors opened, Fotis shirked backward. As per the advice of her mentor the cabbie, she picked Fotis up and placed him in the elevator before she dragged in the shopping bags. As it lifted to the third floor, Fotis hit the floor splayed out from the sensation of increased gravity.

The hotel room smelled like cloves and vanilla. The décor was contemporary shades of white and beige, like a high-end spa.

Fotis was panting, his eyes wide.

"I bet you're thirsty," she said. Crouching down, she rifled through the bags, searching out the Bubble-Wrapped ceramic French bowls. Busting open the plastic of the first one, she carried it into the spa-like bathroom, turned on the faucet and waited, testing the water's coolness before filling the bowl.

Fotis watched.

She tottered out with a topped-off bowl, careful not to spill as the water sloshed dangerously close to the rim. She placed the bowl onto the carpet by the bed.

The dog began drinking furiously. Water cascaded over the rim, splashed over the sides from his tongue, drenching the sand-colored carpet.

"Shit, shit, shit." She scurried into the bathroom and grabbed a plush white hand towel and began blotting the floor.

He emptied the bowl and looked at her.

"More?" His ears twitched, brow furrowed in confusion.

She lifted the bowl—realizing she'd used the one marked "food" in French—but shrugged and stepped in to refill it. This time she lowered it down onto the travertine bathroom floor. Fotis sniffed the bowl again and then, after several more healthy slurps, looked up at her, water spilling profusely from his mouth as he walked out into the carpeted suite to explore.

"Jesus Christ." She followed with the towel, trying to catch water dripping from his whiskers, lips. Who would have thought drinking water would be such a sloppy enterprise?

"You hungry?"

Fotis watched as she peeled the Bubble Wrap off the second bowl. Tearing open the dog food bag, she poured in kibble to the rim. She lifted the bowl to entice him. "Yum." She raised her eyebrows. Fotis didn't seem impressed. "Here." She placed it down next to the water on the bathroom floor.

He didn't move.

"Aren't you hungry?"

Fotis looked right and left as if checking for cars and then strolled over to the bowl. With a cursory sniff, he looked back at her with an expression that made her laugh out loud.

"What?" She lifted both hands. "You don't like it?"

He glanced at the bowl again and then turned away.

"Okay, so spanakopita it ain't."

He barked sharply. It echoed off the bathroom's stone walls.

Paula startled.

Fotis stared at her with bright eyes, limbs stiffened as if ready to jump.

Her skin prickled.

She was a little frightened of this strange excitement. He didn't even blink. Alone with a large-toothed furry creature she didn't understand; maybe this wasn't such a great idea. Such an intense stare, primed to pounce.

"Spanakopita?" she asked sheepishly.

He barked again.

"Okay, okay. Shhhh." She held a finger up to her lips.

His ears stood up, even the floppy one.

"Kathe se," she told him to sit in Greek.

His butt hit the floor, face alert as if he was proud of showing off his skills. She turned and began rummaging through the shopping bag to grab the package of hamburger-shaped treats. Ripping it open, she handed one over.

Fotis gently took it.

"Kalo skilo [good dog]."

His tail thumped the carpet.

It stunned her how obvious this was: Fotis understood Greek.

"Pa me exo?" she asked if he wanted to go out.

Fotis woofed softly and hurried excitedly to the door, rubbing the latch with his muzzle.

"Okay, okay, okay." She chuckled. "Tha paou [let's go]." There was a Greek food cart near the dog park. She suspected the owners were Albanian, however, since whenever she spoke Greek to them they'd stare. She often ate there when working late since the stand was open past midnight.

Grabbing Fotis' leash, she rifled through the bags for the pooper-scooper. As she took it out of the bag, she chuckled at the dangling tag that illustrated a three-step process of how to bend down and pick up dog shit.

Armed with the scooper in her purse, they raced down two flights of stairs to the lobby and over toward the square. As they neared the food stand Fotis started pacing, excited by the smell; a thread-like line of drool seeped out of his lips. Paula ordered two rounds of souvlaki and a double spanakopita. Fotis stood tall as the food was being assembled, watching as Paula paid and the paper dishes were handed over. She quickly pried lamb chunks off the wooden skewers and set them along with half the spanakopita pie into the paper dish. He quivered as he watched her. She chuckled at how sincere he looked, like a man vying for a first kiss.

She set down the paper dish. Fotis wolfed the pie down in seconds and looked up at her. She was amazed. He'd eaten in the shelter, but then again he'd vomited in the cab. She set the rest of her food down and Fotis finished it off. She went back and bought another souvlaki. He eyed it as she started to eat.

"Hey, I need to eat, too," she said, but then conceded, "okay, okay." Yanking off half of the lamb cubes, she arranged them in her palm. Cautiously, she lowered her hand.

Gently he vacuumed up each cube and then licked her palm.

After, they walked a block down to the dog park. She'd never had a reason to enter before but would see dogs chasing and playing in the grass, their owners congregating and chatting as they seemed to enjoy watching. She looked around. There was one other person and dog in the park. Paula sat down on the bench. Fotis watched the other dog. The owner waved from the other side of the park and started to approach.

"Hi," he said. "Haven't seen you here before."

"Yeah, it's my first time," she said. Fotis pulled to the e nd of the leash, sniffing toward the other dog.

"Cool dog. What is he?"

"Don't know. Just got him today."

"You're kidding," he said. "He seems so comfortable, like you belong together. That's a good sign." He gave a thumbs-up.

"Thanks." She didn't know what to say.

"You can let him loose. Minnie's a Lab. Totally friendly, is he?" he said as the two dogs sniffed each other.

"Not sure," Paula said. Looking at the owner, she unclipped the leash,

"She's an old girl, going on fourteen. Old for a Lab. Think we're heading home now; she's tired."

After sniffing Fotis, the man's dog squatted to poop. Paula watched as the owner skillfully used one of the plastic bags furnished by the park.

"You make that look easy," she said after he dropped the bag in the waste container.

He winked. "You'll get the hang of it."

He gave a little whistle and clipped on his dog's leash. "Good luck with your dog."

Paula watched as Fotis explored the park. He sniffed carefully around the bases of several trees and then would look over in her direction, searching out her figure on the park bench. Once reassured, he'd dash off. At one point he rolled over onto the grass, wriggling with such delight it made her laugh.

Then he stood and circled before assuming the position the other dog had assumed to poop. Paula looked toward the wastebasket, weighing the option of using the scooper or using the bag like the previous owner had. "Please clean up after your dog!" the sign said in four languages. She pulled out the scooper and walked over. Flies had already discovered the pile; holding her breath, she squatted and reached for the load, shoving the turd onto the spoon before gingerly carrying it over to the waste container. Stepping on the pedal, she lifted the lid and shook off the spoon. Most of it just fell off. But then she looked at the plastic scooper. How would she clean it off before bringing it back to the hotel room? She hadn't thought this through.

"Shit." She looked around the park for paper towels or something else to wipe the thing off. She bent and tried wiping it on the grass. *Damn.*

"Eh, fuck it." She chucked the damn thing in the trash and walked back to the bench. Crossing her legs, she leaned with her chin into her palm. Funny how there were so many benches in New York, but she rarely sat down to look around. Fotis was amusing to watch, like a bear sniffing and lumbering about. She thought of the view from her office window around the corner in Washington Square Park and how last year she'd spotted an older, well-dressed woman sitting down on a bench. The woman was tearing up a loaf of bread and scattering it for pigeons and crows. Not far away sat a homeless man with a dog, watching. The woman ignored him. Paula had begun to feel agitated and then angry. But as the woman left, Paula noticed two paper bags on the bench. One appeared to have a loaf of French bread. Days later she noticed the same two people as she sat reading e-mail, the same little ritual of each not acknowledging the other. The woman fed the birds before leaving two grocery bags. The man would wait until she was far enough away before making a move. Sandwiches and tubs of deli food and always something for the dog, too.

Paula had done the same with Sophie, a homeless woman who lived in the alley adjacent to Roger's brownstone. Sophie used the alley as a latrine and changing room. Paula would leave tubes of toothpaste, rolls of toilet paper and old clothes in a plastic bag. She'd left food in the beginning, but Sophie never touched it. For ten years they'd never spoken—except once when the woman issued a grunt that gave up her name. Paula had done the same and reached out to shake hands, but Sophie ignored it. That was all the help Sophie wanted.

Fotis sniffed around the entire perimeter of the fence, taking particular care in some spots. After a while he came back and sat on Paula's foot; craning his head all the way back, he looked at her upside down. She laughed. "You're so funny," she said in Greek. Her heart rushed open like a child's embrace.

"Ella, micro mou," she said endearingly; "come here, my little one," surprising herself by kissing his muzzle. His tail thumped the dirt and he licked her face.

"Ready to go back?" she asked, so tired she could barely move her legs. It was after nine by the time they got back to the hotel; her cell phone rang as she opened the door.

It was Celeste.

"Hey," Paula said. "I think I've left you a hundred messages."

"Sorry, I've been swamped."

"I figured. Did Eleni locate Theo's nephew?"

"I'll have you know Eleni stepped right up to the plate, pit bull that she is. Peter Fanourakis came forward and claimed the body and all is arranged."

"Thank God."

"Tell me how you made out with the dog?" Celeste asked.

"I'm sitting here looking at him."

"You took him home?" Heavenly hooted.

Paula moved the phone away.

"No. You know Roger with his allergies. I'm staying at the Soho."

"You're staying at the Soho Grand with a dog from the pound?" Heavenly shouted.

"Why's that so funny?" Paula asked.

"It just is; you're such a goof," Celeste said, and Paula heard her shouting the information across their apartment to Tony.

"Heav, he got a bath at Pets du Jour."

"It's still hilarious. So why didn't you just take him home, ply Roger with a couple of Benadryl? Maybe it would help him find some new Law of Relativity."

Celeste had no clue. No one did.

"I fed him Greek food. You know that stand by my office—souvlaki, spanakopita. He wouldn't eat dog food—"

"Would you? Why do you think the Hump turned into such a fat wad?"

They both laughed.

"Seriously, what are you gonna do?"

"I—." Paula looked at Fotis. "I'm not sure."

"I'd take him, but with the cats and the Hump we don't have room. Hey—I've already begged." It sounded like she was cupping the phone with her hand. "Tony gave me the death stare."

"That's okay. I'm thinking of keeping him."

"You're gonna keep him?"

Paula moved the phone away from her ear.

"I'm thinking about it."

"With Mr. Roger's allergies?"

"Yeah, well, I'll stay here a few days, think about things. Maybe I need a break."

"A break."

"Yeah." The idea just came to her as she said it. "A break."

"From Roger?"

"Among other things."

"Does Roger need a break?"

"I don't know what Roger needs."

Silence.

"Which means . . ."

"Which means I don't know." She thought of Roger's car sitting in the garage on Lexington. Too bad she didn't have the keys, or maybe it was better that she didn't. "Tomorrow night he's off to France, Cern, the Collider. Another eight-week project. So—call it a natural break."

"Okay . . . ," Celeste said slowly. "So why not just take your break at home?"

"I won't stay in that house," Paula cut her off. Just being able to see the corners of the hotel room was relaxing.

Neither said a word.

"I need to go on a drive, Heav." The idea took form the instant Paula said it. "Out of the City, maybe even out of state. Go visit some friends in California from grad school."

"I'm not saying you shouldn't."

They were both quiet with their thoughts.

"What'll you do with the dog?"

She looked at Fotis. "Take him."

She was still in contract with friends from Berkeley, including Bernard Kalgan, her major professor, and had driven back and forth to California so many times she'd come to know the I-80 exits by heart. She'd heard Bernie was getting ready to retire. Talking to him was soothing, not to mention helpful; he had a way of asking the right questions.

"Roger always hated driving anyway," she said.

"Interesting use of the past tense," Celeste remarked. "Kind of a crazy day to make decisions, don't you think?"

They were quiet for a few moments.

"It's not a rash decision."

"Keeping a dog's a big decision, on top of everything else."

"Maybe."

"And what about the conference?"

The conference.

"Paula, are you okay?"

She couldn't answer. Everything rushed in on her at once. Her throat became a spasm of grief.

"I don't know," she eked out.

They were quiet.

"Breathe," Heavenly said. "Take a couple breaths. Want me to come over?"

Paula shook her head. She'd call Guillermo; he could handle the conference. He was practically acting director anyway. Then she'd call Christoff. Tell him she needed time off.

"I can't do it anymore."

Celeste waited for Paula.

"I just can't."

"Who are these old friends from grad school?" Celeste asked.

"Bernie Kalgan. You and Tony met him. Eleni met him, too, when he walked me down to get my Ph.D."

"Oh yeah," Heavenly remembered. "We all had dinner at that twenty-four-hour Chinese place that served free refills on margaritas."

"That be the place," Paula said. "The others are old friends. We peer-review each other's articles."

"How long since you've seen them?"

"Saw Bernie this past March."

Her opening statement at the March conference had been awkward. As she began to present her findings on why English-language acquisition was more rapid among Arabic-speaking populations than Spanish, her heart clattered against her ribs. It felt like the audience could see everything, every moment of her life with Roger, on the surface of her skin, documenting her own humiliation. She fought to swim against the undertow of layered emotions, her eyes focusing on her PowerPoint slide, reaching for it like a life preserver.

"We exchange Christmas cards."

"You're gonna show up on someone's doorstep from Christmas cards?"

"I'm not *showing up* on anyone's doorstep, Heav," she said. "I'll call—tell them I'm in town." She hated the desperation in her voice. "Things aren't right, Heav." The partial confession eased her. "Someday I'll tell you."

"Anytime." She could hear Celeste waiting.

"I just need to take a vacation. Get away, to think. For some reason this dog is important."

"So you're taking a road trip," Celeste announced.

"Yeah," Paula said in surprise. "A road trip."

"Shit, I wish I had more time off."

Paula could almost hear Celeste calculating. But while traveling with her would be fun, Paula needed time alone.

The more the idea sank in, the more excited she felt.

"What about a car?"

Paula shrugged. "I don't know—rent one, buy one."

"You're taking the dog?"

She looked at Fotis, who'd been circling the room, sniffing. He instantly looked back at her.

"I don't know why that makes me feel better, but it does," Celeste said. "Will you at least call?"

"Of course."

"When are you leaving?"

"Don't know." She wanted to leave that instant. "I'll call you tomorrow after I talk with Guillermo, call the Dean."

"And call Roger . . . ," Heavenly said.

"Of course."

The joy of the last few moments tarnished quickly. Call Roger. He was probably fuming at her for pulling a "stunt" like this. Her chest burned with resentment like an acidy burp. Shit, what would she even say?

Just as she'd ended the call with Celeste, Roger called. Even the ringtone sounded pissed.

"Okay—you win. Where are you?" he demanded.

She looked at Fotis.

"I'm staying with a friend."

"Celeste?"

Let him think what he wanted.

"Okay, so what's happening, Paula? Why now, the night before I leave?"

"I need a break."

"So come to France with me," he said, sounding relieved. "Take a break there. You can stay as long as you want."

"I don't think—"

"Look," he said in his low, advisory tone. "I know things have been tense."

Were they?

"And I know you've been unhappy for a very long time."

He did? Her heart softened.

"So come to France," he urged. "Give me a chance to make it up to you. I love you, Paula. You're the most beautiful thing on earth."

She couldn't believe what she was hearing. He never said things like this. Declarations of love. Why say it now? She looked at Fotis. Why this day, when so many things were happening?

"Please, Paula, I'm your husband. Give me a chance to make it up to you."

But she felt sorry—for what she wasn't sure.

"I know you're my husband." She wanted to say she loved him but couldn't.

They were quiet for a few moments.

"I just need a break from our life," she said. "From the house, the mess. Normal people don't live like this."

"Oh, come on, Paula." He laughed. "You're a social scientist; 'normal' is a relative measure."

His laughter changed in a way that let her know although she'd pushed too far she was on the right track.

"Well now, don't forget that some of that mess is yours, too," Roger said with a scolding reminder.

Her chin dropped. Disappointment was eclipsed by confirmation. It took too much effort to hold up her head.

"Right, Roger." She was too exhausted to start.

"Think about France."

"Thanks, but I'm staying here."

"Think about it anyway."

Right.

"So what will you do on your break?" He sounded nervous.

"Maybe take a drive."

"With my car? Who with?"

She didn't want to say much.

"With the dog."

"You met someone online, didn't you?" he said. "I've been afraid of this."

She sat up. What a strange thing for him to say, much less be afraid of. Like anyone would want her.

"Roger—"

"You did, didn't you?"

"Oh please." She wouldn't indulge such craziness. Yeah, I met him on the downstairs couch a couple of years ago. "Call me when you land so I know you're okay."

"I love you," he offered. She'd usually say it first.

"Me too." She ended the call and turned off her phone for the night.

She looked at Fotis. "Are you sleepy?" She unrolled the dog bed, setting it on the floor next to the king-sized bed. Fotis watched.

"Here's your bed," she said in Greek. Kneeling down, she patted the surface. "Look how soft it is."

He looked at her like she was crazy.

"Very soft. Ummm." She lay down on the soft bed, trying to lure him beside her.

After a few moments she stood up.

"Okay, under the window instead?" She dragged the bed to the glass and smoothed the surface. "You like this better?"

He didn't move.

"Aren't you tired?" she asked.

He stared at her.

"Look, I'm sorry about Theo," she said, yawning. "But I'm beat." She walked to the hotel bed, kicked off her sandals and lay back.

She flinched as the dog vaulted up, on top of her. Her skin prickled in fear as she cried out. "Ahh!" She cringed and shielded her face.

Fotis tromped in circles before plopping down beside her, groaning contentedly. He sighed as if he too was weary from the day.

The pressure from his spine felt good. It surprised and pleased her.

As she relaxed she thought of the Center. If Guillermo agreed to manage the conference, who would take care of the birds? They'd think she'd abandoned them. But maybe it would be okay. Maybe when she returned she could lure them back.

She'd started thinking of Roger. The room had grown cold from the air-conditioning; she'd wanted to slip under the covers but didn't want to break contact with Fotis. She flipped up the edge of the bedspread to at least cover her feet.

Pressure from the sleeping dog's back made her eyes fill with tears. Such a trusting gesture to give a stranger who, just hours before, had thought of a million ways to pawn him off on someone else.

As tired as she was, she couldn't sleep. Paula thought back to her wedding night. Roger had tossed and turned before finally switching on the light. Raising himself onto one elbow, he tapped her shoulder.

"What, what, what?" Her eyes stung like bees from unwashed mascara and eyeliner. "What's wrong?"

She'd pushed her legs between his, cuddling up. The tiny diamond and sapphire pendant she always wore tickled her neck as it fell to one side.

"It's your breathing, sweetie," he'd said, and rubbed his face. It released the scent of his aftershave, making her twitch again with desire.

"My breathing," she said. With her finger, she'd traced the valley in his chest where the breastbones came together.

"Yes. It's keeping me awake." The skin around his eyes looked deeply lined, ashen.

"Well—uhh—am I snoring?" She'd burrowed her face into his chest, not wanting to entertain the image of her drooling mouth.

"No. Breathing," he said as if that were somehow surprising.

"Oh. Would you like for me to stop?" She was such a plucky young thing back then, but the seriousness of his expression made her stop.

"Am I moving around too much?" she asked in a conciliatory way, to show him she took his comfort seriously.

"No—it's your breathing." Roger leveraged himself up to a sitting position. He put on his glasses and turned to face her. She chuckled at his white silvery translucent skin, like a fish wearing Coke-bottle glasses. She loved what a nerd he was.

"When I get knocked off my sleep schedule I can't work." He shot her a look, both eyes magnified through the lenses like cerulean planets.

"Oh." She was at a loss for words. "Is my breathing that loud?"

"It's keeping me awake."

Paula rolled the platinum chain between her fingers. No one had ever complained about her breathing, not that she'd wanted to point *that* out on her wedding night.

He must have slept with other people. At fifty-two, Roger had never lived with anyone, always joking about how he'd "skillfully avoided it." He'd called her his dream girl, those first few months. Over the previous year their relationship had been much confined to her apartment, which she didn't find odd. He was off so frequently at particle physics conferences or working on grants or as a consultant overseas that they'd not slept together often. She'd thought nothing of it at the time—assuming that once they were married it would all even out. Cuddling with your man is one of those assumptions that brides don't think about.

"Maybe my nose is stuffy," she'd sniffed, wrinkling it as she tested the airways. "I bet there's plenty of dust in here," she'd said innocently, looking around in his bedroom at heaps of objects and cardboard boxes in the dim light. "Maybe once we move all this out and clean up—" She'd halted mid-sentence, feeling a sneeze coming on.

"I've already cleared things out." He'd looked hurt. 'Plenty of things," he said with finality.

Her eyes shifted to stacks of boxes, then back at him. He wasn't joking.

This marked a pivotal moment in their life. A messy bachelor, Roger was never home anyway and had promised he'd clear out the brownstone before the wedding. The only doubt she could remember was a feeling only days before the ceremony, as she signed the lease termination form on her apartment. There'd been something about watching her wet blue signature bleeding into the paper.

After her fifteen years as a faithful tenant, Mr. Mahoney had rented her apartment that same afternoon. You'd have thought he'd give her forty-eight hours or so to think about it. During all those years of waving to her every morning through his ground-floor window where he'd sit reading the paper, she'd never neglected to wave back. The next day she'd mentioned her feelings to Roger. He'd looked at her with such a rush of tenderness and emotion that all was put to rest. "Last-minute wedding jitters," he'd postulated.

"So, uhh . . . what do you propose we do about the breathing?" she'd asked.

Roger just stared at her, like the burden was hers. Then his eyebrows rose, and he flashed his goofy smile that always made her concede.

"Okay, okay, how 'bout for tonight and tonight only," she'd offered, her generosity betraying her like a friend spreading lies, "I go sleep on the downstairs couch?"

Roger smiled in a way that gave her goose pimples. She'd felt frightened; she was his wife now. It must have been that change in Paula's expression that caused Roger to tilt his head in his endearing "polar bear" way. Assured by the afterglow of the wedding, she pushed back the top sheet and swung her legs over to reach the floor.

"Just until you get back on your sleep schedule, of course," Paula mewed as softly as a lamb.

"Of course." Roger's features had formed a new expression: relief, conquest.

We never know precisely when a bargain is struck. Sometimes it just feels like being reasonable and bighearted. Many bargains are not retractable and must run their course. Sometimes they expire quickly; other times they are taken to the grave. Like the eighty-seven-year-old widow who openly weeps; everyone thinks, *How moving,* but she's grieving for all the years she never did one single thing for herself.

Paula had grabbed a pillow and a quilt from the foot of the bed. She felt like a kid swinging too high in the playground, not sure whether to grip tighter or let go.

She'd looked at his face. A nose that had at first seemed too large now made perfect sense. His thinning hair was clipped too short for her taste, but his large hands could cradle her spine like she was the most delicate thing in the world. She could be reasonable, understanding. It was an adjustment. They were both older. And after several more days on the couch Paula crept upstairs at bedtime, but Roger refused her and she started to cry.

"Of course I want to sleep with you, too, Paula—" He'd laughed nervously, touching her tears. "You know I want to. Just let me get on a better sleep schedule." She'd counted that as his first lie.

She settled in on one of his downstairs couches. The couch from her old apartment was still turned on end in the living room where the movers had left it (and where it would remain for a decade). Her books and belongings were heaped on top. She didn't have much, balancing the number of possessions by what she thought of as her "Bedouin mentality"—if she couldn't load it up on a horse did she really want it?

After two months of begging, she'd stopped asking. It was humiliating. She'd vowed to wait until she was invited. "Don't you miss me?" she'd kept asking in her Minnie Mouse voice, repulsed by her own groveling. Didn't he crave her warmth, her smell? Wasn't it natural to want those things? "I want to smell you," she'd insisted. He'd laughed, turning it into a joke as he raised his arm and fanned himself toward her. She'd pull away, hurt by his mockery.

A month before their one-year anniversary, as they were both reading in separate spaces cleared in the dining room, Roger said, "Hey—why not move into one of the upstairs bedrooms? You could fix it up, make it your own."

She peeked around a pile of newspapers at him.

"Seriously. I could clear it out." Roger sprang up from his chair, energized and ready to bolt into action. But Roger couldn't fake anything; this had been his plan all along.

"You could fix it up—get a bed for yourself."

And you could get fucked.

She'd felt him turn in her direction, his lovely blue eyes searching her out.

"You know, sleeping on that old couch," he advised, "you're gonna wreck your back.

You wrecked my life; I'll wreck my back.

"I didn't get married to sleep alone," she'd said quietly. She didn't look up from her book.

"Oh?" He stood and turned toward her, surprised. "I thought you were okay with this."

Paula stopped breathing. Sleeping on the couch felt temporary. Having one's own bedroom smacked of acceptance. And although every few months Paula would revisit "the issue," the outcome was always the same: "I don't have time for this now; let's talk tomorrow." It seemed her installation had been complete. Like some specialized part in one of Roger's neutrino sensors deep in abandoned gold-mine shafts in the flats of North Dakota. This had been his plan. At first such possession had made her feel safe, to belong to someone. She'd relaxed into Roger's solid frame in a way she'd not had with anyone. He'd had a certain heft to him; "good old peasant stock," he'd refer to his burly frame, thumping his chest as it made empty sounds until she laughed.

From that point on, her energy was funneled into developing the Center, and academia was only too happy to slurp up all that passion and drive. As the Center rose in prominence, her marriage withered—what Paula's colleagues would have call an inverse relationship. But as focused as she was, the moment she entered Roger's brownstone she became drowsy—as if she could sleep for a thousand years and still wake up exhausted.

Paula finally fell deeply asleep next to Fotis. The filmy hotel curtain blew with breezes from the window. It was one of the most peaceful sleeps she'd had in years, waking only once to the tickling of feathers on her cheek. She brushed it off and looked up. The room was still, silent. Fotis looked up at her, his entire body illuminated by the moonlight. Something was different.

CHAPTER 4

By eight the next morning she'd spoken to Christoff. While he'd been correct about her level of stress, he hadn't counted on her request for an emergency leave of absence.

"S-s-six weeks?" he stammered.

"Uhh—might be more like eight, Peter."

"For *that* you'd need to apply," Christoff said with administrative disdain.

"For an *emergency*?"

She hadn't taken as much as a sick day in years. He reluctantly gave his approval; Christoff didn't ask about the nature of the emergency.

She'd phoned Guillermo early that morning, not expecting him to answer. Paula imagined he was well into a good sweat, running on the treadmill in the basement gym of his Brooklyn co-op.

"Paula," he said. "So early?"

She mentioned a sudden, unexpected "family emergency." She was ready with a lie in case he asked, which he didn't; there was only the sound of his feet trudging on the rubber bed of the treadmill. Trying to divine the nature of his silence, she figured he was fist pumping a "yes" viva el Guillermo.

"But Paula—" His *Mommy, don't go* tone surprised her.

She'd buried her fingers in Fotis' thick fur.

"Just some things I have to take care of." Her voice was

soothing, even maternal. "You'll be fine while I'm gone—look how well you've already handled everything; hell, you're practically acting director now, Guillermo."

She listened as the pace of his gait moderated, as if his feet were doing the thinking.

"Think of it like this—I'll be out of the way," Paula said, waiting for him to offer up a joke to counter her self-deprecation. "Now you guys can finally get some work done."

"What about selecting presenters?" he asked.

"That's your call," she instructed. Guillermo had disagreed with Paula's direction and emphasis of the Center. While she'd kept it global, he'd wanted to narrow it on Latin America. "Choose from the paper submissions."

"But—"

"Look, Guillermo." Her voice softened, as if encouraging the child she'd never have. "You've got a Ph.D., right? You're a smart guy. Why do you think I hired you?"

"How long will you be away?' He sounded nervous.

"Six weeks, maybe eight."

He was silent.

"I'll let you know if it's longer."

She'd wanted to end with something clever but couldn't think of it.

She'd never walked away from anything. Typically she was the one up all night drafting to-do lists—cross-referencing them with other to-do lists—plagued by details lest the Center appear less than world-class. Her baby was now left in foster care.

She thought about her parents. What would Vassili have said? Or, God forbid, Eleni? She'd have to tell her mother something. Eleni, who still reported at 8:00 am sharp to the furrier, sometimes working past 9:00 pm to fill orders for fall collections in Milan. Only hospitalization for gallbladder surgery ten years ago had prevented her from completing a coat.

Paula left a message on Roger's voice mail to call when he landed the next day. Clapping her hands on her thighs, she sat up. Fotis looked up the instant he'd felt her eyes. "Well, thank God that's over with." The early sunlight filtered through the sheer ivory-colored drapes. "Ready to go buy a car?"

Fotis slowly wagged his tail. His ears lay back as he looked toward the door and then back at her, clearly with the sense something fun was about to happen.

The nearest dealership was uptown in the west fifties on Eleventh Avenue. It was about a three-mile walk, two hours at city pace, considering traffic lights and construction detours. Since it was a cool, dry morning she figured a brisk walk might help to clear her head.

First they visited the dog run. This time Paula used the City scooper as she briefly chatted with other dog owners about brands of food. None of the other dogs picked on or bullied Fotis. Perhaps it was the size advantage.

After the park, she and Fotis headed west on Canal Street, walking vigorously. As her heart began pumping it felt like the toxic fumes of the last few months were beginning to burn off.

Wholesale storefront windows overflowed with merchandise. Some had freestanding dismembered mannequin parts—legs sporting hose and stockings in every shade, color and texture, arms with cotton patterned gloves of different lengths, some wrist length, others theatrically past the elbow. She'd thought of the white cotton gloves Eleni had made her wear to church. Who wore gloves anymore?

Merchants across Canal Street sat in lawn chairs smoking. Small dogs had been tied to the merchants' chairs. There was a grandmotherly Chinese woman smoking a cigar with legs crossed like a man. Several shops were still gated shut—either too early to open or deserted—their jail-like bars were padlocked. The locks looked rusted shut. Chunks of curb were missing like a giant had bent over and taken a huge bite. Jackhammering echoed from building edifices, bouncing off every direction as they broke past striations of asphalt to brick and to cobblestone dating back to the horse and carriage. Discs of chewing gum covered the sidewalk, flattened as if by a steamroller. The coolness of the previous evening had caused the gum to set, but in the warmth of the sun they'd soon be gooey, tacking onto people's soles.

Paula and Fotis walked beneath block-long caverns of tangled metal scaffolding, over sidewalks of makeshift plywood through Tribeca, on up toward Ninth Avenue and the car dealership. They cut west over to Eleventh Avenue. It was another two miles north to the dealership and she figured they'd make it there by lunchtime. Her breakfast had been sketchy; she was hungry though it was not yet eleven.

Aromas of cooking meat and curry stew from clusters of street food vendors lured her across the street. A slice of pizza and three frankfurters later, she looked for a place to sit.

A vacant bench felt good; she wasn't used to walking so fast in one stretch. Fotis stood drooling. "You have to learn to eat your dog food," she said halfheartedly as he eyed the pizza, a spindle of drool streaming from his lips. Paula folded the slice of pizza and took a bite while she fed Fotis a frankfurter.

He gobbled it down so fast he almost nipped her fingers. "Jesus." She yanked back her hand. "Ciga, ciga," she told him. "Easy." She readied the second frankfurter, holding it like a torpedo. He took it more gently, having realized his overzealousness.

"Much better," she said as he swallowed the third dog.

They walked briskly past a block of shady currency exchange storefronts. Hindi and Asian alphabets covered up what had once been storefront windows. These places didn't seem open for business except she spotted a man scurrying across the street toward a windowless door that opened just enough for him to pass through.

The last mile led them to a walkway overlooking the Hudson River. Runners, people pushing strollers, pedestrians with no apparent goal other than enjoying the sights.

She noticed that Fotis garnered a lot of attention. Perhaps it was his size. Some would take one look, scowl and then turn a shoulder against him as they crossed mid-block. Others would slow and gravitate toward Fotis, saying, "Can I pet your dog?" and often asking what kind of dog he was. A few young men softened the instant they spotted him. It pleased and surprised her. "Cool dog." A man with forearms tattooed with sleeves of flames and skulls, metal dangling from every loose flap of skin, was on the verge of tears. A severe-looking older man wearing an expensive suit leaned over to pet Fotis. The man started to cough as if breaking into a fit. He explained how Fotis reminded him of Susie, his childhood dog. As a boy he'd slid his bath towel under Susie's hips to help her down the back stairs out into the yard. She'd had crippling arthritis. Paula felt moved as he recounted how the dog had suffered indignity and sadness as she was robbed of the smallest comforts. "I can't bear to watch anything suffer like that again," he'd said. Paula had touched the man's shoulder.

Fotis had granted entry into a world that until twenty-four hours ago had been hidden. Had she not taken Heavenly's phone call or if Theo had died a month earlier when she'd been in Greece with Eleni, Paula would still be holed up in her office, sleeping on the couch in Roger's brownstone. Yesterday seemed like ten years ago. She looked in the direction of the dealership. There was a car to buy, a call to make to Bernie Kalgan and the start of a drive out west. Each free day would be a precious jewel.

The dealership was located in a glass multistory building. Paula pushed open the front door to the smell of rubber tires, car wax and vinyl.

"Okay if I come in with my dog?" she called.

A large man nodded, swallowing his lunch as he approached, waving her inside. "Of course, no problem," he answered with a slight accent she pegged as Serbian. "I am Aleksey, but call me Alex," he said, wiping his hands on a white paper napkin before extending to shake.

"I'm Paula." She extended her hand and pointed to an orange stain next to his shirt pocket.

Alex looked down and wiped it, nodding.

Fotis pranced in circles, his nose in the air.

"Nice to meet you, Paula." Alex shook her hand and then squatted in front of Fotis. Alex extended his hand, a move that Paula now recognized as one of experienced dog owners.

"My, you are big guy," Alex remarked. "With big teeth, too," he added, and laughed.

"And who is this fine creature?" Alex asked.

"Fotis."

"Hello, Fotis," Alex said as Fotis nosed his fingers.

Alex just happened to have a doggie treat in his shirt pocket. He flipped it up like he was doing a magic trick.

"Can you sit?" Alex asked, and stood.

Fotis watched with rapt attention.

"He doesn't speak English," she said.

"My wife, Marina, says same thing about me."

Paula laughed.

He handed over the treat. One crunch and it was gone. Fotis looked for another. Alex raised his hands and shrugged. "Sorry."

Paula grinned. She knew it was all theatre but was smitten anyway.

"He always seems hungry," Paula said.

"Dog always hungry," Alex said. "Even Pomeranian always hungry."

The man's paunch strained the buttons of his shirt and his black tie gave the illusion of being too short for his body. His face was generous, with a soft smile. She liked him.

"How can I help you, Paula?"

"I need to buy a car," she said, and drifted toward a small SUV. She touched the curve of its smooth, shiny fender. "Today," she added.

"Today, eh," Alex said in a joking voice. "What's so special about today?"

She smiled mysteriously and blushed, enjoying the teasing. "I need a car that's good for *my dog*."

"We have many good models for dog." Alex gestured throughout a showroom that filled the entire city block. Cars were peppered between glass desks and poster-plastered kiosks covered
with action shots of SUVs.

"What about this one?" She smoothed the surface of the door
with her hand; it reminded her of a Japanese lacquererware box.
On the rear, the chrome logo said: "Ford Escape."

"This is next-year model—*very* popular." Alex nodded as he said
it. "Great gas mileage—it's hybrid."

She nodded. "I'm going on a long drive."

"Then Escape would be perfect." Alex stepped toward the
driver's side, opening the door and gesturing for her to sit. "Please."

Paula climbed in and sat. Fotis looked up at her as she leaned
back. It was as comfortable as a living room chair.

"Lumbar support, heated seats, the works." Alex walked around
to the passenger side and opened the back door. He folded down
the backseats, creating a platform.

She watched over her shoulder.

"Backseat folds flat." He patted the the space with his meaty
hand and looked at her. The flesh of his ring finger rolled over his
gold wedding ring.

"Perfect spot for Fotis." She was impressed Alex remembered
the name. "We have many other good SUV model." He gestured
for her to climb out and follow him.

Paula didn't budge. "If it's okay," she said, "I think I'll just take
this one."

"Wouldn't you like to take Escape out for test-drive?"

"Thanks, but that won't be necessary; I'll take it."

Then he shrugged. "You don't want to look at other models for
comparison?"

She shook her head.

"Escape is great car. There are other great cars, too."

"I want this one. I like the color." Black was always her color.

"Oh, so you like color, eh?" He leaned over as if letting her in
on a secret. "Tuxedo black—new color."

She wasn't aware she'd been gripping Fotis' leash so tightly. She ran her hand along the top of the dashboard; it felt good behind the wheel. Safe.

She smiled. "Can I buy this one?" She gripped the steering wheel for emphasis.

Alex raised his eyebrows. "Let me check if car is reserved. It was delivered yesterday. Escapes are going fast. Nice, compact size for city street parking." He raised his eyebrows.

She hadn't thought about parking; Roger had only one space. She'd figure it out when the time came.

She watched Alex scurry around to the front and look at the windshield. "No tag under wipers. Good sign." He raised his eyebrows. He peered at the dashboard and began writing down a number on a piece of paper from his shirt pocket. "Cross your fingers." He motioned for her to wait. "Paula, enjoy car; I'll go check inventory."

She watched him walk over and sit down at what she presumed was his desk. Paula had a good view of his face as he typed into a laptop computer, and she tried to read the set of his brows as his expression changed. Finally, he stood up, the chair moving out slightly. Her stomach jumped.

Fotis studied her sitting behind the wheel. He sniffed at the door.

"Ti skeptisai?" she asked what he thought. Fotis' tail swished once. "Eh, you're so easy," she said in English, chuckling. "You like everything." He smiled and started panting.

She watched Alex walking back with an orange ticket. He held it up like a magician and then brushed it with his other hand. The ticket disappeared. Then he approached and reached behind her neck where she was sitting and pulled the ticket from next to her collar.

Paula gasped.

"Escape now reserved for you." Teeth like tiny white pearls shone as he smiled broadly.

She clapped and squealed, embarrassed by the noise she'd made but delighted at not caring. She wondered what Roger would say when he saw the car. She wouldn't tell him she'd bought it right off the floor. She'd heard of people looking for months—trolling about from borough to borough, bickering here, there—sometimes even making a pilgrimage out to New Jersey for the sake of five hundred dollars.

"Okeydokey," Alex said, and climbed into the passenger seat beside her. "Let me tell you about your car." He began summarizing the car's features, cubic inches and drive trains; she nodded as if she understood.

She loved the smell, the feel of the seats. As Alex kept explaining she reached up to touch the ceiling. Even the roof felt plush.

"Ready for paperwork?"

She nodded.

"Let's move to my desk," he said. "Will you be applying for financing?" he asked as he climbed out of the car.

"I'll give you my debit card." She slipped out of the car.

"Even better, you get cash discount." He led her to his desk. "Please have seat."

On his desk she noted two glass jars, one filled with dog biscuits and the other with M&M's.

They were quiet as he typed in her name, details, and finally began printing out all the purchase forms and agreements.

"Can I take it today?" She gave a slightly embarrassed smile and bunched up her shoulders. Her cheeks burned like an embarrassed twelve-year-old's.

"The car?" He gave a hearty laugh. "Oh no—soonest is tomorrow afternoon."

"Okay," she conceded.

He looked up from the screen. "You look like early bird, right? Maybe you can get it before eight. After that it gets crazy busy. You need car delivered?"

"You deliver?"

"Of course, no problem." He lifted his hands.

Alex's printer churned and Paula signed each form while on

hold with her insurance agent, who'd been a neighbor in her old building. Roger had switched to him after they got married. She kept glancing over to admire the car, still not believing it was hers. After the agent put the new insurance policy in force, she handed Alex the phone to fax over the certificate of insurance. Paula stood and walked over to the car.

"It's ours, Fotis." She felt as if she'd squeal.

Fotis lifted his leg and peed on the tire.

"Okeydokey, now I need a valid driver's license." He held out his hand without looking up. The transaction cleared except for the vehicle registration. For that she needed to produce a valid New York State driver's license.

Providing Alex with an abbreviated version of yesterday's events, she explained how her driver's license had come to be in Queens.

He thought for a moment, playing with his upper lip. "Okay." He looked around the showroom floor and back at her. "Tell you what. How 'bout we take Fotis for ride in your new car to Queens Hospital and get driver's license?"

"Now?"

Alex smiled as he nodded.

"I drive to hospital," he qualified. "You get license; then you drive back. Give Tommy fifteen minutes to pull car out." Alex walked away carrying the paperwork.

He turned back. "Help yourself to coffee, donut," he said. "Give Big Guy donut, too." He leaned over exaggeratedly, talking to Fotis. "Make her give you coconut." It sounded like "cuckoonut." "They are best."

She took out her phone to call Celeste.

The moment they pulled up to the circular patient drop-off Celeste stepped out of the hospital's revolving door to greet them. Fotis took over the backseat, his face sticking out the driver's side window. For the first few blocks out of the dealer garage Fotis had looked a bit queasy, his eyes slightly unfocused—but as soon as he stuck his face out the window and felt the wind he was fine.

"Hi, Fotis," Celeste called his name.

The dog looked straight at her.

"Paula, he's adorable!" Heavenly was petting him before they'd come to a complete stop.

Paula stepped out and the two friends hugged each other.

"I'm so glad you're doing this," Celeste said into Paula's hair. "To anyone else it might look crazy," she said, and then let Paula go. "But I have a good feeling."

"Thanks."

"You look good, *miksa mou,* " Heavenly said.

"Shut up; I look like shit and you know it."

"You look beautiful. Happy." Celeste smiled in a proud way, like the day she and Tony had flown out to Berkeley with Eleni to see her graduate.

"What does Tony think?"

"It doesn't matter what Tony thinks."

She could tell Celeste was making an attempt to stay neutral about Roger, but from the way Heavenly was smiling Paula guessed that Tony approved. "He gives you his best."

Tony had never cared for Roger and Paula knew it. She was one of the few who could read Tony, maybe because she'd known him since high school.

Celeste stepped back and looked at the Escape. "What a *gorgeous car,*" Heavenly said, running her hand along the hood. "Ah shit— wait till Tony sees it. He's gonna want one."

Paula introduced Alex. He hopped out and walked over to shake Heavenly's hand, palming a business card like another magic trick, flipping it, making it disappear and reappear just behind Celeste's ear.

"How did you do that?" Heavenly demanded in astonishment.

"Secret." He winked.

"They deliver, too," Paula added, a member of the team.

"I always discount car for good friend." Alex winked and then got into the passenger side of the Escape.

Celeste began to pet Fotis through the window.

"My gosh, he's *huge,* Paula, but so sweet."

"Yeah, he is."

Celeste looked at Paula. "Roger called earlier."

"Shit."

"Several times."

"Sorry."

"Nothing to be sorry about," Heavenly said, "though he grilled me for almost a half hour."

Roger was no match for Celeste.

"He's convinced you've met someone."

Paula looked at the dog. "Yeah. We slept together last night."

"So how was he?" Celeste asked with the precise inflection she had used when they were younger.

"Big and furry," Paula said.

They both cackled.

"What should I do with your papers?" Celeste asked.

"Dump them," Paula said. "The bag's a piece of shit anyway. Guillermo's already got the articles."

"Wow. Guess we gotta give the little fucker credit for something," Celeste said.

"No, we don't."

Celeste chuckled. "Yeah—you're right."

Paula took the hospital ID tag out of her purse and handed it over as Celeste handed her back her license.

"Promise me you'll call," Celeste said.

"Always."

CHAPTER 5

The car was delivered at 7:00 am just as Alex had promised. Paula and Fotis had finished breakfast via room service at 5:00 am, a fruit cup for her, a plate of ham, eggs and sausage for him. It was nice to share meals. They'd sat on the coverlet of the bed, from City services to room service over the span of a few days.

After a trip to the dog run they were packed, checked out and waiting curbside. A robocall from the dealership confirmed the Escape was on its way.

Paula's black skirt had become as comfortable as a pair of well-worn jeans. After a good washing in the bathroom sink the skirt had finally yielded to her form.

The previous day a voice had hounded her, *Go pop by the brownstone and give Roger an obligatory good-bye kiss. No hard feelings for refusing his offer to come to France,* and, *Go get the suitcase; pack some clothes and things for the trip.* Yet her clothes, shoes, even her jewelry felt polluted. Roger would try to talk her out of both Fotis and the trip. He was good at that. And while buying new clothes seemed like a waste of money, it was better than facing Roger and the brownstone.

After a hippie head shop burned down near NYU earlier that year, she began having dreams about fire. Not nightmares, just dreams. Such dreams weren't far-fetched. The floorboards in Roger's bedroom seemed to groan for liberation under the weight of his stuff. She'd heard of instances where firefighters would give up and let the house fire burn in a controlled way. As it would be with Roger's staircase, three-quarters blocked with piles of *Finan-*

cial Times newspapers, it wasn't worth losing valuable personnel to a hopeless pile of paper.

Then the widow fantasies started. In America widows are seen as noble; in Greece they're considered bad luck. But there'd be no graceful exit. She couldn't help Roger, but maybe she could save herself. She suspected that even firefighters with their sharpened axes couldn't hack through to Roger's common sense.

So instead of going back to the brownstone, she bought new clothes from a Burmese vendor staked out on a street corner. "Genuine" ladies' Calvin Klein merchandise was stacked neatly by color and size on aluminum card tables. She'd picked up enough knockoff underwear, tops and jeans for a week, enough to get her to Bernie and Jeannine's, plus a pair of sunglasses for the drive.

The vendor was pushing a "genuine" Louis Vuitton duffel bag—which upon closer inspection Paula swore was used, though it looked surprisingly authentic. Celeste's sister-in-law had given them tips during a drunken birthday party about how to spot real Vuitton by examining the lining and balance of the logo print.

"This is not new," Paula alleged with her *you've gotta be kidding* look. She pointed inside the bag to traces of white powder. Talc? Cocaine? Heroin? The man took the bag and inspected the lining. He looked genuinely annoyed and turned it over, spanking its bottom to rid the bag of whatever substance had dusted the lining.

"See?" he'd said, and smiled. "Only dust. New, not used." He handed the bag back for Paula to inspect. "Dusty from transport."

"Don't you have another?" She bent down as Fotis sniffed her hair, and perused the merchandise beneath the aluminum card tables.

"No," the man answered quickly. "Only one." He held up a finger for emphasis. "Is new, not used," he'd insisted testily. "My lip to God ear, lady." The man touched his mouth, then pointed up.

Paula pulled out her wallet and paid. What the hell, she'd give it to Celeste for her sister-in-law when she got back. As far as she knew, drug-sniffing dogs weren't manning America's tollbooths.

Eleni believed that the instant a person is born their Tihi, or destiny, is written down in a book kept by the Moirai, or the three goddesses of Fate. After Vassili died, Paula imagined the cunning old hags dreaming up all sorts of miserable scenarios for Eleni. Paula's marriage to Roger had always seemed more like a factory error than cursed. But Eleni had gotten a different version of the same raw deal—a young widow with no other marriage prospects. Maybe it was bad luck. Bad luck men, bad luck dishes, bad luck pots and pans, forks, spoons and knives. But then you see people like Celeste and Tony, happily married for more than twenty-five years, weathering every crisis together.

Paula didn't believe in luck. Perhaps the Moirai had put blinders on her, laughing at her evaluation of Roger as husband material. He'd passed every suitor test as she stumbled headfirst onto the biggest land mine of her life. She never would have predicted that, weeks after the wedding, Roger would stop sleeping and eating. She had to walk him up and down the street at night to calm him. Trembling, he'd cling to her arm as she told him, "It'll all be fine; it's just a rough patch; you really should go see someone." She'd become his best friend, his comforter, and she shut up about the sleeping arrangement, the squalor in the house. It would have been like beating up a puppy. "For better or for worse," maybe she'd gotten the worse part up front, she'd reasoned. Soon their sleeping arrangement became institutionalized. Divorce was never a thought, so she'd backed off, squelched her desires, shut down and turned her attention to the Center, accepting whatever hand the Moirai had dealt.

The first sign of trouble materialized on moving day the week of their wedding. Before leaving for France earlier that summer, Roger had neglected to give her a key.

"I'd like to start moving some things in," she'd said a month before his departure.

"Well, I'll need to do some rearranging." It sounded perfectly reasonable. "I'm reorganizing." He'd smiled sheepishly. "I have a lot of stuff, in case you hadn't noticed."

"Why don't you let me help?" she'd offered, scooting up to the edge of her seat. "If you give me a key I can work on it this summer."

He'd looked at her in a way she couldn't read. "Uhhh—I'll clear out as much as I can, but some things'll have to wait till I'm back."

"I can help clear it out."

"It's not the sort of thing you can do for me." He flushed. He wouldn't look at her. He'd looked embarrassed or ashamed. "*I* need to sort through things," he'd reiterated. "My parents' things."

"But you won't be back until the week of the wedding," she'd protested. "My lease is up. I have to move."

"Sweetie," he'd crooned. "I'll be back in time. I'll do what I can before I leave, but it can wait till then."

She couldn't stop worrying about it. "Hey—if you changed your mind, Roger, that's okay," she'd offered her get-out-of-jail-free card. But Roger laughed the whole thing off. She'd even phoned overseas, afraid he'd met somebody else. "No, of course not," he'd say. "You're my dream girl," he'd reassure her. "What's a summer when we have our whole lives?" True. Sensible as always.

"You worry too much, Paula," he'd said from France. "You gotta have faith in life. Trust the future, our future."

Move-in day finally came after he'd airmailed a key from France days before the wedding. "Oh thank God," she'd muttered, and laughed nervously.

The three movers (cousins of a Malaysian graduate) had stood with their work gloves on, sizing up the ornately carved front door.

She depressed the thumb latch and pushed. It budged a sixteenth of an inch. With her shoulder she gave it a hefty shove. It opened a full inch, just enough to register the smell of musty paper and the briny sting of mildew.

"Phew, it stinks," she admitted, thinking it might lessen the embarrassment. The door opened finally. "He's been gone all summer," she'd offered. "Give me a minute—I'll air the place out."

It would take longer than a minute. The movers shot glances at each other; one of them looked at his watch and then out to the moving van, double-parked on the narrow street. He said something in Malaysian to his partner.

"Lady, we got three more stop," he said.

"Oh," was all she said. She stood there, stunned. Roger had sworn that he'd cleared it out. Decorators were scheduled for tomorrow. Her eyes watered. What was she getting herself into? Why would Roger lie? She thought of hijacking Eleni's car to speed out to Montauk, stand at the end of New York and smell the salt air, dilute her terror. She felt twisted. Her apartment was rented, the dress bought, tux rented, invitations out.

"He's been gone all summer." She began climbing over debris and boxes, searching for windows, coughing. She unlatched the ones she could reach.

The movers listened politely, having seen it all before. Two or three times a week they'd worked on contract with the Department of Health to evict hoarders.

"You *sure* this right house, lady?" one of them asked

She'd nodded at him—what a strange thing to ask.

"This look like hoarder live here."

"What?" She wrinkled her brow.

They covered their mouths with their hands and stepped outside, their heads shaking.

"Place is full," one of them said. "No space." He'd motioned like an umpire at a Yankee game: *You're out.*

"This was his parents' place," she'd said. "We're combining multiple households," she'd explained. "You know, from two into one, getting married," out tumbled the excuse.

"You probably see this every day."

Their expressions worried her. Different from when they'd loaded up her things, joking, trading jabs as they'd packed up her old apartment. Her nature always put people at ease, especially immigrants. Paula'd never forgotten that Vassili had been a waiter, Eleni a seamstress.

One of the movers pointed to the space between the front window and the wrought-iron fence bordering the sidewalk. "We unload you here." He pointed. "Your husband help you move later, okay?" he said, looking at his watch.

"No, wait—tell you what." Paula looked up at the swollen rain clouds. "It'll take me a second to clear a spot—I swear." She lifted a finger. "Please wait—it'll take me a second," she assured.

She stepped inside and quickly began moving boxes; shoving piles of cartons onto other piles, she heard the clanking of bone china, the chiming of a pendulum clock. She tripped over a pile of folded Oriental rugs to clear a footprint for the contents of her life.

She'd had no furniture except for a couch she'd purchased just before meeting Roger; everything else she'd tossed. "You can build a whole room around a couch like this," the home décor specialist had advised.

Paula and Roger would decorate and remodel the kitchen and bathrooms, make it "Our Home," Paula'd glowed to Eleni and Celeste, turning her cheeks pink in a way no one had ever seen. A girly happiness she'd finally allowed herself. "This is the real marriage," Eleni had sworn to Celeste during the bridal shower, pointing to goose pimples on her forearm. "See? It's a sign. This one's gonna stick, you better believe it." Even with Paula, a forty-year-old bride, Eleni had bragged, "The older the hen, the thicker the juice." And she had stood to dance as the priest's wife popped in a CD of Greek music.

It had all seemed too good to be real. Your stars align, the right people are there and your time has come. But according to the Old Ones, that's precisely when the Moirai come hobbling along to crack open the book of your fate. So went Paula's longing for a loving home. Lovely, elegant wedding, not a dry eye in the house—Roger'd cried; she'd cried; they'd all crooned, "After all she's been through, at last she's found love." She'd felt absolutely transcendental as the Greek priest placed one floral wreath upon her head, the other on Roger's, connected by a satin ribbon to symbolize eternity.

It took little time for the movers to pile Paula's boxes on the spot she'd cleared. They'd balanced her couch up on one end, propped it against a pillar in the foyer where it would remain for a decade.

One of the movers was on the verge of speaking up when the other tapped him and motioned with his thumb to the truck. In the time it took for Paula to pull out an envelope of cash for a tip, the men had left. She'd stood on the porch with money in her hand, wondering why they were in such a hurry to leave.

She'd planned the entire wedding that summer in Roger's absence. "Do whatever you want," he'd say. "I know it'll be beautiful." And while she found his confidence reassuring, it felt a little like she was marrying herself.

From the curb in front of the hotel, Paula waved down the Escape the minute she spotted it, followed by a dealership car with advertising stenciled along its sides. The driver pulled over and parked, handing over two sets of keys and a packet with a car manual, certificate of insurance and registration. "Any questions?" he'd asked.

Temporary license plates had been affixed to both front and back bumpers. She was legal enough for now. On the passenger seat lay the GPS manual and a road atlas with a red bow and a note from Alex. "Have a great trip," he'd written in quasi-Cyrillic script. It made her smile; she hadn't thought to buy a map.

She lowered the backseat, tucked it down flat as she'd seen Alex do and then unrolled Fotis' bed. "Kano." She patted the bed. Fotis jumped up. She rolled down the window just enough for him to stick out his head.

After tossing in the duffel and shopping bags, she climbed in and adjusted the driver's seat. The instrument panel lit up brightly in the dim morning light.

"Bye, New York." Her voice was a whisper as she put the car in

gear. She lowered her chin. "See you in a few weeks." Her stomach didn't believe her. The rims of her eyes stung. *Eonia I mnimi.*
She slipped on the knockoff Hermès sunglasses. Butterflies took
flight in her stomach, a mix of sadness and relief.

When Paula was eight years old watching her father's casket
being lowered, she'd remembered a joke. "Know how many
people in there are dead?" her father would ask when they'd drive
between the cemeteries that flanked Grand Central Parkway.
Paula would shrug, though she knew the answer. "All of them!"
Vassili would exclaim, snorting, wanting her to say the punch
line with him. She'd marveled at the knife-edged precision of his
grave, all sides looking more like rich brown velvet than dirt. The
priest, in a black robe that touched his shoes, flanked in layers of
gold-embroidered regalia, led the chant of "Eonia I mnimi."
She'd remembered the priest being aggravated by the November
winds that kept blowing out the chunk of incense in the *livanistiri,*
the golden jingling incense burner. It had taken two altar boys to
prop her mother up through the ceremony.

Paula sat in the Escape, waiting to calm down. A knock on the
window startled her. The hotel bellman tapped again and gestured for her to clear the spot.

Okay, she mouthed.

"Bye, New York," she whispered. "Eonia I mnimi."

Tapping the gas pedal slightly, she pulled away from the curb
and headed west on Canal Street toward the Holland Tunnel,
under the Hudson River, out of the City into Jersey and all points
west.

Paula touched the cover of Alex's road atlas; she decided to take
I-80, the northern route to Berkeley. She'd never been near the
Great Lakes, the Dakotas and Montana, and she could cut south
to Berkeley if she got bored. She'd planned to call Bernie's office
when she got to Pennsylvania, since there was a three-hour time
difference. But she was too excited to wait; she'd leave a voice mail,
hoping he wasn't on vacation. During a traffic pause she searched
her phone directory and punched Bernie's office number.

"You've reached the voice mail of . . ." It was someone else's voice.

"What?" Ending the call, she looked at her phone, surprised. She checked the directory again. *Damn*. That *was* his number. She'd just seen and spoken to him that past March in Montreal. He'd made jokes about retiring, but surely he'd have sent her an announcement.

She looked at her watch, calculating Pacific Time. It was too early to call his home. She'd call the main sociology office later, when it opened. She'd be well into Pennsylvania by then or, if traffic kept crawling, barely into New Jersey.

Paula flew out of the Holland Tunnel into the early colors of the morning. Gas pedal depressed, windows open, her hair blowing, the faster she accelerated the better she felt. Getting up to eighty, then ninety, she thought maybe the wind would whisk her thoughts away.

Jersey was a blur except for periodic traffic congestion; Pennsylvania went on like a past life. The faster she drove, the clearer the sense became that there was somewhere she needed to be. It wasn't California or New York. It wasn't a place. The map was nothing but lines, numbers, destinations. Wherever she was meant to be, she'd know it when she got there.

At a McDonald's in the middle of Pennsylvania Paula bought Fotis three burgers. She fed him all three in the parking lot and then offered him dog food. An obese woman wearing a housedress was sitting in the open door of a minivan watching.

"You gotta eat this, too," Paula said, holding up the bowl in a conciliatory way.

"Hon," the woman began. "Pardon me for butting in, but you know if you keep feeding him burgers he ain't gonna eat his dog food. Make him eat the kibble first."

"How do I do that?"

"Don't give him nothin' till he eats the dog food."

Paula looked at her.

"You just got that dog, didn't ya?"

Paula nodded. "Hon." The woman smiled. "He ain't gonna starve, you know. Just hold out until he chows on the kibble, then give him a burger."

"Thanks," Paula said. "I'm Paula."

"I'm Evelyn. Good luck with your dog. He's a cutie."

"Thanks."

Paula walked Fotis around on the grassy areas, past the playground where children squealed and she let him sniff and lift his leg. He signaled her by looking and then half-dragging her toward the Escape, waiting for the door to open and then jumping up onto his bed, quickly getting settled into his position at the window. The glass was already smeared and dotted with dried drool.

She drove for another hour and then decided it was time to call. It was nine in California. Pulling over at a rest stop, she sat at a picnic table and looked up the department number in her phone directory.

The administrative assistant explained that Bernie had retired unexpectedly after the Montreal conference. The woman wouldn't give any more details, but Paula did manage to wrangle a phone number.

She dialed his number and sighed with relief when he answered.

"Paula!" Bernie exclaimed. "So nice to hear from you."

"It's great to hear your voice." She felt his warmth.

"Sorry about not being able to make your conference in New York."

"That's okay; I'm not going to make it either," she quipped.

"What?"

"I'm taking some time off."

"You're missing your own conference?" He paused. "Is everything all right?"

"Yes and no," she said. "How's Jeannine?"

"Recovering."

"Oh my goodness, from what?"

"Didn't you get my e-mail?" he asked. "She took a bad spill about a month ago on the bike, broke her ankle."

It was probably buried in the hundreds Paula had neglected to open.

"Shattered a couple of bones. I figured it was time to retire anyway. She's always hated Caly. It was time years ago. I'm just a stubborn old Canuck. So we came back to what we used to call our 'summer house' and now we're staying."

Fotis was nose to nose with another dog at the next picnic table. Their bodies were stiff as they sniffed each other and then started to wag their tails.

"How is she doing?"

"The boot comes off in a few weeks. She had surgery, pins, but she'll be fine. A bit of physical therapy and she'll be back on that damned bike of hers."

"I'm so sorry I missed your e-mail; I would have called."

"We were just talking about your conference. We're back up in Thunder Bay. Ontario. Followed our three kids," he explained. "We've got seven grandchildren. We're busy spoiling the heck out of them, turning them into brats to get back at our kids."

She could see it. Bernie always made her feel safe; he and Jeannine were like kin.

"So tell me why you're missing your own conference."

"Oh Bernie." She felt about to cry. "I'm taking a bit of leave, don't know for how long."

"I wondered how long you could keep up that pace," he said. "You're always running."

The words stopped her in her tracks. He'd never said anything like that before. How long had she been running? Her tears indicted her. Years she could never get back time spent striving for recognition, working tirelessly, when all she really wanted was Roger. It felt like she'd awakened to find that someone had died.

She closed her eyes and rested her forehead in her hand. Fotis sniffed the top of her head. The words hurt. Bernie wouldn't have known about Roger; he couldn't have. Yet in one sentence he'd identified the core of her dilemma.

"I think maybe you're right," she said, struggling to gain composure. "So I'm taking time off." She paused. "Driving out west to surprise you and Jeannine, maybe look up Karen Richards and John Timmelman, too."

"Well, we're sorry that we'll miss you. Jeannine'll be disappointed. You two always clicked," he said. "It's wonderful being back, though. Beautiful country up here, Paula; I'd forgotten. Who else are you planning on seeing in Caly?"

"Uhhh, just really you." She felt embarrassed and crushed.

"Where are you?"

"Pennsylvania. Just approaching the Pocono Mountains exits," she said. "You know, honeymoon country." She tried to make it sound funny.

"Is your schedule flexible?"

She laughed out loud at the question, thinking of Roger in France.

"Very."

"Well, how 'bout coming up to see us?"

"Really?"

"When you get to Chicago, head north and spend some time with us." She could hear the Canadian accent replenishing itself. "We've got plenty of room. Mind you, it's a long drive—"

"I'm already on a long drive, Bernie."

"Perfect. So it's decided."

"Yes."

She heard Jeannine's voice in the background.

"Jeannine wants to know if you have your passport."

Everything was back at Roger's. But wait. Unzipping a compartment in her purse, she felt the sharp edge of the passport cover. She closed her eyes and sighed. Thank God she'd forgotten to give it to Roger after she and Eleni returned from Greece. Funny he hadn't asked for it; Roger liked to keep all the documents.

"I almost can't believe it, Bernie," she said, surprised by her good luck. "But I do—I have it."

"Good. Then you'll come."

"Yes. Thanks. I will."

"Then it's settled. Head north to Wisconsin when you get to Chicago. Call me if you get lost." He chuckled. She'd spent years in graduate school driving around California, lost. A direction disaster, she used to call herself.

"Drive through Wisconsin until you hit Lake Superior. You'll know when you hit it because you'll run out of land," he joked.

"Yuk, yuk, you think I'm some kind of city idiot, don't you."

"You said it," he teased.

"I have GPS, Bernie," she said, looking at the Escape.

"Oh my, I don't believe it," he said. "Paula has GPS," he called to his wife. "She says, 'Thank God.'"

"So what happens when I run out of land?"

"Go west along the lake to Duluth," he explained. "Follow the lake on Sixty-two all the way up the north shore. You'll hit Two Harbors, Silver Bay, Grand Marais; keep going. Then up into the Boundary Waters and into Canada and we're the first big city. Your GPS'll take you right to our door. You can't miss it."

Paula felt like she was going home. They'd feed her, take care of her; she'd tell Bernie everything.

"It's about seven hundred miles from Chicago," he said. "Probably more than twelve hours. Now don't try to tackle it all in one day."

"I won't."

"Plenty of places to stay."

"Okay."

"That'll give us time to get clean sheets on the bed."

"I'm bringing my dog."

"Ooo," Bernie said. "Now that might complicate things at the border. You wouldn't happen to have his current rabies vaccine papers, would you?"

She looked at Fotis and thought of Theo. "As a matter of fact I do, Bernie." Buried in the Vuitton duffel bag in the back of the Escape (she now felt worried about the "dusty" lining) were Fotis' papers from the shelter, including the proof of vaccine.

"Wonderful. How fortuitous."

"How fortuitous indeed."

"How perfect that you got a dog," Bernie said.

Paula smiled in a puzzled way. What a funny thing to say. And Bernie hadn't asked about Roger. Getting back in the car, she braced herself and dialed Eleni's number. Now was as good a time as any to explain.

CHAPTER 6

Black birds with massive wingspans soared above the tree line on either side of I-80. She saw Fotis' profile in the mirror. "Ti vlepis?"

Fotis had seen the birds, too. She reached back and scratched his cheek as he leaned into her hand.

"Einai omorfos, neh?"

The birds captivated her. She watched them bank off the wind; hand out the window, she angled her fingers trying to simulate how the birds used air currents with their wingtip feathers. With the slightest shift they'd plummet and then swoop back up, gliding in what she knew were thermal pockets. How huge they must be in order to be visible from so far away.

Maybe they were eagles. Or maybe "just turkey vultures," as Roger used to say. They'd see large dark birds circling on the drive to a Long Island beach house owned by one of his colleagues. Roger would say it as if belonging to their particular species was a bad habit rather than an adaptive niche. "You always know there's carrion nearby." He'd wrinkle his nose disapprovingly.

Billboards along the Pocono exits portrayed dewy-eyed, giggling young couples clinking champagne glasses in red heart-shaped tubs. Paula thought of how Heavenly and Tony had gone to the Poconos. Maybe that had been the key to their happiness—they had the same sense of humor. "Fall in Love with Us!" or "Rediscover Each Other," showing older couples (more champagne), with bleached-white teeth and salt-and-pepper hair. Their faces seemed to exclaim, *Hey, we're old, but damn it, we still know how to have fun in a heart-shaped bathtub!*

Paula pushed her platinum wedding band down to the end of her finger, goading it to slip off out the window. It was a reckless dare; she felt a strange mix of excitement and fear. Not trusting her mood and whatever sick little taunt was egging her on, she reached into her purse, unzipping the side pocket, and let the ring fall in.

Heavenly had warned against making snap decisions, but removing the ring wasn't a decision; it was a breather. Still, guilt oozed through the cracks in Paula's logic. She looked at the empty finger; the skin looked younger.

This wasn't about Roger. Why did it have to be "about" anything other than taking a long drive? Roger was the one who'd chosen to lock her out of the bedroom that first week, deciding not to share his bed or get help when she'd asked him to. She couldn't sleep on that rose-colored mohair couch another night if her life depended on it.

She'd warned him five years ago that her feelings were changing. "We need to go to a counselor," she'd warned. But acknowledge and ignore—that was Roger's strategy, thinking he could smile in that adorable way of his and pull his wife back whenever he wanted her. He'd tap her shoulder on late Sunday afternoons (after she'd already eaten too much ice cream) and invite her up to lie down with him on a space he'd cleared for lovemaking. She'd cringe, try to break down her defenses, conjure up a mystery man in a fantasy that would get her through however long it would take. "You're so beautiful," he'd say every time as if that were the only phrase he knew. But still, her heart rushing blindly with hope—*he loves me.* Even when it was more like masturbating on each other's bodies, she'd stare at the plaster medallion on the ceiling rather than face the disintegration of their marriage.

Early on in their marriage when Roger had been at a particle physics conference in Frankfurt, she'd gotten a call from the Staten Island Police. A neighbor had lodged a complaint about shutters banging against a house after a windstorm. Paula had known that Roger owned investment property there but had never seen it. So she phoned Roger, who told her to call the property management company. She asked about a key. "They have one if they need to enter," he said briskly, "But they won't need to; it's the outside shutters."

After a phone call, the company insisted on meeting her at the house where their representative would assess the damage. She could have picked it out even without an address. The downstairs curtains were drawn; towels were tacked over the upstairs windows. A new roof and gutters had been put on earlier that season after Roger had received a citation. From time to time he'd get notices from the authorities, neighbors fed up with the abandoned house that was an eyesore. This time it had been an easy fix. The company reattached the loosened shutter to satisfy the complaint from the neighbors, and as their truck pulled away, Paula had stood watching the house until a few minutes later, wondering what she was waiting for to happen.

During the first weeks of their marriage Roger caught Paula "snooping" around the brownstone. She'd hoped to find something of his mother's, since he spoke so highly of her. The mountains of his parents' belongings seemed to be layered with antiques.

She followed a "burrow" path into a side room and discovered a box containing delicately embroidered tablecloths and napkins. Sifting through the box, she pulled out an embroidered table runner; chilly puffs of mildew made her turn and cough. The linen had been marked with the tracings of mice teeth, and the runner fell open in her hands like a cut-out string of paper dolls. Elation turned to disappointment after she found that the whole box had been similarly chewed and stained with mouse urine.

"What are you doing?" Roger had asked in a voice that startled her.

"Oh." She'd dropped the cloth and yanked out her hand, hopping back down onto the burrow path. She'd looked up at him and smiled, trying to regain her poise. "Just looking around. I live here now, remember?" she'd kidded, thinking humor might diffuse the strangeness. "Did your mother embroider these?"

"Just leave it all," he'd said. "I'm taking care of it."

She looked at the box. "Wouldn't it be wonderful to display some of your parents' antiques?"

But Roger didn't answer. While he'd made strides, moving around boxes in those first few months, she often wondered where he'd put them. Nothing ever seemed to end up on the curb. The attic was locked. When she asked he'd say, "You don't have to worry about it."

"I'm not worried." She'd offer to help, but he'd refuse with a look that was both pained and fearful. Then after another break-down, followed by weeks of him hiding in his darkened bedroom watching the science-fiction channel, the boxes slowly migrated back downstairs.

"Give me a weekend and a Dumpster and I'll clear this place out," she'd shouted.

"Don't even think about it," he'd yelled back, his voice trembling, his bottom chin quivering. That was the moment when she knew she'd pushed as far as she could push.

Coming up to one of the last exits for the Poconos, she thought back to her first marriage, at eighteen years old, to Joey, an iron-worker. When Eleni had tried to bribe her into coming to work for the furrier, Paula instead went to work at Pet World, her dream job since second grade.

She lost her virginity on her first date with Joey, a guy she'd met on the bus. The next week he proposed. *Better take it,* she'd thought at the time. *No one else'll want you now.* Eleni had always been far more worried about what was between Paula's legs than between her ears. It was an Island thing, remnants of a past Eleni had drummed into her daughter's head since girlhood. Even the use of tampons was prohibited, as was bike riding, lest it make her a "bad" girl.

Sex was love. Paula and Joey married within the month.

The problem with Joey was that after the rings slipped on, the gloves came off. Unable to sustain an erection on their wedding night, he put his fist through the plasterboard above her head.

"That's okay; don't worry about it," she'd tried to console.

"Shut up," he'd yelled.

"Why are you getting mad? It'll be okay," she cooed, only it seemed to make him even angrier. Too bad his bout with impotency hadn't struck on the first date before all that cervix-banging sex.

After five months of Joey hollering so close to her face she could smell what he'd eaten for dinner, Paula plotted her escape. Once he kicked in the bedroom door because his toast had gotten too dark. "How come you're so fucking good at pissing me off?" It was news to her that she was good at anything.

Waiting until Joey left for work one morning, she stuffed her things into a paper grocery bag, surrendering the thin gold wedding band on the night table, and left without leaving a note. Papers were filed. Eleni arranged for a Greek lawyer. "Be careful now," Eleni had warned. "Men use divorced women."

Marriage number two at age twenty to Marco came and went just as quickly. He'd come into Pet World looking to buy an iguana, claiming to have been an experienced iguana owner. He'd wandered around the store talking about how much he loved animals. The way he'd pick up the hamsters and softly stroke them made him seem like such a gentle soul. A few days after his iguana purchase Marco came back, just to see her and visit the animals. Even Mr. Sanchez, the owner, nudged her. "He's sweet on you," he said, and his wife agreed.

Within days Paula and Marco had taken several tumbles between the sheets, talking to each other in their own baby-talk sort of hamster language they'd invented, and they were quickly inseparable. When Marco proposed it surprised her, but his puppy-dog eyes won a "yes" out of her. Besides, Eleni's voice of practicality echoed in Paula's skull: "Better take it. Who wants a twenty-year-old divorcée? You might never get asked again."

But a week after the wedding, a very pregnant woman came into Pet World asking about food for iguanas. She tearfully explained how the love of her life had disappeared and left her with his pet iguana. "So what was the guy's name?" Paula asked. "Marco," the woman said.

That evening Paula laid it all out before him. "I *was* gonna tell you." He'd broken down and started to cry. She'd just stopped taking the pill that morning at his insistence and sat mortified. She'd run into the bathroom and swallowed one, half-coughing and choking on it. "Don't leave me," he'd cried. "I love you."

She'd assured him and waited until he left for work the following day and then packed up her things. "Stupid, stupid, stupid," Paula said in time with each yank of her T-shirt, bra and underpants from the dresser drawer he'd so graciously cleared. She set the gold band on his dresser next to the jar of quarters he'd collected, pocketing just enough for bus fare.

She'd headed back to Eleni's. Thank God she'd kept her job at Pet World despite Marco's insistence that she quit to stay home. Sitting on the bus, she dug her fingernails into her forearm, leaving little half-moon-patterned bruises.

After the second marriage fell apart, Heavenly called from the pay phone in her upstate college dorm. "Hey, *kukla mou*," she sarcastically used Eleni's nickname for Paula of "my little doll." "Stop marrying every guy you fuck, okay? Break out of that old-world bullshit. Get a boyfriend."

Twenty and divorced twice. Paula was far too ashamed to date, finding ways of keeping relationships platonic. Instead, she turned her sights toward academia—the coldest, most unavailable suitor this side of the moon. Community College of New York, then CUNY, where she made dean's list every semester, and then graduate school at Berkeley. She figured if she was in school she was safe. Academia asks no personal questions and is only too happy to suck the marrow out of all the little sublimators like her, hiding out.

It took eight years for Paula to rack up as many degrees as institutionally possible at Berkeley and land an academic position at NYU. Each degree served as an evidentiary hearing about her self-worth, and the further she went in school, the more she felt exonerated. Maybe she wasn't a loser. But Eleni, in her self-appointed role as one-woman Greek chorus, warned, "Stop with the education, already. Men don't like too-smart women. Be smart, but not too smart."

Roger's early criticisms (which he insisted were mere observations) were "you talk in paragraphs" and "you certainly do swear a lot."

"Does it bother you?" she'd asked, fully prepared to never utter "fuck" again.

"I don't know what I think about the swearing." He'd tilted his head in a thoughtful way, mulling it over as she waited.

As for her shameful marital past, as she called it, he'd not batted an eye. After a few dates of "really, really, really liking him" the whole confession came tumbling out in a dark restaurant ironically called The Monastery. After two glasses of wine and the sordid tales of Joey and Marco, Roger had sweetly touched her hand. "Consider them the warm-up act for me."

To a starving heart such words were narcotic. Some call it love, but acceptance is the most potent drug there is. It creates a loyalty that's as blinding as it is liberating. Like March's first bright, warm day after the dark introspection of winter, it's an affirmation that indeed there is safe harbor and possibly, after all, even a God.

After six months of dating, Roger took Paula to Gdańsk, the Polish city on the Baltic where his parents were born. And then he proposed. "My parents would have loved you as much as I do," he'd declared in the shadows of the massive shipyards. He'd stroked her hair and fingered one of her curls. She'd shied away, aware of how the ocean air turned her hair into Brillo. "What, sweetie?" He'd laced his fingers between hers. "What's wrong?"

"Oh," she'd said in a worried tone, pulling on her coiling strands. "It's just that my hair is so ugly right now."

Then he'd softly chided her and their bodies melted together to form a new synthesis, or what Roger had called the urge to merge. "Everything about you is beautiful—you are the most beautiful thing on earth."

She realized that he really meant it and for a second she could see herself as he did. Then he'd whisked her off to Brussels, the diamond capital of the world. He introduced her to his colleagues in the United States, France and England. His awkwardly large frame would curve and almost cup around her as if to give shelter. "This"—he'd pause—"is Paula," a name his body language translated to mean "the most precious substance in the universe."

Just outside of Toledo, Paula called it quits for the night and fell asleep quickly in a hotel room. She'd forgotten to wriggle under the coverlet or close the drapes. The morning sun woke her and the scent of bacon and toast lured her to the hotel lobby. She'd left Fotis up in the room. Hungry guests politely elbowed their way closer to heaps of scrambled eggs, bacon and sausages. A nearby basket of fruit looked as perfect as a still life. She pressed a fingernail into an apple's red skin just to make sure it was real and then pocketed it for later.

She loaded a paper plate with bacon, scrambled eggs and sausages. "Whoa ho, hope you left some for the rest of us," a man with a Green Bay Packers jersey teased.

After Fotis ate he and Paula spent half an hour walking down a dirt path through a little grove of trees behind the hotel. Soon she didn't even hear the steady din of the interstate. Fotis paused to look up at the trees like he'd never seen so many packed together before.

"Dhen birazi." She gestured with her arm to follow. "Tha pao."

Littered along the path were crushed beer cans, a few amber beer bottles and an empty Doritos bag.

Paula called Eleni after retrieving the message: "I'm your mother; call me."

"Hi, Mom."

"I still don't understand why you're driving all the way to Timbuktu," her mother continued as if she'd been talking nonstop since their previous conversation.

Paula strolled down the path as her mother continued. No "Hello"? No "How are you?" "You could've gone out to the Island, to the beach, if you wanted to take a break," Eleni said. "It's gorgeous out."

"It's gorgeous here, too, Ma," Paula countered as she watched Fotis sniff a Snickers wrapper.

"Your husband called me twice from France," Eleni said. "In ten years he doesn't call me once, and now he's called twice."

"Did you ask him what he wants?"

"Of course not," Eleni said in her scolding way, as if Paula were still thirteen. "He left messages saying it's important, and he needs to talk to me."

"So answer it next time, see what he wants." Paula shut her eyes, picturing Roger's face.

"I don't wanna answer it," her mother said. "It might be Stavraikis." This was an elderly man who'd come over to watch TV with Eleni on weekday evenings. While she enjoyed his company at times, Stavraikis would often fall asleep almost immediately and snore so loudly that she'd have to turn the volume way up to hear anything else.

"He wants his wife, is what he wants," Paula's mother said. "I want him to stop calling."

"So answer it; tell him to stop."

"I'm not gonna tell him that." Eleni's sheepish tone surprised Paula. She'd often thought Eleni was either afraid of or maybe in awe of Roger, the astrophysicist. "A Real Scientist," Eleni would say, and raise her eyebrows. She knew there was something fishy about them as a couple; Eleni's bird-like eyes saw everything.

Paula's preemptive Saturday afternoon visits to Queens always seemed to assuage Eleni's curiosity. "You know I've never once tasted your cooking," she would say with a sly and suspicious eye. Paula would take Eleni out for birthdays, Mother's Days, buy her new purses, shoes, outfits for Christmas and Easter.

"Sorry Roger can't make it; he's busy with work," Paula would apologize.

"Dhen birazi," Eleni would say. "Husbands work. That's what they do."

"Look, Ma," Paula continued. "I'll call from Chicago. I'll be there sometime later today."

"*Christos kai Panayia,* Paula, Chicago?" Eleni said. Paula guessed her mother had crossed herself. "That's so far."

"Ma, I told you. I'm driving to Bernie and Jeannine's in Canada."

"Why Canada? It's so far." If you left New York you must be running from someone.

Paula hated when her mother fretted. It stirred a deep sense of responsibility to protect the aging woman. "Mom, I've told you," Paula sighed.

"Hhhh. Canada?" Eleni asked. "What if something happens?"

"To me?"

"No, to me."

"Call Heavenly; call Stavraikis."

"But Stavraikis doesn't always answer; he can't hear good."

"So call nine-one-one, Ma, I don't know." She hadn't thought to make arrangements for someone to check in on Eleni. "No, Paula, I haven't died in my sleep," Eleni would say as if her daughter's calls were bothersome, but God help Paula if she forgot to call.

"I was just in Montreal this past March for that conference. Remember? It's the same thing."

"It's not the same thing." Eleni sounded more afraid than angry. "That's work."

Paula had nothing to add.

"I don't like this, Paula, don't like it one little bit." Eleni's mistrust was contagious. Fotis looked up at Paula from the base of a tree.

"I didn't like it yesterday when you told me about this cockamamie scheme and I like it even less today."

"There's nothing cockamamie." She almost added *and I'm not doing anything wrong*. "I have Theo's dog with me."

"Uch ooo, Christos kai Panayia. That Theo and his dog." Paula could picture her mother's hand covering her face. They'd exhausted the topic of Theo's nephew and the funeral by the time Paula made it to Ohio. "Why now go see this *advisor*?" Eleni grilled.

"Bernie's my old advisor from grad school," she said. "The one you met in California with Jeannine, his wife. Remember you flew out?"

"I know who he is; don't talk to me like I'm senile."

"I know you're not senile."

"Why there?" Paula's mother asked.

"Because they invited me."

"You leave your husband to go off looking for some advisor you had in college?"

"We're colleagues, Ma—I'm not *leaving my husband*." Her voice rose as she cradled the top of her head as if to protect its contents. Guilt seeped in. That old-world subservient crap, as Celeste called it.

"Roger's in France *every* summer," Paula reminded Eleni.

"But usually you go with him, right?"

"For *part* of it," she corrected Eleni. "I'm just not going *this* summer; I'm taking my own vacation." She labored to soften her voice.

"A woman doesn't go on vacation alone unless she's asking for trouble."

"I'm not leaving my husband," she repeated, and could have kicked herself for sounding so defensive.

"Well, suit yourself. You'll do whatever you want because you always do."

A confusing silence held them on the phone.

"Look, Ma, I've got a long drive ahead of me," Paula said. "I'll call from Chicago."

"All right," Eleni said. "I'm your mother and I worry."

"I know." She ended the call. All of a sudden she felt mixed up. Her previous feeling of conviction and excitement began to sour in her stomach.

A sob gripped her so suddenly it made her sink; squatting on the dirt trail, she grasped her knees. She missed her mother. She hated Roger for what he'd done, yet she missed him, too. She looked up at the trees; what the hell was she doing in Ohio? Fotis began sniffing her head and then, more specifically, the roots of her hair. She stopped sobbing, looking around to see if anyone could see. Finding her breath again, she touched his fur for safety.

"Everything's gonna be okay, good boy."

Heading back to the interstate exchange, she sat at a stop sign. Two I-80 signs—one west, the other east. A wilted feeling urged her to back down and go home. Show up at the Center, look stupid for a couple of weeks, then get over it. She could deal with Roger and the brownstone head-on and refuse to give up the dog no matter what.

"Fuck." She grasped the steering wheel as her stomach lurched. Her head dropped forward until the car behind her beeped. She hit the blinker and continued west.

Bernie sounded blasé when she phoned from Chicago. Maybe he and Jeannine were having second thoughts about the sudden company. "Now just keep going till you hit water, Paula. That would be Superior/Duluth."

"I know, Bernie." She tried to rekindle the enthusiasm of the previous day. "I'll be there tomorrow, early evening about five."

"Fine, fine, Paula, no rush." He sounded distracted.

Her hand migrated toward her purse until she remembered that she'd smoked her last cigarette in New Jersey. After Eleni had cast aspersions on Paula's "cockamamie scheme," everything was doubtful.

The sun had set by the time she reached Eau Claire, Wisconsin. The fresh, cold night air made her shiver. Looking at the dashboard, she began pressing buttons, searching for the heat. Who would have thought she'd need the heat on in late August? The wrong button triggered the windshield wipers.

"Shit." After a blast of air-conditioning and a squirt of blue fluid blurring her windshield, warm air finally started flowing in through the vents.

She was road weary. No matter how she shifted the electronic seat controls, her bones ached. The last time she'd spent this much time in a car was twenty years ago in graduate school, driving back to New York for Christmas. Tall brightly lit hotel vacancy signs were visible from the highway—better take one or risk driving through miles of nothing but woods. It seemed darker by seven here than in New York. The farther north she drove from Chicago, the more dramatic the autumn colors.

After getting the last room at a Days Inn, she watched the desk clerk switch on the NO sign. Entering the room, she pulled down the blankets and climbed right into bed. Fotis nestled up against her and she welcomed his warmth through the covers. She'd neglected to close the drapes, brush her teeth or slip off her jeans. To her surprise the sun woke her for a second morning in a row.

Early the next afternoon Paula caught her first glimpse of Lake Superior; the water's blue-whiteness erased any evidence of a horizon. The illusion was perfect.

As she drove through the city of Superior toward the bridge that crossed the twin ports into Duluth, Minnesota, and then onto Highway 61, the buildings reminded her of depressed towns in New England. Or even Long Island City before infusions of big money had turned it into a funky upscale artists' community where the average person could no longer afford to live.

What struck her most were the huge rusted structures along the shoreline, spanning into what appeared to be rivers and estuaries. Paula felt the weight of a different kind of urban blight. Tall beige granaries densely packed the docks; boxy prefab warehouses and imposing rusted structures dominated the landscape. Just over the bridge in Duluth she turned to ask a young man standing on the other side of the gas pump, "What are those?"

"What are what?" The tall college kid turned.

"Those rusty-looking things," she said.

"You mean the ore docks?" He'd wrinkled his nose, then glanced at her temporary New York plates.

The giant structures fascinated and terrified her. They looked like huge mechanical creatures that could spring to life at any moment and tromp across the landscape as the ground quaked.

Roger had called early that morning before she left Eau Claire. It was as if they were sitting in a restaurant somewhere on the West Side, mulling over the day's events. One of his colleagues had had too much to drink on the flight and slept in such an awkward position he couldn't fully straighten his neck after they landed. Fotis barked at someone at the door. "Scasai," she told him to shut up.

Roger'd spent hours driving the man to a chiropractor in a provincial village. He prattled on about the research facility, concerns over security, and nothing about their marriage or her trip. Maybe he didn't want to know.

The outskirts of Duluth were behind her. She glanced out the passenger's side window at Lake Superior; the quiet color of the water slowed her mind, her thoughts. Her chest and neck muscles seemed to let go. There was no place to pull over, though the lake demanded complete concentration. Even her breathing interfered with her ability to absorb its depth.

Roger's phone call had left her unsettled, but she was soon distracted by the first sighting of rock outcroppings in the water;

cliffs; boulders and spiky evergreens. She sought out the view in each clearing, catching herself weaving like a drunkard toward the center yellow line, staring at something breathtaking—but everything was breathtaking. She was frantic to take it all in, to know it before it disappeared.

Across the road, cliffs of red granite jutted up in cylindrical shapes. Evergreen trees grew out of the rock at angles she'd not thought possible. Drill marks like stripes were still visible along the face of the cliffs where road crews must have tucked in sticks of dynamite. Within a five-mile span she'd passed through two long tunnels. Though they were not as long as New York's Midtown Tunnel, the lighting and the vanilla-colored subway tiles were identical—her mind kept tricking her into expecting either the Long Island Expressway or 34th Street at the end.

The farther up the coast she drove, the more dramatic the scenery. In places it reminded her of the coast of Maine, or Northern California or Ireland, yet it had its own delicate yet rugged sensibility. She placed her hand on her chest without even realizing, searching for a spot to pull over and get a better view, but the road closely hugged the narrow edge of the shore. Finally she veered off in the town of Two Harbors into a red dirt parking lot. She saw a sign for BNSF's Allouez Taconite facility and wondered if this was one of those ore docks she couldn't stop thinking about.

Climbing out of the car, she grabbed Fotis' leash. They walked down a narrow red path through wispy pine trees lined up along the edge of a steep cliff. To her left a covered railroad bridge spanned the highway, feeding out onto a trestle. The ore dock extended for a quarter mile over the lake.

On top of the ore dock was a line of railroad cars; the structure was so massive they looked like toys mounded with reddish rust the color of the dock. To her amazement a giant tanker was roped to the side of the dock; its engines murmured quietly as men on deck signaled to one another with their hands. The side of the dock was composed of narrow rusty louvered chutes. Each was gently lowered by chains along the length of the ship; some chutes groaned as they were lowered, crying like a suffering animal.

After the chutes were in place, reddish pellets of iron ore began sliding into the cargo holds. Each chute emptied in turn along the ship's length. She watched as the white markers on the outside of the ship lowered into the water slowly and evenly as the cargo holds filled. Once the chutes were raised, activity buzzed on the ship's deck with men sealing off top hatches. The water surrounding the back of the ship turned a teal color and slowly the ship pulled away. She'd never seen anything like it. It filled her with wonder—what the lives of those men must be like.

She looked at her watch; an hour had passed. And while this place was restful, she thought she'd better get driving. The thought of being on the highway to Thunder Bay after dark with deer catapulting in every direction made her cringe. She'd die if she hit one.

Paula liked the tall evergreens packing the tops of red granite outcroppings, like spectators craning to see the outcome of a football game. The air was chilly. Through her windows it felt thin and clean.

She thought about calling Celeste but didn't believe she could talk. In that moment she understood jewelry. Embedded in the mystery of an aquamarine jewel was this lake—a drop of seawater trapped in stone, believed to have properties that could save a sailor from drowning. Greek women would give their men stones as talismans. Paula wore an aquamarine ring on her right hand almost every day, except for the day Celeste had called. Maybe Paula had been drowning, too, and it was why she'd reached for the same ring every morning. As she gazed into the blue-green stone during staff meetings, on the subway or flying to conferences, it stilled her. The lake, surrounding cliffs—all of it hundreds of millions of years old—had been created by the same earthly forces.

Approaching the next little town, called Beaver Bay, she pulled off into a Culver's. She'd seen several of these—their sign advertising the "Home of the ButterBurger." Recreational vehicles filled the parking lot, like sailors lured by the sirens of Greek myth, but here the ButterBurger did all the seducing. She drove up to the window, ordered a coffee for herself and two ButterBurgers for Fotis (what the hell). She figured she'd park and walk around.

The sound of chain saws had drawn a crowd. She had a ringside view of "Chainsaw Treasures"; a yellow banner was planted into the grass next to the Culver's sign where a man wielded his chain saw like a dance partner. No storefront window or display case, only the open tailgate of the man's dented truck. Wooden sculptures of eagles in various poses perched atop the back gate, along with wolves and a few bears. The taller sculptures, three feet and above, stood on the grass in front of the banner.

Sitting down on the curb next to the Escape, Paula watched. Sawdust blew in swirls, and as sunlight broke through blustery charcoal clouds it sparkled like gold. The scent of freshly cut wood was intoxicating. With only a few strokes, the beak of an eagle emerged, a wingtip, then its chest. On the front the artist managed to whittle little wooden points to resemble feathers. Bark was left intact to look like the feathered back. The carver then triumphantly lifted the chain-saw blade skyward, signaling his creation was complete. Applause exploded. The buyer lifted his sculpture, looked it over and then held it up as people pushed in for a look. A man stepped up and put his money down. Paula sipped her coffee; the cement curb was warm from the sun and felt like a heating pad. She figured five more hours if she drove straight through, but then her pace was slowing the farther north she drove. She yawned as she walked toward the Escape. They climbed in and got back on the road. Maybe she'd stay one night in Grand Marais, find a hotel and call Bernie, make plans to see them tomorrow. What was a day when she had eight weeks?

She rolled down her window to smell the air. What she thought was smoke drifting across the road, obscuring the shoreline off to her right as she approached Silver Bay, was maritime fog. Banks of it wisped through the trees, obscuring the taillights of the car ahead, as thick as any fog out on the easternmost parts of Long Island. The quality of this fog was different, gently layered like bolts of thin organdy fabric as if someone were standing on the other side of the road, unwinding it across the land.

A road sign partly obscured by a pine branch said thirty miles to Grand Marais. A line of cars was backed up behind her as she followed a large RV. Ordinarily she'd have been among those jockeying to pass, but instead she let the others take on the dense fog and winding roads.

It was late afternoon by the time she saw the Welcome to Grand Marais sign. Drowsy, she took her cue from Fotis, who'd stood and shaken off, ready to get out of the car. Another cup of coffee would be nice. Spotting the Angry Trout Cafe in what looked like the center of town, she pulled into an empty parking space.

"Okay," she said as she turned off the engine and unbuckled her seat belt. Fotis looked out the window, waiting for her.

She grabbed his leash and they headed toward a long line at the Order Here sign. Standing behind a blond Scandinavian-looking family, whose adolescent children were already a good head and shoulders taller than her, she wondered if they were tourists until she heard them speak unaccented English. She looked out at the water; the Grand Marais Harbor was a half-moon shape, the beach extended all the way out to rocky points on either side. Concrete and boulder jetties had been built across the harbor. A lighthouse-type beacon stood on either side of the jetty, marking the entrance to the harbor. Along the left side she could make out a U.S. Coast Guard station by the signature white buildings and red metal roofs. On the right was a marina filled with sailboat masts, cabin cruisers and networks of docks.

Fog began creeping into the harbor. One of the lighthouses was enveloped and mist was dreaming its way across the passage. People congregated on the beach, benches loaded with children, small dogs yapping, family reunions, couples laced arm in arm as if seeing Lake Superior for the first time. Lined up on the walk-way along Harbor Park, people took photos of the sunlit drifting fog. The sky was steel gray as the sun poked though.

She too couldn't take her eyes off the water, not noticing she was up next at the Order Here window.

"What can I getcha?"

"Umm. . . ." She looked at a painted wooden menu posted on the back wall, feeling pressure from the people behind her. She'd been too caught up in the harbor to make a decision and picked the first two listings.

"How 'bout an egg salad sandwich, two brats and a coffee, please."

"What size coffee?"

"Medium?"

"It's about a ten- or fifteen-minute wait," the young woman apologized. Paula was taken aback by her sincerity. The woman was dressed in a navy blue polo shirt and a gingham checked blue and white kerchief.

"That's fine," Paula reassured. She looked at the overhead clock, almost four.

There was an empty picnic table on the beach near where she'd parked. Hurrying over to claim it, she muttered to Fotis in Greek, "You know you really have to start eating the dog food, too," as if it were his fault he'd been living on ButterBurgers and brats. It felt mean to starve Fotis to get him on dry kibble. The stuff looked like the pellets she'd pour into the bowls of guinea pigs at Pet World.

She thought to call Bernie while waiting but instead decided to clean out the Escape. She tied Fotis' leash to the table and stepped to open the passenger's side door. The dog was torn be-tween supervising Paula and watching the other dogs on the beach.

Reaching in, she grabbed two crumpled-up Doritos bags and inadvertently dumped orange crumbs onto the passenger seat. As she began brushing them out, images of the rose-colored mohair sofa flashed before her. It had belonged to Roger's parents, Josef and Katya. Paula had covered it with bedspreads so the wool wouldn't itch; shards of Doritos would poke through as she'd turn in her sleep—snacks instead of Roger to pass the night. She often wondered what Katya would have said about her son banishing his bride on their wedding night. Maybe Katya wouldn't have cared. From what Roger said, she and Josef also had separate bedrooms—very continental.

Paula reached for wadded-up paper gasoline receipts. She'd lost most of her anger at Roger long ago. When had that happened? She paused, thinking back; emotion pulsed in her hands. Whenever it was, it seemed her soul had quickly followed.

She'd been a girl with pluck, Roger used to say. But all her rough edges had worn as smooth as the small stones that washed ashore on Jones Beach, eroded after ten years of living in a junk pile. But she'd stayed. She'd stayed. She'd only wanted what other women want. She'd not been greedy.

Someone tapped her and she jumped.

"Sorry to scare you, miss," an older man asked, "but are you okay?"

"Oh yeah, fine. I'm fine. Just clearing out some garbage." She smiled. "Been on the road for a few days."

The man didn't look reassured but nodded and continued on his walk.

Paula bent over and grabbbed a McDonald's bag stuffed with wrappers and coffee cups. She clasped the trash against her chest and headed toward a gray rubber garbage can buzzing with a thick cadre of yellow jackets. A newspaper lay on top. It looked as if someone had just set it down. Shooing away the yellow jackets, she dumped the trash, picked up the newspaper and tucked it under her arm. Something to read while waiting for her food; she'd not seen the news in days.

Fotis greeted her as if she'd been gone for a month. "Hey, cutie pie," she said in a voice that made his ears lie back and his hind end wiggle. She sat down with the paper still tucked under her arm and gave the sun-bleached tabletop a cursory read. Initials corralled with hearts and "IF *YOUR* NOT OUTRAGED, *YOUR* NOT PAYING ATTENTION." It made her chuckle. Just as she turned to read the newspaper, her name was called.

"Paula?" another young woman called from the "Pick Up" window, making tentative eye contact as she held up a white paper bag.

Paula stepped to get the food. Fotis followed to the end of his tether; a tiny stream of drool trickled from his lip.

"Here we go." She sat down to arrange the brats on a paper plate. As she bent over to put the plate down in front of him, she saw a man sitting at the adjacent table recoil in disapproval. The brats were gone before the plate was even down. Maybe Fotis had a tapeworm; she'd heard of colleagues picking up things while researching in parts of the developing world, their only symptoms being perpetual hunger and weight loss.

Fotis began licking at the paper plate.

"Hey, hey, hey." She leaned over, chuckling, and took away what was left of the plate. "God, don't eat the plate, too," she said in Greek.

She'd expected a comment about hungry children or obesity in dogs, but the man said something to his wife instead.

Fotis turned his attention to her sandwich.

"Uch ooo," she continued in Greek. "You're a bottomless pit."

She took a bite and chewed, trying to ignore Fotis' eyes. "Shit." She handed over the other half of her sandwich. She could starve to death before he'd lay off.

"Now shut up," she whispered. "That's all you get." As she took another bite a blob of egg salad dropped onto her chest. "Damn." She wiped at it with a napkin, which made it worse.

She unfolded the newspaper: *Cook County News Herald, the local news of Grand Marais.* Next to the masthead was a sketch of a bear leaning against a tree stump, relaxing with the newspaper as a bird sat on his head reading along. She took another bite of the sandwich and folded the newspaper back to read an ad in the classified section that was circled in blue ink: *Wanted: Part-Time Wildlife Rehabilitator of Raptors and Mammals.*

Without thinking she took out her phone and dialed. "I'm sorry; you must first dial the area code or hang up and ask for assistance."

"Shit."

She asked the nosey couple if they knew the area code.

They looked surprised.

She dialed again.

"Yes?" The man sounded out of breath.

"Oh, hi," she said. "I'm calling about the ad for the wildlife rehabilitator."

"And?" he said.

"Well, uhhhh . . ." She stumbled on her words, caught off guard. "Can you tell me more about it?"

"You work with raptors, wild canines, before?" His voice was gravelly.

"Two years, nine months of working with birds—not so long with canines." She looked at Fotis.

"What kind?"

"Parakeets, macaws, parrots, cockatiels, finches—"

"Sounds like you worked in a pet shop." He hadn't laughed but might as well have.

She still visited Pet World on Saturdays when going to see Eleni. The spicy smell of cedar bedding for the guinea pigs, mice and rats hadn't changed, nor the homey crackling feel of the waxed linoleum tiles as the aging floor gave with each step. The same huge faded paper posters of exotic jungle birds were joined by plastic inflatable palm trees that Mr. Sanchez had added recently to frame the new tropical aquarium fish displays. He no longer replaced birds as they'd sell. Fish were easier, he'd told her, since he was even more stooped over with crippling arthritis since his wife, Berta, had died. Paula would take out the last few remaining macaws and parrots and let them sit on her head and shoulders as she helped Mr. Sanchez clean out bird, rodent and reptile cages. When his high school part-timers didn't show up, she'd help ring up customers if the shop was busy. The old cash register had taught her basic math, since it didn't provide "cash back."

"I've fed, cared for and trained birds," Paula spoke up as a point of pride. "Also worked with guinea pigs, chinchillas and iguanas, snakes and other reptiles."

"Look," he cut her off. "Either you're a bird person or you're not."

"Would I bother calling if I wasn't?"

No answer. She looked at her phone.

"Lotsa lifting," he said like she couldn't handle it.

"I'm strong."

"Ever swing a hammer?"

"Of course." It had been fifteen years since she'd put up shelves in her old apartment.

"The work's more with wild raptors."

"Well, I've fed and cared for wild birds." A pang hit her as she thought about the sparrows, finches and cardinals on her office window ledge.

"What kind?"

"All kinds." She knew she sounded full of shit.

"Hey—can I come over and talk to you about the job?" she pushed.

"Doesn't sound like a good fit."

"Can I at least see what's involved?"

More measured silence. "Rehab's not for everyone," he said.

"Well, let me at least find out more."

"I'm pretty busy right now."

"I won't get in your way. How do I find you?"

There was a pause. "Highway Sixty-One north till you're almost out of town, make a right."

"Street name?"

"Last one on the way out of town. Can't miss it," he said.

"Go right and then what?"

He'd ended the call.

CHAPTER 7

The phone call left her hankering for a cigarette. She spotted an IGA grocery store across the street. She'd grab one pack of cigarettes, not a whole carton, and then change into her last clean blouse before going to see about the job. Rolling down the windows enough so that Fotis could stick out his head, she kissed him between his ears. "You stay," she explained. "I'll be right back."

Opening the back door of the Escape, she felt for the collar of her blouse and pulled it out. Wrinkled, but wrinkled was better than blotches of egg salad. Folding it up, she stuffed the blouse into her purse.

She felt the dog's eyes on her through the glass doorway of the IGA. The smell of old linoleum made her think of Roger. Half-unpacked boxes of merchandise in the aisles made her smile. Why hadn't he called?

Instead of charging straight up to the register and the overhead racks of cigarettes, she began strolling the aisles of the cluttered little store. There was Roger's shaving cream, a Gillette brand that stores in New York sold out of quickly. She grabbed six cans, thinking to stock up, and tucked them in her arms before noticing there were several more. She'd come back tomorrow morning before leaving for Thunder Bay. Roger would be happy; she'd tell him when he called.

Then she saw a display of Canadian Club sparkling club soda—it was his favorite. She'd always thought the brand old-fashioned. On Fridays she'd make him a scotch and soda after work.

She thought sadly about their little routine of dinner while watching the news every evening. Although they'd spent the better part of every summer on separate continents, this separation felt different. He should have been with her on the cliff in Two Harbors, watching the men load the tanker.

Fear tickled beneath her collarbones; something unnamed was threatening to take away her polar bear. She clutched the cans of shaving cream, needing to know that everything was all right, but something about taking Fotis had been divisive. Yet it wasn't Fotis. She could blame him or blame herself for standing her ground. Fotis was like those two diminutive lighthouses in the harbor illuminating a passage to safety—the part of her for which Roger had made no room in their marriage—reissuing what hadn't fully withered, though God knows she'd tried to kill it off. Working to death, hoping those needs would shrivel away and die if she lost herself in the Center and the next big publication. "You can't get everything in life," friends would say, and she'd chalked up not having Roger be a "real" husband as one of the casualties of that adult axiom.

But still she'd longed for the feel of his arms at night, his scent, to hear the subtle surety of his breathing. It bothered her not to have an arsenal of funny sleeping stories about his snoring to share at dinner parties. She'd sit there mute while resentment gathered in her throat like a pile of partly digested food.

And strangely, for the past day she'd felt no impulse to phone and leave Roger lingering messages gushing about the beauty and majesty of the rocky outcroppings or the mystical loveliness of horizonless Lake Superior with its bridal veil of fog. These things were hers alone. Maybe Eleni had been right; something about the whole drive was beginning to feel disloyal. Paula thought about the mythic Penelope who deceived unwanted suitors by asking them to wait until she finished knitting a garment, then by night secretly unraveling whatever she'd completed during the day. Was she also buying time?

While Paula grabbed a stick of deodorant and a large tube of toothpaste, it dawned on her that she hadn't shaved her legs since her last morning in New York. She grasped a pink package of razors and looked around for a basket. She'd only come in for a pack of cigarettes.

The cluttered aisles were punctuated with boxes of unfinished stocking jobs, price guns with stickers (stores in New York hadn't used those in years); it looked like someone hadn't shown up for work. A carton of toilet paper was left half-unpacked. She strolled through the meat and dairy section, which proffered an assortment of locally caught smoked whitefish and trout, homemade brat sausages and large basted shrink-wrapped bones, presumably for dogs. Would Fotis know what to do with one? She picked up two, figuring it might keep him occupied while she went to see the bird rehab guy.

As she approached the checkout the deodorant fell, clanking on the floor. A can of Roger's shaving cream hit and began rolling away from the checkout station. Leaning over the rubber conveyer belt, she unloaded her items onto the surface and bent to retrieve the others. The overhead cigarette rack was calling her name.

"Jeez," Paula said as she stood, noticing an older woman who had stepped behind the register. "Didn't think I needed so much."

"This it?" the older woman asked. The smell of her perfume was familiar.

Paula kept her eyes level, ignoring the cigarettes. "Like your perfume."

"Why, thank you, dear."

Judging by the older woman's wrinkles, Paula figured they might be just a few years apart.

"My husband gave it to me for my birthday."

"Nice husband. Better keep him," Paula said as the woman chuckled at an inside joke.

"You wonder sometimes, don't cha?"

Paula nodded, her eyes widening. She liked the accent people had had since she entered Wisconsin, like Canadians.

"It's Avon," the woman added. "I'm Maggie, the Avon Lady." She nodded slightly to introduce herself and then pointed to her matching pearl earrings and pendant. "These are Avon, too," the woman said with pleasure.

"I'm Paula," Paula said, staring at the pendant. "Wow, that's pretty." She looked at the woman in surprise. "I didn't know Avon even existed anymore, much less had jewelry." Something about the woman's pride made Paula want to wear Avon jewelry, too. She remembered one of the Philoptochos ladies from the church had come over several times to their apartment and lined the top of Eleni's hand with stripes of lipstick.

"Well, my, that's pretty, too." The woman pointed to Paula's Edwardian pendant.

Paula touched her neckline.

"Thanks."

"Was it your mother's?"

"Oh no." Eleni owned little jewelry, except for pearl earrings Paula had given her on her seventieth birthday; she would wear them to church on Christmas and Easter when she wasn't feuding with the ladies Philoptochos. Eleni had made it abundantly clear that she "would never wear anything antique, since someone might have died in it." Paula'd always felt that a woman without jewelry is like a woman without love.

"Something I found in a little antique shop years ago." Paula touched it.

"Avon makes all sorts of things these days," the woman said. " 'Not Your Mother's Avon,' they say."

The woman's coiffed short black hair hovered on being old-ladyish yet looked stylish enough to skirt the divide, shiny, straight, not one hair out of place. It was clear she took pride in her appearance. The clinking of three silver bangle bracelets stamped with Native American motifs, along with the woman's Asian features, made Paula wonder if her checker was American Indian.

"On vacation with your dog?" The woman picked up one of the shrink-wrapped bones. The scanner beeped as she set it into a plastic bag. Paula scooted the rest of her items toward the cash register.

"Ummm—sort of," Paula said.

"Been down to the water yet?"

"Yeah." Paula glanced outside across the street at the changing color of the sky and lake. "It's so peaceful."

The woman chuckled as she scanned the pink package of razors. "Come back in a month when it hurls boulders the size of small cars up onto the beaches."

"*That* lake?" Paula turned to look.

The woman just looked at her; her eyes twinkled. "Fall can come with one good storm."

Paula wondered what she meant.

"It always starts with vacation groceries," the woman teased. "Then warm coats and boots from the Ben Franklin." She gestured next door with a can of Roger's shaving cream. "It gets harder to leave, and before you know it you're looking for a job."

"Funny you should say that," Paula said, laughing. "I just called about a job."

The woman smiled. "What job?"

"Part-time wildlife rehabiliatator, out on Highway Sixty-One?"

"Oh." The woman chuckled in a way that put Paula at ease. "That would be Rick. You must have experience with birds."

Paula looked out the storefront window at the Escape. Rick. So the voice had a name. He sounded too sour to be a "Rick."

"Looks like a nice dog."

"He is. I'd better go."

"I slipped an Avon brochure into your bag," Maggie said, lifting her hands like "just in case."

"Thanks."

"They're introducing a new vintage jewelry line you might like," she said, keeping an eye on Paula's pendant. "I don't have the brochures yet, but if you end up getting the job give me a call. My number's stamped on back." She pulled out the brochure. "I just got in the autumn products, candles, spice packs. Tell Rick that Maggie says 'hi.' "

"I will."

"He's been short staffed for a month; his part-timer left for school in The Cities. Got a job down at the university's Raptor Center."

"The Cities?"

"Minneapolis/St. Paul. Happens every summer, he loses his interns. Gets 'em trained and then releases them back into the wilds of the university." She chuckled. "Winter's hard, though God knows he's done it for years."

"Is his place hard to find?" Paula asked, fishing for better directions.

"Go north on Sixty-One till you're practically out of town." The woman gestured. "Rick's the first right. He's the only fire number on the lake side. "

"Fire number?"

The woman studied Paula for a moment. "Those blue signs with white numbers. You can see 'em from the road."

Paula slowly nodded.

"Where you from?"

"East Coast," Paula said.

"New York?"

Paula nodded and pointed at her. "Good guess."

"Well, it's a pretty distinctive accent." Maggie looked at her. "Rick'll be glad to have help." She looked out the storefront window. "What's your dog's name?"

"Fotis."

"Fotis," Maggie repeated it. "What's it mean?"

" 'Light.' Like light." Paula pointed to the sky.

"Pretty," Maggie said, her voice drifting a bit as if she'd been reminded of something. "What language?"

"Greek."

"You're Greek?"

Paula nodded.

"Knew you were something or other," Maggie said as she

chuckled and raised her eyebrows. Paula felt the woman studying her features.

"So this guy Rick's okay, then." Paula looked at her in a way she thought was universal.

Maggie looked back in a funny way.

"Okay?"

"You know." Paula joked out the serious question, "Not a psycho killer?"

Maggie laughed and slapped her thighs with both hands as her shoulders shook. "Oh my stars, you're a hoot." The woman patted her eyes as if to protect her makeup. "You just say it right out there, don't you?"

Paula bunched up her shoulders and raised her arms. "Why not?"

"You just made my afternoon," the woman said.

"Sorry," Paula said. "I'm new, just thought I'd ask woman to woman."

"Oh God no," Maggie said, though still savoring Paula's comment. "Rick is decent. Known him for a decade; no one's gonna argue he's got quite an edge," she said. "Comes with the territory."

What territory? Paula had wanted to ask. "Well, thanks." She wanted to coax out more information but was afraid of sounding too curious.

"Well—good luck," Maggie said. "Let me know what happens." She turned to put away Paula's basket. "Don't forget to say hi to Rick."

Placing the grocery bags in the back of the Escape, Paula pulled out one of the bones and began peeling off the plastic wrap.

Fotis focused on her hands.

"Here." She held it out. It left a greasy residue on her fingers. She looked around. There was nothing to wipe them on. Fotis sniffed and then took it. He turned over on his back and began gnawing on one end.

It was impossible to tell where the town ended. Rick and Maggie had made it sound obvious, but it took Paula three passes, looking for the last turnoff. Finally, she spotted a slight hint of a driveway; the blue fire number was obscured by branches.

She took the turn and drove toward the lake. The water shimmered so brightly from the angle of the late afternoon sun that it was blinding. To her left was a large log home weathered dark gray by the elements. Surrounding the front yard were several round gazebo-like structures, only where open space should have been there were closely spaced wooden slats.

A man was hammering nets up around one of them. Inside, two huge birds were flapping and screeching. She parked and walked toward him, with Fotis on his leash. The dog smelled the air before pausing to pee on a tree.

As the man straightened up, he set down the hammer, put his hands on his hips and looked at her. He had thinning sandy gray hair, pale blue eyes—almost colorless—and was short, about her height, and deeply tanned, with weather-beaten face and hands from too many years of not caring how much time he spent in the sun. She guessed he was probably sixty, though the skin made it tough to narrow down.

"Hi." She extended her hand. "I'm Paula. You must be Rick?"

He didn't offer an introduction.

"I called about the job?"

He frowned and looked at her torso, seeming irritated at having to stop working. He assessed her short skirt, temporary NY license plates, sandals with the patent-leather straps, red toenails.

"First put your dog back in the car." It was the same crotchety voice, thin but not weak.

"Right, sorry." She turned and walked toward the Escape. "Don't know what I was thinking," she mumbled an apology as she led Fotis back. He was only too happy to hop up and resume his work on the IGA bone.

She and Rick walked side by side in silence toward a large metal building; his clothes smelled of fabric softener. Inside a heavy green metal door was a space that looked like an examination room. A metal table was covered by what looked like a towel. There was a stainless sink, a centrifuge and a refrigerator. Drawers were labeled with various supplies. A large computer monitor sat on top of one of the refrigerators, its screen divided into squares of closed-circuit TV that monitored birds.

"Stand there." He gestured to the examining table. She moved into position. "You said you have experience with wild birds."

She nodded.

"I'm short staffed today. Suzanne, my intern, just left for school."

"Stand here?" Paula asked.

"Put these on." He set a pair of heavy leather gloves on the examination table. She slipped them on and tried to bend her fingers. It was hard to flex, the suede was so thick. The tops reached up to her elbows.

She watched as he stepped over to a cardboard box that looked large enough to house a washing machine and gently unclipped and rolled back a sky blue bedsheet, fastened on all sides by multicolored plastic clothespins. He bent over and reached in. When he straightened up, in his arms was a bald eagle as tall as Rick's torso. Holding the eagle by his yellow feet, Rick shifted his hands to cradle the raptor's enormous body. His talons looked as long as the man's fingers, only curled and razor-like. The eagle opened his wings. Each wingtip almost grazed a side of the small room. The bird turned and looked right at her; the clarity of his gray-yellow eyes against his white face stopped her breath.

She blinked in wonderment. Aetos Dios—the eagle of Zeus—the legendary golden eagle that became the god's trusted personal messenger. Paula had seen depictions of the huge bird portrayed on statues in the Metropolitan Museum's antiquities collections as well as the national museums in Athens.

Paula had never seen an eagle this close and was astounded by his size.

The bird began to struggle.

"Adult male," Rick said. "Around thirty."

"Years?" she asked.

He looked at her like she should know this. She looked away.

"How can you tell it's a male?"

"Because he's small. Females are much larger." Rick said it like she should have known that, too.

The eagle opened his yellow beak and arched toward Rick as if about to attack. The man yanked back, avoiding the beak that seemed capable of ripping off his nose. Paula shuddered to think of the softness of a man's flesh in that beak.

"Lead poisoning. Was brought in yesterday. It's okay; it's okay, old man," Rick said calmly. The eagle responded to Rick's voice by lowering his head and settling onto the man's gloved arm. He rested his chin on the top of the bird's skull.

"This is not characteristic," Rick explained. The top of the eagle's head was tucked under Rick's chin. "He's hallucinating from toxins. Ordinarily they're docile. In the wild if they're on the ground sick you can pick them up using your coat. They offer no resistance. Fearless at their own peril," he explained. He sounded like a colleague, an academic, which surprised her, especially after the phone call, which had consisted of a series of grunts. "They're always assessing what's around them, who is food, who is not. They have no natural predators, except us. We're the distortion at the top."

"How was he poisoned?" She thought of peeling paint in the older buildings in New York.

"A deer carcass with lead shotgun pellets or a fish with lead sinkers in its belly. I see more of these in winter. Deer entrails," Rick explained. "Hunters use lead ammo for whitetails. They leave their gut piles in the woods. After the lakes freeze, it's slim pickings, and gut piles are an easy meal. It kills many of them. It's needless suffering for these birds—an easy fix if hunters would switch to lead-free copper bullets and fishermen would use bismuth-tin alloy tackle and nonleaded sinkers."

"Why don't they?"

He glared at her like the eagle. "For every eagle we find, there are nine more we don't. That suffer and die needlessly." The bird became agitated and began turning his head from side to side, the arc of his neck reminding her of the mosaics she'd seen in the museums in Athens. He pulled back as if getting ready to take a swipe. The man pulled back in anticipation, talking to the bird until he calmed. He stared eye to eye.

Then the eagle turned to Paula. She'd never felt so examined; his eyes were so clear, as if there were nothing between them. As though the beat of her heart were visible through her neck as well as the pulsating blood running through her arteries.

"He looks scared."

"He's delusional," Rick corrected. "See the green stain on his tail feathers?" He raised the eagle so she could see.

"Yeah."

"Lead." Rick looked at her. "But this guy's luckier than most. They die a long, slow death as the iron depletes them, interferes with the digestion process." They both looked at the bird. "Folks saw him on the ground yesterday in a campground. Just out of town. They threw a blanket over him and called the DNR. Ranger brought him yesterday evening."

"Will he live?"

The man didn't answer.

"Come closer," he said.

She couldn't; her body felt like stone. She wasn't afraid but in awe.

He scooted aside.

"Surround my hands," he instructed.

She found a place within that wasn't frozen.

"Now grasp his ankles as I let go," Rick said calmly. She circled the raptor's yellow ankles, his three-inch talons just inches away. She clutched as best she could through the stiff leather gloves.

"You got him?" the man asked.

"Yeah." She blinked and nodded. Her stomach fluttered like the Escape had just crested a steep hill and gone momentarily airborne. She was surprised by how light the bird was, ten pounds at most. But as he spread his wings it was like trying to hold on to the wind. Her muscles burned; her bangs lifted off of her forehead.

The man shifted one hand away, cradling the bird's neck. "Now grasp with your other hand."

She nodded.

"Okay," he signaled.

She felt the man let go, though he immediately grasped the eagle's body, laying the enormous bird, almost three feet tall, down onto the table.

"I've got to pull another blood sample," Rick said, and picked up a syringe from the table. "Lead levels were off the charts yesterday. Been giving him fluids he's so dehydrated. Dosed him with anti-toxin last night, hoping it wouldn't kill him. Sometimes the cure kills 'em before the disease," the man explained. "Gave him anti-toxin again this morning. Want to see if it's made a difference at all."

"You can tell so quickly?"

"Hold him re-e-al steady," Rick said. He moved the bird's enormous wing aside to get at an artery. Pulling the cap off with his teeth, he inserted the needle and filled the syringe with blood.

She was surprised by the color. Not that she'd thought it would be green; she'd just never thought about birds having blood.

The eagle turned and went for her face. Paula reared back without letting go of his feet as the yellow beak missed. She held on, struggling as he writhed and fought to get free, his wings brushing her ears, creating their own wind. The stronger the eagle resisted, the deeper she found the resolve to hold on. Muscles burned from her fingertips all the way up to her neck.

"Shhhh," she whispered.

His eyes were practically the size of a baby's. But he would rip her apart if given the chance. She'd never seen anything like it; she felt like a wide-eyed virgin.

"Endaxi, endaxi," she found herself comforting him in Greek and purring from somewhere deep within, mimicking Rick.

The bird calmed and she felt him relax onto the table.

"Now with your elbow, help me brace his torso." Rick looked at the quantity of blood and then placed the syringe on the side table. "I just got a lead analyzer," he explained. "Now I get results in seconds. This guy beeped off the charts."

Then Rick took out a brown glass bottle. "Ca-EDTA," he said, and picked up another syringe. Paula held the eagle's feet and braced the bird's wings against the table with her forearms. "Anti-toxin," Rick said. "Draws out lead."

The eagle pushed up and spread his wings. They thumped against the table, knocking off the syringes of blood onto the floor. Her face was enveloped in the curve of his torso, where the wing extended. The wings were so massive it felt like a dream.

"You got him?" Rick asked.

"Yeah," she said.

He drew medicine as Paula held on.

"You sure?" he said with a little laugh, but she didn't take it as mean.

"Yep."

He injected the bird. "He'll get one of these three times a day."

"Will he make it?" she asked again.

It took Rick a while to answer. He sighed deeply before he spoke. "He's in pretty rough shape."

Her heart felt as if it would burst for the eagle, his raggedy-looking feathers, crazed demeanor. She felt helpless.

"He's lost lots of weight. Muscle wasting," Rick said, over his shoulder as if he didn't want the eagle to hear. "Bones where muscle should be." He touched the bird's breastbone. "His keel. Feel," he said, and reached to secure one of the eagle's feet so that she could let go.

Paula reached and felt the bone.

"You shouldn't be able to feel that," Rick said, watching her face carefully.

He then smoothed over the bird's head and wing feathers, feeling the sharp angles. "I'm afraid his organs may have begun to shut down. Came in pretty dehydrated. Started an IV on him right away yesterday when he first came in, was up with him most of the night," Rick said.

He gently pinched the skin on the eagle's chest. "Seems more hydrated. We'll try and tube-feed him."

She looked at the curve of his neck where the white feathers met dark brown and wondered how and why nature had drawn such a definitive line.

"You're a real fighter, old man," Rick said to the bird, his voice suddenly riddled with warmth.

He then surrounded Paula's hands with his. "Now let go."

She didn't want to.

"It's okay," he said. "I got him."

She released her hands and Rick took the eagle from her.

"Let's leave him for about thirty minutes, let the medication absorb. We'll come back to tube-feed him."

Rick lifted the bird. He spread his wings again, grazing just over Paula's head. Her skin prickled with the sense of it.

The man carried the bird back to the cardboard box, gently lowering and then covering him with the bedsheet.

"Can he get out?"

"Nope."

Funny how something as fragile as a cardboard box, an old bedsheet and eight clothespins was enough to contain such a creature.

"It's like a nest," Rick explained. "A cocoon. It calms them, makes them feel safe."

She already ached for it—longed to climb into the box, curl her body around it to give comfort as Fotis had done for her that first night in the hotel.

Paula was drained; her arms were empty tubes of flesh. In all the years she'd spent studying society, trying to understand why people do what they do, or don't do, more understanding had passed through that eagle in a split second than over the course of her lifetime of study.

"Well." Rick took off the long gloves and looked at her without a change in expression.

She waited.

"Consider that your job interview," he said. "By the way, your shirt's buttoned crooked."

She looked down but was too electrified to even care. She'd never felt so drained yet so alive.

"You smell like cigarettes, too."

"I haven't smoked since New Jersey," she said with such defiant conviction he burst out with a laugh.

"Smoke kills birds, so knock it off unless you're gonna chew."

She frowned before realizing he'd said it to shock her.

He motioned for her to follow. "I'll show you the mammal side before we come back to tube-feed this guy. Don't take a lot of them, but can't turn 'em away either," he said, talking into the air as she hurried to catch up.

They walked toward a chain-link area that contained a litter of three orphaned otters swimming and twirling around in a large pool. Their bodies were slick; one swam backward while another slipped under and then resurfaced, jumping on top of the other in play. Paula's body felt as light as the eagle's. Three tiny heads bobbed up and then down before turning to look at the newcomer.

"They're just about ready for release. A couple more days," Rick explained.

"What are their names?" she asked in a playful way.

He stopped and glared. "They're never named. You name it, you claim it." He then turned to the fence, holding it open for her to follow.

That night she'd slept in the Escape at a public campground on a half-moon beach next to Lake Superior. She'd combed the area for over an hour looking for a room before giving up; two young desk clerks had searched online before shaking their heads. But all she could think of was holding the eagle, the feel of his weight, worrying about him surviving the night until she could see him again.

Before she'd left that evening, Rick had let her take the eagle out of the box. Rick showed her how to slice fresh trout into tiny chunks and mix it with baby food in the blender. Then he'd shown her how to gently snake a feeding tube down the eagle's esophagus into his stomach as she held on to his body. Tomorrow Rick said he'd let her try.

She'd driven back to the IGA to buy a rotisserie chicken to share with Fotis, hoping that Maggie was still there and she'd get some advice on places to stay. Maggie was gone for the day, but the IGA clerk gave Paula directions to the public campground, where there was access to a bathroom and a shower. So she drove up and parked next to a small hut, which looked like it would house a parking attendant.

"You're in luck," a burly man said. "Someone just left. The wife's water broke. One of the lakeside spots, too. You got a camper?" The man looked out the window of the small hut toward the back of the Escape.

"Just my car."

"How long you plan on staying?"

She shrugged. "A couple of nights?"

"There's a pile of firewood behind your spot. Five bucks a bundle, the honor system, 'you take some, leave some'—envelopes are right here outside the window." He looked over his glasses at her.

She smiled.

"Need your license or photo ID."

She rifled through her purse and handed it over.

He wrote down information and then looked up at her.

"Long drive," he said. "You drive straight through?"

"Oh God, no." She laughed. "Two stops. Ohio, Wisconsin."

"Visiting friends?"

"Sort of."

"I just need to make a copy of this." He held up her driver's license. "Homeland Security requires it this close to the border."

"Really."

He looked up at her. "We're an hour by car from the border, twenty minutes by boat."

She looked out to the harbor. It was dark except for a bright full moon shimmering on the water and light from the beacons on either side.

"Showers are behind you there." He pointed. "Bathrooms in the same facility."

Paula pulled the Escape up to face the lake. The front tires touched a sliver of the red rocky beach. She hoped the tide didn't get much higher. There was a long asphalt walkway bordering the campground starting from a rocky outcropping and continuing from the marina to downtown Grand Marais. Each campsite had a picnic table. The grounds were lit up like a baseball field. People had set up the equivalent of their own living rooms: folding chairs, tablecloths, bottles of ketchup and mustard, glass jars holding wildflower arrangements.

The neighbors at the next site waved; she waved back. Their dog barked at Fotis, but he ignored it. Paula felt so different, chosen; she wanted to tell everyone she'd held an eagle. How many people get to hold an eagle to their chests?

She climbed onto the picnic table to sit, holding the leash and looking out toward the lake. On the asphalt walkway an older man, shaggy hair and beard, soft looking around the middle, rode a child's bike. The man sat tall on the seat and looked embarrassingly excited, like a ten-year-old trapped in a seventy-year-old body.

He accelerated and then turned and rode back.

"Grandpa, you fixed it!" His grandson jumped with elation before running, speeding up as the man egged his grandson to chase.

"You should get a bike, too!" the boy exclaimed.

"Nah, I'm too old to ride."

"But you just did!" The boy squealed as he threw up his arms.

"Nah. Too old." The man pulled over and dismounted, abruptly offering the handlebar to his grandson.

The boy's shoulders wilted, confused as to why his grandfather was suddenly irritated. "Well, thanks for fixing it," the boy said in defeat.

Paula's heart sank. The boy took off and rode down the path, putting one hand pensively into his pocket. She watched the grandfather watching him. *Get that bike, Papou,* she'd wanted to say. *Just do it for God's sake; your grandson is asking you.*

She left Bernie a message apologizing profusely for not calling earlier, telling him she was going to be a few days late. "Nothing bad," she assured. "Just different. Interesting. Amazing, actually," she'd said. "I'll call you again early next week."

Then she called Celeste and blubbered on about the entire experience.

"You what?" Heavenly asked. Paula could hear *NCIS* blaring from the TV in the background. It was one hour later in NYC.

"What was she holding?" she could hear Tony carping.

"A bird, an eagle," Celeste had said.

"A what?" Paula heard Tony over the TV.

Paula was excited and knew she wasn't making much sense. "I'll call you tomorrow."

"All right, but be careful that damn thing doesn't poke out your eye," Celeste said, and signed off.

Still ignited by the experience, Paula walked Fotis up and down the waterfront until late that night, hoping to calm down enough to sleep. As she stepped out onto one of the shoreline boulders, Paula remembered the Greek myth about how Aetos, the eagle of Zeus', had fallen on hard times. The bird had once been a beloved and respected King. But all of the adulation from the King's subjects had roused the jealousy of Zeus, who realized the people loved this King more than him. After planning to incinerate the King's family with a thunderbolt, Apollo softened Zeus' resolve and convinced him to turn the King into an eagle. So while the King made love to his wife, Zeus snuck in and turned the man along with his wife into golden eagles.

Slipping off her sandals, Paula dipped her feet into the water. It was surprisingly cold. She thought it would be like the lakes in Upstate New York, lakes that turned pleasantly tepid during the summer; this felt as cold as the ocean. Fotis sniffed the rocks and then touched a paw into the water.

"Don't like *nehro*?" she asked. She was tempted to splash him with her foot to play but thought he might not like it.

He looked at her. She thought back to his bath in Pets du Jour; was that only days ago?

She and Fotis walked the town streets past couples, arm in arm and packs of friends, laughing and sitting on benches with take-out food. Loud music blared from a live band at the Gun Flint Tavern. Cars were parked along the beach. Several of the galleries had their front doors propped open. People paraded in and out or stood outside restaurants reading menus taped in windows. "A forty-five-minute wait . . . ," she heard bits and pieces of plans being made. Families walking the sidewalks, eating ice cream off of waffle cones that were dripping more quickly than the people could lick.

The sky was still illuminated as if some giant searchlight were burning. After she and Fotis had walked back to the campground, Paula again sat on the picnic table in front of the Escape. It was well after midnight, the waves had started to calm her and a feeling of exhaustion set in.

Climbing into the back of the Escape, she used her dirty clothes like a blanket. The plummeting temperature surprised her, along with the dampness. She huddled against Fotis in the cool night air. Her arm, chest and back muscles had just started to throb, but she'd fallen dead asleep before having much chance to notice.

She dreamed that Fotis was growling at a horse. Deep, low

growling like the rumbling of thunder, primal and terrifying. She could hear the horse clomping about, munching on leaves, stripping vegetation from bushes and small trees. In her dream, the dog's snarl through the window drove off the horse.

CHAPTER 8

Paula shivered awake in the damp morning air. She felt like she'd slept through to October. Her shoulders ached as she turned. The windows were fogged up, not enough light from the RV park to read her watch. Fotis licked her face. Her phone was in her purse on the floor of the front seat. Reaching up, she fumbled for the dome light, pressing until it switched on. Just tilting her wrist to check for the time hurt—Rick said to be there by seven. It was a little after five.

"Shit." She sat up too fast, bumping her head on the ceiling.

She'd had no heavier clothes; it was summer when she left New York four days ago.

Armed with the spa white hotel towel she'd pilfered from the Soho Grand and the plastic IGA grocery bag containing shower items she'd sorted the night before, she opened the door and climbed out, Fotis tagging along on his leash. Tiptoeing barefoot, she spotted the outdoor lights of the dimly lit wooden shelter marked "Private Showers." "Ow, ow, ow," she mouthed quietly, brushing one foot off on the other as she hurried. She should've looked harder for her sandals.

It took several minutes in a hot shower before she stopped shivering. She prayed the attendant wouldn't cut off the hot water. As her body came to life, her forearms, shoulders and chest muscles hurt even worse. Fotis was tied to a pillar outside, guarding the doorway. The tip of one of his paws was visible.

"You guys hear that bull moose rooting around last night," she heard one of the campers. Why was he yelling? Hot water cascaded through her hair as she lathered up.

"You hear that dog stand the thing off?" another said; the rest of them murmured in agreement. "That thing was a beast!"

"Yeah," someone else piped up.

"By that black SUV on the lake," Loudmouth lowered his voice. She looked at Fotis' toes, remembering the dream.

"My wife was more terrified a' that dog than the moose," Loudmouth continued.

A few of them chuckled.

"Probably a calf," another man's deep voice contended.

"Good thing it ain't rutting season."

"Yeah, they can get kinda testy, you know," the other said. "Even here in town. Worse than the bears."

Bears? Their speculation had the ring of competitive argumentation, each trying to out-folksy the other with his knowledge of wildlife habitat.

"A time or two the wife and I were up on Isle Royale," Loudmouth began, "a packa wolves came sniffing around the campsite one night."

"Probably raccoons," another called over.

"You get a look at 'em?" a muted voice asked.

"Was too dang tired to care," Loudmouth said. "The wife saw a moose calf. Horrendous, though. You see them moose with scarring all along their haunches. Like stripes. Wolf attacks, trying to bring the damn things down."

"One time up on the Alcan Highway . . . ," someone else began.

Paula'd seen moose crossings indicated in the road atlas up by Thunder Bay but figured the ones in Grand Marais were more marketing ploys by some Chamber of Commerce. Far out on Long Island during summer you'd see Lobster Crossing signs, too.

Now her only task was to slip out invisibly with Fotis before one of them discovered that the shower was running ice cold.

Fotis stuck his head out the window as they drove out to Rick's place. His lips made slapping sounds against his teeth. She turned at the partially obscured fire number and pulled in, driving along a line of birch trees. The early air smelled sweet and chilly as she entered a pocket of mist nearer the water. The lake looked like a translucent shelf, dormant as it waited for the sun. She was unsure where to park and even less sure of where to report.

"You stay here for now, okay?" she assured Fotis. The dog watched, his eyebrows furrowed with concentration, supervising as she stepped out and unwrapped the last bone. Paula placed it alongside the one he'd been working on.

Armed with two extra-large coffees and her purse tucked under her arm, she walked toward the metal building. Her new neon watermelon–colored sweatshirt made her feel like a walking billboard. She'd picked it up from the Gunflint Grind Coffee Company that morning. The baristas had been gracious enough to find a pair of scissors so she could snip off the tags and slip it on.

There was no way of knowing if Rick was a coffee drinker, but she ordered the second coffee anyway.

The air was musty with wood smoke. The moon was still visible, half-blurred into the lightening blue-white of the sky. A line of birch trees surrounded one side of the property, their leaves like gold coins, tittering with the slightest breeze. You couldn't help but get lost in seamless pink and golden sunrise reflections from the lake. She thought of what Maggie had said about the lake hurling boulders the size of small cars onto the shore.

Up a slight incline a log home perched above the shore. Paula remembered it from yesterday; though rustic, it looked posh for someone living on what must be a shoestring budget. Working with wildlife couldn't be a moneymaker, but then again maybe property here was cheap. The soil smelled wet, like peat, from a recent rain or heavy installment of morning dew. Pinecones crunched under her feet as she approached the house. Though leaves were turning red and yellow, there was still enough brush to obscure any view of a neighbor.

Warmth from the coffee gave her courage. The coffee was bitter, even with cream and sugar. Her lipstick now marked one as hers.

Movement from inside a chain-link enclosure near the house made her turn.

A man looked up. Maybe somebody else worked here, too? Paula stopped. The same rip on the left shoulder seam, but he looked older than she remembered. His hair seemed more sun bleached yesterday; now it looked like matted beach grass. She walked toward the enclosure. He did seem more attractive yesterday. She caught him looking at her, too, and wondered if he was thinking the same thing.

He was pouring liquid onto an animal shaped like a flattened basketball with spiky fur.

"What is that?" she called as a greeting, approaching the fence with the coffee.

He took her in. "You coming to work or meeting a friend for lunch?"

She felt foolish and looked down at her black patent-leather strap sandals. In the shower she'd noticed the red nail polish on her toes beginning to chip off. She felt clownish.

"How 'bout coming with real shoes tomorrow," Rick said.

She was about to say, *These are real shoes,* when she realized that it might come out wrong. His words smarted; it surprised her that she had to blink several times to clear her eyes.

"Might wanna check downtown at the Ben Franklin," Rick said, backing away from the bite of his earlier words. "Otters and fox pups'll chew your toes," he said in a teasing voice. "The birds'll peck at your earrings and necklace," he said in a way she took as an apology. "Might wanna take them off if you care about 'em."

She thought back to the eagle's yellow beak. The bird could probably shear right through a platinum chain.

"How is the eagle?" It was hard to tell if Rick lived alone.

"No worse," he said. "Was up with him all night. His levels dropped a few points."

She wondered if Rick had administered the anti-toxin yet. Maybe he wasn't aware he was wearing the same shirt as yesterday.

"Was waiting for you to give him the meds." Maybe his wife didn't do laundry. Or if he lived alone, maybe he was waiting until he ran out of clean underwear.

"We'll check his levels again," Rick said. "Dose him and then tube-feed him—"

"After thirty minutes again?" she asked.

His brow relaxed, eyes smoothed. "Yes." He looked up at her as if deciding something. "After thirty minutes." He looked down at the animal. "Later I'll have you prepare his food like I showed you," Rick said. "You remember?"

"Yes." Of course she did.

"Weigh each feeding first; enter it on the spreadsheet on the laptop."

She nodded. She'd memorized every detail about the eagle, running it through her mind last night as she walked Fotis downtown, wanting to tell her story to everyone she saw.

"I'm flushing out a wound with a saline solution," Rick finally offered. "When I'm done with this little girl, we'll go to the medical room."

Paula set the coffee on the ground and took off her earrings, unclasped the necklace and tucked them both into a zipper compartment in her purse.

"I'll get better shoes today," she promised, feeling renewed as she lifted the coffee cups. She held one out for him, but he was busy treating the wound.

She withdrew the cup and waited. Neither said a word for several minutes and she began to feel uncomfortable. Maybe he thought she talked too much. Maybe she did. He made her feel foolish and shallow, full of herself, a bullshitter.

"When you get a place, leave your dog home. Barking scares birds," Rick said.

She turned to the Escape. Fotis hadn't made a sound. "I'll show you where he can stay after I'm finished."

Rick wrestled with the animal. She grunted as he turned her over, her quills clicking as they brushed together. Paula moved closer to the fence.

"Porcupine," he said.

"Oh."

"A tourist found her three days ago, hit by a car. They don't often cross, but when they do they're slowpokes," he explained. "Someone brought her to town in a Styrofoam beer cooler. Maggie gave them directions. There's another one in here that's ready for release. We'll do that tomorrow."

"Oh—I met Maggie yesterday and I'd forgotten to tell you she said 'hi.'"

He glanced at Paula with an expression she couldn't read.

"I brought you a coffee."

"Heard you're staying in the campground," he said, examining the animal's other side.

"I guess news travels fast."

He shot her a look. "Need a place?"

She nodded and slurped her coffee.

"I've got a summer rental that's vacant. It's a ways down the shore. People just left. Haven't had the place cleaned out, but you're welcome to it unless you find something else."

She thought it unusually generous.

"Thanks. Maybe so."

He set the animal down. She waddled off into a wooden shelter, favoring her right side. Rick peeled off a latex glove and tossed it into a trash can before walking out of the enclosure and removing a long leather glove from the other. He reached for the coffee.

"You're welcome," Paula chided.

He smirked. His eyes were pale, like the moon against the sky.

"Nice dog," he said, raising his cup toward the Escape. "Quiet, doesn't seem to bark. You have him long?"

She didn't answer as she followed Rick toward the Escape.

Fotis looked through the window and then stood. With the exception of last night's campground incident and one short bark at the door of the hotel room when a maid had come in, the dog had been silent. "I guess he doesn't really bark."

"Where'd you get him?"

"Animal Control on Northern Boulevard."

"Can I see him?" Rick seemed curious about something.

"Uhh . . . I guess. Sure." She opened the door and grabbed Fotis' leash. The dog jumped down.

Rick set the coffee cup on the roof of the Escape before squatting to pet Fotis. He checked the dog's teeth, ran his hands down both of Fotis' front legs and then checked his skull.

Fotis jumped up on him, placing his paws on Rick's shoulders. It surprised Paula; she'd not seen him do that.

"Off," Rick said. He stood back up before calmly kneeling down, lowering Fotis as he squatted eye level, allowing the dog to sniff his ears and hair.

"You've got a hybrid. Your dog is part wolf."

"You're kidding." She thought back to comments at the shelter, the groomer. "Is that bad?"

"It just is. Which is why his teeth are so big, his skull's so broad and he doesn't bark. Looks part husky, but you're seeing wolf," He patted Fotis' head. "Probably crossed with some herding type, Aussie shepherd, Border collie maybe. Seems stable enough, though." He stood up and took his cup from the roof. "Good-natured, too."

She wondered how Rick spent his days. He had the relaxed air of a man who owes no one a thing.

"His name is Fotis."

Rick picked up the cup. "Coffee's not bad either." His brows arched into a furrow as he studied her sweatshirt.

"You don't have to say it, you need sunglasses to look at me, but hey—the yellow one was even worse," she offered. She was tempted to ask if the color would scare the birds.

His expression was a couple of standard deviations from a grimace. His features gave him a look of perpetual consternation.

"At least their coffee's better than that other place," he said. "Bring your dog." He turned toward the house.

"Before we treat the eagle, I'll need your help. Someone dropped an owl off by the mailbox. I found her this morning," he explained, leading her and Fotis to a fenced yard.

"Some kids found her on the ground," Rick began. "Thought they'd keep her as a pet until their mom found out. The woman got my name from the Sheriff and left the box and a note," he said while opening the gate and leading Fotis into a large fenced area on the other side of the log home.

Fotis began sniffing the enclosure.

"You feed him yet?" Rick looked at her.

"Uhhh, kind of."

"How 'bout I get him something quick," Rick said, and began heading toward the log house. "Looked the owl over quickly," he said. "Broken femur; been shot, too. We'll take her to Darryl's for X-rays."

He disappeared into the back door of the house.

She waited outside. What a strange man: not unfriendly, but not friendly either. Before long Rick emerged with two metal bowls of what looked like wet dog food and fresh water. He motioned with his head for her to follow around the back.

The house was much larger on the lake side than was visible from the driveway. It was set on a ridge with a staircase leading down to the lake, a prominent deck with tables, chairs, a bank of windows and a million-dollar view. What looked like a large husky began running excitedly around in the yard; Fotis responded with a jerk on his leash.

"He can play with Sam today; Sam's a good old boy," Rick explained. "We think his mom was killed by a hunter or a car. He was found on Sixty-one at only a few weeks old. A family took him, thinking they'd raised him to be a good family pet, and when it didn't turn out that way, he'd already imprinted. Too late to be released," Rick explained. "Either a game farm or euthanasia. Been with me ever since."

"That's a wolf?" She stopped dead. Her face wrinkled into a question mark.

Rick didn't answer. The animal was tall, with long knock-kneed legs, yellow eyes and a thick ruff around his neck, just like on TV.

"You've gotta be kidding; you're gonna put Fotis in with a wolf?"

She stared at Sam, expecting him to start snarling.

"Both of these guys seem pretty good-natured," Rick said. He unlatched the gate and stepped inside. "Come in." He put down the bowl of food and waved her in. Fotis dragged her toward the food.

Rick made a hand signal and Sam sat down.

"Shut the gate," Rick said.

She reached behind her and flipped the latch.

"Birds come in with broken bones all the time," he went on, ignoring her shock. He unhooked Fotis' leash and draped it over the fence. She watched in amazement as Fotis began to gobble down whatever it was Rick had set before him. Sam sat calmly, waiting to be released.

"What's in there?" Paula laughed.

Rick smiled. "I'll give you some to take home." Fotis licked his chops, looked up at Rick and then began furiously drinking the fresh water. After he was done, the dogs began circling each other, sniffing.

"Let's get to work." Rick herded her out and latched the gate. Paula turned and looked at Fotis. He was lost in play.

"Come on," Rick said over his shoulder. "They'll be fine." He started toward the raptor ICU.

Paula didn't budge. What would Theo, God-rest-his-soul, think if he knew.

"Sam's gentle. I use him as a foster dad," Rick called back.

She watched as the dogs frolicked, their limbs loose, happy like two puppies she'd seen in the dog park just off Washington Square. Then she hurried to catch up with Rick.

"She can't fly, but her weight's good," he explained as he and Paula walked. "Her mate's probably been feeding her until those kids took her yesterday," he continued. "She's distressed."

"Does she have babies—uh, I mean chicks?"

His eyes narrowed. Another thing she should have known. "Raptors nest in January, February," he said. "Raptors mate for life. The males are just as attentive, in some cases even more so than mothers. Some of my best foster parents are males."

The metal building was in sight.

"I'm sure her mate's distressed." Rick looked up into the trees. "Wouldn't surprise me if he's followed and is watching."

She couldn't make anything out but leaves.

"How will they find each other?" She looked at Rick.

His face relaxed with the urgency of her question. "They will," he said. "He knows she's here; she knows he's around, somewhere. They navigate all over the world, migrating thousands of miles from the Arctic to South America. They return every spring to the very tree and nest where they were born."

"God," she muttered, shaking her head in amazement. She continued scanning the branches. "How long will it take for her to heal?"

Rick lowered his voice. "Depends on what we find."

"Could she die?"

"Maybe. But probably not." He wrinkled his nose and shook his head slightly. "It takes a few weeks for a bone to heal. Scotch-tape it together and in a few weeks they're ready for the flight room."

"Flight room?"

"The tall part of this building. You can't see it from here," he explained. She looked at the tin roof, bright-colored leaves already gathering in the divots and ridges. "Tall perches. We bait them to fly, build up their muscles—physical therapy for raptors."

"Can I see it?"

He looked at her in a way she didn't understand, as though suspicious of her enthusiasm.

"Maybe later if we have time." He looked at his wristwatch—an older-looking 1930s golden-faced dial with a brown leather strap. It could have belonged to her father.

"Raptor bones are hollow, better blood supply than mammals, which is why they heal so fast." He reached for the doorknob. "For now we'll tape her femur, check her body for pellets and draw a blood sample to test for lead."

"So how do these animals find you?"

"Police, rangers, birds in backpacks, chicks in baseball hats," he said.

"Are you a vet?"

"I studied and spent time in wildlife biology before law," he said as they reached the metal building. "Was out in the field most summers. Did a lot of this." He reached for the doorknob and held it open. "No vets up here specialize in wildlife, but Darryl's a good man. Helps me with surgeries and X-rays." He said it like she knew Darryl. "Folks can specialize in birds or mammals," Rick explained. "Up here that's a luxury. If I can't treat it, I call Darryl."

She immediately noticed another small cardboard box next to the eagle's. She imagined him inside, curled up like a dog, his yellow feet tucked under him in the pink blanket. She so badly wanted to peek.

Rick touched the eagle's box. "Let's look the owl over first; then we'll treat and feed him," Rick said. "Some weeks we're twenty-four/seven around here; others it's quiet. I fed him around two this morning."

"Where do you get the fresh fish?"

"Fishermen drop it off. In winter, ice fisherman drop off what they don't want. Hunters drop off deer and bear hearts, especially after the lake freezes. Fresh roadkill will do. No pork, though."

She chuckled. "Oh, a Jewish eagle?" she joked.

He looked at her with no expression. Either he didn't get the joke or he didn't think it funny. "Hope you're not squeamish."

Was she?

"Sometimes it's a deer, squirrel, anything. They drop 'em off if they're close. Sometimes we have to drive. Lotsa legwork."

She nodded and walked toward the boxes.

"Gloves first," he reminded as he slipped one on. "Always." He pointed toward a wooden box. "They can tear you up."

He was just about to open the owl's box when Paula's phone rang in her purse. *Shit.* Her gut told her it was Roger.

Rick noted her reaction. "Might as well take that." He pulled back from the box. "Next time turn off your phone."

Paula looked at him. "Sorry." She took off the glove and walked toward her purse, hurrying outside before answering.

Roger started right in. "I just talked with Celeste," he said. "She says you're working for *some guy.*"

"Well, hello to you, too," she said.

"Where'd you meet him, Paula?"

"Roger—"

"Online? Just tell me."

"From an ad in a garbage can, okay?" she said, though she doubted he'd heard.

"Are you wearing your wedding ring?"

She looked at her hand. He got her.

"You aren't, are you," he confirmed.

There was silence.

"It's in my purse. I'm working with birds," she said. Roger had never worn the wedding band she'd bought him and it had always bothered her. He claimed it was too restrictive.

"I knew things had to change," Roger started. "They've not been good for a long time—we both know that—" His voice kept cutting out.

Did we? Roger was mired in so many protective layers that he'd always characterize marital kerfuffles (as he called them) as *her* problem, *her* time of the month, *her* starting *the change,* nothing remotely resulting from the effects of his illness on their marriage.

"—but God, Paula, are you sleeping with this guy?"

She laughed and was tempted to say something nasty like, *What do you care? You had your shot,* but didn't.

"You're having sex with him?"

"Oh God, knock it off," she said, almost flattered. "I'm working here," she said.

Roger struggled to calm his voice. "You sure?"

"Roger, for God's sake I'm sleeping with the dog."

"I don't know what you're doing out there with this dog—whose damn dog is it anyway? Did you have to take it all the way to Minnesota, for God sakes?"

"Excuse me, Roger"—she had to stop herself from laughing—"but you're in fricking France. What difference does it make where I am?"

"This makes no sense at all. Why don't you just fly here, Paula? We can talk."

It was true he wasn't one for the phone.

"I've looked into it. There's a nonstop from Minneapolis to Paris. Just come for the weekend. We can talk it out—I've told you I'll make changes; I told you before we left New York."

"I must have missed that conversation, Roger." It felt like a coldhearted thing to say. She looked at her phone; it was down to one bar. Holding it out in front of her with both hands, she began walking the property searching for a beam from some cellphone tower. "Look, we need a break," she said. "*I* need a break."

"Paula, I love you," he said. "I miss you." His voice was shaky in a way she'd never heard. She guessed he wasn't sleeping again.

"Well, I love you, too," she said, laughing in a way that might have included ice cream too.

"Come to France. I miss you."

"Well, I miss you, too." It began as an obligatory thing to say but then she started to feel it.

"Why are you pulling a stunt like this?" he asked.

A stunt?

"Look," he said. "I'll do whatever it takes, whatever you want."

Her stomach squeezed. "'Whatever *I* want,'" she stated. "Like someone's put a gun to your head and is forcing you to sleep with your own wife?" Her face felt hot, the top of her head like a geyser. "I can't even talk, Roger. For ten years you haven't missed me." Tears came up from the painful knot in her throat. Two weeks ago she'd have been on her knees with gratefulness at such a concession. She'd have gone to church with Eleni, lit a candle, crossed herself and kissed the icon of Panayia (the Virgin Mary).

"Sweetie, of course I've missed you." He tried to pull it off, but his voice was syrupy.

"I can't talk about this now."

"I'm sorry, sweetie; that came out all wrong," he said, tripping over his words. "Maybe I didn't realize how important it was to you—"

She started laughing. "Look. I can't have this conversation now. We'll talk when we're back in New York." Just the thought of it made her feel gray.

So many years of disappointment, then hope, then more jewelry to soothe the disappointment. A week ago felt like someone else's life. Asleep for a decade to awaken with nothing except a perpetually sore back, wrinkles, more gray hair and a trove of old jewelry. And while Roger was never one for grand overtures before, she didn't want to decide anything. The next weeks were hers. All she knew was that she couldn't continue living as they had. Roger was so good at eroding her resolve. What scared her most was the possibility that once back in New York she'd collapse, unable to save herself. Even if her marriage was lost, the last few days suggested that she was still alive.

She glanced around to make sure Rick hadn't snuck out to hide in the trees, like the male owl, listening, watching.

"I miss you," Roger said. "Please reconsider. Come to France."

"Look." She gained some composure. "I have to go."

"Go where?"

"I'll call you tonight," she conceded.

"There's an awards ceremony in Paris tonight."

"So miss it."

"I can't. I'm presenting."

"So call me after."

"There's a banquet."

She shook her head. He got her again; she felt kicked down-stairs, relegated to the couch.

"Good-bye, Roger, I have an owl to save." She turned off her phone, disgusted with herself. She dashed to the Escape and threw her purse through the open window onto the driver's seat, then ran around the side of Rick's house to check on Fotis. The two animals were lying side by side in the morning sun, panting. She then raced back to the metal building and the birds.

"I'm back." She closed the door with too much force. Rick's eyebrows rose. He was peacefully sitting in front of the laptop entering vitals. She felt foolish but grabbed the glove and put it on.

He looked up before standing up. "Ready?"

Rick began walking over to the smaller box. Opening the lid, he lifted the owl out of the box, and she was the most beautiful thing Paula had ever seen. The bird's feathers were the colors of fall leaves and tree bark, yet when Paula touched the owl she was softer than Paula had imagined. The owl's eyes were amber, an eye color Paula had never seen at close range.

"Do you ever get used to the beauty of these birds?"

One look from him told her, *Never.*

"Great horns don't have horns," he said with the same gentle-ness she'd heard the previous day. "They're tufts."

He laid the bird down on the table. She looked up at Paula.

"Hi, sweetie," Paula said.

"Here," he said, holding the owl's feet with one hand. "See how this wing moves? Now watch the other one."

She could see the difference.

"Broken femur. But see this blood clot?" He pointed.

Paula saw what looked like three black knobs among the feathers. "Shotgun pellets. I need for you to hold her, while I feel the rest of her body."

Paula grasped the owl's feet with her gloved hand. The bird offered no resistance. After examining the torso, he shifted his hands back. "Now you feel. Feel for things that don't belong with feathers."

She touched the bird with her bare hand; the feathers were so soft she could barely feel them. The owl's body was surprisingly tender as Paula could feel rough bumps that were irregular in distribution. The bird didn't even seem to mind being touched.

"There's something here." Paula looked up at Rick.

He nodded.

"And another here."

"Keep searching."

Paula's hands felt around the owl's entire body.

"All right. Hold tight," he said, reaching into the drawer for a syringe with his bare hand. "Hope it's not lead buckshot."

"Hope not, too."

"Even if it is, depends where they've been shot. In some parts of the body it becomes toxic; in others a pellet remains inert."

Paula wanted him to explain more, but he didn't.

"She's stressed," Rick said, pulling blood into the syringe. He held it up, seeming satisfied it was enough. "But that's because she's separated from her mate. Wanna make sure it's nothing else."

Paula thought about it.

"You're sure they'll find each other?"

"If she makes a full recovery, we'll release her."

She pictured her mate waiting, searching, distressed.

"You got her?"

"Yeah." Paula nodded.

He moved over to one of the machines on the counter. "Just got this thing, used to have to send samples off to the Twin Cities and wait." She watched him program the tester and set up the sample. "This gives lead levels in minutes.

"When we come back, in that fridge over there is a blue plastic bag containing two deer hearts. I need you to slice 'em up into tiny cubes to feed the outside eagles. Think you can do that? Later we'll put 'em in the flight cage for some exercise."

She froze, thinking of deer on the highways. She looked at Rick and nodded.

"Aren't a lot of happy endings in wildlife rehab, so gotta revel when they happen."

She looked at him.

"Most don't make it; they're euthanized. Sometimes they can't be released, because they've imprinted or are blind or can't fly well enough to hunt."

"What happens to them?"

"Some go to large rehab facilities as teaching birds. University vet schools take them. Or they go to conservation facilities somewhere, to live in captivity."

The machine beeped.

"Music to my ears," he said. "It buzzes differently when the levels are abnormal." He lifted the owl and walked back to her box. He turned to Paula. "You wanna try getting him out this time?"

Her stomach jumped. With her ungloved hand, Paula folded back the bedsheet and looked in. "Kalimera," she said in Greek. His yellow eyes immediately took hold of hers as she reached down, using the blanket to get ahold of him. She clutched his feet and placed him on her arm, purring before holding him to her side. "Eisai oraios," she said. The eagle seemed pleased to be told what a beautiful creature he was, as she carried him over to the table. Rick helped her lay the bird down as he drew blood.

After the tube feeding, Paula carried the eagle back to the box and set him down on his feet, as Rick had instructed, on the pink blanket. She covered the box and clipped it. Rick was quiet as he lifted the smaller box and carried the owl out of the building. They didn't speak the entire two-mile drive to Darryl's and somehow Paula didn't mind. She was unspeakably happy.

By one that afternoon they'd returned from Darryl's vet clinic. She'd stood for almost two hours watching as Rick and Darryl removed pellets from the owl. Luckily they'd been only superficial wounds. The break in the wing hadn't needed to be surgically pinned, so his treatment of Scotch tape would hold as a splint until she healed. Paula held the owl, talking softly to her in Greek as Darryl and Rick washed her wounds with antiseptic fluid in the sink.

At the end of Paula's shift she and Rick walked toward the house. She veered off toward the back fence to get Fotis. Once their eyes met, Fotis squealed and rubbed his flank against the chain link in anticipation.

Her heart rushed—to feel so wanted, so found.

"Ella, micro mou," she clapped her hands and called in Greek. Fotis started wiggling.

Rick looked at her, puzzled. "So what brought you out here?" Sam took off for the back of the yard toward a small grove of trees, still shy of Paula.

"Oh, just wanted to visit some friends." She knew it sounded flaky.

"You know people here?"

"Up in Thunder Bay." It reminded her that she needed to call Bernie, explain as best she could and maybe drive up to visit next weekend.

"Family?"

"Friends."

"So how long you plan to stick around?"

"For a while." She grabbed the leash draped over the fence and snapped it on Fotis and then guided him out of the gate.

"Where'd Sam go?" She looked around.

"Probably hiding in the trees."

She looked toward the wooded area but didn't see him.

"So you worked with birds in New York?"

"Yeah." She wondered how much to fudge the truth.

"Where in New York?"

"Mostly the City."

"You grow up there?"

She nodded. "Pretty much." She didn't want to get into parsing boroughs.

"And where was it you've worked?"

"Uhh . . . at NYU."

"You worked with birds there?"

"Jeez." She turned and looked at him laughingly. "I feel like I'm being cross-examined."

His face had a strange look, but he backed off, folded his arms and became quiet. "Just trying to figure out where you materialized from. Out of nowhere," he said without a smile. "As an employer."

"Not much to find out." She shrugged, realizing how sketchy it sounded. "How do most people end up here?"

They stood at the fence. It became an awkward silence. Paula didn't like the way he peered at her, like the eagle examining her, looking into the pores of her skin for answers and information.

"So," he said, and stepped back, tucking his fingertips into his jeans pockets. "You still looking for a place?"

"Sure, if the offer's still good."

"How 'bout an even swap?" he said. "My guesthouse in exchange for labor."

"Deal." She held her hand out to shake.

He nodded and looked down at Fotis.

"Tomorrow I'll have you fill out some paperwork."

"Like what?"

"Application form, waiver of liability, W-2."

"Thought we were doing an even swap."

"Tax purposes."

On one hand she could understand the formality, but it felt like a tether.

"Okay."

He turned sideways, pointing. "Drive down this road." He pointed. "It's at the end by the lake."

"Do I need a key?"

"Nope."

"All righteee then." She smiled and thumbed toward her car. "Tell you what," she said, stepping backward toward the Escape. "I'm going to go check the place out."

He watched carefully and she thought a bit too long.

"Guess maybe I'll see you later," she said.

It was a relief to get away. But the more questions he asked the more evasive she became. It felt like prying; she was used to living in hiding, an undercover human of sorts.

The driveway was a grassy path through more groves of birch trees; she spotted what he'd called his guesthouse. It was like a miniature log cabin version of his home. A small satellite dish was attached at the peak of the roof. Fotis led the way to the front door. Inside was one large room with stairs leading up to a tiny loft. The staircase was made of irregular planks. She climbed the stairs and peeked into the loft: a bed, an overhead light, nothing remarkable.

The interior was sparsely furnished—a rough-hewn couch that looked like it was also a futon, flanked by two matching end tables with wrought-iron lamps. The shades sported alternating images of moose and bear.

It had a small efficiency-sized kitchen with an RV-sized fridge, stove/oven and microwave. A small, round bistro-sized table with two chairs was placed in front of a large picture window that looked on to Lake Superior. Paula sat down and set her keys on the slate tile surface. The lake was hypnotic. She could have sat there for years. Fatigue washed over her: good tired, not the mental weariness she felt on the subway ride home.

Fotis sniffed around but paid extra attention to places Paula assumed there must have been a dog.

"You have fun with Sam today?" she asked in Greek. "I'm gonna have to enroll you in ESL classes."

A TV was perched on a stand across from the couch and a tiny bathroom was located just off the living room area. A wood-burning

stove was tucked into the corner of the room, standing on a platform of flagstone. Photos of raptors in birch bark frames and
scenes of rocky outcroppings from downtown Grand Marais were
hanging on the walls.

Fotis lay down next to her on the wood floor. She took out her
phone to call Bernie. No reception. How could anywhere in
America not have cell-phone reception?

She looked at the clock over the TV. It was only two, but it felt
more like six. The sun was lower or at a different angle, making
the shadows cast oddly. But it was too early to sit around. Standing, she clipped the leash back on Fotis and headed out to the car.

They were in Grand Marais before she needed to shift into
fifth gear. She pulled in front of the IGA and saw Maggie through
the front window at the cash register.

"Be right back." Paula petted Fotis and flipped him his bone.

Maggie was handing someone their change when Paula walked
in the door.

"How's the new job?"

"Amazing," Paula said. "I hope I don't get you in trouble for
talking."

Maggie laughed.

"Don't know if your boss'll ride your ass."

"It's nice of you to worry, but my husband and I own the store.
I ride my own ass." She laughed.

"Oh, sorry," Paula said, embarrassed.

She started telling Maggie about the eagle, owl, porcupine and
abandoned otter pups.

"I have to buy boots, some clothes, for work."

"Ben Franklin's a few doors down." Maggie looked out from
behind the register. The store was empty. "You got time for coffee?"

"I'd love some." They walked toward the coffeemaker next to
the rotisserie chicken oven. "It's quiet in here."

"Mid-afternoon lull," Maggie explained. "Folks out on the water, hiking." She paused. "Screwing," she said, and sighed. "God
bless them."

They both laughed.

"Here." Maggie pulled an Avon brochure out of the pocket in her smock. "Flameless candles are scented this year," she said with added significance. The cover was decked with jack-o'-lanterns and stalks of corn. "Circle what you want on the order form; I send it in on *the computer.*" She raised her eyebrows. "Takes about five business days, sometimes less. Something to spruce up that guest cabin." Maggie winked.

Paula hadn't mentioned Rick's guesthouse.

Maggie handed Paula a Styrofoam cup and pulled out two display camping chairs, each with armrests and cup holders. They dragged the chairs into the center aisle, turning to face the half-moon beach. Sales tags and instruction booklets dangled from each frame. Firewood was bundled and stacked beneath the front windowsill.

"Jeez, it feels good to sit." Maggie plopped down, the cup in her hand, exhaling as if she'd been on her feet for months. "I'm getting too old for this crap."

"Comfortable chair," Paula remarked, looking out to the Escape parked on the street.

"Last two," Maggie said, looking at the dangling tags. "Everyone sits here. Kids, old ladies like me with swollen ankles—"

"Well, I'm right behind you."

"Probably can't sell 'em," she said, picking off something that looked like hardened chewing gum.

Paula thought of the merchants on Canal Street, taking in the early-morning sun before the day began, and the Chinese woman she'd seen smoking a cigar.

"For the love of Pete, will you look at that?" Maggie looked as if there'd been an egregious assault on reason. "Forehead prints. From people looking in to see if we're open."

Paula would have never thought the oily splotches were from foreheads.

"Jesus Christ, you'd think if the damn lights are off we're closed. Now I've got to get Bobby Ray; he's my bagger; you'll meet him"—she made a little motion toward her head—"to wipe them off when he comes in. Poor guy's got some problems, sort of slow. He's Marvelline's nephew from Gotebo, Oklahoma; he's a kind soul." Maggie said, shaking her head. "So we're shorthanded and I'm doing all the stocking right now."

"Well, the coffee's good," Paula said after she took a sip and started leafing through the Avon catalog. "Thanks."

"Ephraim says it's turpentine."

"God bless turpentine." Paula raised her cup in a salute.

Maggie laughed. "Sort of torques up your innards, don't it, though?" Maggie said, and they both began to chuckle

"So what's the story with Rick?" Paula asked.

Maggie turned in her chair. "Funny thing, he asked the same thing about you last night on the phone."

Paula touched a bundle of firewood with her toe, playing with the clear shrink-wrapped wood, embarrassed. Maggie had her loyalties and Paula had overstepped her bounds.

"So what'd you tell him?"

"Told him I knew what he knew. Says you got a way with the birds." Maggie got up to put more cream in her coffee.

"Says you're picking things up fast, got that inner calm he looks for in a rehab person."

Paula felt Maggie studying her.

"He said that?" Paula glanced up, hoping it was true and that Maggie wasn't just being nice.

Maggie nodded and shrugged.

Paula looked into her lap, trying to hide how pleased she felt. "Thanks." Paula felt herself beaming.

"Don't thank me. Rick said it."

"But you passed it on."

Paula looked down at the brochure with the candle selections. "Don't think I'll go for the flameless candles," Paula said. "I mean, what's the point."

"I'm with you, but you'd be surprised how many people burn down their own damn houses."

"You got a point."

They sat sipping the piping-hot coffee as they thumbed through the catalog. The sun had shifted direction, shining onto Paula's knees, and the warmth felt good.

"You see," Paula started. "I'm on a leave of absence from my job in New York." It was a good place to start. "Was driving to Thunder Bay to visit friends when I stopped here to get some coffee, let Fotis out. I picked up a newspaper for something to read," she explained. "And saw Rick's ad. I've always loved birds, so I figured what the hell?" She left Roger out of it.

"What kind of work you do in New York?"

"Uhh . . . I'm in education."

"A teacher?"

"Yeah, among other things." She was reluctant. Some people found professors intimidating and she didn't want it to distance her from Maggie. So often they'd clam up or shy away, thinking they were not in Paula's league, whatever league they thought that to be. The moment she felt that distance, it hurt. "Oh, you're a *professor*?" Some would squint, reassess her features, scrutinize her as if looking for signs of assumed superiority. But in her heart she worked alongside Eleni, cutting out furs, and cleared tables with Vassili. Paula could suddenly see herself pitching in if Maggie was busy, learning to work the second register, walking the aisles with a red pencil to mark down day-old bread and aging vegetables before they were too wilted to sell. She'd felt more at home in the past forty-eight hours than she had in twenty years.

"Hope you don't think this is totally stupid," she qualified, "but it felt like fate." Paula hoped Maggie didn't think she was foolish. "Fate's a big deal in Greek culture," she added, thinking of Eleni.

"I love this work." Paula looked up at Maggie, feeling like she'd cry. "I've never loved anything so much." They turned to look out on the lake. She could feel Maggie waiting for her to go on.

Paula shifted the camping chair a bit to face her. "I've worked in the same place for almost twenty years, Maggie." She struggled

to gain composure. Another word and it might all come tumbling out.

She felt Maggie studying her.

"So who's the somebody you left behind in New York?"

"Damn, you're good," Paula said, and they both laughed. "He's
in France for six weeks."

"Think you'll go back?"

Paula looked at her knees. "At some point," she said, and tried
to relax, but a dark mood seeped in on the heels of her happiness.
Memories and obligations pecked at her. No one walks away un-
encumbered.

Paula wanted to be enveloped by the smell of old linoleum in
Maggie's store, the cluttered shelves of beauty products, potato
chips, breakfast cereals, refrigerated shelves of smoked fish and
the fun of thumbing through Avon catalogs.

"Sounds like you and Rick are good friends," Paula said.

"More coffee?" Maggie offered, raising her cup as she stood to
refill her own.

"No thanks."

"Rick blew into town ten years ago. Sort of like you," the woman
said, looking at Paula in a funny way. "Unhappily married, not
that you are, though I suspect most folks are." Maggie raised her
eyebrows.

Paula looked at her naked ring finger.

"—unrewarding career," Maggie started to explain. "Came
here with some buddies for a fishing weekend and basically never
went back."

"He never went back?" Paula looked at Maggie.

"In a manner of speaking," she clarified. "Never *looked* back—of
course he went back, bowed out of his partnership, settled his
affairs, sold his house and bought the new one."

"What partnership?" Paula asked.

"His law firm. Rick's an attorney. From the Cities."

"Oh."

"Apparently had done quite well for himself," Maggie explained. "He turned sixty last month; we've got the same birthday."

"Kids?"

"Nope, but that's another story." Maggie glanced sideways at her in a way that said there was a whole hell of a lot more to it. "You know." Maggie turned to face Paula. "Sometimes there's no starting over because the stuff that you're working with is just plain bad. Rearranging bad never turns it good unless you develop a taste for bad. Some of us gotta start fresh, walk away. Alcohol, bad love, shitty life, whatever. No one faults a person for that. And the ones that do are bitter 'cause they don't have the guts to do it themselves."

"Oh." Paula couldn't move, as if she'd gotten hit by a blunt object. As if Clotho, one of the three Fates, and the spinner of the thread of life, had borrowed Maggie's mouth to cite line and verse from a page of Paula's fate. It was so clean, so pointed, she felt as though Maggie knew everything.

It took Paula a few moments to recover.

"I don't have kids," Paula said. "You?"

"Four of 'em. All grown. Some days I say, 'Thank God they're grown'; others I miss their sweet baby smells so bad it kills me," she said, and looked down at her knees. "All of 'em moved away— Chicago, the Cities."

"You must miss them."

"Every day." Maggie looked at her hands. "Ephraim wants to remodel the store, 'update.' Says it's ratty."

"Doesn't seem to bother customers any." Paula looked around at the shelves that looked to be in need of perpetual restocking.

Maggie sighed. "I'm ready to retire. Ephraim says retiring kills ya."

Paula thought of Vassili, who'd never lived to find out, and Eleni, who said the same thing. The IGA was a gold mine. The only grocery store in a tourist town aside from a few health-food stores that sold meat, real toilet paper, plastic forks and spoons, Campbell's soup, Coke, Pepsi, hair dye and ibuprofen.

Maggie sat quietly, thinking. "Maybe in the next few years. Travel, maybe move back to Red Cliff where we're from, see the grandkids."

"How long have you lived here?"

"Ephraim inherited the store thirty years ago."

"Would one of your kids take over?"

Maggie laughed in a dark way. "Hon, that conversation's long dead."

"Does Rick still practice law?"

Maggie gave her a look. "Why do you ask?"

"Oh, nothing—just curious. He seems like a smart guy." She shrugged, wondering what the big deal was.

"Well, hon, I'd say you're no slouch yourself," Maggie countered. "Let's just say he works on special projects."

"Oh." Paula got the sense she'd entered forbidden territory.

Just then a family with four giggling adolescent girls entered the store.

"Well, break's over." Maggie stood and began shoving the chairs back against the front window to clear the aisle.

"Well, thanks for the coffee." Paula tossed the empty cup into a wastebasket by the door. "I'll fill this out and bring it back." She held up the Avon order form in her hand.

Maggie smiled and nodded back as the mother asked about mosquito repellant.

Paula walked out to the street. She could see the top of Fotis' head. He was either napping or busy with the bone. Walking down two doors, she found the Ben Franklin and waltzed in.

CHAPTER 9

Next morning she thought nothing of driving up the steep incline from the guesthouse to Rick's. Scent from a wood fire along with the nutty smell of burning leaves got stronger as she approached. Thick gray clouds like sooty cotton balls hung low over the lake, setting off the yellow leaves to glow brighter than the day before.

"Stay here," she said to Fotis, and parked. Closing the door, she clomped off in her stiff new work boots in search of Rick. Last night she'd taken Fotis on a long walk. Blisters already brewed on three toes; her big toe was at the mercy of the bend in the leather boot, while two others had just begun complaining. She wanted to tough it out, but the thick wool socks provided no cushion at all as she walked toward sounds of Rick foraging about in the otter enclosure.

She was primed and ready to show off the new work attire. Hair pinned back, face free of earrings and necklace, black and yellow plaid flannel shirt, sleeves rolled up to her elbows. The tag in the back was irritating. She reached in and yanked; threads popped and a tiny patch of yellow came out. She stuffed it into her jeans pocket. A thick black polar fleece jacket had replaced the hideous sweatshirt. She pushed up its sleeves.

Each step hurt worse; it would be a long day at this rate. There was a first-aid kit prominently displayed in the raptor room. Band-Aids might help. Thank God she hadn't walked to work; it was at least a quarter of a mile. She'd have been barefoot by the time she got to Rick's. The Ben Franklin clerk had suggested moleskin pads, "to cover those tender areas during the break-in period," but Paula had taken the advice as some sort of marketing ploy, though the clerk had shook his head as if to say, *It's your funeral, lady.*

As she approached the otter enclosure, the smell of damp hay and warm mammal became thick. A garden hose snaked through the chain link. She spotted Rick bent over, cleaning. He wore grimy olive green rubber boots. The top of his sandy gray hair sprang in damp curls from the effort; the only clear view was that of the two back pockets of his jeans. "Okay if I put Fotis in with Sam again?"

"Any reason you drove?" Answering a question with a question—she was getting used to it. Rick sounded more amused than peeved.

Paula looked over to his house; the lakeside glass wall of windows sparkled like sheets of polished quartz. No sign of a lady friend.

The lake mirrored a sky with no horizon. It was hypnotic.

"Sam's already out," Rick called back.

"Okay."

"There's food in each kennel. Didn't know if he'd eaten; just open the doors. They'll go in."

"All right, thanks."

"Shut each gate; wait till they're done before you let 'em out," Rick instructed.

"I will."

"Once they're settled come on in," he said. "I want to talk to you about something."

Fotis dragged her toward the backyard where Sam stood motionless, tall and shaggy like a cartoon version of a wolf. As they neared, Sam dropped down onto his front elbows and emitted a squeal before running off, inviting Fotis to chase. She stood watching the two of them romp like best friends. Her throat cramped; happiness hit so sharply it hurt. She breathed and looked up to the trees. They were noticeably barer than the day before. The freshly fallen yellow leaves formed circles beneath the drip line of the trees. As the dogs rustled through the leaves, she closed her eyes. She wanted to remember this scene forever.

"Okay, you guys," she called, and clapped her hands, walking toward the kennels. Sam ran toward her and Fotis followed. When she opened the gates, each ran like a bullet to his respective food bowl.

Closing the gate to each kennel, Paula waited. Fotis' rabies tag clinked on the side of the bowl. He finished first and looked to Sam, who finished and glanced back as if clocking in. "You guys done?" She unlatched each gate and Sam dashed off to the trees with Fotis chasing after.

"Okay, I'm back," she announced before opening the otter gate to step inside. "How's the eagle?"

"Had a rough night, but his lead levels dropped a few points."

"Thank God."

"He's not out of the woods yet." Rick stopped scrubbing and looked up to get her attention. "Remember yesterday when you started to play with the otters and I told you to stop?"

She nodded.

"Do you know why?"

She looked down at her boots.

"You invited them to imprint," he said.

The animals were irresistibly cute.

"They're not stuffed animals," he said, scolding. "You play, they imprint, you've ruined their lives." He went on. "Imagine one of them approaches someone's kid in a campground and bites to initiate play." He studied her for a few moments. "It's seen as an attack and the animal pays."

The scenario played out in her mind. She nodded and looked down at the crease in her boot.

"I see."

"When they're imprinted, we become peers. They look to humans for food, for a mate." He stood up, hands on hips to stretch his back, keeping his eyes on her. Foamy cleanser smelling like Pine-Sol dripped from his scrub brush. "Imprinting begins at birth," he began. "Parents identify what to eat, how to hunt, who's a mate. Human contact screws it up."

"Then what about the eagle?" She looked toward the metal building. Rick hadn't shut her down as she'd murmured and stroked the bird's chest feathers.

"Adult raptors don't imprint. We treat them, comfort them as best we can. Release is the goal unless injuries impair their survival. We want them well and back to their territory, their mates—therein lies the payoff. You'll see when we release."

She thought of the eagle, alone in the box.

"Wild turkey vultures on the other hand"—Rick turned and pointed with the brush to a large black bird with a bald red head of wrinkly skin—"are a different story. Which is why Sigmund here never goes away."

"He's got a name?"

Rick smiled wryly. His lips were a bit crooked. "Too bad they're not good to eat."

"Hhhh—" She looked at Rick. "You don't mean that!" One glance said he did.

The vulture was a few inches shorter than the eagle; his head resembled fresh hamburger meat.

"Why's his head so disgusting?" she asked.

"Easy, you'll hurt his feelings," Rick said.

She laughed.

"He's got a crush on you," Rick said.

The vulture tilted his head to sustain eye contact.

"Don't let it go to your head, though; he falls in love with every female who works here."

"Seriously, his head looks like a giant hemorrhoid!"

Rick suddenly bent over, laughing. It pleased her.

He straightened, wiped his eyes and said, "If you had to stick your head into the rib cages of rotting, dead things for a meal you wouldn't want a head full of feathers gathering bits of bacteria and rotting flesh either."

A mild gag reflex kicked in. Perhaps she was more squeamish than she'd thought.

"After a meal they sun themselves. It burns off the bits of bacteria and dead flesh. They're important players in the cycle of the forest."

She studied his expression. A bit of a smile turned his lips. Aside from sun damage, his skin was pitted in acne scars that had merged into wrinkles with the aging process. When he was talking about animals, twenty years peeled off; he became fresh, so alive.

"Here." Rick held out a pair of rubber gloves along with a pair of rubber waders that looked like overalls with attached rubber boots. "We're cleaning this morning."

Sigmund took a few steps toward her. She stepped back even though there was a chain-link fence between them.

"Vultures get a nasty rap, but they're really quite gentle."

"So I could just walk over and pick him up," she dared. Sigmund tilted his head as if displaying his best angle.

"Go ahead. He'd love it." Rick's voice was low, almost a gurgle at Sigmund's love-starved expression. "If he doesn't he'll vomit."

Paula looked at Rick. "Delightful."

"The stench from their stomach is so vile it drives away everything except for the females—they seem drawn to it."

"Yum."

"They also urinate on their legs to kill off lingering bacteria. Their urine is acidic for that purpose."

"Oh goody."

Rick looked at the otter shelter. "Imprinting's only a threat with the young," he went on to explain. "So we limit contact to feeding and handling only for medical procedures. Even with caution, imprinting is a risk."

"So how do you avoid it?"

He bent over and picked out twigs, leaves, from the bottom of the otter pool. The three otters hid from him in the wooden shelter. "Very carefully."

One of them peeked out at her and then withdrew.

He motioned for her to wait and stepped to close the door to their shelter.

"I try not to even speak around them; I'm breaking my own rule," he whispered.

"They seem afraid."

He looked at the shelter.

"Avoidant. Which is how they should be."

She looked toward two eagles sitting in the sun, each tethered to a stand by leather jesses on their feet. One puffed out his belly and leg feathers seemingly in bliss.

"Does he like the sun?"

Rick looked. "Animals love the sun. These two are flightless. Both about twenty years old. One's a bald; the other's a golden. Been with me for years. Normally we don't get goldens up here; don't know where he came from. He's mostly blind, too blind for the wild—some sort of head trauma—the other lost part of a wing. He can't hunt. Mixed it up with a power line over near Two Harbors. Sometimes they get so fixated on a field mouse they miss power lines, barbed-wire fences. These guys have 'sanctuary'; we'll see who outlives whom."

She wondered if Rick's parents were still alive. He seemed so much more robust than Roger.

"Both came in as adults, so they've not imprinted. They're my foster dads."

"Dads?" She looked up as she unlaced her boots.

"Males are often more attentive. If we get a young eagle while you're here you'll see," he said. "They feed, raise the young, teach 'em to hunt."

"Even the blind one?"

He nodded. "These guys have successfully reared dozens of chicks."

They were quiet for a few moments. Everything was contrary to what she knew about birds.

She leaned against the fence, happy to step out of the boots and into the waders. She massaged her foot.

"You mind if later I use some of the Band-Aids in the first-aid kit?" She made a face. "Blisters."

"Didn't Clyde at the Ben Franklin get you some moleskin?"

She said nothing.

"Check to see if there's still some in there. Works better than Band-Aids anyway. Let me know; I got some up at the house."

"Thanks."

Paula thought about the owl as she stepped into the rubber boots and secured the waders around her waist.

"Imprinting with wild canids, wolves, foxes, is serious," he went on to explain. "They'll have no fear of humans. They'll approach to play or think you have food for them. Imagine if a ninety-pound wolf walks out of the trees and approaches your five-year-old."

She cinched the straps tight on the waders.

"Curiosity is natural; familiarity is deadly. They watch us all the time." He looked out to the woods. She looked, too, searching for pairs of eyes. "It's the people who try to keep them as pets that get into trouble."

"Like the people who had Sam?"

Rick nodded. "They get unruly, so people dump 'em, thinking they'll *go back to the wild*," he mocked. "Instead they starve."

She hadn't thought of instinct as something that could be lost.

"Someone sees a pup or a chick and they think it's abandoned. Often the parents are just out finding food. Just think how those parents must feel when they can't find their young." There was something so earnest about his face it made her want to comfort him.

She mirrored his silence, imagining Sam wandering the highway.

Rick then bent down and grasped one side of the otter pool. Paula took his lead. Together they lifted and dumped out the remaining water.

"These guys were found in the woods," he said.

"You think their mother was killed?"

He shrugged. "Hard to know." He took a long pause. "It's rare to find otters so far from a water source."

She wondered what circumstances had befallen them. It would be tempting to cuddle and keep them; she could see how someone might try.

"After a few more checks this week, we'll take them down to the shore." He motioned west. "Several otter colonies there."

"Will they be okay?"

He didn't say directly. "If they don't come back I'll take it they're fine."

She turned and looked at Sigmund. He spread his huge wingspan with the suddenness of Dracula's cape and turned around to exhibit himself.

"Oh brother," she said with disgust.

"He's going for it," Rick said in a singsong voice.

Once the pool of water was empty, Rick handed her a scrub brush and a bottle of disinfectant.

"You have the honors," he said. "Scrub out all the slime and anything that feels suspect." He let himself out and began walking toward his house.

"Suspect?"

"Yeah. You'll know what I mean when you start scrubbing," he called over his shoulder.

"Where are you going?"

"Fish for the raptors."

She was covered up to her midriff in rubber boots and up to her elbows in rubber gloves. The sun felt good on her face, and like the eagles, she stood absorbing it before bending on all fours to scrub.

Later that afternoon they treated the eagle again and tested his blood. He seemed more listless than the day before and she mentioned it to Rick; he said that the treatment could be rough on them. He put salve on the owl's wounds. Though her blood blister looked ugly and serious, it was too dangerous to lance.

Holding the owl was like holding the world. Though she was huge, Paula could feel the owl's hollow bones and skeletal body in her arms as light as air. The feathered tufts on the bird's head tickled Paula's face as Rick used a giant syringe to suck up a baby-food jar of pureed liver and deposit it into the owl's stomach. Next time they'd give her a mouse as a test to see if she was ready to eat. Rick taught Paula how to move the tube down the owl's throat in the correct position, slowly releasing the food into her stomach and not the lungs.

"You're going to be okay," Paula said as she lowered the owl back down into the box. "You'll see. Rick says maybe six weeks or so you'll fly back to your home." The bird looked at Paula. Yellow eyes that mirrored her own: mysterious, clear-sighted like the eagle. Paula could see how people would impart all sorts of qualities onto this bird—wise and precognitive, secret keeper. She covered the box with the bedsheet, fastening it with clothespins.

She was unaware that Rick was watching. He'd left to walk back to the flight room and she hadn't heard him return.

"Oh," she said. "I didn't realize."

"You did that really well," he said.

She looked at him and smiled, too humbled to even thank him. Moving toward the sink, she disassembled the components of the tube-feeding apparatus and began scrubbing it in warm water.

"When you're done, come on up to the house," he said. "I have some forms for you to fill out."

She nodded.

⁓

The front door to Rick's log home was wide open. No screen. Sigmund followed, teetering on his scaly pink feet as if racing her toward the opening. "Don't go in there." She tried to shoo him away, chasing him out of the doorway, but he walked inside, making himself at home. "Sigmund," she called. "Get out of there." But the vulture disappeared deep inside the house.

The home had the feel of a 1920s Adirondack lodge. She knocked on the open door; it was so thick her knuckles barely registered a sound. There was no sign of a doorbell.

"Hello?" she called. She didn't know whether to walk in like Sigmund or wait out on the deck. What if Rick was taking a shower?

She stepped inside the foyer and called again.

"Hey, Rick?"

There was a stirring from somewhere in the house.

"Come on in," his voice echoed. She stepped inside and looked up. Vaulted ceilings, exposed beams, huge skylights lined the top near the peak of the roof.

The inside was larger than it appeared from the outside.

"Sigmund's in here," she called.

"Ah, that's okay. I leave the front door open or he'll scratch off the finish."

She looked around, imagining the disgusting bird making himself at home in the luxurious great room, and then spotted him sitting on the back of a leather sofa, looking at her as if inviting her to sit down.

The interior smelled like pipe tobacco, old leather jackets and wool. Weather-beaten leather furniture, iron floor lamps, tribal-looking Oriental rugs, wall hangings that looked Native American. Large logs and beams framed the interior ceiling. The inside walls were the same weathered dark brown as the outside.

"Wow, this is amazing," she said to no one. It was so tidy she imagined someone came in to clean.

She spotted Rick down the hall. Brown reading glasses dangled on the tip of his nose. He waved at her to follow him down a long hallway to a room on the far end of the house.

Bookshelves with legal books lined one wall. A massive cherrywood desk filled practically a third of the room, along with computer equipment and paper files. He sat down behind the desk as she stood.

"Maggie tells me you're an attorney," Paula said.

"So they tell me," he said absentmindedly, gathering forms for her to sign.

"What kind of law do you practice?"

"Have a seat," he said. It felt like being in Christoff's office.

She down sat in a leather chair opposite the desk. Photos of birds covered the walls.

"Did you take these?"

He turned as if having forgotten what was hanging on the wall behind him.

"Some. Here, sign where I've indicated." He pointed to yellow stickers with red arrows. It felt like she was buying another car.

"What's this?"

"Waiver of liability."

"For what?"

"If you get hurt on the job."

"I'm not expecting to."

"No one expects to."

She looked up at him, the glasses dangling from the tip of his nose, the same shirt he'd been wearing for two days.

"Okay, but I have my own health insurance."

"Congratulations."

There was a twist to his voice that put her on guard. It hurt her feelings a little. She was unsure how to respond and felt foolish, younger, unschooled, as if a few days working with birds had disarmed her. She couldn't think of one bitchy comeback. It seemed she'd forgotten them when she'd grasped that eagle's feet the first day. Her chin dipped. Maybe she'd imprinted with a species other than her own early on. And maybe it was the same for this weird, contradictory man.

Rick handed her a pen. "Print your name, sign and date here," he said, as if instructing a client.

She briefly read the statement and then signed.

He rotated the documents. Rick smelled like soap. "And this one's for the rental agreement."

She signed.

"And sign this W-4, put your social here and then print and sign your name here."

She was about to question why this was necessary since it was an exchange of rent for labor but didn't bother. Reaching over, she filled out the form and signed.

"Okay then." He looked at his watch.

"Guess I'll see you tomorrow," he said.

"Guess so."

She was about to ask if there was a back door she could use to retrieve Fotis but decided against it.

Instead she walked out the same way, feeling stung. She eyed the log walls and stone fireplace. Sigmund was still planted on the sofa like a Basilias, Greek for king. She hopped down the front steps and was grateful to be out of there. The air smelled fresh with sweet grass, campfires and the delicate spice of water plants.

"Asshole," she muttered, as if that would cauterize her feelings. How could someone who exhibited such gentleness and compassion with mammals and birds be such a jerk? Walking around the side of the house, she spotted Fotis and Sam waiting at the fence.

"Hi, guys," she gushed, bending over in a goofy play stance, relieved to be suddenly enveloped by love and welcoming. She unlatched the gate and stepped in. Fotis rubbed her, turning against her chest as he basked in her scent.

Sam made a beeline for the stand of mature birch trees in the farthest part of the backyard.

"Hey, Sam." The wolf's ears perked up as he loped quickly away. He stopped a ways off to watch her, hiding behind one of the trees, peeking out, still not making up his mind. It hurt her feelings, too. *Like father, like wolf.*

"Let's go have fun," she said to Fotis in Greek. Leaning over, she began playing, feeling excited about something for no apparent reason. He started wriggling.

"Let's go to the IGA and see if Maggie's there," Paula said in a playful voice. "We'll get a rotisserie *kota,* maybe some ice cream, a new bone and some *psomi.*" At the sound of *psomi,* he stopped. "Yes, bread." She nodded. Bread was his favorite; he'd go through a whole loaf in one meal. She'd taken to buying the long baguettes Maggie stocked. He'd lie in the car on his back, holding the two-foot-long bread between his front paws like a flute as he chewed away.

"Let's go," she said, and began to run, racing Fotis to the Escape.

Later that afternoon, just back from Maggie's, Paula found Rick's driveway filled with cars. Shiny, identical late-model BMWs, without a speck of road dust, not the type of trucks and cars she'd come to recognize as local. All had Minnesota license plates.

She played with her lip as she scoped out the cars. Rick's front door was shut, inside lights were on. Maybe he was having a dinner party. She felt miffed but was glad she hadn't been invited.

Just then her phone rang.

"Heav," she said. "Let me call you back." The signal was weak. Yesterday, while talking to Eleni, Paula had discovered a place with good reception, out on the water in front of the guesthouse, on a boulder. She could get three bars. Maybe the signal was bouncing off a tower across in Canada or maybe Wisconsin.

She situated Fotis with bread and a bone in the cabin and walked down to the shore, rolled up her jeans and stepped through the knee-high icy water. It made her breath catch as she slogged toward the boulder. Getting a foothold, she climbed up and checked the signal.

"Hey—Tony's got info on the guy," Heavenly said.

"Already?"

"Christ—has all that fresh air killed your brain cells, Paula? He's a detective for Christ sakes."

"I know, but still so fast?"

"We're concerned, that's all. We love you. Doesn't hurt to check—hey, Tone?" She was handed over.

"Hey, beautiful," Tony's voice prompted a pang of homesickness.

"Thanks. I needed that," Paula said. It was so good to hear his gruff voice.

"Richard Erik Gunnarsson," he began. "Last name two *n*'s and *s*'s. Jeez, we don't get a lot of names like this in New York." She'd noticed the name on the papers she'd just signed. "Northern Lights Wildlife Rehabilitation," he continued. Rick was a member of both the Minnesota and Wisconsin Bar Associations. His name was also found in association with legislation in both states as well as federal legislation to restrict breeding and selling native birds. It also covered export of raptors and native songbirds unless by controlled facilities licensed by the federal Wildlife Protection Act.

Aside from a few speeding tickets over the past few years, a long and ugly divorce battle that was over eleven years ago, there was nothing else. His property was assessed at almost $2 million; his taxes were fifteen thousand a year. This was his only residence, and he had no reported income other than capital income.

"Lots of photos with legislators, animal advocates," Tony said. "He's helped with updating the Endangered Species Act; Migratory Bird Treaty Act; Bald and Golden Eagle Protection Act, Jesus, I could go on. Guy's an animal nut."

"He's hardly a nut, Tone," Paula said in the middle of a yawn. Tony then read off Rick's registration number with the state of Minnesota as a wildlife rehabilitator.

Paula missed Tony and Heavenly, missed being known. It was

a strange experience that people looked suspiciously at her. In New York life moved so fast that few were suspicious for their mere presence. But here she was the mysterious newcomer. Materializing out of thin air with few possessions other than a wolf dog who understood Greek, she'd landed a job and cozied up to the local grocer for information about her new employer.

"You talk to Roger lately?" Tony asked.

"Yesterday," Paula said. "He's busy with the collider. I think we're on a talking hiatus. "

"We miss you, dolly," Tony said. "Here's Heav."

"So tell me what Mr. Rick Gunnarsson looks like?" Heavenly said.

"Forget about it, Heav; the only thing hot for me is a turkey vulture."

"A what?"

"Forget it. Had to be there."

"So what are you doing now?"

"Right now? Sitting on a boulder in the lake talking."

"You're what?!"

"It's the only place I get a signal."

"She's sitting in the middle of the fucking lake," Heavenly called to Tony.

"I'm hardly in the middle, Heav," she said.

"That's all right; it makes for a good story," Heavenly said. "So what's this town like?"

"It's cute. Scenery's gorgeous."

"You're right near the border."

"I know."

"What happened to going to see Bernie, your advisor?" Heavenly was relaying everything back to Tony.

"I'm going to make it up there one of these days."

"How's that precious dog?"

"Oh, he's doing great," Paula said. "Having the time of his life. He's got a buddy now."

"You got another one?"

"No. This guy Rick's gotta"—she wondered what to call Sam: a house wolf?— "one that's Fotis' size."

"Cool."

"Hey, I better go. I left Fotis alone at the cabin I'm renting."

"We love you; stay safe," they called into the phone.

After ending the call she sat on the boulder, looking out to the horizon. Except for Fotis, there was no urgency to get back. The sun was beginning to shift into rich late afternoon, bathing everything in its color. Everyone kept noting how the days were growing shorter. She pulled up her knees and tucked into a ball. It felt like she was inhaling the beauty of the sky, the aquamarine horizon, all of it so serene, so quiet. She sat there a few moments longer until she missed Fotis and headed back to take him for a walk.

Early the next morning, cars from Rick's houseguests were still parked out front, covered with a fine layer of pollen and dust. As she walked Fotis down the grassy path she'd noticed the lights were on in Rick's home.

It was after seven and Rick wasn't out yet. She put Fotis in the back gate and walked toward the main building to begin preparing food for the eagle and the owl. There were no entries on the clipboard; this would be the first feeding of the day. She carefully weighed the food and noted the amount as Rick had instructed so that they knew exactly how much each was eating per feeding. As the blender was going, puréeing fresh fish into a consistency that would go through the feeding tube, Rick walked in with his contingent of guests.

She turned off the blender out of courtesy and looked up.

"Paula," he acknowledged. His voice sounded different. Quickly he rattled off their names, none of which she caught. They watched her closely, as if waiting for a reaction. Each nodded as they were introduced and she nodded back. Paula felt uncomfortable.

"They're in town for the day; I'm showing them around."

"Rick tells us you're from New York City," one of them said in a way that hit her wrong.

"Guilty as charged," slipped right out of her mouth.

They seemed taken aback.

"I have a cousin in Brooklyn," one of them said.

"Well," Paula said as they began milling about. "Have a nice visit; looks like you'll have beautiful weather." She'd picked up the standard weather talk from Maggie: "When you got nothing to say, there's always the weather."

She turned the blender back on, hoping they wouldn't interpret it as a hostile act.

"Mind if they stay to watch you feed the owl?" Rick asked, after the food was ready.

"Doesn't bother me." She walked over to the box, unclipped the clothespins, bent over and lifted the owl.

There was a bit of a collective gasp.

"I'll hold, you feed, this time," Rick said.

"Sure." She transferred the owl to him. She immediately looked to Paula.

"You hungry, sweetie?" Paula asked. Loading up the feeder, she filled the plunger with food and pressed out all the air.

Rick held the owl against his chest, each leg secured in his hands.

Paula parted the owl's beak and slowly, carefully slid the tube into the esophagus and down into her stomach.

She looked up to check with Rick.

He nodded.

She pushed slowly on the plunger.

"Wow," a woman with pearl stud earrings said. "You've learned this in just a couple of days?"

After she removed the tube, Paula glanced toward the woman. Something about her was bothersome. "Don't quite have my Ph.D. yet in raptor feeding," Paula said, unable to mask the slap of sarcasm usually reserved for unreasonable colleagues. The sharpness surprised all of them.

The owl blinked as she looked at Paula. She smiled and smoothed where the owl's feathers had gotten ruffled due to Paula's inexperience.

She stroked the owl and lowered her head to feel the feathers on her nose. It was like getting kissed by nature.

Paula looked more closely at the woman. Maybe she was Rick's girlfriend. Didn't seem like it, though. Aside from being too uptight, they didn't exude the lush vibe of lovers that's difficult to hide.

"I'll show you the otters we're going to release on Friday," Rick said, turning to place the owl back in the box. "I'll be back in a little bit to feed the eagle."

The group huddled together before turning to leave the building, exchanging information in low voices.

After the door closed, Paula slumped. She felt like she could cry. She'd sounded like a bitter, aging bird-woman. How long had it been that she'd been exiled from love? It felt like a century. And what the hell was she doing here? She should've kept driving to Bernie's. Maybe she should go to Thunder Bay on the weekend, get some perspective. Yet she was unsure about the eagle. He wasn't doing well; he'd seemed more listless last night. Rick did say that the anti-toxin was hard on them, but she was scared. She yearned for the eagle's defiance, his yellow-gray stare, and for him to live that she might see him released and not fighting for his life in a cardboard washing machine box from Sears. She peeked into the box. He didn't look back; he was lying on his side, yellow beak parted, and he was panting. "Hold on, oraios," she whispered. Tears burned her eyes to see him fighting to breathe. She covered the box again and went out to the flight room.

After she cleaned the flight room, Rick motioned for her to follow him and help feed and medicate the eagle. She hurried to catch up with him.

Sigmund caught sight of her and tottered after, flapping his wings and grunting. He was courting her, as Rick had pointed out.

"What do you want from me?" She turned to the bird, opening her hands. Sigmund seemed to take this as encouragement and hurried to her side.

"Hey, Rick." She finally caught him. "So tell me about your friends?" she asked.

He stopped. "What about them?"

He'd been so polite when they'd been there. "I don't know," she said. "It all seems very formal, like you're having meetings."

He seemed to wonder if he should answer her. "They're people I work with."

"Are they attorneys, too?" It was a strange position, knowing so much about him but not letting on.

"They were impressed with your level of skill."

She got the sense it wasn't meant as a compliment.

"Why do you say it like that?"

"They were wondering where you've worked with raptors."

"Maybe I'm just a natural," she said. She put on the leather gloves and walked toward the cardboard box. Unclipping the bedsheet, she rolled it back and looked in.

"Hi," she said. "You gonna let me pick you up today, *micros mou, esai oraios.*"

The eagle opened his eyes but made no effort to raise himself up.

"Hey, Rick?"

He quickly stepped over.

"He seems worse. I checked him after you left."

"Pick him up and let's look," Rick said.

She bent over, supported the eagle's body with one hand and grasped his feet with the other. He looked over at Rick.

"Hey, guy," Rick said.

Paula carried and then laid the eagle down on the treatment table.

"Doesn't he seem worse?" she said.

Rick said nothing but quickly checked the bird over. Whether Rick wasn't one for false optimism or the eagle was worse, he gave no indication.

"I'll draw blood," he said. "You go on and run it over to Darryl's. I'll call him, have him check for white blood cell count. Sometimes these birds have subcutaneous infections that go undetected."

She looked at Rick. "Are we going to tube-feed him?"

Rick seemed to be thinking about it.

"Let's see if he can eat solids."

Paula laid the eagle down on the treatment table, gently securing him with her forearms. The bird was as long as her torso.

"It's okay," she purred to him. The eagle stopped pushing back with his wings at the sound of her voice.

"We're gonna check you again," she explained. "See if you're getting better."

She could've sworn she caught a hint of a smile on Rick's lips as he drew blood. Afterward, Rick wrapped the eagle in a blanket to secure his talons and held the eagle against his chest. Using a pair of long tweezers, Paula picked up the fresh fish she'd cut into chunks for the eagle to grab.

"Hold it closer so he can reach."

"Can't he smell it?"

"No. They have a poor sense of smell, not like turkey vultures."

She moved the fish closer, and tapped his beak. He still didn't take it. She looked at Rick.

"Press it harder against his beak," Rick said. "He's still a bit confused. Probably never been hand-fed by a bunch of people before."

She tried again. To her surprise the eagle grabbed the fish and almost the tweezers, too. She pulled them out of his mouth and grabbed another chunk of fish, offering it up.

"Wait for him to swallow; then offer more."

He grabbed it in one chunk. To her surprise, he ate most of the fish.

"Either he's full or he's getting tired," Rick said. As soon as he said it, the eagle seemed to wilt. "I think enough for now," Rick said, and carried him back to the box. "This was good.

"I'm going to check him again in a few hours. Will you be around?"

She looked at her watch. "I'll make a point of it."

"Good. I'll call Darryl. Start him on some antibiotics."

Paula loaded up Fotis. After she'd dropped off the tube of blood at Darryl's she drove a few blocks to the IGA to get another rotisserie chicken and bread. She hoped Maggie was there but was disappointed to see a young woman, maybe high school age, marking down packages of blueberries. The girl looked up as Paula entered.

"Hi," Paula said. "Is Maggie here?"

The girl motioned toward the back with the wax pen she was using.

Paula found Maggie rearranging the meat shelf in the refrigerator section.

"Hey, Maggie," she said.

The woman turned; she was wearing winter gloves and a sweater.

"Hi, Paula." She smiled. "I'm glad you stopped by; did Rick mention the potluck at my place tomorrow evening?"

"No."

Maggie sighed. She sounded frustrated. Paula hadn't seen her like this before. "I told him to have you give me a call."

"Oh, what's up?"

"In a couple of weeks the regional rep's stopping with that vintage jewelry line I told you about. Already told some friends from Two Harbors and Silver Bay. I'll make dinner; this way you can meet some of the women in the area," she said. "Tomorrow night it's just some local friends. You game?"

"Yep," Paula said, delighted at the invitation.

"Good. So you'll come on over around six?"

"I'd love to."

"Remind me to give you directions before you leave."

"Want me to bring anything?"

"Just yourself."

Paula looked at the winter gloves.

"Whatcha doing?"

"Damn refrigerator section broke down again." Maggie looked at the unit as if it were a noncompliant employee she was thinking of firing.

Paula'd never thought about grocery store equipment before.

"Was checking out a customer at lunchtime and his bologna was room temp," Maggie explained. "So I went back and sure enough, the damn thing stopped working."

Paula watched as Maggie emptied packages of lunch meat into blue plastic bins.

"You need some help?" Paula put down her purse and pushed up the sleeves of her long-sleeved T-shirt.

"Would love some if you're offering."

Paula smiled. "Where's Bobby Ray?"

"Oh, he's not so good," Maggie said. "Hospitalized in Duluth. Last night he started hallucinating. Took his shirt off in the housewares aisle after he took a box of kitchen matches and started striking them one by one, examining his skin, convinced there were poems written on the surface. He's worked for me two years. Watched him struggle with this mental illness. So young to struggle like this, but he'll be back, probably in a couple of weeks. It's happened before."

"Poor guy," Paula said.

"So I'm down one person today. We're moving the lunch meat, the smoked fish, all the ready-to-eats over to the dairy section until Jim gets off of work. Jim's my fix-it guy," Maggie explained. "He'll figure it out."

Paula walked up to the shelves, awaiting direction.

Maggie pointed to an empty plastic bin.

"Use those plastic bins and just load the packages in there. We'll store whatever we can fit in the back refrigerators. Don't worry about the order." She gestured to what she'd done so far. "We'll sort it out later."

Paula began unloading. Bologna, tiny Oscar Mayer wiener frankfurters, olive loaf: she hadn't seen this packaged stuff in the grocery stores in New York for years.

"This damn thing's probably forty years old," Maggie said. "It was old when we bought the store. I told Ephraim it needs a new motor, not just Band-Aids." She sounded aggravated. "But he's such a cheapskate. He says, 'Why put a new motor in an old refrigerator?'" She looked at Paula as if to garner her support in a decades-long running argument. "They don't make parts for it anymore. It's an antique." Maggie chuckled. "The damn thing breaks every few weeks. He'll feel it when we start losing product, that'll fix his wagon."

"What are you gonna do?"

Maggie looked up at her with a wry little smile. "I already talked to Jim. He's ordering me a new motor on the Q.T. There's some things, hon"—she winked—"a husband just don't need to know."

Paula looked at the bin.

"So Rick didn't mention to call me?" Maggie seemed steamed about that, too.

"Nope," Paula said. "But then he's been busy with people at his house."

"Oh yes, that's right," Maggie said, and looked at Paula.

"Looks like they're having meetings."

"His friends from D.C.," Maggie said as they emptied the last of the pre-packaged lunch meat.

"Want me to clear some space in the yogurt section?" Paula walked toward the dairy section.

"You're reading my mind," Maggie said.

"It looks like there's room to consolidate the flavors."

"Good thinking. I wish those high school kids"—she gestured with her chin toward the front register—"would think like you," she said. "You want to work part-time through Apple Festival for me?"

"You serious?" They were already through the first week in September, Paula's second week of working for Rick.

"Damn straight." Maggie looked at her. "First two weeks in October are our busiest time of the year. I'll need someone to keep the shelves stocked when the high school kids are back in school.

"We'll pull in the bulk of our revenue—our busiest time."

"I'm in," Paula said. "Thanks, I'd love to." She beamed. Being part of the store felt so familiar.

"Just come by when you're done at Rick's."

"Deal." Paula extended her hand and shook Maggie's glove. "So who are these D.C. people?"

"Part of some legislation he's working on for animals," Maggie explained as Paula made room on the yogurt shelf. "He's trying to put puppy mills out of business. There's one guy in the area that's really bad," Maggie motioned with her chin. "And the breeding of raptors."

"Raptors?"

Maggie looked at her and made a disapproving noise. "You'd be surprised what people want to collect. They think they're being cool having a wolf or a hawk as a pet."

Paula thought of some of the things that Rick had said about people trying to raise chicks in captivity.

"And the puppy mills are despicable," Maggie said, shaking her head.

Paula had never thought about it.

"I tried to ask Rick," Paula said. "But he won't share a thing."

Maggie stopped working. She looked at Paula as if deciding whether to say something.

Paula waited.

"Okay. I'm done keeping people's secrets; I'm getting too old," Maggie said. "He's suspicious."

"Of me?" Paula touched her chest. "For what?"

"Thinks maybe you're spying for the other side."

"What other side?"

"The puppy mill lobby," she said. "People who illegally breed wildlife—they're all bundled together under one fancy name that hides who they are and what they do."

"Puppy mill lobby?" She stopped working, her mouth agape.

"He's not sure who you are," Maggie went on. "Here you show up out of the blue, no luggage, New York plates, he's got no idea of where you came from, what your agenda is."

She looked back at Maggie, realizing that she wasn't sure either.

"My agenda?" She laughed at the preposterousness of it. She thought of the birds on the ledge in her office in New York. She thought of the downstairs couch, how scratchy the mohair upholstery had been all these years and how some mornings she'd awaken with an imprint of the piping from one of the cushions embedded across her cheek.

"He thinks maybe," Maggie paused and looked down at her gloves, "you're working for a lobby."

"He thinks I'm working for a lobby?"

Maggie said nothing.

Paula felt the woman gauging her reaction.

"Then why did he hire me?"

"Maybe 'keep your friends close and your enemies closer.'"

Paula was stunned. She looked at the bin of Lunchables that she'd just unpacked from the shelf. She thought of Tony, of Heavenly. Thought of her friends who loved her, trusted her; it was odd to feel misunderstood. Her stomach turned. The smell of the refrigerator made her nauseous. She wanted to go back to the cabin, load up Fotis, her things, and drive to Thunder Bay that evening. Bernie knew her, knew that she wasn't a spy. This was craziness.

Tears unexpectedly filled Paula's eyes. "I just love the birds." She started to cry.

Maggie set down two packages of smoked whitefish, stepped over and hugged her.

"Do you think that about me?" Paula asked.

Maggie shook her head and motioned to follow her into the back room.

As Paula sat down on a shrink-wrapped box of Campbell soup, she began blubbering about Roger, about Theo and Fotis, NYU and the Center, about everything.

CHAPTER 10

It was early afternoon when she got back to Rick's. The cars were gone. She put Fotis in the yard with Sam and went to check in on the eagle. Rick's front door was wide open; Sigmund stepped out as she neared.

"Oh great," she mumbled. She stopped and looked at the bird, wondering if he'd try to block her entrance.

Sigmund stayed put. She shuffled around him and into the foyer; the finer hairs on her body prickled as she moved.

"Rick? You here?" After several moments, she headed out toward the raptor ICU. Sigmund followed, grunting.

"Get lost," she muttered. He looked up adoringly.

Rick's truck was in the driveway. She saw the raptor ICU door was closed but not latched.

She pushed it open. "Rick?" she called.

"In here." The eagle lay faceup on a towel on the metal table, panting. "Darryl called. His white count's sky high; something's going on."

She walked up to the table and touched the bird's shoulder. "That was your hunch."

He turned toward her. "Yeah. Glad I started those antibiotics."

The bird pivoted his head toward Paula and blinked. She stroked the brown feathers on his chest with her index finger. His eyes closed. "Ella, oraios mou." With the other hand she began smoothing the feathers on the top of his head. The white head feathers always looked wet. The bird opened his eyes again, too weak to turn his head back. Hard to believe it was the same fierce creature of the other day.

"Hi," she said. The bird seemed to like her touch, plus Rick didn't tell her to stop.

"Gonna be another long night," he said, and began to set up a tiny bag of IV fluids. "He's pretty dehydrated. Tubed him some fluids earlier, but this'll be more direct." He moved toward the counter, opened a drawer and took out a tiny needle with what looked like an attached valve. He set the needle into the eagle's side. The bird didn't jump.

"Doesn't it hurt?"

"Not a needle."

Rick then wrapped the bird's torso unwinding a roll of white gauze to stabilize the needle, and then several more times with what looked like an Ace bandage to hold the valve in place. "I'm afraid he's got pneumonia," Rick said as he exhaled. "High lead levels can cause respiratory distress."

"Will the antibiotics help?"

He raised his eyebrows, looked at the eagle's face and sighed. "Hope so."

Paula watched the bird, head turned toward her, too weak to protest. How could lead buck shot and sinkers down such a majestic creature?

"Why don't hunters and fishermen just switch to nontoxic?"

Rick looked at her. "You tell me."

"They should be forced to watch this bird suffer," she said angrily, her voice close to a holler.

"Shhh," he said. "Shouting upsets him."

"Sorry, it just pisses me off."

Rick looked sympathetically at the bird.

"Think he'll make it?"

"He's pretty weak." Rick pulled up two tall wooden stools. "I've seen too many die. Unless we get this secondary infection under control there's no telling."

Paula scooted up the stool, leaning on the metal table to get closer to the bird. As she leaned over, her hair touched his brown feathers. She noticed it was the same color. His feathers were coarser than the owl's.

"It's too bad, too, 'cause his lead toxicity levels were dropping nicely." Rick connected the IV bag to the needle, elevated the small pouch and handed it to Paula.

"What else can I do?" she asked.

"Just do what you're doing; it's comforting." His eyes softened as he handled the animal.

As she stroked his feathers, the eagle would open his eyes and look at her, blinking a few times before closing them.

It had gotten dark between treatments, Rick settled into a well-worn green armchair off to the side. Under a reading lamp he reviewed what looked like thick legal briefs. Brown tortoiseshell-colored glasses balanced on the end of his nose. Paula remained perched on the stool close to the eagle, wondering what life would be like with a man like this. Long silences. Even longer spaces with nothing to say, no compulsion to fill them with empty chatter as she often did with Roger—deficits in the restaurant menu, critical comments about the wine list, just to make small talk.

But with Rick there was peacefulness, no anger lying in wait to ambush her. When he had nothing to say, he said nothing. Yet Paula guessed that Rick would never have found her attractive ten years ago for all the reasons that Roger had.

Rick was real. Had she been grounded, she would never have slept on a couch or let Guillermo push her around. Yet Paula believed the better part of her was real, too—the part that was reaching for liberation or absolution. That she could recognize the real in others gave her hope. Fotis had seen it in her. The eagle had looked inside her, too, holding the truth within his gaze long enough for her to feel it stir.

She looked around the ICU. For once she was not reduced to

her hair, her clothes, her jewelry, her accomplishments or, most important, the woman who thought so little of herself as to allow her husband to shun her.

"You might as well take off for the night." Rick's voice pierced the quiet. "Go tend to Fotis."

"But what about this guy?" She wanted to be both places and touched the eagle's keel again to ensure he was breathing.

"I'll be here all night."

She looked at the bird; his pinkish-white tongue was visible. If it weren't for his panting he'd look dead.

"I wanna stay, too." She looked at Rick. "I mean, if it's okay."

He nodded; his brows rose slightly. "I'll go round up Fotis and Sam. Feed 'em and bring 'em into the house for the night."

"Thanks."

"They can have a pajama party," he said as he headed toward the door.

She hadn't heard that expression in years. What a funny thing to say.

"Old Sigmund'll keep 'em entertained." Rick turned with his hand on the doorknob and looked at her.

She thought about his "house vulture." "Will Fotis bother him?" she asked.

"If he does, Sigmund'll fly up to the beams."

"Or vomit."

He smirked. "Or that." The way he said it made her laugh.

She imagined Sigmund projectile vomiting on "Mr. Redford's" couches and tribal rugs and watched the curve of Rick's back and shoulders as he slipped out the door.

The wall clock said almost five; hard to believe she'd been sitting there for over two hours. She'd thought to mention her earlier conversation with Maggie, but somehow it didn't matter. Let him think whatever he wanted.

As she pulled the stool closer to lean over, the thought occurred to tiptoe over and peek at what he was reading. She looked at the ceiling. It would be just her luck that he had some sort of camera rigged up to catch her snooping. The cold metal table felt good on her sinuses as she faced eye to eye with the eagle. She continued smoothing his head and stroking his keel. The bird blinked. "Aetos, esai palikari," she told him to be brave and fight. His yellow feet were curled in the pink blanket. She reached down and held them; they were leathery and rough. Feeling his toes in her hands, she moved her fingers down to feel the curve of his talons, like fishhooks. She covered them with the blanket in case they were cold.

He opened his eyes to face her. Compassion with ferocity. He had what looked like yellow lips where his beak attached along the side of his head. He blinked a few more times and then seemed to doze. She was dozing, too.

She awoke with a start as Rick opened the door. For an instant her eyes and the eagle's opened into each other's, momentarily free of the awareness of respective species, awake in the aliveness of the other. She sat up, not wanting Rick to think her foolish.

"Fotis and Sam are fine," he reported. A rush of chilly air followed him in; a jeans jacket and an oatmeal-colored ragg wool sweater were tucked under his arm. "Getting brisk out. You cold?" He held them up for her to choose.

"Thanks." She chose the sweater and slipped it over her head. It smelled like his house.

"Brought some sandwiches, too," he said, depositing a plate on the counter, "in case you're hungry."

"Thanks." She wasn't but looked anyway. Maybe she should nibble at one as a show of thanks.

"Egg salad, turkey. Take your pick," He gestured to the food. They looked like leftover catered sandwiches from his earlier meetings.

"You gonna eat, too?" she asked.

"I could have a bite," he said, walking into a little alcove just off the hall leading to the flight room. She heard the clunking sound of a coffeemaker. "How's he doing?"

She was surprised to be asked.

"I think the same," she said.

Rick walked over with the glass coffeepot in his hand to take a look. He studied the bird and then felt the eagle's chest. He sighed, gently pinching the skin near the bird's neck to check hydration.

"Can't he just drink water?" she asked.

"No. They get fluids from the food they eat." Rick sighed as he walked to the sink and filled the pot.

They sat in silence as Rick read his stack of legal documents. Each time he stood up she noticed the seat and back were molded with the impression of his body. With his glasses on the tip of his nose, he periodically got up, checked the eagle and then walked over to a laptop to enter his notes.

Hours later Rick disappeared near the flight room. She heard him wrangling with something down the hall.

"You need some help?" she called.

He dragged a folded aluminum cot from one of the hall closets. "For when you get tired."

"Thanks." She watched him unfold it.

"Blankets in the closet down by the flight room," he said. "Tomorrow, you'll need to do laundry, bird blankets and towels. Soap, everything's by the washer."

She'd seen an old washer and dryer down the hall by the flight room.

"I can start it now if you want."

"No, no," he said. "Noise from the machines'll disturb him. Just stay with your buddy tonight."

He plopped down again in his chair, popped his glasses back on and resumed reading.

They sat in silence until later when he looked at his watch and stood. "Let's tube-feed him."

"Even when he's this sick?"

"Especially when he's this sick, with muscle wasting and the danger of his organs shutting down. Get those deer hearts from the fridge," Rick said. "They're in a black plastic bag. I'll show you how to section and weigh them before we put 'em into the blender. Always weigh everything like I showed you and record the amount he actually eats, not the amount you prepare, on the laptop. We have to know what's going in. This guy should be eating between three and six hundred grams."

She headed to the refrigerator and pulled out the bag. The hearts weighed heavy in her palm.

Rick handed her a pair of latex gloves. "Remember, always wear gloves," he said, and put a pair on, too, and then began to show how to section out certain parts for specific nutrients. She placed the meat on the scale and then scurried over to enter the amount, date, time into the eagle's file. She tossed the pieces into the blender, whirling it to a puree fine enough to pass through the feeding tube.

"This time you hold him, I'll feed," he said.

She lifted the eagle as Rick watched. The bird was practically inert and offered no resistance; she had to hold up his head.

Rick gently placed the tube down the eagle's throat and dispensed the contents.

"We'll do this about every hour or so until dawn and then assess how he's doing." He motioned for her to place the bird back down. She stroked his feathers as Rick listened to the eagle's heart. She waited for an update, but he gave none.

Paula moved over to clean up the counter, put the remaining meat back into the refrigerator and washed the tube-feeding equipment in hot soapy water.

She stayed, leaning over the eagle, until late in the night. They awoke several more times to treat him, getting up to check his vitals, give more antibiotics as the eagle panted, gasping for air. Each time Rick would shake his head. "Done all we can for now." He collapsed into the chair, rubbing his face. She saw how despondent he was.

Paula woke to clicking noises. She didn't remember falling asleep on the cot beside the table, much less sitting down. More noises. She opened her eyes toward the sound. On the edge of the metal table, the eagle stood, the midsection beneath his wings still wrapped like a mummy. The outline of his shoulders and wings shadowed her like those of an archangel. His talons clicked as he moved along the edge, staring intently as if willing her to awaken. Standing straight and tall, he was alert, seemingly amused by her.

"Rick." She sat up. "Rick?"

A rustle from the chair.

"Rick, look."

They stood slowly.

"Hey, buddy," he said, his voice light in a way she'd not heard.

"Ti kanis?" she asked, as if the bird would answer and tell her how he was feeling.

"It's always amazing when they bounce back like this," Rick said, and moved toward the table. "So often you awaken to a dead bird."

"But you're not, are you?" she said in a goofy voice.

The eagle spread his wings. With an eight-foot whoosh, his wingtips swept everything off the table. Stethoscope and syringes pinged as they hit the floor. Even his pink blanket whooshed off the table and onto the floor as his wingtips grazed the walls of the crammed examinination room.

"Easy, big guy," Rick said. "No showing off just yet." But in defiance, the eagle spread his wings again. "You've got a *long ways* to go." Rick drew out the last few words in a tone-deaf singsong.

"How long?"

"Two, three months, maybe four. Till he's well enough for release. Providing he has no long-term neurological damage from the lead poisoning. This was a pretty severe case." He nodded at the bird.

"Could he get sick again?"

Rick looked at her with relief. "Let's hope not."

She wondered how Rick held up doing this kind of work.

"Let's check his levels," he said.

In one motion, she reached for the eagle and lifted him, grabbing hold of his legs, grasping his ankles and gently securing the bird against her chest, restraining his wings with her arms.

"That was pretty damn good." Rick nodded, crouching and leaning toward the bird to draw blood, the cap of the syringe between his teeth. "You're getting better."

"Thanks." Even Rick's scalp was tan in the spots where his hair was thin.

"Hang on." He stepped to the lead analyzer and deposited a few drops of blood. The machine hummed. "Now one more dose of antibiotic." She watched as he drew another syringe and injected the bird. He then pinched the eagle's skin.

"How is it?"

He nodded and lifted his eyebrows. "Feels okay." The machine beeped and he went for the reading. "Huh." Rick sounded surprised.

"What?"

"Still high, but it fell several points overnight." He adjusted the dosage of anti-toxin and injected the bird again. "How much you wanna bet he'll eat solid food. Set him down and go get that fresh fish in the fridge."

She set the eagle down to stand on the table. "Now stay." She pointed at the bird as if talking to a dog.

Rick rolled his eyes and shook his head.

"This fridge?" she said, hurrying back toward the flight room, thinking she'd cut the fish into small pieces. Something made her look back.

He nodded, looking at her with something she hadn't seen since she'd arrived: trust.

After they'd treated the eagle and fed him, Rick insisted she take the morning off. She was too elated to sleep. Instead she changed into her sandals, grabbed her fleece jacket and loaded

Fotis into the car. She'd wanted to walk out onto Artist's Point, a local tourist attraction, to watch the early sunrise. People raved about the hikes along the jetties, out to a lighthouse in the center of the harbor.

She parked downtown, realizing she hadn't brushed her teeth or looked in a mirror since the previous day but didn't care. She felt jubilant about the eagle. It felt like a miracle.

As they walked past the IGA Paula glanced inside, mindful not to press her oily forehead against the window, but there were no store lights indicating that Maggie might be there. They crossed onto Broadway and walked until it ended at the Coast Guard parking lot. Evergreen bushes lined the grounds for several yards and smelled like Christmas trees. A sign marked the trailhead, noting that the trail was "for Coast Guard navigational purposes" and that people traveled at their own risk. It stated that a small boreal forest overlooked the East Bay and Lake Superior. Homeland Security Border Patrol boats were docked like a tiny fleet along the pier.

A few people sat out on the rocks, watching the horizon as the sun rose. The lake was perfectly still. The sky was clear except for high, thin layers of clouds and the sunrise was promising. She breathed a rush of cold air as she neared the shore. Fotis pulled and hopped up onto the first boulders; he practically dragged her over the strange ancient lava formations that made up the shoreline. It had eroded into strange three-dimensional rectangular towers that looked like clumps of massive crystals. Boulders, rocks, all broken into the same shapes like some gnome had sat for centuries tapping with a hammer and chisel to form each one. The flatter rocks were piled up into various formations along the beach, a watery field of them.

In places people had stacked up the broken rocks into *inukshuks,* or cairns, marking the fact that they'd been there, the ecotourist's graffiti.

Slabs of lava rock looked like paved walkways, having been

smoothed by the melting glacial waters and hundred of years of pounding by Superior's waves. The stone was mottled with bright orange and green lichens that looked as if someone had randomly walked through and splattered bright-colored paint. In spots the flat rock shoreline was hollowed out into perfect concentric whirlpools. Seagulls swooped wildly as the sun rose, diving for fish. Mist from the harbor illuminated by the rise of the sun gave everything a pink cast. In the distance she saw elevated cement walkways, three or four feet tall, some with rope railings, some without. They looked terrifying. She headed out to Artist's Point, thinking she'd sit on the concrete base of the lighthouse.

Up farther she stepped up onto the break wall. In some places the wall was so narrow that only one could pass. She wondered what people did when it was crowded with tourist traffic. Either backtrack several yards to let someone pass or else jump off into the pools of waist-high frigid water of Lake Superior. Some sections had rusted iron handrails, others loosely strung rusty cables or nothing at all.

Fotis didn't seem to be bothered by any of this. Once they'd reached the lighthouse, she sat down on the concrete slab and wondered how deep the water was. It was so clear she could see down to huge boulders and rocks in the frigid teal-colored water. It was so hushed and peaceful she wanted to call Roger, tell him how lovely it was, but she remembered she'd left her phone in the guesthouse. It would have been nice to share the events of the night before, but he was probably underground in the collider by now.

As she walked back the town started coming alive. In the parking lot across from the Escape, people were setting up tables, opening tailgates to boxes packed with merchandise, some holding art-glass vases and dishes, others wooden sculptures, boxes and burled bowls.

"What's this?" Paula asked a blond woman unpacking and setting handblown glass vases on a table.

"Craft Market," she said. "We started a day early. Tonight begins the Fall Harvest Festival. Today, tomorrow, winds down on Sunday."

"Sounds like fun. What time does it start?" Paula asked.

The woman looked around at the other people and gave a laugh. "I guess as soon as we all set up. It's going on all day until about midnight. Music starts about noon, out of respect for the tourists. But look around; people are starting to set up on the sidewalks," she said. Paula noticed trucks unloading, kiosks and booths being erected.

"Just holler if there's something you want to see," the woman said. On one table Paula watched a man with a beard like Andrew Weil's setting out finely carved wooden bowls, wine stops and puzzles.

Paula approached a table being set up out of the back of a white van. A woman with blond hair began unpacking boxes that her husband had unloaded onto the table, carefully unwrapping painted wooden plates. "Nice-looking dog you got there," the husband said over his shoulder as he placed another box on the table. His hair was the same color as his wife's. There was not one ounce of tension as they worked together.

"Thanks." Paula picked up two plates and looked at a large box. "These are the most beautiful things." The woman paused; Paula's comment seemed to surprise her.

"It's Norwegian," the woman said. "Haven't you seen rosemaling before?"

Paula shook her head.

"Learned it from my mother and grandmother. You see hundreds-years-old steamer trunks with dates on them. Plates, bowls all painted with these designs, some have sayings, some dates and people's names. The designs are based on techniques from differing parts of Norway. Families pass them along. "

Paula was enchanted. She picked out a few plates and the large box. "Can you hold these? I have to run and get my wallet from the car."

"You on vacation?" the woman asked.

"Actually I'm working for Rick Gunnarsson on Sixty-One—Nothern Lights Wildlife Rehabiliation."

The woman turned to her husband. "She's working for Rick." She turned back. "We know Rick. His house is filled with our stuff." The woman chuckled, gesturing to the other dealers. "She's working for Rick," she announced to the other dealers.

"I'm Paula." She extended her hand.

"I'm Karin. Didn't Rick mention the festival?"

"No."

"That's surprising," the woman said. "He's usually a fixture. His whole staff, too."

Paula didn't know what to say.

"The whole downtown turns into one big party," the woman said. "Restaurants open their doors; everyone gathers on the beach; there's live music; it's the biggest hoopla of the year," the woman said as she laughed. "Sort of a good-bye-to-summer party."

Paula bought a wooden plate for herself, one for Celeste and a few carved wooden wine stops for Roger and Tony. Roger was impossible to buy for, but she thought he'd appreciate the fine wood craftsmanship. She bought Eleni a matching glass pendant and earrings in the Santorini blue colored glass (the hue of the Aegean Sea) that her mother loved.

"Well, thanks for tipping me off about the festival," Paula said.

The woman looked puzzled.

"I'd better get back, just taking a break," Paula said. "I'll be sure to come down later."

"Good," the woman said. "Tell Rick Karin says 'hi' and that I better see both of you down here tonight."

"Oh, you'll see me all right." Paula headed back to the Escape with her purchases, thinking about Bernie. She phoned him. "I'm so sorry, Bernie; something's come up," she said.

"Jeannine figured you got waylaid by some boyfriend or something." Bernie chuckled.

She told him about Northern Lights Wildlife Rehabiliation.

"Well, we'll be here, no rush, Paula. Jeannine's been making noises about wanting to go to Grand Marais for dinner in the next few weeks; maybe we'll see you there."

The call ended, her guilty feelings assuaged. Excited, she started the Escape and headed back to get ready. She found Rick outside the otter enclosure.

"I just hiked out on Artist's Point," she said. "It's amazing. And then saw everyone setting up for the festival."

He looked over at her as they walked toward the raptor ICU. "I'm surprised you didn't crash after the long night."

"Couldn't sleep. How's he doing?"

"So far okay."

"Someone named Karin and her husband say 'hi.'"

Rick smiled.

"Are you going to the festival?"

"Maybe for a little while."

She'd wanted to ask him why he hadn't mentioned it but didn't want him to feel cornered.

Later that afternoon after she'd finished her duties with the animals, hand-fed the eagle and had her daily chat with Eleni and Celeste she discovered a stackable washer and dryer in one of the closets plus laundry soap. It felt good to have clean clothes.

She left Fotis in the guesthouse with the lights and TV on along with three fresh bones so he wouldn't feel lonely. She'd thought about taking him along but then wasn't sure. "Bye," she said. The dog didn't look up.

She ended up parking almost as far away as Rick's place, but on the other side of downtown. Music carried all the way from the heart of the town as she hurried, her pace accelerating as she got closer. Crowds of people lined the promenade; sidewalks were filled with displays of photographs, paintings and fabric sculptures— she didn't know where to look first.

Then Rick tapped her shoulder. "Can I buy you a drink?"

It surprised her. He was wearing a brown plaid shirt, khaki shorts and sandals. His hair look freshly washed and fluffy on top, the sides still wet.

"Love one," she said.

"Beer? Wine?"

"Wine. White's perfect."

He led her toward the Gun Flint Tavern, which had a make-shift bar on the sidewalk. The smell of barbeque, grilled fish and potatoes was intoxicating. On the way Rick was stopped numerous times by people calling him over, talking, chatting and slapping him on the shoulder. A few men swapped plans regarding a kayak expedition they were planning that winter in Patagonia. "Take Kate along," someone said to him, and he laughed it off. Some made plans to kayak to the caves along the Superior shore that next weekend and a Boundary Waters trip in early October, weather permitting.

Each time she was introduced as the new trainee someone would make a scrappy comment about Rick, and she could tell people really liked him. This other side of him was dumbfounding; she kept blinking to recalibrate her senses.

They finally made it to the bar. Paula watched the outline of his shoulders as he negotiated the deal. Then he turned, carrying an amber bottle of beer and a glass of wine.

"Let's go sit over there by the water; it's quieter." He motioned with the glass of wine.

She followed him across the pebbly shoreline toward the marina as he carried both drinks.

He waited as she sat down on the pebbly beach before handing her the glass. He crossed his ankles, lowering himself into a cross-legged position next to her, tipping back the beer bottle as he landed.

All around them the benches were occupied; families and couples had set down blankets to watch the harbor. A few kayakers were demonstrating Eskimo rolls—tipping underwater and then upright again, performing as the crowd applauded.

"That's an old law-school buddie of mine, Derek, showing off," Rick said.

"Can *you* do that?" she asked in a flirty way.

"What do you think?" The way he said it reminded her of men at graduate school parties at Berkeley. "You see Maggie and Ephraim yet?" he asked.

"No. I didn't. I haven't met Ephraim yet."

"Just saw them over by the brat stand at Sven and Ollie's." Rick laughed. "Ephraim's quite the character. Fell off the roof last winter trying to shovel it and broke a leg."

"Shoveling a roof," she stated in disbelief.

"I keep telling him it's time for a metal roof rake, but he's a stubborn cuss. Cheap as the day is long. Calls me from the hospital where they're pinning his leg back together and asked me to bring his ninety-seven-year-old father, Chester, his 'staples'—a gallon jug of muscatel, packages of summer sausage, bags of Brach's dinner mints and a case of Archway oatmeal cookies. The old man still has a place, next property over from them."

"What an awful diet." She had no idea what summer sausage was.

"The guy's pushing ninety-eight; the rest of us should be so lucky."

"Why didn't Maggie bring them?"

Rick laughed. "The old geezer grabs her ass every time she's alone with him."

Paula looked down at the pebbles, laughing.

"The old guy's losing it, but you gotta give him credit," Rick said, setting his beer bottle into the pebbles.

Thank God she had clean clothes and makeup. Her knockoff designer tank and shorts felt loose from days without ice cream.

"Pretty sunset," she said.

"There's a big storm front coming in, not till after midnight, though."

"Is it always gorgeous like this?" she asked, watching a fog bank dreaming in again, slowly, gently like a promise.

"Got me to move here."

"I can understand why." She turned and looked at the outline of his profile against the changing colors of the sinking sun.

"Lake's thirteen hundred and thirty-two feet deep, with two thousand, two hundred and twenty-six miles of shoreline," he said.

"Not quite the drive from California to New York."

"And takes one hundred and ninety-one years for all the water to replace itself," he said. "Hundreds of shipwrecks dating from the seventeen, eighteen hundreds. Fun to dive. Because of the low acidity levels, the wooden hulls are amazingly well preserved. They're protected historical sites."

She looked out at the lake, thinking of the depth.

"How's your wine?" he asked, looking at the lighthouses.

"Great, thanks." She raised the plastic cup and looked at it. "So, I'm curious," she asked. "What's a *marais*?"

"It's French for 'safe harbor.' This was a stop for fur traders. They hired French voyageurs to transport pelts from Lake Athabasca to Montreal. Have you ever felt a fox pelt?"

She chuckled. "My mother's worked for a furrier her whole life. She still does," Paula said. "On Sundays when I was a kid sometimes after church we'd go there. I'd watch her work when there was an important job. She was proud, still is." Paula thought of Eleni. What other eighty-year-old woman was still working? "I used to put the raw fur pelts on my head as a kid and pretend to be the animal."

Rick looked at her and she looked out to the lake, feeling her face flush. She'd forgotten that memory.

"The voyageurs used birch bark canoes, May through October, working the waterways until they froze. They needed *marais* when storms blew in during the fall—like Artist's Point." He said the word *marais* with a French accent.

"You speak French?"

"My mom's French-Canadian. Spent summers in Montreal. My father was a surgeon in the Cities. They didn't get along."

"Fotis speaks Greek."

"Yes, I've heard him."

She laughed. "I've got to teach him English commands."

"He's picked them up all right." Rick then looked at his wrist-watch. She liked the fluffy sun-bleached hair on his brown fore-arms. "I can't stay too much longer. Got people coming in."

"More mysterious guests, eh?" The wine made her brave.

She felt his eyes as he turned to look at her. "How are they 'mysterious'?"

"You're all so hush-hush." She pulled up the neckline of her T-shirt in jest to hide her face like a spy.

"We're working on animal welfare legislation."

"I know."

He turned to examine her. "You know."

"My best friend Tony de la Rosa's a detective, NYPD," she admitted. "He checked you out."

"Well, I ran your plates before you'd even left my driveway that first day."

She looked at him. There was a wry smile as he sipped his beer.

"Immigrant studies at NYU," he started. "Paula Makaikis, resides on West Twenty-fifth Street, Manhattan, married to a one Roger xyz, Polish last name I won't even begin to pronounce, par-ticle physicist, Columbia."

She started laughing, looking down at the rocks that for some reason made the whole thing seem even funnier. "Got me there." She wiped her eyes.

"Criminal law," Rick said. "Prosecutor."

"Yeah, well, that explains a lot."

He took another swig of beer.

"Maggie says you think I'm a spy." It slipped out of Paula's mouth before she could button it.

She watched his face carefully. He seemed to formulate his thoughts.

"Animal welfare's a lot more complicated than you'd think," he said. "Anytime there's money involved, people get ugly."

"You still think I'm a spy?" Her voice softened.

"Not competent enough," he said conclusively but with a smirk. Finishing the last of his beer, he looked around as if deciding whether or not to get up and get another. "Wasn't sure at first." He looked out to the horizon and then back at her. It made her feel funny; maybe she was getting drunk. Wine on an empty stomach.

They sat a while longer. She asked him about growing up in Minnesota and he asked about NYC. She told him all about how she'd gotten Fotis from Theo and how worried she was about Eleni. How surprised she was at loving Grand Marais.

"Curious, what made you answer my ad?" he asked.

She thought for a moment. "I don't know." She looked at him. "I didn't even think about it; I just called." She looked away. For an instant she felt him wanting to kiss her.

"Well," he said, and stood. "Better go get ready to meet my mysterious guests." He raised his eyebrows twice in quick succession and held out his hand. He pulled her up as she brushed off her legs. "We're finishing legislation that'll outlaw puppy mills." He pointed west with his empty beer bottle. "Like that bastard up the road."

"Who's that?"

"This guy not far from here. Ships to dealers throughout the U.S. He's moved his operation around. Buys old farms, sets up the barns with hundreds of breeding pairs."

"That's a lot of dogs," she said.

"See ya." He saluted with two fingers as he walked off toward his truck.

The festival was winding down just as the wind began to pick up. Napkins blew off the makeshift bar in whirlwinds of white paper. Dealers hurried through transactions; empty soda cans, plastic folding chairs and some of the lighter makeshift tables blew over with each gust. Paula stayed to help a few artists pack up.

By the time she drove home, after midnight, twigs and small branches were strewn on 61; rain blew in torrents across the pavement. Wet leaves covered the road like papier-mâché.

Turning into Rick's driveway, she noticed his house lit up, with even more cars parked in front than last time.

As she drove down the grassy path to the guesthouse, a gust from the lake hit the Escape. The car lurched, frightening her. Her headlights flashed on her front door and she noticed a pile of firewood stacked under the porch overhang that hadn't been there when she'd left. Another pile stacked off to the side was covered by a plastic tarp, its corner whipping in the wind like a flag. A fire in the wood stove sounded wonderful, though the only fire experience she'd had was lighting the pilot light in Roger's kitchen stove.

She parked and ducked inside. Fotis jumped up, overjoyed to see her. She knelt and hugged him around the middle, shivering from the cold front while water gushed off the metal roof.

"Hi, good boy, sorry I left you." She climbed the loft stairs and crawled under the down comforter in her damp clothes. Fotis stepped up and settled beside her. The pinging of rain against the window and crashing of waves against the rocks below began to lull her.

Just as she was drifting to sleep, a loud bang made Paula jump up. The ceiling logs groaned; she turned on the lamp next to the bed. Fotis had sat up, too.

"Hope we don't wake up in the lake." She reached to pet Fotis. It wasn't clear who the gesture was meant to comfort. The cabin had seemed sturdy enough, though rattles, creaks and crashes revealed the structure's vulnerabilities.

Another thud of branches startled her awake.

A loud crash down in the bathroom followed. She sat up. "Shit." The rain sounded louder. Maybe a screen had blown in; she should have checked the windows. She looked at the clock on the night table. One am. Fotis listened for a few moments but quickly lost interest and groaned in a contented way as he leaned against her hip.

"Damn it." Paula got up and descended carefully. Each stair felt colder than the next. The noise got louder as she set foot on the main floor. It was so much colder all of a sudden; the intensity of the draft made the hair on her body stand on end. Something was in the bathroom. Then a flash of raw hamburger and a pile of feathers on the couch—like a crime scene—made her scream.

Sigmund looked up and began vying for her attention with his huge wingspan. Feathers scratched the walls. The table lamps went crashing over; photos on the wall thumped off.

"What are you doing here?" she shrieked, her heart pumping madly.

Whipping open the front door, she chased Sigmund around the living room, flapping her arms and yelling until she'd shoved him out the door. Locking it, she put the chain on, too, as if Sigmund could articulate the front latch and pick the lock. She then ran into the bathroom, quickly cranking shut the casement window and locking it. The window screen was on the floor along with a few telltale feathers.

Then, hiding behind one of the living room drapes, she peered out the front window.

The bird had perched on the woodpile just under the eaves by the front door. The slump of his shoulders made her feel sorry for him, but not sorry enough to let him back in. His profile looked haggard, forlorn, in the outdoor light as he looked out into the rain.

"What the hell am I feeling sorry for?" she cried. Reluctantly she climbed back upstairs. She tried but couldn't fall asleep.

"Crap." She crept back down after about twenty minutes and peeked out again to see if the bird was still there. Sigmund made eye contact the instant she looked. She exhaled in exasperation and placed her forehead against the door. "Oh shit."

Finally she opened the front door and Sigmund tottled foot by foot back in.

CHAPTER 11

Two weeks had passed when Eleni called one afternoon.

"Hey, Mom," Paula said, walking back to the guesthouse with Fotis after her shift. Her head still swirled thinking about the eagle on his first day of rehab in the flight room with Rick. As soon as she'd set the bird down, he'd swooped up in one motion; her heart had taken flight with him. His wings made flicking sounds, and he landed effortlessly on the top rung of the flight cage.

"Impressive," Rick said, "considering." She'd been amazed, too. "Bravo," flew out of her. The eagle had then turned to look down at her, presiding from his new vantage point. Later that day she and Rick had dragged a fresh deer carcass—roadkill dropped off by a construction crew—into the center of the room. The eagle had soared down and landed within inches of her, claiming the carcass. The sudden whoosh of air made her turn. The eagle's expression seemed to say, *Yes, we're friends, but this is mine.*

"What's up, Mom?" Paula asked immediately. Eleni only called when something was wrong. It always was Paula who called, knowing Eleni lived on such a limited income.

"I don't know, Paula." Eleni's voice was small. Paula looked at her phone, but the signal was strong enough.

"Ma?" Paula stopped walking. She glanced down at the scattering of orange leaves as if they would help sharpen her hearing. "Are you okay?"

"It seems I made a mistake."

"A mistake," Paula repeated. "What kind of mistake?" It was a word she'd never heard from her mother. She saw ambulances, critical-care units, thinking the worst. Paula's heart banged her ribs. "Is everything all right?"

Eleni was quiet.

"Mom?"

She began to explain. It seemed that Slimowitz the cutter had gone on vacation and forgotten to cut the last two coats for Eleni to finish. In a pinch, Eleni had offered to cut the pelts so they could meet the deadline. Even though she'd worked as a cutter for Pappas' late father twenty years earlier, the current boss had forbidden her from touching the pelts until he could find another cutter. Two days had passed with Eleni sitting around, twiddling her thumbs and obsessing, counting down the hours until the runway show in Milan. After the third day, she defied her boss and cut the pelts.

"I thought I was helping out." Eleni paused.

"It sounds like you were." Paula listened, eager for Eleni to wade through the prolonged silences and get to the point.

"Oh, Paula." Eleni's tone was upsetting; Paula had never heard her mother sound so beaten.

"So what happened?" Paula fought to stay calm.

"I used the wrong pattern—a different designer's patterns."

"So couldn't you just get more fur from the supplier?" Paula asked.

"It was a special order."

"Shit."

"The designer hit the ceiling, Paula. Pappas said my time is over."

Months ago Eleni had mentioned that Pappas had begun relegating her to the less important jobs, sewing labels, linings, alterations.

"He fired me," Eleni whispered. "He fired me, Paula." Eleni's voice broke. "Told me to get my things and get out. Just like that." Paula heard Eleni snap her fingers. "He stood over me, Paula, waiting." Her mother began to cry in spastic gasps. "Like I was a criminal. Almost fifty years working for that family—for his father, God-rest-his-soul, giving my all to them, working weekends, holidays. And then this kid fires me, standing over me like I'm some dirtbag."

Paula's fury rose in an instant. She wobbled with rage.

"I'll call the son of a bitch myself."

"No," Eleni almost shouted.

Paula'd always despised the younger Pappas and in fact had hated the entire family since she was a teenager. They acted like Greek royalty. They'd give her mother orders as if she were a scrubwoman and not a highly esteemed tailor and seamstress known throughout the City's fur industry. As if it were a duchy, the wives and daughters would waft through the workroom in chiffon and pearls while Paula's mother sewed—still hunched over her work after they'd all left for the evening in their Lincoln Continentals. Young Paula would sit on the showroom floor doing her homework as her mother worked, or she'd fall asleep using a pile of ranch mink for a pillow until Eleni's nudge that it was time to go home.

Even now Paula's stomach tightened whenever her mother talked about work. The place was a sweatshop. They paid her almost nothing—docked her check if she had a doctor's appointment. One peep and they'd start to make noises about outsourcing. And what Paula found most revolting was how Eleni would cower in gratitude when talking about the Pappas Fur Empire, as if standing in church before the very icon of Jesus, waiting to make her cross and kiss it.

But the job had made Eleni proud of not being a *klossa*, or sitting hen. While the women around her had grown fat, idle and mean, Eleni had supported her young daughter and herself well into old age without anyone's help. And for that she'd greeted each day with a place to go, a job to do and beautiful creations that came to life out of nothing but skins.

Paula closed her eyes. Her heart sank as she pictured Eleni alone in her dimly lit apartment. Vulnerable like the great horned owl who'd helplessly flopped about on the forest floor, yet different in that Paula and Eleni had no mates to protect them. Paula could have cried right there and then, for her mother, for the eagle and for herself—for all the years she'd spent alone and abandoned as a girl, then as a wife.

"Mom," Paula said. "I'm so sorry."

"Eh, Akri, Paula, einai akri," Eleni minimized the depth of hurt, claiming that only the edges of her body were injured, but Paula knew better. Time would drag on forever in Eleni's darkened apartment with no one to talk with except Stavraikis, who heard practically nothing.

"Mom, listen. Let me fly you out here," Paula offered. "You can stay with me—like a little vacation. You never take vacations; going to Greece is not a vacation." Paula lived by the clock in Greece, feeling she'd earned at least a paycheck after enduring days of family visits. "I'll arrange it all. Just pack a few things—I have a washer/dryer," Paula encouraged. She started to feel excited. "It's beautiful out here, Mom. I'll get you a ticket; you can fly out tomorrow. I'll arrange for a car to pick you up, take you to the airport."

Eleni was crying. Humiliation crying, the kind you want to hide, only your shame has become larger than your pride.

"Aww—don't cry, Mom." The instant she said it, Paula wished she hadn't. "It's a hell of a lot easier flying here than to Greece." She tried to make a joke. "I've got plenty of room." She looked at the outside of the guesthouse. "It's a cozy little place." Eleni could have the bed or the futon if she was too nervous about the stairs. "I'll meet you at the airport, Mom; you don't have to worry about a thing. We'll drive along the shore together to my place. It's a beautiful drive, Ma. Like nothing you've ever seen. We can talk, visit."

She could hear her mother thinking.

"You always did love to drive," Eleni said.

"I do."

"You still have Theo's dog?"

"Of course."

There was silence for a few moments, as if that was the decid-ing factor.

"It was very sad, Paula. Only me and Fanourakis, his nephew, showed up." She began to cry again. "Nobody else came. Nobody."

"Yeah, I know, Ma; you told me."

She could hear her mother's breath. "I'd have to pack and all."

"Yeah, I know. I've got a washer and dryer."

"I'd have to get to the airport."

"I'll arrange it all."

Except for Greece, Paula's mother had never been out of New York. She sounded frightened.

"Ma, we have toilet paper, refrigeration, electricity out here."

Laughter interrupted Eleni's crying.

"You have an iron?"

"Sure." She didn't but was sure she could buy one at the Ben Franklin. Maggie or Rick would have one she could borrow.

"If I can find a flight, Ma, would tomorrow give you enough time to pack?"

"You're a good girl, Paula," her mother said. "Yes. That's plenty of time."

At ten o'clock the next morning at the Duluth airport, Paula spotted Eleni on the down escalator heading toward the baggage claim. Paula had never seen her mother outside of New York or Athens. Eleni stood out on the crowded escalator stairs, high cheekbones, her face retaining that classic, stoic look though her dyed red hair looked matted after the long flight. The color clashed with her dark olive skin under the airport lights, yet she still had an accidental poise that came natural to her. Despite her age, she was a dignified, old-world elegant woman, a type you rarely saw these days. Wearing dark yet stylish-looking clothes, she was handsomely formal, unlike the midwestern informality. Paula spotted the long, thick gold chain that was Eleni's trade-mark, brightly announcing her life, as it held Vassili's wedding ring, an Eastern Greek cross, a bright blue evil eye and a pendant of the Parthenon. While Paula was struck with pride, it also hurt her to see how dramatically her mother stood out—the alien, still the foreigner. Paula rushed to get to Eleni quickly. Before the others noticed how out of place she was. Even the form and outline of her body, proportioned differently, was vivid and distinct, like an apparition from an early 1900s photograph of immigrants flooding New York Harbor but Photoshopped onto an escalator, passing under the post-modern neon-lit sculpture of a moose suspended from the ceiling.

"Mom," Paula cried, elbowing her way through a group of people. Eleni turned. Pain wrenched her face as she reached for Paula. They grasped like they hadn't seen each other in years.

"Thank you," Eleni uttered into Paula's shoulder.

"For what?"

"For understanding."

"You've done the same for me."

"Yes. I have."

All those years ago, when Paula escaped on the subway with a shopping bag full of her clothes after husband number one had taken a swipe at her. Eleni had asked no questions as she'd opened the apartment door and taken the heavy bag from Paula's hand, her daughter collapsing on her shoulder.

"Thank you for coming, Mom." They stood there for several more moments.

"Paula," Eleni whispered, and clutched her tighter. "My Paula."

"It's gonna be okay, Mom," Paula said. "I promise. You'll see; everything's gonna work out." She had nothing to go on but strong conviction.

The loud buzzer in the baggage claim startled them both, a warning to stand clear. People pressed in as suitcases and duffel bags began to stream out. The two women still held on. Paula spotted Eleni's bag. Without letting go, Paula reached for it but missed. Instead, she'd surrendered to the hug, figuring the bag would come around again.

Her gesture prompted a nice-looking man to turn and ask, "You need help?"

Paula nodded. "You mind grabbing that green bag that just got away?"

The man sprang into action, grabbed the bag and placed it next to Eleni.

Paula mouthed, *Thanks.*

Eleni let go and turned. "What a nice man you are."

Paula loaded Eleni's suitcase into the back of the Escape and opened the passenger door, helping her mother up onto the seat.

"Nice car," Eleni said, and began scoping out the interior. "Is it yours?" she asked as Paula helped her locate the other end of the seat belt.

"Yep," Paula said. "All mine."

"*Uch ooo,* Paula, this must have cost a fortune."

She felt her mother glaring over at her.

"Not as expensive as some."

"But expensive enough. Where'd you get this kind of money? Does Roger know you spent all this?"

Paula sighed and didn't answer. As they headed toward the parking ramp exit, Paula explained that the car got good gas mileage. Eleni tried to sound cheery about it but seemed to give up before they reached the parking attendant. She seemed tired, indifferent or both. Eleni didn't even flip down the sun visor or at least feel for a mirror on the back to fix her hair and check her lipstick, which she always did in her own car. Sometimes she'd drive with the visor down—more concerned about getting her eyebrow pencil right than missing a traffic light. But now Eleni's eyes were dull; her prying questions about the Escape lacked the usual bite that would have progressed into a critique of Paula's spending habits. Eleni was a toothless dragon.

They reached the parking exit and Paula handed over two dollars. The gate lifted and they headed toward downtown Duluth, and then toward Highway 61.

"This is it, Mom," Paula said with feigned exaggeration. "You're in beautiful downtown Duluth." Her hand gestured across the windshield and she got a smirk out of Eleni. "Are you hungry?"

"Not really." Eleni looked passively out at the trees and at a multistory black iron drawbridge on the lakeshore that caught her attention.

"The drive's a bit over an hour," Paula explained. "We can stop if you get hungry."

"I'm fine for now."

"The seat tilts back if you're tired, Mom."

"No, I slept on the plane," Eleni said, taking in roads, trees and buildings as if it were her first day on earth. She limited the usual running negative commentary as she scanned for threats and opportunities. More like a butter knife now than her usual stiletto self.

"Doesn't look as cramped as I thought," Eleni said as something caught her eye and she followed it.

"Cramped?"

"Small towns always look cramped to me."

"Oh." Roger's brownstone came to mind. Paula could almost smell the musty stacks of astrophysics journals. She shuddered. So far she'd battled such thoughts, New York had been kept safely under lock and key since her arrival, and she intended to keep it there for another three weeks.

Cramped. She wondered what Eleni would think of the tiny cluster of buildings hugging Grand Marais' half-moon harbor.

Her reaction to the first glimpse of the lake surprised Paula, especially since Eleni had spent so much time on the Aegean, Mediterranean and North Atlantic.

"Oh my." Eleni stared out as if she couldn't believe what she was seeing. "You weren't kidding it was gorgeous."

"I wasn't," Paula said. It was a clear, warm late September day. Eleni fiddled with the window control until the glass lowered.

"It smells good, too. I can't quite place the scent, but like some kind of spicy perfume."

"I thought you'd like it."

"Is your town near this lake?"

"It's right on it, Mom," Paula said. "The place I'm staying is on the shoreline, too."

Eleni raised her eyebrows and turned to Paula and clicked her tongue in disapproval. "*Uch, popopopo*—that must be expensive; why are you going through money like water now? How are you paying for all of this?"

"Actually, Mom"—she felt giddy as she revealed the bargain with Rick—"it's free."

Eleni glared sharply at her with those bird eyes that, had she been a falcon, could detect mice under layers of snow.

"I swear—it's a trade. I work and get a free place to stay."

"Your work with the birds," Eleni confirmed.

"Yeah."

"I bumped into Mr. Sanchez last week. He's closing the store," Eleni said.

"Aww." Paula felt a pang.

"I told him about what you were doing here and it made him very happy. Says you finally found your calling. Will I get to see your birds?"

"They're not *my* birds, Mom, but of course you can see them. My boss rehabilitates them and releases them back to the wild. Right now we've got an eagle, an owl and some mammals. There might be something else by the time we get back. You never know."

"So who's this boss of yours?"

She told her all she knew about Rick, the property, the guesthouse.

"So is this Rick married?"

"He was."

"Kids?"

"Apparently not."

"A girlfriend?"

Paula took her eyes off the road and looked at Eleni.

"You interested, Mom? I could probably hook you up."

Eleni laughed. At last Paula had caught her mother off guard.

"Just curious," Eleni says. "That's all. I want to learn about your life out here."

"Well, my life out here ends in three weeks. Two with you, one more after that and then it's back to New York."

Paula could feel Eleni studying her for a very long time.

"What?" Paula asked, her eyes on a logging truck that had just pulled out in front of her.

Paula glanced at her mother, but Eleni dropped her eyes.

Thick storm clouds rolled in later that afternoon, drenching everything on and off for the rest of the day. Fotis had greeted Eleni at the door and she'd bent over talking to and petting him. After Eleni unpacked they drove to IGA to meet Maggie. On the way, Paula mentioned the upcoming Avon party that Maggie had been hyping for weeks.

"I don't know, Paula," Eleni hedged in the car. "I'm not sure I'm up for a party. Why don't you go ahead? I'll be okay; I brought plenty to read."

"Why don't you wait and see how you feel?" Paula suggested.

At the IGA, Eleni picked up her brand of instant coffee and creamer, and blueberries from Ephraim's orchard. Paula introduced her to Maggie and Bobby Ray, the bagger, stocker and janitor who was the twenty-year-old nephew of Marvelline, who ran the Oklahoma Café. Bobby Ray was slow, as they called it, yet he was as smart as could be. It was as if he'd been in a litter of puppies and while in utero the others had squashed him way in the back. Even Paula couldn't figure it out, since he was always attentive, though shaky, as if doped up on some kind of meds, some days more so than others. And everyone had the sense that Marvelline had rescued him from some bad situation back in the small town of Godebo, Oklahoma, where they were from. Yet Maggie extolled Bobby Ray's virtues—a hard worker the likes of which she'd never had. Missing not one day in two years, unlike many of the high school students who'd last a few months and then disappear.

"Hi, Paula," Bobby Ray said.

"Hey, Bobby Ray. How's it going?"

"Pretty good. See your mom's visiting."

"Yeah, she is. Did you meet her?"

"Just did." Bobby Ray nodded to Eleni and walked away. Pencil thin, his body moved in one piece with minimal articulation of his limbs, and he had short crew-cut hair. He returned to finish blocking the cans of soup that he'd just stocked.

"So I see you have one of those little blue evil eyes, too," Maggie said, spotting the jangle of charms on the end of Eleni's necklace.

She picked up the chain, holding the blue eye between her fingers. "They sent me this from the village the day Paula was born. To protect and bring luck."

A lot of good it did. Paula pressed her lips together.

"I've never taken it off," Eleni said as if that were a major life accomplishment.

"Well, you know," Maggie began. "The evil eye is very hot right now in jewelry. Necklaces, bracelets, earrings all with those staring blue eyes. I have to confess, I find some of them a bit creepy."

"They're supposed to be," Eleni explained. "They bounce back people's envy and ill will, protecting the wearer." Eleni went into a detailed explanation about the importance to Mediterranean people.

"Would you be our featured guest at the dinner this Saturday?" Maggie asked.

Eleni looked at her as if trying to gauge the woman's sincerity.

"I'd be honored if you'd come share all of this history at the potluck," Maggie asked. "Marvelline's closing up the Oklahoma Café for the night and we're having our semi-annual Avon party there. Regional reps, the works." Maggie turned toward Eleni.

"Truckers all got their undies in a bundle, but Marvelline told 'em they're more than welcome providing they buy makeup. That shut 'em up."

Paula laughed. Eleni wasn't sure what it all meant.

"We don't often get someone from your background up here," Maggie said. "I know my friends would be very interested in a talk about the evil eye."

Eleni paused, considering the invitation. "Why, I'd love to," she said, her voice having a lightness that surprised Paula.

"We have samples of pendants, necklaces," Maggie began. "Makeup demonstrations, plus Avon's regular line of products," Maggie explained. "Wait till I tell the others; they'll be so tickled. They've wanted to meet Paula, and now they get to meet you both."

Maggie looked at her watch. "Too bad I don't have someone to cover now or we could all go down to the Oklahoma for some lunch. I got that new night manager, Amber, coming in around three and I gotta stick around for training."

"She looks Turkish to me," Eleni said as she and Paula walked back to the Escape during a break between rainstorms.

"I told you she's American Indian."

"I know, but she still looks Turkish. I had a cousin, Despina, up in Thessaloníki who was a cop and used to paint her fingernails blue. She could be her twin. Lots of Turkish-Greeks up there."

Eleni stopped on the sidewalk. "How 'bout I make spanakopita for the Avon party on Saturday? Think they have filo and feta up here?" She began searching the storefronts.

"Well, if they do, Maggie's got it."

"You have a full kitchen?"

"Yes, though I've never turned on the oven," Paula said sheepishly.

Eleni glared at Paula, hands on hips. "Now why doesn't that

surprise me." Grabbing Paula's sleeve, Eleni turned her around, walking back to the IGA with the excitement of a teenager. "Come on. I'll bring fresh spanakopita to Maggie's and that Marvel lady's party. Maybe I'll even spring for some baklava. You can help with that."

Paula smirked. As they entered the store, Eleni pulled out a shopping cart.

It rained the entire rest of the day, so they hunkered down in the guesthouse with Fotis. They dozed, ate and watched old reruns of *The Donna Reed Show.* "I always thought that woman was such a phony," Eleni said, sipping coffee and petting Fotis' head with the other hand. "Ella, Fotis mou," Eleni said, amused as she studied the dog's face. "You know he looks like one of Theo's dogs."

Paula thought back to the dogs of his she'd known.

"They all have the same expression," Eleni said.

Paula glanced at Fotis as he looked up. She didn't remember the dogs that well.

"Like they're really people in a dog's body, God rest his poor soul. Maybe he'll come back as one and be happier." Eleni looked at her watch.

"You got a train to catch?" Paula teased.

"You're such a smart mouth." Eleni chuckled and pretended to smack her. "I'm just trying to figure if I'll be back in time for his *mnismosino.*"

Paula remembered that forty days after death the priest would perform a ceremony that released a person's soul from the earth.

As Eleni started to pet Fotis, he leaned against her leg. "Aww— you're such a good boy, aren't you," Eleni said, and hugged him.

Paula practically did a double take. "I didn't know you liked dogs." She'd never seen Eleni touch a live animal.

"I love dogs," she said.

It was news to Paula. "Then why didn't you let me have one?"

"*Uch ooo,* that was Vassili," Eleni dismissed with a wave of her hand. "'All I see is filth, fur and money down the toilet,' he'd say."

"You asked for me?"

"Of course I did. For me, too. I wanted a dog," she said, and laughed in a way that made Paula feel a pang of disappointment. "But as much as I tried to get him to say yes he'd shake his head. 'Ochi, Ochi, case closed,' he'd say. 'Don't ask me again.'" Eleni imitated Vassili brushing his hands. "And then after he died," she said, "I was lucky I could feed you. Thank God you ate like a little bird."

CHAPTER 12

Eleni insisted on tagging along with Paula the next morning. First they visited the eagle. Paula gently grasped both of his feathered legs to secure his talons, lifted and tucked him into the crook of her arm. As she walked out of the enclosure, talking to him in Greek, Eleni gasped.

"Oh my God." Eleni stepped back and unconsciously covered her mouth.

"Yeah, they're big, aren't they?" Paula said. She was proud of the eagle and even prouder to be holding him.

"My God, that thing's as long as your whole body," Eleni remarked, studying his head, his eyes.

"I felt the same way when I first saw him," Paula said.

"'Magnificent' doesn't even describe it," Eleni said, putting a hand to her forehead. "No wonder Zeus chose one as his companion."

The eagle shook his head, as if shaking off snow.

"Do you believe two weeks ago he almost died?" Paula said.

"Aw," Eleni said, and to Paula's surprise her mother reached to touch him. "Can I pet it?"

Paula laughed, astounded by how brave her mother was to touch Aetos Dios.

"Sure, but touch his chest." Paula motioned down with her eyes. "If you pet his head like a dog he might nip."

Eleni slowly reached out her hand. "Go ahead." Paula held on to the bird. Her mother touched his chest with first one finger and then her whole hand, feeling his breastbone.

"That's called his keel," Paula explained.

"I'm feeling the chest of an eagle." Eleni shook her head in disbelief and wonder. "Aetos, parakalo, sou eisai oraio," her mother purred to him. "It's so soft."

"Wait till you feel the owl, Mom." Paula punctuated the words with her eyes. "She's a great horned owl, but the horns are only tufts of feathers. We'll feed her after this guy."

"Is the eagle a boy, girl?"

"Rick thinks he's male because the females are twenty-five percent larger."

"Larger? *Uch ooo,* how different from nature."

"No, that *is* nature, Mom. And what's really cool is that after they've been flying, then land, you can see them catching their breath. How many people get to see an eagle catching its breath?"

Eleni looked at her daughter. "You really love this, don't you?"

Paula nodded. She returned the eagle to the enclosure, walked back to the refrigerator and retrieved a fresh whitefish. Carefully cutting the fish into sections, she then weighed it and placed it near him. "Just a snack to keep his body weight up," Paula explained. "When he's done we'll transfer him to the flight room for another day of rehab. Gotta get his muscles conditioned and his stamina up after being so sick. After five or six months of rehab, Rick says he might be ready to be released back to the wild." Her heart banged against her ribs as she said it. As she watched the eagle eating sections of the fish, the bird turned and looked at her as if he'd thought of something. She almost couldn't bear the thought of never seeing this creature again. For Rick the bird's release would be success; but for her, sadness. It made her dip her chin and turn away.

"What, *kukla mou?*" Eleni noticed.

"Nothing," Paula said, hiding a sense of grief that had come out of nowhere.

Her phone rang. It was Rick; he was over at Darryl's with an injured fox. Darryl had just surgically pinned the leg back together and Rick was about to transfer her back to the small mammal ICU for recovery.

꙾

An hour later Rick pulled into the driveway. Both women watched as he retrieved a small portable plastic dog crate from the passenger's side of his truck and headed toward the small mammal ICU.

"Rick, this is my mom, Eleni Makaikis."

"Nice to meet you, Mrs. Makaikis. Rick Gunnersson." He held out his hand to greet her.

Once inside he set the carrier down and with a gloved hand reached in to check the fox. Paula had never seen a live fox before.

"Can you get another heating pad and set it into the cage so I can move her in?" Rick directed Paula to a cabinet.

She placed the pad into the metal cage, smoothed it and then plugged it in. "What setting?"

"Low," Rick said. "Cover it with a soft blanket, too."

"She's so petite." Eleni used her fingers to illustrate her surprise. "I've never seen one alive."

He shot Paula a glance.

"My mother's worked for a furrier," Paula explained.

"Oh, that's right." He snapped his fingers. "You told me."

The fox stirred as they began to move her. Paula supported the animal's head as Rick held her body, transferring her into the wire cage. Paula could smell his breath as he quietly filled her in on the details of the surgery and resulting care the fox would need in the next forty-eight hours. During the weeks he and Paula had worked closely together not once had she felt self-conscious, until the moment she felt Eleni's eyes. Paula hoped her mother wasn't getting the wrong impression.

"So is the fox sick?" Eleni stepped up as if to break the spell.

"She just had surgery," Rick explained, pointing to the splint on the fox's hind leg.

"Oh, I didn't see the leg," Eleni said.

"Darryl, the vet I work with, just pinned her back leg together. She's still a bit groggy."

"So who pays for all of this?" Eleni asked.

Rick shot her a *what do you care?* expression.

Paula's eyes dropped to her boots. His expression was reminiscent of her first days on the job.

"I mean, I'm just curious," Eleni softened her tone. She pulled the cardigan across her body and folded her arms.

"Well . . ." Rick's gravelly voice lowered, pausing as if about to begin reading a bedtime story to a child. But first he folded a small fleecy cloth and rested it under the fox's head before closing the wire gate. "Funds come in a variety of ways," he answered.

Later that morning they started work in the raptor ICU, where Rick had just admitted a barred owl. The bird was brownish gray with brown and white bars across his chest and head. A newspaper reporter for the local *Cook County News Herald* had brought the bird in after he'd found him struggling to stand up in the middle of the road. The reporter had taken off his fleece jacket, wrapped the injured bird and called his office. They directed him to Rick.

Eleni watched as Rick unfolded the jacket and carefully lifted the barred owl. He was much smaller than the great horned.

"Hey, big guy," Rick said as he looked the owl over.

The young reporter stood next to the table. "Does it look bad?" He crossed his arms and rubbed his chin. He shifted his weight from foot to foot.

"Don't know yet."

"It just happened, not twenty minutes ago," the young man said, still shaken. "I saw the whole thing."

"I'm Rick; this is Paula."

She nodded at the introduction.

"Jason."

"Hey, Jason, it's good you came right over," Rick said, and began to examine the bird.

The owl's eyes were swollen shut. His shoulders bunched with pain. While the bird could stand, he didn't move. Paula's heart broke as she watched Rick work. As much as she wanted to take the owl into her arms, she knew it wouldn't help.

"I'm guessing his skull's fractured." Rick handled him gently, as he tried to look into the bird's eyes.

"Is that fixable?" Jason asked. "I mean, can he recover?"

Rick examined the bird's eyes. "You'd be surprised how many do." He made eye contact with Paula, pointing to a small cardboard box. She retrieved it, opened the flaps and set a flannel baby blanket on the bottom.

"Okay, fellow," Rick said. "We're taking you for some X-rays."

Paula held the box level with the tabletop as he slowly lowered the owl. "There you go." Rick looked up at the young man. "I'll take him right over to get x-rayed; we'll know more then."

"Is it okay if I call?" the young man asked. "Find out how he's doing?"

"Anytime," Rick said. "We're here. And if I'm not, you can talk to Paula."

"Thanks."

"Thank *you* for stopping."

"Well, of course," Jason said, looking perplexed. "Who wouldn't?"

"The person who hit him." Rick said.

"No, they didn't." The young man's gaze dropped as he shook his head, closing his eyes. "I'm glad you guys are here," he said, visibly moved as he walked toward the door.

"Tell you what." Rick walked toward him, folding his arms. "How 'bout writing a story about your experience? Let people know we're here, what we do."

The reporter's face brightened. "That's a great idea. I'll pitch my editor today."

"Hey, Jason." Rick handed him the fleece jacket he'd left on the examination table.

"Thanks," Jason said, and turned to get one last look at the box on the way out.

Rick speed-dialed Darryl and they traded information.

"Good," Rick said to Paula. The machine's free. Be back soon," Rick said to Paula, hurrying to enter notes on the laptop.

Eleni stepped over to the box and peeked in.

"So how does an owl get hit by a car?" Eleni asked in such a way as to blame the owl.

Rick stopped typing. He studied her for a few moments and then began explaining about how they swoop down to catch prey "sometimes so focused, they're oblivious to oncoming traffic."

"Thank you. I would have never known that," Eleni said humbly. "So what would happen to these animals if you weren't here?"

"Most would die." Rick looked at her straight on.

Eleni held his gaze. "That would be very sad."

"I think so."

Eleni followed Paula for the rest of the morning. Rick pulled back into the driveway just as Paula was returning from the flight room. He rolled down the window. "His skull's fractured."

"So you guessed right. What now?"

"We tube-feed, load him up on pain meds, keep him quiet, hope for the best. It's a hairline. He's got a bad concussion. Time will tell if he's got any long-term impairment."

"He's so sweet." She thought of the owl's face.

Rick looked over at Eleni. "You two ladies up for joining me for lunch at the house?"

"That would be nice," Eleni said in a voice that made Paula's head turn. Her eyebrows arched at her mother's formality.

Rick checked his watch. "Let's tube-feed this little guy, start the pain meds and get him comfortable."

Paula moved into action.

"Can I come and watch?" Eleni asked.

"Sure." Rick sounded surprised. "How's the fox?"

"The same," Paula said.

After the animals were settled, Paula and Eleni followed Rick up to the house. Eleni lagged behind as they headed up the incline, but she nudged Paula once she saw the house. Once inside, she bumped Paula's arm again; her eyes practically bugged out of her head.

"Anything you two don't eat?" Rick called from his kitchen, pulling open the double doors of a stainless refrigerator.

"Pichti," Eleni offered as a challenge.

Rick looked to Paula.

"Pigs' knuckles," she translated.

"Well, Mrs. Makaikis, I hate to disappoint you, but there's no danger of being force-fed *pichti* on the premises," he said. Eleni laughed in such a genuine way it made Paula laugh, too.

"I like his humor," Eleni said as if Rick weren't there.

Paula spotted Sigmund teetering in the open door. "Oh shit," she murmured, touching her forehead and averting her eyes. She cringed to think how Eleni would react once she saw the vulture. But before Paula could explain, her mother spotted Sigmund.

"And who might I ask is this?" Eleni slowly approached Sigmund, who turned his head to get a better look at her. Eleni bent slightly.

"That's Sigmund," Paula said.

"Oh no, he's not." Eleni shook her head. Paula and Rick glanced at each other. "Slap a handlebar mustache on that face and *boom*." Eleni clapped her hands. "It's Panagiotis from the village."

They laughed in relief.

"Your great-uncle from Kos, Paula," Eleni explained. "His face was all pitted like that." She pointed to Sigmund's head. "Bad acne—pizza puss, they'd call him. It drove him to America thinking Americans were kinder. But once he discovered they weren't— *boom*—back to Greece. The weather's nicer."

She then launched into the story of how, later in life, Panagiotis would sit outside the *kafenio* (men's saloon) playing cards, drinking ouzo and making passes at all the village women. For reasons Paula couldn't ascertain, Eleni seemed funnier than she did in New York, hamming it up for Rick; and Rick's face was alight, his smile crooked, as he listened, littering the counters with cheese, tomatoes and a loaf of uncut bread. His stove beeped after Rick pressed a button, and he seemed at a loss as to know how to turn it on. Paula squelched a laugh; he looked so awkward in the kitchen.

"But then all the men did that," Eleni said. "My mother used to have to go looking for my father and then drag him home for supper. *Uch ooo,* men, you're all alike."

Rick looked up at her as she said it. "Mrs. Makaikis—"

"'Eleni,' please."

"Eleni," Rick corrected himself, "Sigmund here's got a crush on your daughter." Paula watched as Rick sliced into the loaf of bread and balanced slices of tomato and cheese on top of what she guessed would become grilled cheese.

"You see, Paula?" Eleni turned to Rick and laughed. "I'm always telling her how pretty she is, but she never believes me."

Paula frowned in disbelief.

※

It was mid-morning on the day of Maggie's Avon potluck when a lone car pulled into Rick's driveway. As Paula and Eleni were heading toward the raptor room to feed the owl, Rick came bounding out of his house to greet the car. Out stepped a woman, a bit taller than Rick, blond and Scandinavian looking. As soon as she stepped out, they hugged. It was a couple's hug, a lovers' hug. Both Paula and Eleni averted their eyes. To watch felt intrusive. But Paula noticed how the couple walked woven together toward the house, nuzzling, talking in low voices.

Paula began to ready mice for the great horned owl as Eleni watched. Neither had spoken, the scene outside having silenced them both. Paula let two live mice into the owl's cage and turned away. She hated this part of the job; each time she rushed with horror, never getting used to releasing the happy-go-lucky creatures to a certain death.

"That's it," she said. "Let's get the hell out of here," and she headed toward the mammal room and the fox.

"Wait," Eleni said. "I wanna watch how she eats it."

"It's revolting, Mom," Paula protested. "Come on; the fox is hungry."

"It's nature," Eleni said.

"So what? Doesn't mean I have to watch," Paula said, and shuddered.

Eleni turned to her with curiosity. "Why are you like this, Paula *mou*?" she asked in a tone of voice Paula'd never heard. "Everything has to eat," Eleni said, as if Paula were a child.

Paula flinched as the enormous owl attacked the mouse and gathered it into her mouth. The tail hung down her face as the bird slowly swallowed. Paula hurried out. Eleni shook her head, chuckling at her daughter as she threw up her hands. "*Uch ooo*, you're such a city girl."

In the mammal room, Paula cut up shards of chicken that Rick had left in the refrigerator and placed them in with the fox.

"What's the difference between the mouse and this? One has a face? This did, too, you know."

"Ma, stop."

"People in the village could never stand it when someone slaughtered a lamb. 'It's barbaric; it's brutal,' they'd say. *Uch ooo*, they'd cover their ears, horrified, but watch them push you out of the way to grab a hunk of that roasted lamb." She brushed her hands together. "I've always thought that if you can't stand to watch something slaughtered, then you've got no right to eat it."

"All right," Paula said. *Fair enough.* "No more about eating animals, okay?"

They were quiet for a few moments as they watched the fox nosing the pieces of chicken.

"Aw, such an expressive little face she has." Eleni reached to touch the wire cage. The fox looked at her. Both women calmed as they watched the fox eat.

"So Ma, when you look at her do you see a coat?"

"Now *you* stop it," Eleni said, and hit Paula's arm, laughing.

"Just kidding," Paula said. It was half-true. "But if you get bored or tired I can always drive you back to the house to watch TV or something."

"Why?" Eleni turned toward her with those piercing eyes. "You want to get rid of me?"

"No, of course not," Paula said. "I'm just saying."

Eleni studied her with a critical eye.

"I swear," Paula said, laughing. The longer Eleni stared, the harder Paula laughed.

"We never get time to talk," Eleni said. "Besides, I love watching you with the animals. It's fun."

Fun? Another word she'd never heard from her mother.

Rick had left Paula a note on the message board to move a deer carcass into the center floor of the flight room.

But first, Paula took out her eagle, carrying him down the hall. "Time for physical therapy, Aetos Dios." She set the bird down and in one motion he swooped up to the top perch.

"Wow!" she heard Eleni exclaim through the screen in the hallway.

As he landed, he turned, looking down to regard Paula. "Eisai palikari mou," she said.

Eleni agreed. "Alithos palikari."

"God, I hope Rick shows up soon to help with the deer," Paula said.

"I can help," Eleni offered.

"Ma, you'll pop out your back. I'll go get Rick." They walked outside as Eleni chattered in half-Greek and Paula went to the outdoor aviary to retrieve the two foster dads. Putting on a thick glove, she approached one. "Come on, Pops, time for a little exercise." She took hold of the leather jesses with one hand and the eagle hopped onto her gloved forearm. She brought him into the flight room and then went to fetch the second. Eleni studied each of the birds with fascination.

Just after Paula had moved all three of the eagles, Rick showed up with the woman.

"I'd like you to meet Kate Larson." Tall, willowy blonde with great jewelry. Paula hadn't expected that caliber of earrings from a country girl.

"Oh, hi, I'm Paula." She extended her hand.

"Hi, Paula. Rick's told me so many good things about you." The woman had the new season's Louis Vuitton bag on her arm. Paula also noticed that Kate had the smallest nose that she'd ever seen on an adult woman; plastic surgery or nature, she couldn't tell.

"And this is Paula's mother, Eleni, who's visiting from New York," he continued. "Kate Larson's a friend from the Cities."

They chatted about New York, Minneapolis, while Kate joked about her fear of birds and overall dislike of bugs, crawly things, as she called them, and made jokes about how she wasn't a big "nature" person. And while Paula was fully prepared to despise her, she didn't. "I've tried to get her into a kayak," Rick said. Kate turned to Paula and rolled her eyes.

"Well, nice to meet you," Kate said without an ounce of malice as she and Rick left arm in arm.

Outside, Paula heard the couple talking about restaurants as car doors shut and the engine started. The sound of tires on gravel reminded Paula she'd forgotten to ask for help.

"Shit." She rested her face in her hand.

"Don't be jealous, *kukla*," Eleni said from behind the screened wall.

Paula stopped. "What? No, Ma, I'm not. I'm pissed. I forgot to ask him to help with the deer."

"Yes, you are, you're jealous."

"Ma, what the hell are you talking about?" Paula bent over, her frustration mounting, annoyed with having been so distracted. She then opened the back door. There it was, the carcass. Placing both hands on her hips, she sized the thing up. It might be easier to move than she thought. Bending over, she grabbed hold of the rib cage and yanked. It budged only a few inches, far heavier than she'd estimated: at least a hundred pounds. "Damn."

Eleni appeared next to her. "Let me help. With the two of us . . ."

"Forget it, Mom."

"I know what I'm doing," Eleni said, pushing her aside as she bent over and grabbed the rear legs, staring at Paula. "Close your mouth or you'll catch a fly. Now come on."

They dragged it partway and rested.

"See? A few more times, it'll be there," Eleni said. They worked up momentum and pulled it over the floor before stopping. Paula gauged the placement.

"Good enough," she pronounced. She looked at her mother. "Is your back okay?" Paula hurried back to shut the door before the birds got away.

"I'm fine." Eleni made an about-face and walked across the flight room, keeping a close eye on the eagles. "I still think you're jealous," she called, and waved her hand over her head. "I know you."

"Well, if you did, you'd remember that I'm married," Paula called back before pivoting the carcass.

"So what?" Eleni called from across the room. "Married people get jealous all the time."

Paula was angry now. "Ma, you're so far off base it isn't even funny."

"Yeah, well, keep saying it, maybe it'll be true."

All three eagles watched from the highest rungs as if deciding who to believe. "Come on, you guys. After all that . . . *eat,*" Paula said. Each glanced at the other and then back at her. It felt eerie to be watched so intently.

"But don't worry, *kukla,*" Eleni said. Her voice echoed off the metal walls of the building. "They're just fuck buddies."

"Mom, will you stop!" Paula coughed in exasperation, feeling she could laugh and cry at the same time.

"What? You're shocked I know such things?" Eleni said. "I know a lot you don't think I do. I hear them talk: the cutters, the finishers; I hear the guys who bag up the furs, I hear it all, things you probably never even heard of."

Paula ignored her mother and peeled off the latex gloves. Sometimes when she didn't have an audience she'd stop.

"I even know what a rim job is—"

"Okay, Ma—you win a medal," Paula cut her off, her hands slapped down at her sides.

"Oh, look at this, my daughter's so delicate," Eleni said to an imaginary person. She seemed giddy.

"You'd better go wash your hands after touching that thing," Paula said, noticing blood on Eleni's hand.

"He's not serious about her is what I mean."

"And so what if he is?" Paula lifted both hands in the air. "Who cares?"

"You care," Eleni said.

Paula blinked in exasperation, looking for a place to toss the gloves. "What happened to all that crap about how I was 'abandoning my husband' and that I was 'asking for trouble' bullshit on the phone?"

"Mothers are obligated to say certain things," Eleni said, taking out a tissue from her sleeve to rub off the blood. "I'm talking strictly woman to woman now."

Paula turned away muttering, "You're insane." Then her eagle swooped down and landed on the carcass, not six feet from her. The whoosh of air startled her.

"Eh, you're so stubborn," Eleni concluded. "Never could tell you anything." Her tone was as if she was declaring herself the victor. "Let's go make spanakopita."

Paula fumed as she followed her mother out of the flight room.

All afternoon long they layered and baked two pans of spanakopita, arguing incessantly about how many leaves of filo dough were needed between the spinch/feta mixture. They fixed one pan for the party and a second for "that nice Rick for taking you in."

Paula's anger rose to her mother's over-sappy concern. "It's an even exchange, Mom; I told you."

"Still, he's helping out my little girl," Eleni said, as if talking about someone else's daughter.

Eleni walked out of the bathroom dressed in the same clothes she'd traveled in. Her church outfit, though rumpled, still looked elegant. Black silk blouse layered over a black and white tweed wool skirt, stockings, heels and her trademark necklace. She wore the pearl earrings Paula had given her on her seventieth birthday. Eleni smoothed her skirt and looked at Paula in the mirror.

"Does this look okay?" Eleni asked.

It was a surprising question coming from Eleni, who never sought Paula's advice on fashion matters. It was usually Paula on the receiving end of an unsolicited treatise on how dumpy she looked, how she should make an effort to look more professional.

"You look great, Mom," Paula said. "You always do."

"What about my hair?" Eleni fluffed her short copperish hair. "I didn't have time to dye it before I left." It was touching to see her so excited.

"It looks lovely. But you don't have to get so dressed up. People here just wear what's comfortable."

"That's okay; I want to look nice for my talk." Eleni checked her reflection one more time and shifted the skirt on her hips. "You have any of your jewelry here, maybe a pearl necklace?"

"Sorry. Everything's back in New York."

Though the style was dated, her mother wore the skirt and blouse well. She still had enough of a figure to make the outfit look classic. Paula knew the other women would be wearing jeans and sweaters.

"I guess it's okay." Eleni eyed Paula again in the mirror for confirmation.

"Mom, you look great." And while you couldn't call her a beauty, in her time, Paula remembered, her mother was quite striking. She'd kept her figure all these years while those around her were losing theirs. She'd walk miles in a given day—to the subway and then again crosstown in Manhattan to Pappas' workshop and back again, refusing to take the bus due to the expense and because she loved to walk. The words of her secret to keeping trim: "eat no bread and walk."

"Okay then." Eleni looked at Paula. "If you're ready, I'm all set." Eleni's eyes had an unusual gleam, as if going on a first date. "You wanna grab the pans for me?"

"Got 'em, Ma."

"The baklava, too?"

"Yep. Got 'em both."

Eleni's cheeks were flushed. Paula hadn't seen Eleni so excited since her husband had been alive. Her eyes were bright but tinged by self-doubt. As she grabbed her purse, Paula felt like she could cry.

Paula had been to the Oklahoma Café other times with Maggie. Marvelline was in her mid-sixties, with a well-boned curvy figure, from the stock that had made the Oklahoma Land Run. A large woman with big hands, she'd kept slim with brisk daily walks out to Artist's Point, the lighthouse and back again. She had tightly clipped hair that was frosted blond to blend in with the gray and a pixie face retaining a youthfulness that shone in her mischievous dimples. Whenever she smiled, her white, slightly buck teeth seemed to bring everyone in on the joke.

The Oklahoma Café had been a 1940s gas station and the roof outline still had a Sunoco-deco line to it. All three sides of the café had been opened with large windows, affording customers both lake, street and harbor views. The exterior stucco was beige, with the storefront sign lettered in the type style of the Wild West.

The tables and chairs were now arranged into one long banquet table—white linen tablecloth, flower arrangements. As promised, Marvelline provided wine, soft drinks, coffee and tea. She'd cleared out the stools and covered the counter with a long white tablecloth where the women had begun depositing their specialty potluck dishes.

"Welcome, welcome." Marvelline stood at the front door in jeans and a silk fuchsia-colored top, glittering with Avon evil eye jewelry.

"Hi, Eleni." Maggie walked out from where she'd been filling out name tags at a card table and introduced her to Marvelline. Eleni's blue evil eye pendant sparkled in the restaurant light.

"Nice to meet you, Eleni," Marvelline said. "Maggie's told me so many wonderful things about you." She paused to shake hands and then give Eleni a hug. "I'm so glad you agreed to be our featured guest." She escorted Eleni over to the banquet table and introduced her to Barb Zimmer, the regional rep. A few of the women were the top local Avon sellers, including Maggie, and many were local women there to visit, do makeovers and buy jewelry, candles and makeup.

Paula set down the pan of spanakopita and baklava on the counter and peeled off the aluminum foil. As she did she watched Eleni, wondering if it might be too overwhelming for her. Eleni rarely even spoke to her neighbors, much less complete strangers.

"Hey, everybody," Marvelline called, waving her hands to get the room's attention. "I want to give a fine midwestern welcome to our guest of honor, Ms. Eleni Makaikis. I sure hope I didn't just slaughter your name, darlin'." Everyone chuckled and then clapped.

"You said it right." Eleni nodded.

"Your English is perfect!" Marvelline said.

"Thank you, but it's not perfect, just good enough," Eleni conceded.

"Eleni has come all the way from New York City," Marvelline said. "She's going to talk to us about the story and the lore behind this enchanting evil eye jewelry we all can't seem to get enough of. Plus she's brought us some traditional Greek food."

There was a rush of applause. Paula glanced at her mother. Rather than being mortified with embarrassment, Eleni smiled shyly and began shaking hands and chatting up the women. Ages ranged from the forties all the way up to Eleni's age. Some introduced themselves as farmwives; others had been or were schoolteachers, librarians, nurses, artists, insurance agents or shop owners.

Eleni seemed to be blossoming. Paula watched astounded as a

small group formed around Eleni and asked about New York, Greece and how old she was when she came to America. Some of the women were so fair that their skin was pinkish. Others were darker, with olive skin and Ojibway features like Maggie. Paula's mother switched into a gear that Paula had never seen—it was like watching a stranger talking about her life.

By the time Paula had worked her way to the food, the spanakopita and baklava were gone. As everyone sat and ate, Eleni reminisced about her years of working with furriers, all the famous designers she'd met. Hermès, Yves Saint Laurent, Lagerfeld and, of course, the iconic Coco Chanel. They sat in awe, listening. Paula was in awe, too. The only part of the job she'd seen was the workshop. She had no idea how chummy her mother had been with these famous people.

Eleni fielded question after question, barely touching her food.

As Paula watched, she was struck with a new sense of respect—to have accomplished all of this without the help of family, a formal education and/or a husband. Her mother talked about how her father had been a shoemaker in Greece until shoes became mass-produced. And after his friends and neighbors stopped ordering shoes, he became the town tax collector, out of spite. The room had a good laugh. She talked about her "Husband Vassili," who had grown up on the tiny island of Kos, where his father ran a *kafenio,* where Vassili remembered standing on a chair, washing out glasses, as a young boy.

The room was silent as Eleni talked; people couldn't get enough of her stories. And from the calm, almost professional way in which she delivered her story, she seemed more like someone on the "talk circuit" than Paula's mother.

Later the other women started talking about their histories. Maggie talked about the Ojibway as several women nodded. About the fur trade, dating from the 1700s. She offered to take Eleni up to the reservation and Grand Portage, about thirty miles west to the historic Fort, the meeting place for native people and Europeans.

Others began talking about great-great-grandparents from Norway and Sweden, stories they'd heard about homesteading. Paula thought of the Center for Immigrant Studies. Here was a living, breathing part of the American experience that she'd known little about—an unfolding narrative about the lives of immigrants who'd struggled on homesteads through the brutal Minnesota winters of the 1800s.

Maybe she'd write a monograph about the area. Yet as she thought about the prospect of beginning such a research project, she was struck with a sadness that she'd never get to it. Perhaps she'd mention it to Bernie when she found the time to drive to Thunder Bay.

After dinner, Eleni spoke for about fifteen minutes on the significance of the evil eye and the Hamsa for the Mediterranean people. Paula looked around the room; many of the women sparkled with their evil eye jewelry.

After Eleni's talk, Barb Zimmer got down to brass tacks about Avon products. Before the individual beauty consultations began, Barb singled out Paula for a group beauty consultation, demonstration and makeover. Though a lighted mirror was set on the table, Barb turned Paula's chair to face the crowd as the women clustered around like a convocation of eagles in a tree. Barb held a magnifying glass up to Paula's skin, discussed her crow's-feet, dry patchy areas and frown lines on her forehead between her brow. One by one the women filed by, poring over Paula's face like some Rosetta stone. As Barb tilted Paula's head, she began a full consultation on older skin. Paula frowned and looked sideways at the woman.

"Look, you see how she frowns?" Barb said to the group. They all leaned in and nodded. Barb turned to Paula. "You have more frown than smile lines. You really should try to smile more," Barb advised. "All that frowning's scored grooves in your skin."

Paula flipped around to look at her face in the lighted mirror.

"Whatever happened to 'character lines'?" Paula shot back.

Barb frowned and glared back at Paula. "Women don't get character lines; they only wrinkle."

Paula was about to argue when Eleni gave her the death stare from the seat across. Paula slinked back. It pained her to let a statement like that go unchallenged, but it was better than arguing with a bunch of Avon ladies, and heaven forbid she rain on Eleni's parade.

Barb shook a bottle vigorously before squeezing a drop of white liquid onto a cotton ball. Then Barb scrubbed Paula's face before studying the fiber with certain disguised pride. Barb then held it out for the ladies to examine. "See the filth on her skin," Barb said.

"Hhhh," the group reacted. Eleni clicked her tongue in disapproval, shaking her head.

Paula frowned and gave Barb the eye. "Uhh—I think 'filth' is a bit strong," Paula said in her defense. A few of the women chuckled.

After the facial scrub, Barb said, "There. Now we have a clean canvas. Moisturizer and foundation come next."

Barb looked increasingly pleased as she layered product after product. Paula's tailbone began to hurt from sitting so long.

Finally, after three shades of eye shadow, layers of foundation, blush and cover-up under Paula's eyes, Barb stood back for everyone to see. "There. Now you're done. Everyone: look at the transformation."

The women were oooing and ahhing in approval. Barb explained Paula's facial flaws and how they'd been corrected.

"Einai Oraio." Paula turned as she heard Eleni pipe up. A sharp look from her said Paula ought to make more of an effort to fix herself this way.

"Now turn around and look," Barb said with an eager smile.

As Paula stood to face the lighted mirror, she almost laughed. *Bride of Dracula* came to mind.

As she and Eleni were driving home Paula was infused with a deep feeling of *endaksi,* or well-being. It felt good to share a sense

of belonging with this new group of people. They'd been so welcoming and open, though her face was itching and she couldn't
wait to get home and wash.

Upon Paula's turning into Rick's driveway, Eleni sighed deeply.
"I like these people, Paula," she said. "Not so much that Barb,
though."

CHAPTER 13

The morning after the Avon party, Paula and Eleni sat in front of the guesthouse on the pebbly beach in two lawn chairs. It was the first day off that Paula had taken since arriving. The calm lake and clear sky were mesmerizing as the two munched on leftover cold spanakopita and plowed through a bottle of white wine Eleni had discovered in a closet.

A plastic bucket served as a makeshift table, separating the two chairs and balancing the platter of food, wineglasses and bottle. Fotis sat beside them, begging for squares of spanakopita, of which he'd already downed two. They ate off mismatched dinner plates from the guesthouse kitchen.

"Ahhh." Eleni took a bite of the cold spanakopita and kicked back, using a rock as an ottoman. "Now this is the life. What a great country—God bless America, *opa*!"

"Yeah," Paula agreed. "Spanakopita always tastes better cold from the pan the next day."

"Agreed," Eleni said, using her fork for emphasis. She took another sip of wine and bunched the moose-patterned throw closer around her hips. "By the way," she alerted her daughter. "Tomorrow I have plans."

Paula looked at her. "What kind of plans?"

"I'm going for brunch with the ladies from the Avon party."

"Not that Barb, I hope."

"*Uch*, no." Eleni gave an emphatic head shake. "With the ladies at the Oklahoma Café. Some of them have names like Christmas cookies, I can't remember. And then after, that funny Marvelline and I are going on a long walk."

Paula stopped chewing. "Really?"

"Why do you sound so surprised?"

"I'm not," Paula lied.

"Yes, you are; I just saw your face."

"No, I'm pleased, Mom."

"What?" Eleni turned toward her. "You don't think I know how to make friends?"

"Of course you do," Paula said, laughing. "I'm happy for you."

"I like the people here." She looked round at the hills, the sky. "You picked a good town."

"Thanks, but I hardly picked it."

Eleni turned to her. "Why do you always give me a hard time?"

"I'm not," Paula protested, looking out at the lake.

"Can't you just say, 'Thanks, *mitera,* yes, I did pick a nice town'?"

Paula let it go.

To prevent her dyed hair from fading, Eleni had wrapped a china blue print head scarf around her copper hair. Both ends were crossed under her chin and secured behind her neck like a forties movie star. Eleni had an elegance about her that Paula guessed her mother wasn't aware of. She wondered if it had been that way all her mother's life. Eleni's eyes were obscured by Paula's knockoff Dolce & Gabbana sunglasses. Since the Korean War, Eleni had worn the same red lipstick, but this morning—upon the advice of last night's beauty consultant—her lips were a coral shade the rep had thought more flattering. Eleni looked like Garbo at a seaside rest home.

"It's a little brisk out here," Eleni said, rearranging the moose-imaged throw from the couch around her legs. Paula guessed they looked more like sisters than mother and daughter.

Once the food was gone, Fotis settled down, but not until he'd licked each plate clean. He was perfectly content sitting beside Eleni, keeping her company as she sat reading through back issues of *People* and *Us* magazines left behind by the previous renters.

Paula pivoted to face the sun and lifted her face.

"Have you already forgotten what the Avon rep said about your crow's-feet?"

"Thanks for reminding me, Mom," Paula said, but didn't move.

"I mean it."

"I know you do."

"Fine. Get like a wrinkled prune, like that Barb said," Eleni said. "See if I care."

Paula smiled.

Though the air was cool, the warmth of the autumn sun was restorative. The water shimmered. Somewhere far out on the lake they heard the drone of a motorboat. It was so quiet you could feel your ears working.

"I like it here," Eleni announced. She surveyed the place like she was considering buying it.

"Yeah, I do, too," Paula said.

"Maybe we should move here and I'll come live with you."

Paula laughed.

"I mean it."

"I'm sure you do, Mom."

"And what about 'that Rick'?"

"What about him?" Paula said dispassionately with closed eyes, up to the sun.

The aluminum frame of Eleni's chair squeaked. Paula could feel her mother's eyes through the dark lenses.

"What a guy, huh?"

Paula refused to take the bait.

"Nice, good-looking, a real gentleman," Eleni said, tilting her head toward Paula and raising her eyebrows.

"Mom?" Paula tilted hers toward Eleni. "Why are you doing this?" she asked quietly. "I have to go back."

"Why?"

"Why? He's my husband."

"So?"

She opened her eyes, not believing what Eleni was proposing. "You know I love Roger."

"Love?"

"And what's that supposed to mean?" Paula met her with a territorial glare, more shocked by Eleni's insistence than the question.

"It means that I've known something's very wrong, that's all." Eleni didn't give an inch. "Mother's instinct."

Paula looked away first. So rigid she couldn't breathe. Though Roger was deep in the periphery of her heart and thoughts, a whole life had bloomed and was establishing itself—the eagle, the owl, Maggie, Rick, Darryl and the craftspeople Paula had started to become friends with, the breathtaking eyeful of landscape that filled every corner of her vision, they'd all opened the way to something fresh and sustainable. A new home had fallen into place.

"Has he called?"

"No. He can't. He's underground in the collider. He won't for another week or so."

They were quiet for a few moments before Eleni spoke.

"You think when my daughter never once has me over to show off her home that I don't wonder?" Eleni asked. "Daughters want to show off their homes, have their mothers over. Even with the first bum you married," she said, "you had me over."

Paula listened with a ready excuse but squelched it.

"You were so proud of how you fixed up that little apartment," Eleni went on, turning to face her. "You'd made a home, Paula. At eighteen. You'd made a home you were proud of. And then your apartment before you married Roger. Remember? We used to get Chinese food every Sunday night and watch *Sixty Minutes* with that adorable Morley Safer. I like him."

Paula looked into her lap. She had no defense.

"But now we meet at restaurants somewhere like it's a job interview."

Paula's whole body stiffened. Eleni knew all; Paula had no comeback.

"Come closer, *kaimeni*." Eleni patted her thigh. "Come here."

Paula's face contorted in the way she'd cry as a little girl. She couldn't stop it; the muscles cramped in agony.

"Come, move your chair closer." Eleni scooted hers, pushing the plastic bucket aside. "You're all bottled up."

"Things have been very sad for a long time." The words hiccupped out of her and she couldn't stop. "I couldn't tell you. I was ashamed, embarrassed."

Eleni patted her thigh. Paula leaned over, resting her head on Eleni's lap like she did as a child. "Go ahead and cry, *kaimeni;* don't be ashamed."

Her chest had been bound with straps so long that the knots were too hard to untie. "Go ahead," Eleni said. After only a few minutes, they loosened and Paula felt better. "There's something wrong with him."

"Did you see it before we married?" Paula hiccupped as she sat up. Her nose was so stuffed; her face felt like it was filled with wet concrete. Eleni pulled a tissue from her sleeve and held it up to Paula's nose.

"Blow," Eleni commanded. Paula blew into the tissue. "Again," Eleni ordered. Paula could finally breathe. "Not so much," Eleni said. "Everyone thought you two looked happy, I did, too. So in love. Even that Elvira, the *pharmakia*." Eleni looked at Paula. "You remember her. The priest's wife who's a sourpuss and a bitch thought so, too. There was such hope, but sometimes hope isn't enough."

They sat like that for some time. The sun began to warm the breeze, the remaining leaves on the surrounding trees so bright it hurt to look at them.

"Oh, Paula," Eleni went on to explain, "when people have been unhappy in love it's easy to spot it in others. You feel it. It's like a sixth sense."

It made Paula sit up straight. Eleni didn't look back but rather pulled out another tissue from her sleeve and handed it over.

"Here, wipe off your mascara," she said. "You look like a raccoon."

Paula chuckled as she wiped; the tissue was black with eye makeup.

"So, you were unhappy with Dad?"

The way the sun shone on Eleni's face Paula could see through the dark lenses into her mother's sad eyes. Eleni then laughed to herself and reached over to touch Fotis' head. The dog looked up. She didn't answer immediately but looked out to the lake. Whether she was reluctant or gathering her thoughts, Paula watched as Eleni studied the blue horizon.

"You see," Eleni began. "Long ago before I worked for old man Pappas, I worked for other furriers. I had just started a new job when I met Vassili and he proposed. I was nearly thirty. No one else had asked and everyone said to take it." She looked at Paula. "Nobody wants an old woman and back then thirty was old. Now at fifty they're half-naked on the beach with those water balloon boobs." She stopped. "Vassili was a hard worker. No one could *ever* fault him for that, ten years older, clean, didn't drink too much. But the month after we married, Thanassis, the son of my new boss, surfaced out of nowhere. Same age as me, an artist, smart and talented, but not right in the head," Eleni tapped her head with the empty wine bottle. "But whenever I looked at him I felt like the world was being created for me."

"Wait, so you were married to Dad then?"

Eleni looked at her through the dark glasses, adjusted the throw around her feet.

"I kicked myself," Eleni said. "Letting the others talk me into it, but how could I have known? The agony of missed timing, bad chances, but that wasn't all there was to it, Paula."

"What do you mean?"

"Thanassis would hear voices. He made beautiful paintings,

but then he'd disappear for weeks. His father would go searching, sometimes finding him in an alley, batting away things that weren't there."

"Sounds like he was hallucinating," Paula said, feeling her mother's emotions toward the man. "Schizophrenic?"

"They'd put him away somewhere out on Long Island. Then he'd come home and seem okay for a while." Eleni suddenly got quiet. "But it was too late by then; I loved him—we were in love." She did not look at Paula, leaving her to think whatever she might.

"You loved him while being married to Dad?" Paula looked into her mother's face.

Eleni looked back as if to say, *What do you think?*

Paula rested her chin in her hand, leaning and blinking, trying to fathom her mother in love. "No way," she said. Her mother having a life other than lighting candles in church for a dead husband—a man Paula could no longer visualize without a photo prompt. "I can't believe it; so what happened?"

"You see, Vassili had this problem—a manhood problem." Eleni raised her penciled eyebrows.

"He couldn't have sex?"

Eleni nodded sharply. "Not so good, anyway. He would get mad. By then I was in love with Thanassis." She took off the glasses and stared at Paula. "And was pregnant."

Paula's hand covered her mouth. "With?"

Eleni nodded.

"Did you have it?"

She didn't answer.

"So wait—somewhere I have a brother or sister?" Paula asked, pondering for a few moments, a brief blend of excitement and bewilderment.

Eleni didn't answer.

"Did you ever tell Dad?"

"Never." Eleni shook her head and turned to stare at Paula.

"So wait. Was that me?"

Eleni's stare remained unbroken.

"H-h-h." Paula covered her mouth with her hand. "So that guy's my father?" She stood, rubbing her face and stepping backward in her bare feet over the pebbly beach.

Paula started laughing bitterly. "So thanks, Mom," she said, her arms slapping her sides, shaking her head. "I can't believe you didn't tell me. All these years you didn't tell me—are you sure Dad didn't know?"

"I'm sure."

Standing there, Paula waited for the shock and agitation to subside, but it didn't. To find a place of calm from which to talk. Stepping into the icy water didn't help; she crouched down and hugged her knees—Vassili's aloofness, her feeling like the pesky neighbor kid who never goes home. The cells in her body suddenly felt different, as if stamped now with a different maker's mark, as if the wind had blown away the memory of a counterfeit existence.

She stood and turned to Eleni and brushed the sand off her hands. "He knew, Mom. Dad knew."

"He couldn't possibly."

"He did. I know he did."

They were silent as two seagulls circled in unison before flying off in different directions.

"Didn't you want another child? One with Dad?"

"He couldn't."

"And you never told me?" Her hands wandered through her hair.

"Only Thanassis knew. Theo, you called him."

"Theo?" she exclaimed. "*The* Theo?" Paula looked at Fotis. The dog looked around as if he knew people were talking about him.

"You know that painting over the couch?" Eleni asked.

Paula thought back to their living room.

"It's the only picture we have. The one in the gold frame? The sea with the big rocks at sunset where everything is bathed in golden light?"

She'd grown up with that painting but had never really looked at it. She'd passed by it thousands of times during the course of growing up but couldn't tell you a thing about it except for its location—on the wall above the couch.

"That's his. He gave it to me when I told him I was pregnant with you. Before they took him away for a long time."

"Didn't Dad ask about it, or get suspicious about a painting that suddenly appeared?"

"Oh—he didn't care or notice what I put on the walls."

They were quiet for a long while, Paula's insides roiling before she laughed it off in a bitter way. "Oh great," Paula snorted, though she was about to cry. "So now I get to grieve all over again for another dead father—*this one I wish* I would have known." Though she felt bad for it coming out that way, knowing what guts it took Eleni to finally tell her, Paula couldn't help it. She'd phone Heavenly later. She had to talk with someone.

But no wonder Theo disappeared. She was suddenly flooded with a billion memories, each one pelting her like a rainstorm, each drop hitting with such velocity she didn't have time to examine them all.

Paula'd always look for Theo on the street, trying to spot him in his long coat. Then he'd show up from nowhere with his endless patience.

"Paula." Eleni's voice was soft. "Thanassis was so kind, like you. He loved you, loved his animals, nature; he did the best he could." Eleni had stood and walked over to her, smiling through tears. "And you look just like him," she whispered, as she brushed back Paula's hair.

"So did anyone know?" Paula asked, her voice muffled through her hands.

Eleni sighed; her arms fell to her sides. "No. I left the place, went to work for Pappas. He paid less, but I had to get away from Thanassis. People talk. Greeks love a good story, and back then . . ."

"Did you ever see him again?"

"Not like that. When I did see him over the years, I'd call his brother, tell him where to go look for him."

"But didn't you miss him?" She turned toward her mother.

Eleni took off her glasses. "You can't imagine." She breathed on each lens, held them up to the sky and then rubbed each clear with a corner of her blouse.

"So why didn't you marry him after Dad died?"

"He was sick, Paula." She held up her hands before putting on the glasses again and walking back to the chair. "In and out of hospitals, what kind of a life would that have been? To drag you through all of that?"

"Didn't you even try to help?" Paula faced her mother, surprised to be so angry.

"What could I do?" Eleni opened both hands, raising her voice.

"He was your child's father."

"I had no money." Her voice rose. "His family did. They got him the best doctors. I lost touch and was afraid to ask, to rouse suspicions. Back then people saw a love like that as being a crime." She laughed airily. "Now it's nothing." She snapped her fingers and shook her head sadly.

"Why didn't you at least tell me, especially after Dad died or when I graduated from high schoool?"

"Because people talk, Paula," her mother said. "Back then people looked darkly on young widows. The men, including the priest, think you're a *poutana*, their wives convinced you wanna steal their husbands."

"Still you had no friends?"

She looked down at her *People* magazine on the ground. She seemed hurt by that the most. "No one knew. I never got too close, never wanted it to slip out and then have the person blab it all around if they got mad at me. For people to say I'm the *poutana* with the crazy man's child. So I lived on the sly," she said bitterly. "But times have changed; now nobody cares." She raised her hands. "And the ones who would are all dead except for me." Eleni laughed at the futility of being released from a shame that had lost its charge.

Paula walked back and sat down next to her mother.

"I love you, Mom." She reached out and hugged her. "I'm sorry I said it like that before; it's just gonna take some time."

"I know you do, *kukla*. I love you, too."

They stayed that way for a while until Eleni let go and said, "I think you should stay here." She broke the contemplative quiet. "You've made such a nice life for yourself."

"It's a leave of absence. I have to go back. To NYU, to Roger."

Eleni looked heartsick for her.

They ate at the Gun Flint Tavern, mostly in silence, and then walked to the beach and sat on a bench.

"Please don't be mad about Thanassis," Eleni said.

"I'm not mad." Paula shook her head.

"You seem very quiet, not like usual."

"I'm just shocked."

"I tried to protect you—"

"And you did, Mom; you did."

"I didn't want people to say bad things about you."

"Mom, they didn't."

"I'm tired."

"Me too," Paula said. "Let's go back."

It was pitch-black by seven. Eleni was snoring softly on the futon before the local weather report was even over. Paula turned off the TV, locked the door and grabbed the ziplock bag with Fotis' old collar and leash from the top of the TV. Fotis trotted past her up the stairs to the loft, racing for a place on the bed. He jumped up and circled before settling into his sleeping position. She took the collar and rope leash out of the bag and set it down on the covers. She looked at him. "Do you still miss him, good boy?" Fotis stretched his nose and sniffed. His pupils dilated. He then tucked his nose back into his tail and closed his eyes.

She placed the folded leash and collar on the pillow beside her, inhaling their musty scent. What Theo must have lived through— she'd wished she could have helped him, gone to see him. She'd have gone looking for him. It wasn't right for Eleni to have kept it all secret; Paula's heart felt fractured with a break that might be impossible to heal. Impossible to go back and be the daughter he might have needed or find the father she'd so desperately longed for. And yet maybe he'd done just that, summoning her during the last few moments of his life.

Tears leaked out of her eyes as she drifted off. Just as she'd begun to doze into the peacefulness of that knowledge, Eleni's voice woke her.

"Paula?" she called up the stairs. "Paula."

Paula jumped up out of a deep sleep so fast she became nauseous.

"Someone's at the door."

But before Paula could get to the stairs, she heard the door open and close.

"It's just Panagiotis; I let him in," Eleni announced.

As Paula peeked over the railing, Sigmund looked up, victorious. Her mother was chattering on in Greek as the bird kept turning his head like he understood.

Paula sat down on the top stair, her chin resting in her hand. Thinking back to all the years she'd spent being angry—each man who'd failed her. But curiously, she wasn't angry with Roger. With a heavy heart she climbed back into bed and fell asleep. She dozed off but quickly woke after having a weird dream that she couldn't recall, feeling around behind her for the surety of Fotis. The bed was empty. "Good boy?" she called. Standing up, she crept over to the rail and looked down into the living room. In the dimness of the hall night-light she counted three forms on the futon. Sigmund and Fotis briefly looked up at her.

"Oh forget it." Paula turned and climbed back into bed.

CHAPTER 14

October brought peak autumn color toward the end of Eleni's second week. Neither woman had mentioned a return ticket, since both knew it would only take Eleni back to a life of isolation. The days had settled into a comforting routine, and the longer the visit went on the more they avoided the topic. Paula dreaded watching the weeks of her NYU leave of absence tick down toward Roger's return from France.

Eleni had fallen in with a regular coffee group of women who met at the Oklahoma Café. Marvelline would pour a cup of coffee, sit down and help herself to the latest gossip. Eleni would laugh, listening to stories about people she didn't even know, recounting the tales back to Paula in great detail. And while it heartened Paula to see her mother so invigorated, it also saddened her, knowing that such camaraderie would come to an end once Eleni stepped foot on an eastbound plane. Their relationship had grown in a way Paula had never thought possible. She swore to herself that once back in New York she'd visit Eleni more often.

Just before noon they'd started food prep inside the raptor ICU with Eleni slicing up a deer heart that a bow hunter had dropped off the previous day. Both had noticed Rick pacing outside and arguing with someone on the phone. They'd caught bits and pieces of conversations, since the morning was pleasant enough to leave the windows open.

"E fonie tou exchi alaksi," Eleni said.

Paula agreed that his voice did sound different.

"Is this the Jailbird's food?" Eleni's nickname for the barred owl. She lifted the tiny pile of meat, handing it over to Paula to be weighed.

"Yep—the Jailbird." Paula chuckled, entering the gram weight into the computer. Another sharp verbal exchange made both women turn toward the open window.

"Ti epethis?" Eleni asked in Greek.

Paula shrugged, "Den Ksero," not knowing what it could be. She'd never heard Rick so agitated.

"Pigo exo." Paula pointed toward the door.

He'd just ended the call as Paula stepped out. Leaning against the aviary enclosure, he played with his upper lip, thinking. She didn't get the sense it was "love" problems with Ms. Kate.

"Everything okay?" Paula approached him.

"No."

"What's wrong?"

"A lot." His phone rang.

"Is there something I can do?"

He looked at the number. "Excuse me; I've got to take this." He crossed his arms and hunched over, walking away from her in measured strides, talking in guarded, hushed tones.

Paula looked at her mother through the window screen, shrugged and made a corresponding *I don't know* face. Both watched a few moments longer before Paula stepped back in to check how much the barred owl had eaten. The bird had just begun eating solid food and seemed to be gathering strength.

"Faiee olli to faito. He ate it all." Eleni was so excited about the owl eating that she said it in two languages. Paula looked inside the box.

"Hhh—hey, little one, you're feeling better, huh?"

The owl swiveled his head toward Paula's voice.

Just then Rick burst into the treatment room. "Hey, Paula?" he called, and sank into the green armchair in the corner near the desk lamp. His hands scrolled through his hair in a troubled way. "I've gotta take off for a while; I'll be back later."

She stopped. "What? Are you all right?"

He didn't answer.

"You don't look okay." She sat across from him on the computer chair, rolling it closer. Eleni pulled the ends of her cardigan together and stepped next to her daughter.

"Would it help to tell me what's going on?" Paula asked.

He sat quietly for a few moments and then looked up at her. "Do you know what a puppy mill is?"

She nodded.

"I've been trying to put this guy out of business for the past few years. He's been reported to the USDA. Numerous violations. Their regulations are a joke. Enforcement is an even bigger one." He stood up and began to pace. "Now he wants out."

"Well, isn't that good?" she asked.

He looked at her. "It would be except for the fact that he's got maybe fifty-five adult purebred dogs stacked in cages that no one wants. Now he's threatening to set the barn on fire and walk unless rescue groups cough up seventy-five bucks a dog to buy him out."

The image was so horrendous it stopped her breath, the wind knocked out of her. To burn down a barn full of caged animals? Dread settled like a sick aftertaste; she wasn't aware that she'd clenched both her fists.

"Dog brokers are up to their eyeballs in puppies; they don't take adult dogs except to sell as breeding stock," Rick explained. "I wish I could say this wasn't typical. They sucker rescue groups by threatening to burn down their operations," he said bitterly. "After they cash out, they start up again in some other godforsaken state. Now he's headed to Iowa, land of the free market."

"This is the legislation you've been working on?"

"Part of it." He blinked and looked down into the creases of his hands.

"So what's going to happen?"

He sighed and rubbed his face as he stood. "I've been arguing with rescue groups all morning. You give the son of a bitch a penny, you give him carte blanche."

She winced. "But then what about the dogs?"

Rick headed for the door. Eleni was silent.

"Rick," Paula called, following him out. "Let me come with you," Paula raised her voice.

He climbed in and started his truck. "Stay here," he called, turning the truck around in the driveway.

"Pa meh." Eleni grabbed Paula's arm and pulled her toward the Escape. Sigmund appeared from nowhere. The bird flew up at Paula, excited by her agitation.

"Get lost." Paula waved his wingtips away from the top of her head.

"Ciga, Panagiotis, ciga." Eleni motioned with her hand for him to back off and he did. Eleni climbed into the passenger side.

Luckily, the keys were in the ignition. Backing around, Paula raced down the gravel driveway, skidding a right turn onto Highway 62. She realized she didn't have her purse but floored it anyway.

The back of Rick's truck became visible as he crested a hill. "There." Eleni pointed.

It was about a fifteen-minute drive. Tall columns of gray smoke were visible long before the turn. Trucks and cars were parked along the sides of the road; Paula followed toward a dilapidated white barn that had more bare spots than paint. Smoke billowed in unnatural cloud formations.

In all the commotion she lost sight of Rick. People ran in and out of the barn, their arms loaded with shivering dogs. Someone had dragged a garden hose and was spraying inside the barn door.

"Ekei." Eleni pointed. Paula spotted him, too, racing past a group carrying large dogs. She parked, flung open the car door and ran after him.

"Paula, wait!" Eleni yelled after her.

Thick gray smoke billowed out the doorway. The cries and screams of dogs were deafening; her skin prickled all over. The smell of ammonia hit her like a vapor barrier as she entered. The urine smell was so strong it seared her nostrils.

Fear gripped her as flames climbed like creeping vines up a corner pillar. Wire cages were stacked into three- and four-high walls of animals separated by narrow aisles. The front third had been emptied, their doors standing open. But as Paula raced deeper into the barn, she found cages jammed with dogs, several packed in each. Spotting three dark figures huddled against one another in the back of a cage, she unlatched the door. "Come on," she called sweetly. The dogs didn't move. "Hey, let's go." She felt for a collar. She then pulled his scruff and the dog yelped. The bottom of the cage was covered with feces and urine, which was also matted in the dogs' fur. "I'm sorry, but you gotta get out of here," she explained, and grabbed the dog by the torso, pulling him away from the other two. He cried out and then braced his feet against the cage, leveraging against her effort.

"Come on," she grunted, easing up to gather the dog's front paws and pull him out. The others followed with no resistance. Someone beside her took the dogs and ran.

The fire began making a humming noise that made her body hair stand on end. Flames snaked up the side wall. Her fear felt like dark fingers flittering in her chest. The urge to tear out of the barn was overwhelming. She fought it and turned to the next cage. Unlatching the door, she climbed in and pulled out three more dogs, pointing them toward the sunlight. "Go, run." Someone behind bent over to lift them.

From the next crate she dragged out three small wiry-coated dogs and set them down. They stood mute, as if it was the first time their feet had touched ground. "Go." She turned them, pointing them toward the door, and gave them a shove. They all shrank back. Thankfully, someone behind her scooped up all three and ran. As she went deeper into the barn, the whoosh of flames crackled and popped as she opened cages and lifted dogs down. Toward the back she saw walls of caged dogs. Paula knew there were far more than the fifty-five Rick expected. Water from the fire hoses began sprinkling like rain through a missing corner of the roof. And while the fire on one side hissed and steamed in defeat, the other side flared into a fury, consuming the dry wood.

She crouched just below the smoke line, crawling toward the back. Smoke was obscuring the outlines of objects. Opening door after door, she turned in to a machine, reaching in, grabbing dogs. Just moving, acting and racing against the fire that had become her rival. The metal latches were hot to the touch. "Go, go," she yelled, shooing out dogs into the arms of others. The dogs were paralyzed with fear. "Shit. Go, damn it!" She crawled into each cage, kneeling across months' worth of accumulated feces and urine.

"Paula." She looked up. Rick was kneeling on top of the stack with two large dogs in his arms. He had his T-shirt pulled up over his nose and she did the same. She reached up to take the first dog.

"I've got her." She grasped a large husky, the dog's underside heavy with milk, and handed her off to another person. Then Rick passed down the second.

"You got him?"

"Yeah." Someone else took the second one.

"Here." Next Rick handed down a litter of six puppies, each no bigger than Paula's palm. "He missed some," Rick said bitterly. Paula transferred them to someone behind her. She followed Rick, taking and lowering dogs while simultaneously working the lower tiers, unlatching cages and pulling out the frightened animals. She looked up. The whole back section of the barn was still loaded. One litter of puppies was isolated in a cage; she picked each up, tucking them into the hem of her sweatshirt. A tall husky in the cage beside them shrieked. Paula opened it, and the dog jumped out, sniffing furiously at the puppies in Paula's sweatshirt. She knew it was the mother. "Come on, Mama,"

Paula said as she handed them all off. "This is their mother," she said to the person who took them.

A man's voice yelled from the back of the barn, "Everyone out; it's gonna collapse." Someone grabbed her arm and pulled her toward the door. The dog screams were deafening.

She wrestled free and ran toward the animal sounds. She caught a glimpse of Rick again, scrambling up and down the top stacks of cages, lowering dogs.

"Rick," she yelled. "These are tied." She pantomimed scissors. He tossed his pocketknife. She slashed the ropes and opened the cage doors.

"Out," she yelled. "Go, go!" she hollered, automatically crawling in, dragging out resistant dogs, shoving them into the aisles, tails so tightly glued under their bodies in fear it looked like they had none.

"Paula," Rick yelled from on top of the stacks, his arms filled. She climbed up to the bottom empty cage and took them one by one, lowering them toward the barn floor.

She climbed up two stacks, lying down on the cage tops to bend over and open the doors. Heat from the metal wire burned hot through her jeans. The cages were up too high for the dogs to jump.

"Aren't there ladders?" she yelled to him.

"He probably took 'em all."

"Motherfucker," she cursed him, reaching in to pull legs, scruffs, whatever she could get ahold of to lower the dogs down. Some thumped to the ground, yelped and then took off running. She looked over at the aisles; most of the cages were empty. Rick was down on the floor. "Get this one," he yelled. She opened the cage and leaned in and pulled out a husky by the front leg.

"I can't get him."

"Just pull the other leg," Rick yelled.

She was able to get ahold of the dog's front to pull him out. Rick knocked over a stack of empty cages and climbed up to reach her. He bent in and grabbed the two adults. She followed

Rick's form; the smoke had gotten so thick she could no longer see daylight.

"Let's go," Rick yelled. The din of people calling one another was drowned out by the roar of the flames, hissing from the water and the thud of collapsing beams.

Just as Paula was about to leave, she spotted a small, dark form through dozens of empty wire cages, obscured by the smoke. Alone, the dog was sitting quietly in a corner cage that everyone else had missed. He was serene, his head slightly lowered as if he had already surrendered to his fate. She knocked over empty cages and climbed up to reach the dog. She opened the latch and reached in. "Come on; come on," she coaxed. The dog looked at her but didn't move. She then reached in, grabbed a hunk of skin and pulled him out under his arms, lowering herself with the dog clutched to her chest. The ceiling was rippling in coils of fire.

A beam came crashing down from the barn ceiling, to her left. Paula jumped down onto the ground. The back wall of the barn started to cave.

"Rick," she screamed. The dog's nails clutched the skin beneath her sweatshirt. Rick jumped down from the top cages, his arms loaded with small dogs. They crawled down the darkened main aisle. She felt disoriented, clutching the brown dog and following the soles of Rick's shoes.

"Paula," she heard her mother shriek as she emerged. She rolled over, gasping, trying to get her lungs to fill with air. Eleni pried Paula's hands from the small dog. Her head pounded, her eyes burned and she began retching. Someone picked her up and carried her off, laying her down on the ground and placing an oxygen mask over her face.

"Now take some real slow breaths," a young man instructed.

She shuddered. Her arms throbbed. The smell of burning hair filled her nose.

"Just relax and try to breathe," the voice instructed.

She opened her eyes expecting to see someone, but all she saw was the blue of the sky. "Are they all out?" she rasped, her voice muffled by the masks. Her throat burned like she'd swallowed embers.

"I hope so." It was Rick. He began coughing.

"You lie down, too," the paramedic directed, placing a mask over Rick's face.

"Paula." Her mother was crouched over her, crying. "Paula."

Paula grasped Eleni's hand. She breathed in the oxygen though it burned and made her cough.

Dozens of others were lying down or kneeling, breathing in oxygen. A loud crash made everyone turn and look. Half the barn collapsed. The fire crew had just arrived. After checking to see that everyone was out they gave up the barn for lost, letting it burn itself out.

The paramedic turned to Eleni. "Are you a relative?"

"I'm her mother," Eleni said.

"First off, I think she'll be fine," Paula heard the paramedic soothing Eleni. "But I'm advising everyone to be seen at Saw-tooth Mountain Clinic in Grand Marais. They're on alert—they know what's happened; they're ready for all of you. A few of the more serious cases are leaving by ambulance, but your daughter's fine to go with you."

As Paula opened her eyes, she started to cry. Tears rolled out from beneath the oxygen mask down the soot-covered sides of her face. "Mom." Her eyes burned. Eleni bent over, hugging her. Paula shivered from the trauma. All she wanted was Roger—his smell, his reassurances, the smooth part of his neck, a place to rest her cheek and breathe. The way he'd always say everything would be okay. If only she could jump into a jet plane and fly back to New York that very moment. But Roger wasn't there.

After she calmed down, her breathing became easier, though her throat and eyes still burned. She slid off the mask and sat up.

"Keep the mask on for a while longer," the paramedic advised.

Instead she stood and looked for the Escape.

"Take it easy," the paramedic said. "You should be sitting."

She ignored him. All she wanted was to crawl inside and feel her quiet car.

Rick followed as she bolted toward her car.

"Paula," he called. But she sped up.

She opened the driver's side, climbed behind the wheel, shut and locked the doors. "Oh my God, oh my God." She leaned her head against the familiar part of the steering wheel, gripping it to stop her hands from trembling. Inside, a humid cloud of urine was overpowering. She sniffed. The windshield was totally fogged, as were the two front windows. Brief shuffling sounds made her turn and look. The back was filled with different sizes and breeds of dogs, every one as still as a photograph. All eyes silently watched her. The small brown dog was in front of the group. She realized he was a puppy. He studied her with the same quizzical, worried look, his brow furrowed as if to ask, *What made you do that?*

Crammed against one another, the dogs pressed backward in one collective gasp to get as far away from her as possible.

"Oh." At the sight of the dogs, tears burned her eyes, which made her nose run profusely. "Well, hello." She choked out a sob, so happy to see them. Some were terrified and shivering; others seemed more curious. She wondered who put them back here.

A knock on the window startled her.

It was Rick.

She looked at him through the glass.

He motioned for her to roll it down. She turned the key and opened the window. Outside the smell of burning wood over-powered the ammonia smell inside. It made her start to cough in a spasm.

"Eleni's driving us back," he said, and broke into a coughing jag.

The driver's door opened and her mother pushed her hip. "Go, Paula, move over." Eleni tapped her again. "Move. I'm driving you both to the doctor." Eleni looked sharply at Rick and motioned with her head. "And you get in, too."

Rick climbed into the back, contorting to fit into a tiny space not loaded with dogs.

"That nice emergency boy told me how to get there," Eleni said. "It's up the hill from Maggie's."

"What about these guys?" Paula asked.

"I'll drop you off first," she said. "Darryl the vet doctor man is going to meet me back home. I just saw him and he said your place is the triage."

They drove in silence for a while, both Paula and Rick continuing to break into episodic fits of coughing, their throats and nasal passages raw.

"You know that was really stupid," Eleni scolded. "Brave, but stupid. But then most things that are brave are stupid, too. If people weren't a little bit stupid then we wouldn't have brave people in the world." She reached to smooth Paula's hair and then back to pat Rick's leg. "I'm proud of you both, but I could kill you for giving me such a heart attack like that."

As Eleni pulled up to the Sawtooth Mountain Clinic, an entire medical staff was waiting with wheelchairs, gurneys. Dozens of other volunteers were being dropped off; two ambulances had raced by them along the highway. People coughing, their faces covered with soot, ash. Paula hadn't realized how many people had answered the call for help.

Hours later, after Paula and Rick had been treated for smoke inhalation and minor cuts and bruises, Eleni walked into the room.

"So what's going on at the house?" Rick asked.

"Your friend Darryl's there with other vets. They unloaded the dogs. People are bathing them in your house and in the small mammal ICU and then they're getting checked," Eleni filled them in.

"What about the little brown one?" Paula asked.

"Oh." Eleni smiled sheepishly. "I took him home. I washed him in the bathtub with your shampoo."

"You what?" Paula exclaimed.

"Fotis smelled him and seemed to like him. Darryl says he's a puppy—checked him all over. Says he's a Lab, between two and three months old. He got shots and Darryl gave him a pill for worms."

Paula turned to Rick. The nurse gave them discharge instructions at the same time, reading off dosages on their bottles of medication. They were told to call if symptoms got worse. It felt good to stand up and walk, though Paula was a bit dizzy.

"That's it; you're free," the nurse joked.

"Let's go," Paula said.

"The car's right out in front," Eleni said. "So what happens to the rat bastard?" she asked as they stood waiting for the elevator.

"Oh," Rick said. "I've made a few phone calls. Buddy of mine's got squad cars posted on every road to the border. If he's headed for Iowa, they'll nail him. Animal cruelty, arson, there's a pile of charges pending."

"Would you take the case?" Paula asked as the elevator doors opened.

"I'll consult more than anything."

"Good. I hope they put the motherfucker in a cage, let him crap there for a month and then set the building on fire." It was the first time she realized she could put a bullet through someone's head and feel good about it. Hate seethed in her. The conditions those dogs had lived in, the fire, their fear as they'd rather have died than come to a stranger who was trying to save their lives.

"You know." Eleni turned to Rick and looked at him in a shadowy way as the elevator doors opened on the main floor. "My nephews know people."

Rick paused and snickered as they stepped out toward the main entrance. "Thanks, but I'm going to let the system take care of this guy."

"Okay, but let me know if it don't work out," Eleni said, glaring at her daughter in a knowing way.

Rick turned to Paula with an expression she couldn't read.

"So where'd you leave the little dog?" Paula asked, more to call off Eleni and change the subject.

"He's sitting in the driver's seat."

"Of my car? You left him in my car?" It triggered a fit of coughing and Paula leaned over. After it subsided she looked up at her mother. "Ma, what if he craps in the seat?"

"So what?" Eleni raised her voice in the puppy's defense. "And if he does, he's just a baby, Paula; he can't help it."

Rick snickered.

"Ah, shit," Paula said. Her arms slapped down at her sides in disgust, pitching her into another coughing fit.

The Escape was parked out in front. Paula could see the top of the puppy's head in the driver's seat, just as she had in the cage. As Eleni opened the door the puppy stood. She lifted him, cradling him like an infant and plastering his face with kisses. "Come here, my little *loukoumi*."

"Uh, Paula?" Rick turned around and looked at her. "I think you just got another dog."

"Oh God." She made a face.

"What other dog?" Eleni protested. "He's mine. *I'm* keeping him. My little *loukoumi*," Eleni said to the dog, hugging him and squashing his face against her cheek, and the dog let her. Then she handed the puppy to Paula to hold up so she could admire him from afar. "Hold him up." She adjusted Paula's arm. "So I can see him." Eleni had an amused look on her face, another expression Paula had never seen. The puppy looked up at Paula with the same worried, quizzical expression.

"He looks at me so strange," Paula said.

"It's because he's suffered," Eleni said. "He's had a hard life."

"Here, Ma." Paula handed the puppy back. "I'll drive back." She made a face at Rick.

"So what are you going to name him?" Rick asked as they headed out to his place.

"Loukoumi, because he's so sweet."

"Cute, Ma, but he's gonna get big," Paula said.

"Labs can get up to eighty pounds," Rick said.

"See?" Paula looked over at Eleni, but she was fussing with the puppy. "How much do *you* weigh, Ma?"

"It's none of your business what I weigh," she raised her voice again. "So what? So he'll be a big Loukoumi then," Eleni said defensively. "I'll train him like people do these days. Take him to the doggie class."

"What does *loukoumi* mean?" Rick asked.

"He says it well, huh?" Eleni elbowed Paula. "You're becoming a real Greek."

Paula explained that *loukoumi* was a dessert, like a square gumdrop, only it was made with sugar and rosewater. When you bit into one of the gelatin squares, dusted with powdered sugar, it tasted like you were eating a rose.

"Well, I guess one is placed," Rick said. "Only a hundred more to go."

As they pulled up to Rick's, Darryl stood outside talking with volunteers.

"We took in about thirty," Darryl reported. "The Duluth and Ashland shelters took the bulk of 'em. Not many litters. We've sorted the few nursing mothers with their puppies. I figure he'd siphon those off before he set the place on fire," he said, and turned to Paula. "Puppies are easy money. Adult dogs in this condition, worth nothing in their world."

They all stood looking at the huddled dogs in the wolf run.

"Seventeen goldens just left with that rescue group from Bemidji. They were in good enough shape to let 'em go."

"Good," Rick said.

"I checked 'em all over. So far, thank God, no signs of parvo, though I'm vaccinating them all," Darryl said. "That's all you need is a parvo outbreak at your place." He glared at Rick. "The Bemidji group washed and flea-dipped 'em all before they left. Malamutes and huskies need to get bathed next. Their rescue groups are on their way," Darryl said. "Probably be here by morning."

"Any mange?" Rick asked.

"So far no, thank God. Probably too noxious in that barn for even bacteria to thrive," he said, squatting back down to resume looking at teeth, gum tissue and skin.

"Boy, this is all so quick," Paula said.

"Well, we've been debating with the rescue groups what to do about this situation for the past few weeks," Darryl said. "The Canine Underground Railroad was alerted. They've got drivers sent from New Jersey and California to be here in the next few days."

"What's that?"

"Networks of individuals across the country who do animal rescue—they pick up and drive mostly rescue dogs, but other species, too, that need transport," Darryl explained. "Each will drive a leg of a journey. Sometimes it's for an hour or six or for a day to connect with the next driver. They'll meet at truck stops or other rendezvous areas to transfer the animals for the next leg of the journey."

It was a whole world of people and purpose she'd never been aware of.

"There are also guys with small planes who'll transport animals."

Darryl turned to Rick. "Just last April a guy flew two eagle chicks from somewhere in Wisconsin to Rick's."

"Sure did." Rick nodded. "Released both juveniles right before you showed up, Paula," he said.

"This is all amazing."

"Yeah, well." Darryl looked at her. "Amazing as it is, that's the easy part. Working to socialize these adult dogs into being more adoptable is the tough work, especially in a case like this. These dogs have never touched leaves or grass. You should have been here when they first arrived. We moved them all into the wolf runs."

"Good," Rick said. "I was hoping you would."

"This was the first time these dogs have felt the earth under their feet," Darryl said, his upper lip furled in disgust. "Five, six, seven years old, they've never been out of that barn. They don't even know what the world is like, what people are like. Some of 'em are terrified. Christ, it took Betsy, the golden rescue person, over an hour to get a few of them out of her van so I could check 'em."

Paula looked around the yard. With the thinner-coated dogs, it was easy to see they were half-starved. Ribs and hip bones poked out from their thin skin like concealed weapons. Their eyes were wide and bewildered as if the sunlight, trees and open space, not to mention people, were just too much stimulation. Huddled together, they wouldn't spread out or venture to explore the space, few moving past the cramped cage space they'd lived in.

"I heard there were plenty of puppy corpses," Darryl said to Rick. "Which is not uncommon in these mills," he directed the comment to Paula. "The cages are so jammed, many puppies can't get nourishment."

One of the older dogs bumped into a fence post and cried as if it hurt to put weight on his feet.

"He's probably barely visual if not blind, too," Darryl said, and looked around, a stethoscope hooked around his neck as he continued examining teeth and feeling lymph nodes in some of the dogs. "Maggie and Ephraim are adopting these two older blind huskies," Darryl said. "With the exception of the puppies, all have evidence of corneal scarring from the ammonia-urine in that barn. Some of 'em will heal; others won't. Most'll have permanent damage, like those older ones. He'd probably kept them around as breeding pairs.

"Their feet have deep scarring on the pads from getting cut up on those wire cages all these years to the point that there's permanent muscle atrophy. Most have burnt feet from the hot metal cages, but that'll heal. They'll have to be watched for signs of infection. But now that they're clean, the chances of that are lower."

"Who would buy a dog from a place like that? I'd call the police on them," Paula said.

"He's been operating within the confines of the USDA regulations," Rick said.

"What?" Paula demanded.

Darryl looked at her long and hard.

"People never see what you did," he said. "Puppies are turned over to dog brokers who clean up the 'merchandise,' as they're called," he explained. "They're then distributed to pet stores across the country. Sometimes they move them to other brokers who sell them outright from newspaper ads—the perennial ad in the Sunday papers, 'All breeds,' usually from anywhere from four hundred fifty up to a thousand dollars depending on the breed. No one ever sees the conditions in which their parents suffer. By the time buyers look at the puppies, the dogs have changed hands many times. Those who die along the way or are overtly ill are written off as merchandise spoilage."

"What about the adult dogs?" she asked, and cringed, looking at some of them shivering in fear, their desperate eyes seeking comfort from someone, anyone. How could Rick have thought she was part of such a scam to spy on him? How could he have ever thought that about her?

"They're breeding stock. They keep males and females together in the cramped cages you saw so that every time a female comes into season she's impregnated. After six or seven closely spaced litters their uterus either withers or comes out. Sometimes they're left to die. Sometimes they shoot them or let them starve."

"I can't hear any more." Paula covered her ears.

"Paula, it's all about the money," Rick interjected. "Millions go on to end up in shelters to be euthanized," he said. "Their lobbies claim it's about 'freedom of the marketplace, freedom from government regulation.' They actually think of themselves as entrepreneurs—businessmen and –women—and they turn it into

a philosophical issue about liberty and the power of free enterprise."

"This is cruelty, not free enterprise; how can you say that?" she
raised her voice.

Rick said. "I'm not saying *I* believe that, but that's their legisla-
tive talking point." There was a cool edge to his voice she'd come
to recognize as rage. Where she'd just explode, Rick turned to
ice. She'd noticed it first when they'd begun examining a second
barred owl they'd admitted last week with a broken wing. The
bird had been blown out of a tree during a windstorm and saved
by a screaming neighbor after a group of kids had tried to kill it
with a baseball bat.

"No one suspects where these puppies come from," Darryl said.
"And brokers play it like the dogs come from happy-go-lucky ma-
and-pa country homes."

"If only people could see," Paula said. "They'd be outraged."

"Or else they'd buy 'em all just to save them," Eleni said.

Paula lowered her head. "Why isn't this illegal?" she asked.

"For the same reason lead sinkers and bullets aren't," Rick
said, his voice getting chillier by the word.

She thought of the eagle and how the bird had suffered with
seizures and organ failure. How Rick had stayed up nights,
holding the eagle while he violently seized, so that he wouldn't
hurt himself. Her eagle was one of the lucky few to beat the
harsh odds of lead poisoning. Yet he had many hard months of
rehab still ahead of him before being released back to the wild, if
ever. And for every bird found and treated, Rick claimed there
were at least five or six more suffering and dying in the woods
alone.

"So why doesn't the NRA just ban lead bullets?" Paula asked.
"I mean it's our national symbol and all," she insisted. "Wouldn't
you think they'd give a shit?"

Both men laughed bitterly. Darryl bent down to resume ex-
aminations. "I gotta stop talking about this shit; my blood pressure's rising and my wife'll fucking kill me if I have a stroke."

"Paula you should come home, go to bed," Eleni suggested.

"No, I want to stay and help with the huskies and malamutes."

"I'll drive her back," Rick said. He looked at Eleni and winked that it was okay.

"Okay, Loukoumi." Eleni turned to the little brown dog. "We'll go back to the house alone," she said in an exaggerated way that made both Paula and Rick laugh out loud.

"Maybe Panagiotis will come keep us company. Come, little one." She climbed into the Escape and shut the door.

Rick ran over to the yard and brought Fotis over, loading him up in the back.

The yard had been divided using bales of hay into those dogs who'd been immunized and checked and those who needed further evaluation and medical treatment. Rick came out of the house, holding two small wet dogs he'd just washed. He placed them in a separate part of the yard. "Two more, Darryl," he called.

Paula crouched down to pet the husky with her pups. She was positive the mother was the same one she'd grabbed from the barn. Rick crouched down beside her. The dog looked up at her so gently, yearning for love and a gentle touch, that it broke Paula's heart. She remembered the dog's shriek as Paula had gathered up the puppies into her sweatshirt. The mother had felt so light as Paula had carried her out—a furry sack of bones.

"What'll happen to them all?"

Rick looked at her. "Oh . . . the rescue groups'll find homes," he said. "I'm sure it's already a high-profile rescue on the Net. People from all over will be wanting to adopt, and rescue groups do a great job of screening to find what they call 'forever' homes," he explained. "They'll probably first sort out those dogs who'll be more easily adoptable and then concentrate on the ones who need more socialization. Some might never be adoptable."

"What'll happen to them?"

"They'll get sanctuary. Just like some of the raptors I have here, just like Sam," Rick said as she felt his gaze on her face. "I figure after this you'd be heading full-speed ahead back to New York City," he said in a way she couldn't read.

"Why do you say that?" she asked. He didn't answer.

"You up for washing this mom and her pups?"

"Absolutely." She stood and launched into a coughing jag.

"You okay?"

She motioned with her hands that she was fine.

"Grab that shampoo bottle and let's carry them into the house," he said. "There's a large crate in the hall. Let's put 'em all in there. Someone said all four bathrooms are full with dogs being bathed, so I'll put on a pot of coffee for everyone while we wait."

He lifted the mother and Paula gathered the puppies.

"As you wash 'em, make sure to saturate their fur and every crease and fold in their groins, armpits," he instructed. "Wash and rinse each pup three times even if you think they're clean."

"You got it."

Just then Jason arrived, walking into the kitchen as Paula placed the puppies into the hall crate with their mother.

"Hey, guys," he greeted Paula and Rick. He began asking questions; another reporter had been on the scene taking photographs. He was assigned to cover the story and check on the Jailbird. He stood taking notes in the kitchen while the coffee brewed.

It was after eight that evening before they'd washed the last of the huskies in Rick's master bathroom. Paula was drenched and filthy. Rick had stepped outside to help Darryl with something when she spotted a folded pair of Rick's cutoffs and a shirt on a chair. She quickly changed into them, wrapping her clothes in one of the damp towels and placing the bundle by Rick's bedroom door to grab on the way out later.

Paula sat down on Rick's bed for a moment. The top covers

were strewn with towels, grooming rakes and brushes along with
dog collars, some used and others with store tags. She pushed the
paraphernalia aside and then rolled flat to stretch her back.

She woke up, the sun shining pink through her eyelids. The feel
of breath was warm on her neck; as she leaned back deliciously, a
body pushed against her. Peaceful breathing was coming from
behind her, pressing against her back with its every rise and fall.
An arm was slung over her hip, with a hand holding her stomach, cradling her. She slipped back into the blissfulness of the
dream of being held, as she'd done on the downstairs couch of
Roger's brownstone—such a sweet dream, until both her eyes
flipped open.

She looked around and jerked up, realizing where she was.

"Shit, shit, shit." Disoriented, she ricocheted around the room
like it had become a pinball machine, bashing into the dresser,
knocking things over in frenzied disorientation. "Shit, shit." She
tried to get her bearings. Here she was, a married woman, asleep
in Rick's arms—so close to smell his warmth, not wanting to get
up. "Oh God, I'm sorry," she said, walking backward, looking for
her shoes. She bumped against the half-open bedroom door. "Oh
shit, I must have fallen asleep. Sorry."

Sam looked up at her from the foot of the bed; Rick glanced
up but then turned over. She raced out of his house down the
slope and toward the grassy road. Hopping as she put on one
boot, then the other, the laces from both trailing behind her as
she ran all the way back to the guesthouse.

CHAPTER 15

Later that morning Rick approached her as she was in the flight room with the eagles.

"Paula," he said with sincerity. "I apologize if I made you feel uncomfortable."

She'd looked down at her shoes. "Hey—no big deal—I forgot about it already." She shrugged it off and made a funny face, nudging the fresh roadkill closer to the center of the room. He bent over to help drag the carcass. She could tell he didn't believe her just by the phony nonchalance of her voice.

"You just looked so peaceful I didn't want to wake you to drive you home," he explained. "So I crashed next to you, like we do in the ICU with the critical all-nighters."

Yeah, but you usually aren't snuggled up to me with your arm around my waist.

"Hey—like I said, no prob." She looked at him like *just drop it.*

A few days later Paula was in the raptor ICU, feeding the barred owl his last meal of the day.

Jason had just left after popping in to check on the bird's progress for his weekly series in the *Cook County News Herald* documenting the owl's recovery. People were calling the paper as well as Rick in support and wanting to make donations to Northern Lights Wildlife Rehabilitation. The *Duluth News Tribune* had picked up the series and it was soliciting phone calls of support from the Duluth area.

The owl was finally out of danger and upgraded to guardedly optimistic, as Rick called it, to the point where they'd started hand-feeding him chunks of muskrat with a pair of tweezers. Rick explained that barred owls don't eat mice; they are known for living on a diet of skunk—so their poor sense of smell, in this case, served them well. With each bite the owl's two dark brown bars arched over his eyes to create an expression of perpetual surprise.

Paula's phone buzzed in her back pocket. Ordinarily she left it off, but since Eleni was back at the guesthouse with Loukoumi and Fotis, making stuffed peppers for dinner, Paula had left it on. Pulling it out, she looked at the number. *Shit.* It was Roger. After three weeks of being underground in the Hadron Collider. She almost didn't answer it but knew she'd just have to face him later.

"Hey," Roger said, his voice elated. "God, I've missed you." She heard the hunger in his voice, but rather than eliciting a rush of desire, it made her feel as if she'd eaten something bad.

"My mother's been here."

"Eleni? You're kidding."

"That's the only one I have." The sarcastic edge in her voice surprised her. "She's been here for seventeen days."

"Jesus. And I haven't read about it in the newspaper by now?"

"Ha, ha, very funny, Roger." The comment made her angry, though only weeks ago she'd have been laughing right along with him. "It's actually been really nice," she corrected him, and it occurred to her she didn't even want to relate the events of the past five weeks. The eagle now being rehabilitated in the flight room, the barred owl she'd been feeding, the puppy mill rescue and watching the husky pups waddle over to their mom in the little wire corral that Rick had set up in his living room. "We've really had a great time."

"Really," Roger backed off quickly. "Well, that's good." He could barely veil his surprise.

An awkward silence followed.

"So how's France?"

"It was great."

Was? "Where are you calling from?"

"Home."

"Oh. I thought you had a few more weeks."

"I did, but I had to come home early. Some sort of ruckus at the department."

"Oh." She didn't have a thing to say.

"God, I can't wait to see you," he said with the conviction men have when they're just about to sit down to a good meal.

Her stomach tightened. It hadn't done so in weeks, and to think that only a few days ago during the fire she'd ached for him. She'd never been one to be fickle.

"When are you coming home?" he asked, only it sounded more demanding.

"I-I-I'm not sure."

"Well, I've got a huge surprise waiting."

"I-I'm committed for a while longer."

"Doing what?" The way he asked implied there was no right answer. Anything she might say would be shot down as inconsequential. "Well, can't you just come back this weekend?"

"I-I'm not sure."

"I'd come out there and drive that car back with you, but I've got to be at Columbia this week. Just store the car somewhere and fly back with your mother. We can always have it shipped or get it one weekend and drive back together. I know how you love to drive."

He didn't even mention Fotis.

"I don't know, Roger. I have my dog, too. Let me think about it."

"I've got an incredible surprise waiting for you," he said, his voice agitated with excitement.

"What?" Her voice was flat—probably another loose, almost flawless diamond from Antwerp.

"Well, it wouldn't be a surprise if I told you," he seductively tried to goad her into begging and squealing as to what it might be, but she didn't.

"Well, okay." He seemed disappointed. "I'll tell you." He sounded embarrassed by her lack of enthusiasm and it made her feel sorry for him. "I've had the brownstone redone."

He continued haltingly, waiting for her reaction. "Last week I got a file of photos from the interior designer. They've worked on it all summer. Thought I'd surprise you, but so much for that," he said. "I'll forward the file right now, you can take a look at it." She could hear him distractedly monkeying with his phone to e-mail it.

"Fine."

"New bed," he went on. "New bathrooms, kitchen, the whole place—you wouldn't even recognize it; I didn't."

"What'd you do with all your stuff?"

"Some of it was yours, too, you know," he said in that scolding-father voice.

She closed her eyes. *Here we go again.* "Whatever, Roger."

"It's all gone."

"Really," she commented. "Where'd you move it?"

"It's gone—I got rid of it."

"Everything?"

"Each room is completely new and refurnished," he said.

"You trashed it all?"

"It's everything you've ever wanted, Paula, I swear," he said; his voice had the eagerness of a TV announcer selling a vacuum cleaner. "I hired that design firm you've always wanted to use."

She felt the quiet space between them expand and didn't know what to say or believe.

"This summer I've done a lot of thinking," Roger broke the silence. "I realized that you've been right all along. It's high time we live like a 'real married couple,' as you always say."

"Oh." Her insides thrashed with guilt. Torn-up pieces were vying to speak. "Well, that's good." *Why now? Why not ten years ago?* The tension between them grew painful.

"So, hey—," Roger broke the silence. "How 'bout meeting me home this weekend? You're not on a schedule or anything, are you?"

"Uhhh—I'm committed for another week, maybe two," she said.

"Doing what?"

"I told you I'm very busy here, Roger," she raised her voice. If it were possible, she would have stalled indefinitely.

"Well, you don't sound very excited," he said.

"I'm just in the middle of something. I'll get back to you later," she said, picking up another hunk of bloody red flesh for the owl.

"Well, okay," Roger said. She heard more disappointment. "Maybe that'll work out better." She heard him thinking. "This way I'll get used to the brownstone, get things ready for your return."

"My return."

"Are you okay?" he asked. "You sound so different."

"I'm fine." It was the first lie she'd told since arriving in Grand Marais. It made her stomach hurt with a familiar ache.

"Babe?" It sounded like he was talking to someone else.

"I'm fine." A second lie. "Look, I'll have to call you back." One thing she knew about Roger was that he wouldn't have the balls to come right out and demand to know what was different.

She ended the call, finished feeding the owl and then sat down, collapsing into Rick's green armchair. It smelled like him. She leaned over, covering her face with her hands. The phone rang again. *Shit.* She looked at the number. It was the guesthouse.

"Hi, Mom."

"What's wrong?"

"Nothing."

"Don't tell me 'nothing.' I heard it the second you answered."

"I'll tell you later."

She heard Eleni sigh. "Rick's here. I just invited him for dinner; it's all ready. You coming home now?"

"Yeah, Ma, I'm coming home. Roger just called."

"Well, come home, *kula mou;* everything's ready," Eleni's voice softened. "Let's eat and we can talk about it. You want Rick to come and get you?"

"No, I'll walk."

"Hurry or it'll get cold."

Eating was the last thing she wanted to do.

The sun was setting noticeably earlier as each day passed. She'd developed a heightened awareness of the changes that each day brought. In New York she'd never been so aware of the season's incremental shift. Kicking through leaves along the grassy path, she hurried back to the guesthouse. All the self-talk in the world was doing nothing to calm her. Even the beauty of the moon rising over Lake Superior and its rippling reflection didn't help to clear her mind and heart.

Rick and Eleni both looked up as soon as Paula entered. She could tell they'd been talking about her. Fotis and Loukoumi greeted her as she entered and shut the door. The guesthouse smelled like her mother's roasted chicken, butternut squash and stuffed peppers with the wild rice Eleni had fallen in love with since discovering the abundant local harvest sold in Maggie's store.

Paula sat down on the futon, afraid to look at her mother.

"And what did my son-in-law have to say for himself?" Eleni asked, handing Rick and then Paula a plate full of food.

"Thanks, Mom."

"So," Eleni said. "Tell me."

Paula paused before talking, wishing Rick weren't there. But as he settled across from her with a fully loaded dinner plate, there was no indication he was going anywhere.

"Roger's back in New York."

"Oh, so he's back early," Eleni said.

"He wants me there." Paula set the plate down on the side table. Elbows on knees, she leaned over, running her fingers through her scalp. "He's had the brownstone remodeled."

Eleni finished serving herself and walked over next to Paula. She tapped her daughter's shoulder and motioned to the plate. "Come on and eat; it'll make you feel better."

Paula lifted the plate and began moving around grains of wild rice with her fork.

"Well," Eleni started. "You can go back to New York if you want," she said. "But I'm not ready."

Paula looked up at her mother, her mouth gaping open. "You're what?"

"Just because Roger wants you back doesn't mean I'm going," Eleni said, and popped a forkful of squash and chicken into her mouth.

"What do you mean you're *not ready*?"

"Well, for starters, I've got two lunch dates lined up for next week at Marvelline's and—*Christos kai Panayia*—it took traveling all this way to finally find someone else who plays Canasta."

"Mom, you can't stay here—"

There was a scratching at the front door.

Eleni stood and stepped to open the front door for Sigmund. The bird stepped in, carefully looking around to check that things were in order.

"Also, I've got a couple of jobs lined up," Eleni said. "Maggie made some calls. Her people on the reservation have fur garments for powwows and ceremonies that need repairing. They'll pay me."

Eleni stared at Paula. "Then on the Grand Portage Monument and Reservation," Eleni said, "they have one of those tourist forts—a historical fur trade place." She looked at Rick for help.

"A historical reenactment of the voyageurs that's open for tourists," Rick explained.

Eleni nodded. "Thank you. They play like old times in these places and Maggie said they need someone who can sew fur clothing and hats."

"What?" Paula was stunned.

"So I've got work lined up there, too, Paula. Then I got a call from Canada—they heard about me from the Grand Portage place. Their place is called Old Fort William—another place for tourists—the North West Company and the Canadian Fur Trade. They do the same thing as Grand Portage. They want me up there for a few weeks to look over their stock, do repairs and make new clothing. It's in Thunder Bay. Isn't that where your advisor guy, Bernie, lives?"

Paula was stunned. "But how are you going to get to these places?"

"It's only a half-hour drive, Paula. I'll take your car."

"But Ma, all you've done for years is drive a few blocks to the grocery store. Highway driving is different."

"Marvelline'll take me; she already promised she would. And Thunder Bay is only an hour away, Paula, closer than the Catskills, for God's sake. She's got in-laws up there. They said I could stay with them while I'm working."

"Mom—"

"It's a huge job, Paula." Eleni slowly nodded. "The fur trade was a big deal up there. They have lots of work."

Paula was stunned. She sat up on the futon to protest, but she didn't have a coherent reply. "Ma, you can't stay here."

"I'm the mother here," Eleni said. "You don't tell me what to do."

"You just can't."

"Of course I can—this is America." Eleni knocked loudly on the table three times. "And a person can do whatever they want." Her sharp eyes settled on her daughter as she chewed a piece of chicken. "You took a break; now I'm taking one."

"Yeah, Ma, but the break is over."

"Says who? Roger?" Eleni glared at her. "For you, maybe."

Paula looked at the ceiling beams, slowly shaking her head; she couldn't believe this was happening.

"But what about your apartment?"

"What about it? It's not going anywhere."

"All your things."

"What things? My furniture? My rent is paid for the whole month. The only thing I want is Thanassis' painting. And for that I can have Stavraikis take it to one of those 'U-mail it' places. He has a key. The rest they can chop it up for firewood for all I care. No one's gonna steal it—and if they want the furniture, *echi o Theos*," she said, and crossed herself. "It's theirs."

"But where would you stay?"

Rick was listening quietly, slowly eating.

"You know, Paula," he interjected. "I sure could use another person here," he said. "Your mom's great with the husky and her pups."

Paula shot him a look of betrayal.

"It'll be at least another eight weeks," he said, "maybe longer, before I can place them, so why not just let her stay? She's been an enormous help."

Looking at Paula, Eleni nodded in thanks, her eyes shining with *Listen to him*.

"She's great with the smaller birds; you know that," he said. "She knows how to prepare the food for tube feedings; she's welcome to stay on in the guesthouse."

"But what about Fotis? My car?"

"Leave them here," Eleni said. "We'll take care of Fotis, plus I'll need your car."

"And then what, Mom?" Paula felt herself about to cry. It was embarrassing to be having such a family discussion around Rick.

Eleni shrugged her shoulders. "I don't know," Eleni said. "Right now I'm very busy, Paula," she said as if brushing off a co-worker. "So why don't we just play it by ear?"

Sigmund flew up onto the back of the futon and nestled behind Eleni, looking triumphantly over at Paula.

"Fuck," Paula whispered. "But what about winter, Mom? It's supposed to be so harsh."

"It's not winter now." Eleni glared at her. Paula could feel Rick watching her carefully.

"But you don't have a phone or anything."

"I'll put her on my plan," Rick said. "I'll get her a phone tomorrow."

"But what if you fall in the guesthouse or something?"

"I'll look after her," Rick said, and turned to Eleni. "Eleni, you're welcome to come stay up at the house with me," he said. "I've got five empty bedrooms."

Eleni looked at Paula. No one talked for a few minutes. They could feel the agony of Paula's confusion.

"Paula mou." Eleni moved closer and put her arm around her daughter's shoulders. Paula wanted to shake it off. "Go back; figure out what it is that you want."

Paula stood and brusquely headed out the door. She didn't want to let Rick see her cry.

She climbed into the Escape and drove to the IGA, hoping Maggie was still there. It was dinnertime and she'd often go home to fix dinner for Ephraim.

As Paula parked and walked in, Maggie was just grabbing her purse from under the register, talking to Bobby Ray.

"Hi, Paula, I was just thinking about you." She felt Maggie read her distress immediately.

"You have some time to talk or are you heading home?"

"Ephraim's in Duluth on orchard business and I was just gonna give Bobby Ray a ride home, so I've got plenty of time. You eat yet?"

"Uhh, no."

"You want to join us, Bobby Ray?"

"N-no. I'll wait here, finish stocking the soup aisle. I've got to block the cake mix boxes also."

"Let's go get a bite at Marvelline's," Maggie suggested to Paula. "Let me check in with Amber before we go." Business slowed down after 7:00 pm, though they were open nights until 10:00. Paula waited as Maggie spoke to Amber.

"Bobby Ray, honey?" Maggie called as she walked over and put her hand on his shoulder. The tentativeness of his movements suggested he was heavily medicated. Maggie always kept a mother's eye on him. "You gonna be okay if I go with Paula to the Oklahoma for a bite to eat?"

"Hi, Paula." He waved.

"Hey, Bobby Ray." She waved back. "How's it going?" Tall, thin, mid-twenties, with short light brown hair, his belt always too high up on his hips, Bobby Ray never missed a day's work.

"It's goin' good," he said.

"Now you call me, honey, if things get busy, you promise?" Maggie asked. "You got me on speed dial; you've got Marvelline, too, right?"

"Yeah, I-I-ll be o-okay," he said. "I promise."

"You want me to bring you something?"

"I-I like their burgers and shakes."

"Chocolate?"

"V-vanilla."

"You got it. Be back in about an hour." She gave Amber a look that said to call if she got overwhelmed.

It was a beautiful but chilly October evening as they crossed the street, walking down toward the Coast Guard station and the Oklahoma Café. The place was full of truckers this time of night and Marvelline was in her glory.

"And look who's walking in the door," she announced over the din of conversation. "And what brings you ladies in tonight?"

"Dinner," Maggie said, and tapped Paula's shoulder. "It's on me."

Marvelline walked over and sat down next to Paula. "Shit, I'm tired. My tootsies are killing me."

Paula noticed Marvelline and Maggie were both wearing the same red crystal evil eye earrings.

"Damn, those earrings look better on you," Marvelline said.

"I was just thinking the same about yours," Maggie said. "Whatcha got for specials?" Maggie looked over the menu.

"That prime rib sandwich, which Earl over there says is killer." She pointed toward his table as he lifted the last bite in her honor. She took the pencil out from where it had been tucked behind her ear and set it on the table along with her order book. "I hear the chili is too."

"I'll have the chili," Paula said.

"Me too," Maggie ordered. "Plus a take-out order of burger and a vanilla shake for Bobby Ray."

"Well, bless my sweet nephew's little heart." Marvelline closed her eyes and smiled. "It's as good as done. How's that boy doing?" She leveraged her hands against the table, hoisting herself up as she yawned and shuffled back toward the kitchen to place the order.

"Bobby Ray's always fine," Maggie answered. "Better than the rest of us." She then turned to Paula. "So what's going on?"

Paula began with Roger's phone call. Halfway through her rendition of the conversation, Marvelline appeared carrying a tray with three bowls of chili, a pile of packaged saltine crackers, a plate piled with shredded cheddar and three sets of silverware wrapped tightly in white paper napkins. It had the feel of eating dinner in someone's kitchen.

"The burger's cooking. Don't let me forget his order before you leave," Marvelline said. "Okay, so go on; I heard half of what you said, and I can probably fill in the rest myself."

Paula began to dump the entire story about Roger, the hoarding, the brownstone, the downstairs couch. Marvelline listened politely. Midway, Paula got the sense Marvelline was pretending she'd never heard it before.

Paula stopped mid-sentence. "So you know."

"Well, of course I know everything, darlin'; you think we don't talk?" Marvelline said. "For starters, I agree, that man is still your husband."

"Makes sense to me," Maggie weighed in.

"Leave your mom," Marvelline said, "Fotis and your car while you go back to New York, sort things out."

Paula turned to face Maggie. "Just out of curiosity, how did my mother happen to land all this work with fur?"

"Uhhh—word spreads fast?" Maggie smiled enigmatically. "A person with those skills up here?" Maggie waved her hand. "Summer tourism's huge up here with that French voyageur stuff."

"Don't you worry none about Eleni," Marvelline said. "We'll keep your mama busy and look after her. Okay, so we got the mama thing solved." She looked up at Paula for confirmation. Paula nodded. "Now on to you. First off, ladies, how's the food?"

They both waved as if too euphoric to comment.

"Here's the thing with the husband, baby doll. When in doubt, check it out. Unless he's beating the tar out of you (which in that case I'd say run for the hills and don't look back), then you need to go back and play this thing out."

Maggie was nodding. "Sounds like you still have feelings. You'll never forgive yourself if you don't give it another shot. You'll always wonder. It'll haunt you, so go and see. You might be surprised."

"But I feel like such a shit," Paula said, and covered her face with her hand. "Here he's made all the changes I've wanted him to for ten years, and for some reason it's not good enough. It's so unfair of me."

"Now hold on, doll." Marvelline held up her hand. "You just said it—you've waited ten years. Maybe the man just plain wore you out. It happens."

"Or else it's you who's changed," Maggie said in a quiet voice. "And all that stuff that was so important no longer is 'cause it's not what you want. The timing may be off. Ten years ago you might have jumped at it, but that was ten years ago."

"But don't you think I'm being an unfair shit?"

"Now quit saying that or we're gonna have to shoot that bird off your shoulder. Unfair or not, it's what is," Marvelline said.

"I've loved him for ten years."

"And that don't mean you won't love him always," Marvelline said. "But living with him, being his wife, is different. People change."

"But can't they change together?"

"Sometimes," Maggie said.

Paula looked at her hands.

"Listen," Marvelline said. "Some loves can take a hit; some can't. I tell you, forty years ago when I followed old Arnie up here from Gotebo, good Lord, I knew I had me a tiger by the tail. But what I didn't expect was for him to take back up with an old flame once we got here. So here I was, didn't know a soul, and he off and leaves me for a whole month to have a fuckathon with little Ms. Prissy. (Lordy, you should see her now!)" Marvelline stood up and walked to the counter, got three mugs of coffee and set them down on the table.

"So what happened?" Paula asked as Marvelline opened two creamers from a little cup on the side of the table and dumped each one in.

"Well, he come back running with his dick tucked between his legs soon enough," she said. "Sweating like a whore in church, begging me, saying, 'Thank God I married the right woman.' I guess there'da been some doubt I wasn't aware of back in Gotebo when he'd proposed. After that he knew better than to pull that shit again, and that was that. Put the whole matter to rest."

"And that was that," Paula repeated.

"But mind you, it didn't go on for ten years." Marvelline stared with a knowing look at Paula while blowing on a spoonful of chili. "I'da been the hell out of there. Now you look at ole Arnie and he's one a these old doobers who can't fit their guts into a booth; I gotta get some of 'em a special chair to sit on the end."

They broke out into cackling laughter. Several of the men turned around to look. One of them called, "Hey, what's so funny, Marvelline?"

"You don't wanna know, dearie," she fired back.

Paula piled cheese onto the surface of her bowl of chili and mixed it in.

"You've been so deprived of what us women need that maybe your little soul just gave up, darlin', and turned elsewhere to stay alive," Marvelline said. "But sitting here speculating'll only make you nuts. Sounds like you ought to go back, take that boy for a ride again, see where it takes ya."

Something had changed. Seeing Theo in the hospital, the moment Fotis looked at her in the shelter, grasping the eagle's feet that first day in the raptor ICU. Whether that change could fit back into her New York life and her marriage to Roger she couldn't tell.

"Besides," Maggie said, smiling. "We get to keep Eleni a while longer." Maggie raised her glass of water like it was gin to toast Marvelline. Marvelline nodded. "And trust me," she said. "Between Grand Portage and Old Fort William, mama's gonna make a killing."

"Just think," Maggie said. "Maybe Ephraim'll have Eleni bring old Chester his cookies and dinner mints just to see if the geezer tries to cop a feel."

Paula laughed.

"That'll be the 'shot that was heard all over the world.'" Marvelline started laughing. "Feathers and teeth flying all over the place." Maggie laughed, but Paula sat like a stone.

"Oh, come on, Paula." Maggie grabbed her forearm and shook it. "Lighten up for God's sake—Eleni loves that dog of yours and that precious Loukoumi. She's cooking Greek food for them and Rick."

"And she's gonna show me how to make that spinach pie thing I can't pronounce," Marvelline said. "I'm adding it to the menu." She looked around at the truckers. "These guys need some vegetables; look at 'em all, probably can't even shit. Them guts like eleven-month-pregnant stomachs."

"You know," Maggie started, "sometimes when people get old and they think life's over, but often it has a strange way of coming around again. Maybe that's what Eleni's getting here. Let her have it, Paula. Don't rain on her parade while you're figuring out which direction yours is heading."

"Yeah," Paula said. "Wow. My mom's new life. Shit. I've created a monster." Her eyes widened, smiling as she shook her head and looked down at the table. "But Chester?" She glanced over. "Really, Maggie."

The three of them cackled so loud, the men from the other tables turned around again. "What're you ladies laughing at again?"

"You," Marvelline said, and made a face. It made them laugh all the more.

Paula suddenly felt excited about going back to New York. She missed Heavenly and Tony, standing in line for the best Italian food at Eataly.

"Go back and see him," Maggie said. "You'll know."

"What if I don't? What if I'm more confused?"

"Than that's your answer," Marvelline said. "Confusion is an answer."

Paula nodded and took a sip of coffee. Nothing felt right. Leaving Grand Marais was torture, but not going back to New York felt wrong, too. As she looked up at both women she knew that each had made up her mind about Roger. Paula could tell. But what she couldn't tell was whether they were of like mind or not. And neither would say—the way people keep silent when they know that everyone must walk that long road alone.

CHAPTER 16

She hadn't planned on taking a hike when she left the guest-house; otherwise she'd have worn boots instead of her patent-leather sandals. Tomorrow her flight would depart from Duluth and her chest already hurt from anticipating the separation—it felt as if the bones in her sternum had been bruised.

For her last day she wanted to take Fotis on a walk, just the two of them. Rick had mentioned that if she followed the small footpath behind the guesthouse it would lead down the steep banks of the ravines onto rocky riverbed. He'd intrigued her with his description of cold springs flanked on either side by red cliffs, gorges and mossy old-growth forests. She'd always been curious as to where the little path went but was usually too tired after work to follow the urge to explore. He'd promised her that following the trail would be like taking a trip back into time through one of the most remote, untouched wilderness wetland areas on the North Shore of Lake Superior.

Walking down the little path, she waded through ferns tall enough to brush against her chin. Fotis pulled her onto the top of the ridge and she could barely see where it dropped off. She lost her footing and fell to her knees onto the spongy rotting bark of a fallen birch. The ravine fell off so steeply that she grabbed fallen timbers, hoping their dry branches would hold. For a second she gasped, realizing she'd dropped the leash. "Oh my God, my God, Fotis," she shrieked.

Fotis wagged his tail from where he stood on the sandbar, the leash draped beside him, the end in a pool of standing water.

"Fotis," she cried. He nimbly dashed up the side of the slope toward her. "Come here," she coaxed, reaching out to try to grab his leash. He tapped her face with his nose and took off.

He was back down on the sandbar again, bright eyed, looking up at her, puzzled by the concern in her voice. She sidestepped at an angle all the way down the steep slope and leapt onto the sandbar next to Fotis. He touched her lip with his wet nose, smiling, with his one ear flopped over.

"God, I thought I'd lost you." She hugged him tightly and then picked up the leash, her chest heaving with relief. He still seemed mildly amused at her worry.

Both sides of the ravine were carpeted with mosses, interrupted and bracken ferns, heavy layers of red and orange leaves and huge boulders covered with sprawling green and orange patterned lichens. Fallen birch and basswood trees spanned the ravine from where they'd toppled eons ago, resting where they'd hit the other side above the river. The smell of fresh water plants and forest soil was intoxicating. The sound of bubbling, running water was everywhere. The air at the bottom was chillier and more humid. Cold underground streams bubbled up from the sand like boiling water, creating their own micro-climate as they fed the river and, ultimately, Lake Superior. Yellow birch leaves floated by as she gained a foothold on the exposed rocks; her feet slipped in the wet sandals—the wrong footwear for the job. She could imagine Rick's commentary about her shoes.

Fotis surged ahead downstream, dragging her as he hopped from rock to rock.

"Wait." Her voice was nervous and panicky. "I can't go so fast." She stumbled and dropped the leash again. She caught her breath, afraid he'd take off and she'd never see him again.

Fotis stopped to look at her and then turned downstream. She could tell he wanted to explore and not be tethered to six feet of red nylon.

"Oh, you're probably okay," she muttered, thinking back to Rick's comment about Fotis being very bonded to her and obedient at coming when called. Despite her worries, Rick said he'd be shocked if Fotis ever bolted. "Paula—he's not going anywhere; who else is going to feed him *keftedes*?" She knew Rick had taken Fotis running free with Sam in the woods.

Fotis looked up at her, his eyes pleading.

"You wanna walk on your own, don't you," she said. "Okay." She crouched next to him. He touched her lip with his nose again. "Okay, but promise me you won't run away. Promise?" She hugged him, feeling the meld between them and how precious he'd become, more precious than almost anything or anyone she'd known. Like they'd already lived a whole life together that Roger could never understand, much less share.

"Okay." Paula unclipped the leash, tied it around her waist and looked up at the late-afternoon sky. Lingering light filtered through the remaining scatter of yellow and orange leaves along the ridge, making the little canyon glow.

Fotis scampered along the curve of the stream, sniffing, pausing to paw a leaf. He'd stop and look at her to make sure she was watching as he began playing and showing off. She laughed and clapped her hands as he dashed farther in the stream and then stopped to wait for her to catch up. Around a bend, she heard him lapping freshwater that had pooled in shimmering areas, reflecting blue sky and autumn color. Scarlet maple leaves floated along, looking as succulent and fresh as the moment they'd detached from their branches.

There was a fragrance like nothing she could place. Inhaling, she tried to describe it—wet soil and a spice she couldn't name. Maggie had mentioned something about the sweetgrass harvest, how it permeated the air on chilly mornings, indicating that winter was not far off.

The stream curved around a bend. Fotis was nowhere. He'd either paddled through the deep water or hiked up along the side of the ravine. Paula stopped and looked around.

"Fotis?" Her voice bounced off the red granite walls. It was a silent aloneness she wasn't used to. Tiny ferns growing out of the rocks listened. Some wore hats of yellow leaves that had fallen.

Panic set in. "Fotis, where are you?" She scanned the steep inclines, quickly looking around. *Oh shit.* Without even realizing it, she drew up both hands to cover her mouth. "Fotis?" her voice quivered.

Then she spotted him. He ran like a ghost atop the ridge, invisible except for the white tip of his tail, scampering sideways down the ravine, negotiating gravity as he made his way toward her.

"How'd you get up there?" Her voice was giddy with relief. As she squatted, he practically dove into her arms, his face beaming. Her chest was heaving. Fotis' eyes were alive.

"I was so afraid you'd run off," she explained. Fotis tilted his head as he listened, oblivious to her worry. Paula cried into his fur like a child, knowing she couldn't bear ever losing him. But Rick was right; it was about trust.

Then Fotis suddenly dashed off again, glancing back, encouraging her to follow.

"Pou pas?" she asked in Greek, wondering where he was going, listening to the thud of his paws as he galloped, zigzagging up and down patterns along the sides of the mossy slopes. She marveled how ill-equipped a human was to follow.

She hoped they weren't lost. Rick had said to follow the water and you couldn't get lost.

She looked down at her patent-leather sandals, crusted with sand, probably ruined. It made her laugh. She took them off and stepped in the pool; her breath caught in her chest at the icy water, as cold as the Atlantic. A pocket of colder, fresh air made her look up. The underwater stones and rocks felt slippery, but the water got no deeper than her thighs as she kept walking. What the hell, if she slipped at least she could swim.

She began to walk up an incline to the sandy portion—funny how water finds its own level. The warm, dry rocks felt good on the arches of her feet.

"Fotis?" she called, and then startled at seeing him somberly standing on a sandbar watching her. His expression was curious, as if he wanted to ask her something.

He watched her clumsily hop atop the last few rocks. "Whew," she said, and leaned over to pet him. His ears lay back and he lifted his head toward her. "You're liking this; I can tell."

As they rounded the bend, orange sunlight lit the side of the cliff face and she entered a pocket of still, humid, suffocating summer air. She started to wonder where they were going. The streambed kept winding in what felt like 180-degree turns back and forth, taking her farther from the guesthouse. Paula stopped. She could go back, but then it might be impossible to find her way back up onto the grassy path. The woods were thick enough to get lost.

She squatted in the moist sand of the streambed to touch the purple, green and speckled rocks, along with a few oval stones shaped like eggs. Then eye level along the bank—growing out of a mossy, rotting log—Paula saw the most beautiful white flower. Her mouth dropped open in awe; it looked like an orchid, perfect as if someone had bought it potted from a Park Avenue florist. She scanned the banks looking for others but saw none. She crept barefoot over to it, crouched silently, afraid she might scare the flower away. The delicacy of the edges, the blooms as long as a finger. There was a faint scent like clean powder.

"You're so pretty," she said, her fingers cradling the blossoms, wanting to press the beauty of it in her mind. It made her think of Roger; this was the first time all afternoon she'd thought of him. How could she describe the flower, the ravines, the sound of Fotis running on the ridges like a phantom, reveling in his freedom? The sight of an eagle foster dad soaring in the flight room or the grateful smile of the mother husky Paula was caring for at Rick's house, her puppies pushing about blindly as they sought her out for food? She wanted to tell Roger how disgusting Sigmund was but how she'd grown to love him nonetheless, how the lead-poisoned eagle had fought his way back and was now healing. She wanted Roger to come here, share her newfound joys, discoveries, and yet she didn't.

"Hey, you," she called as Fotis came running back, splashing through the water, his belly fur dripping with wet strings. He ran over to her and shook off. She held up a hand and laughed, then circled his neck with her arm, kissing him on the muzzle. After she let him go, he gently sniffed the orchid, too, as if knowing it was something fragile and rare.

Through the trees was the vast blue expanse of Superior. Paula walked to where the river met the lake, watching as pools and currents swirled and collided.

She sat down on the sandy beach; the sun was setting west over the horizon. Fotis sniffed and bit at the water. The last ten years felt like a chronic illness. A reluctant husband, a married bachelor—she cringed at her own shame. She could barely feel what it had been like sitting behind her desk at NYU for all those years. Ten years she'd never get back, but maybe it didn't matter anymore. Maybe time had stopped the moment Theo said her name.

She looked at Fotis.

"So, what do you say? Wanna walk back along the beach?" she asked, and stood, brushing sand off her damp shorts. He started trotting back down the shore toward the guesthouse. Tomorrow she'd be in New York. There was nothing to lose because, in a way, she'd already gained everything by having lost it all.

CHAPTER 17

Rick and Eleni drove Paula to the Duluth airport long before there was even a hint of dawn. Though Eleni tried to make small talk, Paula was so engrossed in her own silence that, after only a few miles, her mother had given up. Even Rick was more silent than usual.

The neon moose sculpture suspended over the Duluth airport escalator seemed even more surreal than the day Eleni had arrived. Like it might come to life, break free of its cable moorings, crash through the glass walls and gallop out onto the tarmac and back to the electric woods of its dreams. But maybe that's what you get when you stay up all night, tossing and turning, looking at the clock every hour. Paula's stomach was a pit of hot coals as she cuddled up to Fotis, holding on to him for dear life.

Paula was leaving with only her purse and the clothes on her back, since her things were in New York. Once through airport security she bought a book, hoping to get lost in a story, but instead gave up after reading the first page twelve times. She gave up and sat quietly at the gate, the book in her lap, waiting to board the aircraft.

She sat dazed during the short flight to Minneapolis before changing planes to New York. On the three-hour flight to La Guardia she tried to sleep, shifting her legs so many times in unsuccessful bids to find a comfortable position that the person in front of her finally turned and glared with irritation.

As the minutes ticked down, she pictured Roger waiting at the airport, big smile and arms open wide with a bouquet of flowers—though he already said he'd be tied up at Columbia all afternoon. But she didn't believe him, convinced he was setting her up for a surprise but also hoping he wasn't. Mixed feelings swirled together like contents in a blender; the reunion was far more complex than hugs and flowers and she knew it. And while she'd meet him at the airport after each summer in France, she doubted Roger would drop everything to reciprocate, even with all the talk about starting married life over again.

Though she was excited to see Heavenly and Tony and share her experiences, it was equally impossible to explain them. In trying Paula ran the risk of hurting the couple's feelings by insinuating that they'd failed as friends. But how real, basic and alive she'd been in Grand Marais—could that be translated into her life in New York? Plus it would be impossible to explain why Eleni had stayed behind, sleeping with a puppy, a wolf-dog and a wild turkey vulture. They'd never believe it; Paula barely believed it herself.

Paula looked down at her knees—so strange how a whole little life had generated all because she'd stopped at a roadside café. What if she'd sat at a different table and missed the Cook County newspaper with Rick's ad sitting atop the bee-swarmed garbage can? The whole thing smacked of a page out of the Book of Fate—the Moirai, Clotho in particular. "You can never miss your fate," Eleni would always say. "Even if it feels like it, it only means that your fate isn't what you thought."

The plane landed with a thump, skidding a bit as the engines reversed, thrusting her back against the seat. Paula sighed in relief and looked at her watch. It was 10:00 am, gray and raining in New York. What a surprise. Puddles and the steady patter of raindrops were a dreary reminder that she didn't have an umbrella. She hit the call button on her phone and Roger answered.

"I'm here."

"Oh good, you landed," he said. "Everything go smoothly?"

"Pretty much. I'm heading toward the baggage claim area now. Are you here?"

"No, sweetie," he said. "I told you I'm tied up all day."

"Yeah, I know," she said with disappointment and relief. "I was just hoping you were lying." She was half-lying herself.

"I'm in the middle of something, Paula," he said gently. "I'll see you tonight; I can't wait—I've got a whole dinner planned."

"How sweet," she commented, still partly convinced he was downstairs in the baggage claim area hiding behind one of the pillars. Even though Roger didn't do surprises, her stomach flew with butterflies.

"Love you," he said, and ended the call.

As she crested the top of the escalator to street level, she scanned the gathering of faces, some eager, others bored and chewing gum as they held up signs scrawled with people's names. Roger's polar bear face was not among them.

She stepped off the escalator and searched for several moments. Again she phoned. "Sure you're not here?"

"I told you I can't," he said in a muffled voice as if he was in a meeting.

"Yeah. I know, but I wondered if you were just saying that." She exited the automatic doors and stepped under the awning of the taxi stand to get in line for a cab.

"I'll be home later this afternoon." The call ended. He hadn't sounded annoyed but indifferent—his work voice.

Then her mind started playing with her again as rain pattered on the awning over the taxi stand. Maybe he was at the brownstone waiting. She stopped herself in the middle of that thought.

After the four people queued up ahead of her rode away in taxis, she was up next. Cabs streamed in like the rainwater rushing down the streets into the sewers. The dispatcher pointed to the next cab and opened the back door for her.

"Twenty-fifth and Seventh," she rattled off, and sank back, turning off the obnoxious promotional TV screen that now threatens the serenity of cab rides in New York. The last time she'd been in a cab was with Fotis. She thought about their hike yesterday, remorseful she hadn't taken him on more during the weeks she'd been in Grand Marais.

The cab sped west on the Long Island Expressway approaching the Midtown Tunnel. Resting her head back, she watched the lights of the tunnel blare by with a mix of dread and curiosity as to what had become of the brownstone. The conference on immigrant adaptation had ended last week. No one had called her. Not even a peep out of Guillermo or Christoff, but then again she hadn't called to ask how it went. Fumes of guilt filled her rib cage, but she ignored them.

After exiting the tunnel, the cab turned left toward downtown. The streets were as shiny as an expensive pair of black patent-leather shoes. She was surprised at how nothing seemed to have changed as much as she had over the past five weeks.

Turning down her street, she spoke through the divider. "Here is fine," she instructed the driver, and flipped him far more cash than the fare. The Indian-looking man turned quickly to look at her.

"Keep it." She pushed open the door and climbed out, glancing across the street at the brownstone. Two large black planters with topiary trees and fall mums were stationed on either side of the front door. The chipped and beaten wrought-iron fence and gate were now a shiny black. Even the brownstone's reddish-brown edifice looked crisper, not as dingy. The rain began to pick up. As Paula unlatched the gate it made the same familiar squeak. She pulled out her keys and, hurrying up the front steps, she ducked under the overhang of the doorway. It was a chilly autumn rain, the kind that makes your bones ache; it didn't help that she didn't have a coat.

The front door looked as if it had been stripped down to the wood and then freshly coated with black lacquer. The once indistinguishable brown-tarnished brass knocker and door latch were polished to a bright mirror shine. Paula could see her face. The dead bolt and corresponding brass plate looked new.

Her key didn't even partially insert. She flipped it over and tried again. Still, it was the wrong key to the wrong lock.

She stood there looking at the door, confused. "Well, what the fuck?" Then she used the knocker. "Roger?" It made a deep thunk that reminded her of Dorothy knocking at the palace of the Wizard of Oz. A brass-framed doorbell was attached to the molding surrounding the doorway. The brownstone had never had a doorbell. She pressed it and heard a chime inside, hoping Roger would answer. "Roger, it's me." She rang it several times and then began jabbing it like an obnoxious teenager, but she was met with only silence.

Funny Roger hadn't mentioned replacing the dead bolt. Paula sighed and rubbed her brow; she was tired and didn't need this.

Looking for an obvious place to hide a key, she felt around in the dirt of the new planters. She searched under the welcome mat and along the window ledges. She tried tipping up one of the planters to see underneath, but there was nothing. "Shit." Turning around, she checked the alignment of the gargoyle on the building across the street, just to ensure she was at the right address, and did a double take. She'd never noticed it was an eagle, its wings arched and mouth open as if calling. She'd lived here ten years and had never noticed it was a bird and not a griffin.

What to do. She phoned Roger and it immediately went to voice mail. Figured he'd turn off his phone; she'd used up her call allotment. Sighing in frustration, she left a message, one hand covering her face. "Hi, it's me," she huffed. "I'm at the brownstone, locked out; call me." She couldn't mask her irritation.

Paula walked out of the gate and around to the side of the building, holding her purse over her head to block the rain as she looked for signs of homeless Sophie. Everything had been removed. The bags Paula would leave, even the Dumpster was gone. Sophie had probably moved on to another little camp somewhere else in the City.

Paula crossed the street and stood under the eagle, turning to get a better view of the brownstone. Sheer drapes uniformly covered the front windows. Daylight streamed in from the side and back; you could actually see inside—it was shocking. "Holy shit," she muttered. That meant the place *was* cleared out.

She sat down on the bottom step of the place across the street and phoned Celeste.

"You're back?" Heavenly gushed.

"Yep," Paula said. "Looks like the place is redone; only he forgot to mention the fucking door hardware's been replaced, so I'm locked out."

"You're kidding."

"Nope."

"So where's Einstein?"

"Who the hell knows. At work, in a meeting, taking a shit, what do I know?" she raised her voice.

"I'd come get you, but I can't right now."

"Nah," Paula said. "Don't worry about it; I'll think of something."

Then she called Eleni's new number, a cell-phone number Rick had given her.

"Kukla!" her mother exclaimed. "How was the flight?"

"Fine, Ma, but I'm locked out of my own house."

"You're what?"

"He's got new locks on the door; my key doesn't fit."

"He didn't meet you at the airport?"

"Ma, don't even start," she raised her voice. It was annoying enough without getting egged on even more.

"Can't you get a key?"

"From whom?"

"From him!" her mother hollered.

"No!" she hollered back. "He's in a goddamned meeting and won't pick up his phone."

"So when's Mr. Important coming home?"

"Nice, Ma. Sometime later." She felt herself getting angry at Eleni for echoing her very thoughts and sentiments.

"Go home to Queens, Paula," Eleni said. "Screw him. Do you have your key to my apartment?"

Paula looked down at her key ring. "Yeah."

"Just take the subway."

"Okay." It felt good to be told what to do.

As crowded as New York was, it felt empty. Fotis was gone, Theo and Eleni, too. As Paula sat on the subway, her skin prickled with emotion; it took all she had not to cry. As the subway rocked her, she remembered leaving her first marriage at age eighteen, all her belongings loaded into a paper grocery bag, going home in defeat to Eleni's. And here she was again, this time empty-handed.

She dragged up the subway steps to Union Turnpike in Queens. Feeling the rain saturating the top of her scalp and tickling, she gave up trying to cover her head. Across the street stood Mr. Sanchez, jiggling the key in the lock of his store. "Mr. Sanchez," she called, and darted through traffic, hurrying toward him. "Mr. Sanchez."

"Paula." He waved and motioned to follow him into the shop. She stepped inside. The store was empty. No cages, no aquariums, no checkout counter or cash register. It felt so sad, so unnaturally quiet, devoid of chirping, frantic movement and the squeak of hamster wheels.

"Mom said you're closing the store."

"Yes, it's time," he said on a sigh. "Way too much for me. I heard you're out in Minnesota now working with birds." His eyes lit up as he said it.

She nodded and looked around at the faded posters of exotic birds and fish still on the walls. It was too hard to explain what she didn't understand herself, so she just smiled.

"I'm happy for you, Paula; you take care," he said. "I'm going to live with Mercedes; you remember my daughter—"

"Of course I do; we were in school together."

"She's back in San Juan. Back to Puerto Rico where the sun always feels so good."

"Yeah, especially on such a raw, cold day like this," she said though she could tell he was sad.

"She's married, I have three grandkids."

"Well, you take care, Mr. Sanchez; say 'hi' to Mercedes for me," she said. Paula moved to hug him. "Bye, Mr. Sanchez." She closed her eyes and leaned over, surrounding the man's bony body with her arms. "Thanks for everything," she whispered, and squeezed just a bit longer before releasing him. She then walked out, choked up, knowing she'd never see him again.

Standing outside the storefront for a few moments, she looked into the empty windows that were usually teeming with cages of busy hamsters, parakeets and cockatiels. It was more than she could handle. Paula turned and hurried the two blocks toward Eleni's apartment.

As soon as she opened the door she noticed a pile of Eleni's mail on the kitchen table, probably from Stavraikis. Her phone was ringing. She hoped it was Roger, but it was her mother.

"Are you there?"

"Yeah, just walked in, Ma. Saw Mr. Sanchez. He's moving to live with Mercedes in San Juan."

"He told me. That husband of yours call?"

"Comedy I don't need, Ma."

"How does the apartment look?"

Paula scanned the place and glanced at Theo's painting above the sofa. Her mother's one plant was drooping.

"The same," Paula said as she walked over to feel the soil. "Stavraikis put the mail on the table but forgot to water your plant."

"Did you see him?"

"No." She eyed the schefflera plant; a few faded leaves had dropped onto the counter. "I'll water it." She stepped over to the sink and filled a glass.

"Good. But don't let it sit in water, Paula," Eleni barked orders.

"I won't."

"Water it and wait for the soil to drain and then dump it out, you hear?"

"Yes, Mom, I will take care of it; I'm not a total idiot."

"You're not an idiot at all," Eleni said. "Call me when you hear from that Roger."

"How's Fotis and everyone else?"

"They're all fine. I think he misses you; he hasn't touched food since you left, nothing. I even made *tiropetes*. Rick says he knows you're gone."

"Yeah, probably so." She sighed deeply and began to study the painting over the sofa.

"I'm looking at Theo's painting, Mom."

"Beautiful, isn't it?"

"Yeah, it is. Can't believe I've never really looked at it before."

"Well, you probably had no reason to," Eleni said. "Turn on the TV; relax until you hear from that husband of yours."

"Okay, Mom."

Theo's painting was smallish, no more than a foot high, no more than two across. It was housed in a bright gold-washed wooden frame. The sea was aquamarine and greenish blue, like Lake Superior. The horizon pinkish as it is when the sun is in play. Paula knelt on the couch and touched the wall on either side, leaning closer. Bold brushstrokes blended into shades of mauve, blue and yellow oil paint to create the seascape. Each brush swirled in arcs, the handwriting of Theo's soul. Each an individual fingerprint filled with emotion. Arcs frothed in an upswing like whitecaps in a rough sea. It was breathlessly beautiful. Paula sighed deeply and looked down at the signature floating in the right corner of the sea. "T. Fanourakis."

So that was her real name, like Theo's nephew. Paula Fanourakis. She'd lived her whole life as Makaikis, the name of a man she'd shared nothing with, not affection and now not even blood. She wondered if Theo'd chosen her first name. She stared at the rough sea, at the swirling clouds in the sky, as stormy as she felt. No one in either Vassili's or Eleni's family had been named Paula. Maybe Vassili had been pissed off at Eleni's violation of the protocol of naming Greek children after ancestors. It was almost always strictly observed and when it was not that was considered a grave insult.

Walking into her old bedroom, she gathered a quilt from the foot of her bed and carried it into the living room. Switching on the TV, she cuddled into the couch pillows and looked up at the painting. She began to doze with CNN droning on in the background.

She dreamed the brushstrokes had become moving fingers like underwater sea grass, undulating with the waves, the tides; the whole painting was alive. She reached to touch the fingers and they were warm, not cold like the sea. Then she saw Fotis running with Sam. It woke her. She was infused with a joy, a peacefulness like the glow of the sun on the rocks in Theo's painting. She held on to that for several minutes, relaxing into it as she peacefully drifted back to sleep, clutching one of Eleni's pillows.

Hours later her phone rang from the coffee table. It was Roger.

"Hi," she answered.

"My God, I'm such a dumbshit!" he exclaimed.

"Uhhh . . . yeah."

"Don't be so quick to agree," he said.

She yawned and looked at her watch in the TV light; it was almost seven. The apartment was chilly, but she was warm under the quilt.

"Jesus, I completely forgot that they'd updated the door hardware, including the locks."

"Yes, they did," she said, pulling up the covers to bunch around her chin to trap the warmth.

"Where are you?"

"I'm home at Eleni's."

"Would you go catch a train?" Roger asked. "I'm home."

She yawned again and then fell back into the pillow. "Would you come pick me up?" she countered.

"Pick you up?"

"Yeah, you know, as in go get your car and come and get me."

"It's all the way over on Lexington."

"So what? I'm all the way over in Queens."

He sighed as if it had been a long day and he wasn't up for this.

"Tell you what," she said, hurt, annoyed, yet relieved at the same time. "Why don't I just see you tomorrow?" she suggested. "I'm tired, didn't sleep at all last night. Sounds like you're tired, too. Just leave me a key under one of the planters and I'll let myself in tomorrow." She'd expected him to take the offer but was disappointed by the speed with which he jumped at it.

"Sounds good." Disappointed but not stricken enough to hustle his ass over to Lexington, fire up the car and drive out to Queens. "I guess what's one more day after five weeks," he offered, chuckling in a way she couldn't interpret.

She could have been wrong, but he also sounded relieved.

"Exactly," she played along. "What's one more day?"

"Jerk," she whispered after she ended the call. What a strange exchange. She got up and turned up the thermostat. The refrigerator was empty, but the cabinets were full. Her mother always stocked them like she was prepared to live through another world war. Paula stood on her toes, sorting through the varieties of Progresso and then selected the New England clam chowder. Opening it, she turned the can over, and the whole thing plopped out in one dollop into the pan.

Her phone rang again. Roger changing his mind? It was her mother.

"So what happened?" Eleni asked.

Paula was almost too disgusted with Roger to even explain.

CHAPTER 18

Paula slept peacefully on the couch under Theo's painting and woke the next morning feeling rested.

Earlier Roger had called to ask how she'd slept and to say he was leaving for work around 7:00 am. Typically, Paula would have trouble prying him out before 10:00. He'd promised to leave his phone on so she could call the instant she entered the "new" brownstone. Their plan was to meet there late afternoon; her stomach tightened, dreading everything except coffee.

Just before eight she left to catch the subway back to the City. In the hall outside Eleni's door she bumped into Stavraikis, who'd stepped out to retrieve his newspaper.

The elderly man startled at seeing her. "Paula," he shouted so loud she jumped. "Eleni's back?" The man's face lit up. He held his hand up to his ear, cuing her that he was hard of hearing, though she already knew.

"No," Paula shouted back. "She's staying on for a while longer."

"Ti?" His voice got louder as he cupped his hand to his large hairy ear and leaned closer, inviting her to shout louder.

"She's staying on a bit longer," she shouted, feeling bad for being so loud so early.

"Oh." He quickly wilted. "She must be very happy to stay longer." He nodded as loneliness settled back on him. Paula nodded and waved as she left.

❧

Standing on 25th Street in front of the brownstone. Paula closed her eyes for a moment and touched the gate for assurance. There was a gap under one of the planters indicating that Roger had left a key. She squatted and slipped it out—gold and shiny like a new piece of jewelry.

The key slid in effortlessly; the lock unlatched, unlike the old one, which required a hefty amount of elbow grease. As she depressed the handle, the door swung open with no opposition.

Paula peered into the foyer in shock. It was someone else's house. She expected a person to come rushing downstairs to see who'd let themselves in.

It smelled of potpourri, fresh paint, new fabric and clean wool, smells of another person's home. A burgundy-colored Persian rug lay in the foyer entrance and she stepped around it, taking off her sandals, though she wasn't entirely convinced her feet were much cleaner.

"Hello?" she called, still not convinced someone else didn't live there.

Opposite the staircase was a porcelain vase with cut flowers set on a Federal-style wooden hall table, above it a gilded mirror. Next to it stood a blue and white porcelain umbrella stand. She lifted one of the umbrellas, looking at it. It looked purely ornamental; she was about to test it but then stopped—bad luck to open umbrellas in a house.

A small crystal chandelier worthy of a grand old house had replaced the naked lightbulb fixture that had been there since the first day she'd moved in. The ceilings were so high they required a ladder to change the bulb, often taking Roger months to dig one out. She'd always shied away from calling someone in for fear of them filing a report with the City Health Department.

The walls were warm, creamy beige and glowing with morning light, the woodwork and moldings fresh, white enamel. Walking down the narrow hall, she turned into what she'd always believed should be a dining room. A long ornate wooden table filled the space; she recognized the carving on each corner from his

parents' table that had long been buried. "Katya," she said Roger's mother's name. Her fingertips traced the grooves of the vines.
Seating for eight and underneath was another large burgundy-
colored Persian rug that was room sized, leaving only the edges of
a wood floor visible. Perhaps these were the carpets she'd seen
folded in tall stacks. She bent down to feel the pile of the wool.
"All this time," she said. So this was what they looked like; she
studied the swirling design after having wondered for so many
years.

"Holy shit," she said. Even stranger to hear her voice echo off
the empty corners of the room. What had happened to the mountains of cardboard boxes and piles of couches? Paula's mouth
hung open, circling the room, feeling like she'd been abducted by
an issue of *Architectural Digest*. The room looked so large and
formal. She couldn't imagine sitting down for a meal here, but
maybe Roger could; maybe he'd grown up that way.

Long, sheer creamy drapes were illuminated by the window
light, pooling in graceful puddles on the floor. The wood floors
throughout looked as though they'd been replaced; the old ones
had been scratched and badly stained with mold. Along one side
of the room was a long, narrow hutch with a display of graceful
old plates with burgundy patterns she'd didn't recognize. Against
the far wall was a matching walnut sideboard, a silver soup ter-
rine and assorted objets d'art. Maybe these were what had clanked
about in boxes every time she'd move or bump them.

Paula walked back into the hallway and down to the living
room on the left. It reflected the same colors. A grand ornate
marble fireplace stood against the outside wall. She'd never seen
the fireplace before, but it looked at least a century old. And to
think she'd sat only a few feet away from it, buried, and never
known it was there. Now the fireplace mantel was the living
room showpiece.

A large ornate Venetian mirror set atop the fireplace mantel,
reflecting light and offsetting the simple, modern furnishings.

Rising up onto her toes, Paula looked at herself. She looked shoddy and out of place, her hair frizzy.

Paula covered her mouth with her hands as she looked toward the back of the building. A wall had been removed. Brownstones typically were long and narrow, broken up into smaller rooms that often served no purpose in modern life. You could see right through to the back windows of the house; how on earth could Roger have allowed this without having a nervous breakdown?

She walked back into what looked like a gourmet restaurant kitchen. White marble counters and backsplashes, stainless appliances, washtubs, vegetable sprayers and spigots, plus an eat-in space built into the back of the brownstone. A table and chairs were framed by a bay window with a window seat—all reflected the same color theme—safe, but stunning. Sunlight streamed in. The house had shed a hundred years; it brought tears to her eyes, though not for her sake. It's what she'd always wanted for the house. Just like her barred owl and eagle, the house too was rehabilitated, resurrected back to life.

The entire second floor was a newly created master suite. The floor was carpeted with plush off-white carpet. Walk-in his and hers closets. Paula was startled to see all her clothes, shoes and bags in one of them. The other closet was Roger's.

Paula spotted her couch that had stood downstairs up on end for a decade. Here it was the focal point of a little sitting area opposite the bed. She plopped down on her sofa and hugged it. "Hello," she said, rubbing her hand on the fabric. Her couch smelled like dry-cleaning fluid; she examined it—the fabric had been cleaned.

At the foot of the bed lay another Persian rug, a match to the one in the foyer. Opposite the bed was a wall-length antique-looking silk tapestry depicting a Tree of Life with colorful birds. It brought her to tears. The room smelled of jasmine and fresh paint. The master bathroom was white marble, the soaking tub lined with vanilla candles, like something you'd find at a resort or in a cheesy movie.

The third-floor rooms were turned into guest suites and two studies—one for Roger, another for her. Their computers, books and work material had all been sorted and arranged into a series of built-in shelf units. They looked like props until she looked closer to see her books, journals and files all neatly organized into bins and drawers. Someone had gone through and organized them with more care and thought than she'd ever given.

It must have cost Roger a fortune, but then again he had one. It was too good, too nice, but he'd done it for her. She sat down in her study on a white-covered chair and phoned him.

Roger immediately picked up.

"I-I can't believe it," she said, and then quickly stood, afraid her jeans would soil the fabric. Leaving the study, she sat down on the top step of the staircase.

"Nice, isn't it?" He sounded thrilled.

"I'm speechless."

"All summer they've worked on it. They finished last weekend."

"I'm in shock." Paula stood and walked down to the bedroom, glancing in the doorway, studying the tapestry. "I don't want to touch a thing."

"I want you to touch it. We'll both be touching it later," he said. The desire in his voice rekindled hers.

"When'll you be home?"

"Around three."

"I can't wait," she said.

"Me neither. I love you; I'm glad you're happy."

She wasn't sure "happy" was the right word. It was too much. She ended the call and scurried downstairs, slipped into her sandals and left—locking the door behind her.

Hurrying over to Madison Square Park, she veered toward a bench. The wooden seat had warmed in the sun and it felt good against her back. She sat dazed and then looked up at the trees as her emotions whirled.

She covered her face and sat for several moments, shaking her head; what had Roger done? How were they supposed to live in that house? It was created for other people. She thought of her little guesthouse in Grand Marais. Even Rick's cabin was homey, with a warm and lived-in feel. This was a dollhouse, and Lord knows, she was no doll.

Birds caught her attention as they flew from tree to tree. She thought of her eagle and the redtail hawk with the broken wing that Rick had admitted the day before she left. Sounds of dogs play-barking in the dog run made her homesick for Fotis. However would he live as a city dog—with all that white linen furniture, the silk duvet on the bed? She thought of him snuggled up in the loft of the guesthouse. Dried bits of mud from his paws, but she hadn't minded. She even missed disgusting Sigmund, though she'd never let him know it, however one keeps such knowledge from a turkey vulture. Maybe Roger had meant to lure her back to New York using the new house. But what about Fotis? In all that splendor she hadn't seen a dog bed or a place for him.

Paula crossed her legs and sighed. She looked at her watch, imagining the eagle in the flight room, struggling to build muscle strength and endurance in order to live as a wild bird once again. The feel of the wind from his wings on her face as he'd swoop down onto a carcass—or watching the bird pant to catch his breath after circling the flight room several times.

Rick and Maggie were both probably scurrying about doing their chores as the day began. "Oh, you can always come back and visit," people had said, even Heavenly. And though well-meaning, the words made Paula angry. She reached into her purse and unzipped the inside compartment, digging around for her wedding ring. She felt Psyche's golden frame; she'd forgotten about the lost cameo and picked up the empty frame, studying it for a moment before tucking it back in. She felt the edge of her wedding ring and slipped it on. It was tight. She pulled out her hand and looked; either her fingers were swollen or they'd grown larger with all the work at Northern Lights Wildlife. In the past it had always been a bit loose. Nothing felt right. A long walk might do her good, and she began the twenty-block hike down Fifth Avenue toward Washington Square and her office.

She slowed as she reached the park, scanning for familiar faces though it was too early for her staff to be out for lunch. Approaching from the park side, she spied her office window; no birds sat on the ledge, at least at the moment, and she thought she saw someone's head at her desk. And while she'd considered popping in to say hi, the specter of two more weeks of leave constrained her. Instead she stood there feeling hollow, studying the outside of her window, the blackened area of the screen where she'd blown cigarette smoke for years. Hard to believe she'd spent fifteen years holed up in that little room. She imagined herself walking down the grassy path along the lake toward the guesthouse—how easily she'd gotten used to that. Taking out her phone, she called Celeste.

"So what happened?" Heavenly answered.

"What didn't?"

"*Miksa*—I'm starving for an early lunch. Hop on the subway; meet me at The Acropolis." It was a Greek dive with every cliché imaginable. For years they'd meet for lunch there since it was near the hospital in Queens and Celeste's office. "I'll buy; you can fill me in. I have a quiet schedule, so we can linger."

≿

Over a Greek salad with too few olives and the waitstaff giving Paula hell for staying away for so long, she spilled the story of Theo and Eleni to Heavenly.

"Shit," Heavenly said, waving a hand dismissively at her. "That was an easy one. I could've told you that day the old guy had a thing with your mother."

"Bullshit." Paula looked up to challenge.

"Excuse me?" Heavenly looked up at her like *what are you, stupid*? "Eleni's brain freeze on the phone?" Heavenly smirked. "Do I look like I was born yesterday?"

"Whatever," Paula said with a full mouth while rolling her eyes.

Heavenly started digging around in her salad. "Shit. Now they're skimping on olives." She looked back toward the kitchen. "First feta, now this," Celeste mumbled.

"Go bitch to Giorgos." Paula motioned with her head toward the kitchen. "He's back there; I just saw him."

"Forget it."

"You're all talk."

They sat awhile before the waitress brought coffee.

"So, how are you doing with discovering that Vassili wasn't your father?" Heavenly asked with her social worker's voice.

"At first it was a shock." Paula stirred in milk from the little white pitcher. "But deep down I sort of always knew."

"It's funny you say that." Heavenly looked up and smiled. "Lots of people in your situation say the same thing."

"I'd watch how other people's fathers treated them. They'd look comfortable around their kids. Vassili was on guard or like he was sitting on tacks when I was in the room, like I was gonna steal a fork or something. Sometimes I'd hide in the kitchen to eat; he made me so uncomfortable."

Heavenly looked sad. "I'm sorry."

Paula took another sip of the coffee and thought of Eleni. "God bless America," she would always say after a sip of good coffee.

"But then a stranger thing happened," Paula said. "After the shock subsided, relief kicked in. I didn't say anything to her, but it did."

Heavenly shifted her position in the booth. "Shit, maybe I'll find out my old man really isn't *my* father," she grumbled. They both laughed.

"It was kind of like a liberation, Heav. Shock, then liberation."

"Or a birthday—'cause let's face it." Heavenly raised her coffee mug in salute. "Vassili was always an asshole to you," she confessed. "*I* remember."

"Maybe now I can look back and say at least it wasn't me."

"Au contraire," Heavenly joked. "We actually now know it

really *was* you." They both started laughing in a way reminiscent of sitting at the Oklahoma Café with Marvelline and Maggie. They laughed until their faces hurt, but it kept on getting funnier the longer it went on, to the point where Giorgos peeked out from the delivery window with a pained expression.

Paula told Heavenly about Theo's painting and the details that Eleni had shared on the beach that day on Lake Superior.

"Sounds like schizophrenia from what you told me before," Celeste said.

"That's what I thought, too."

"Poor guy."

Celeste looked unimpressed as Paula told her about the brownstone's transformation. A wry little smile crossed Heavenly's mouth. "So where do you think it's all stashed?"

"What?"

"Einstein's crap."

Paula looked dumbfounded and then lowered her eyes. She'd been caught up in the Roger zone after seeing the bed, talking with him. "I asked him back in Grand Marais. He says he's gotten rid of it all."

"And you believe it?" Celeste held Paula's gaze. "All right then, so you know he didn't just snap out of it one night after much careful consideration." Heavenly snapped her fingers. "It's mental illness, Paula. Like Theo but different. The hoard's been stashed elsewhere."

"Where?" Paula asked. Roger's hoard could be anywhere. There were so many storage warehouses throughout the City, it would be impossible to track down.

They both sat thinking. "Too bad you don't have more time today, Heav; you gotta see this place. You wouldn't believe the change."

"I just remember when the two of you first started dating, shit piled up in the foyer; I couldn't even see inside. I swear to God, I thought he was moving in—all the boxes, the chaos. Check out the cellar, attic."

"I will."

"But from what you told me after you left, there was a lot more than would fit into an attic or cellar."

"Probably so." Paula sighed deeply. "Some of it the designer repurposed, like the Persian rugs, the dining room table, plus some other things I recognized." Paula looked at her watch. Maybe she could snoop around before Roger got home.

CHAPTER 19

It was almost two by the time she got to the brownstone. And just as she opened the front door, Roger came sailing downstairs with open arms. Their eyes met and she melted, having forgotten how he made her feel. He led her upstairs without either of them saying a word.

They began making love in the beautiful new bedroom where he'd already drawn the shades, only there was a terrible sadness about it this time. His face and eyes were even more striking than she'd recalled and it hurt to look at him. Afterward as they dozed, the doorbell rang.

"Stay here." He dashed naked into the bathroom. She'd forgotten how fit and muscular his body was for a man his age, when all Roger did was sit day and night in front of computers and scientific instruments. He walked out wearing one of those thick white terry-cloth robes that upscale resorts provide and headed downstairs. She heard him talking.

He came right back up and knelt on the bed with an impish smile. She sat up, reaching for him, and snuggled against his neck. "Everything's being prepared," he said. "Relax, take a bath in the new bathroom and dinner will be ready." He crawled back under the covers with her. Her throat stung with tears as she grasped him.

"Hey, hey, hey," he said, pushing back to look at her face. "What's all this about?"

She didn't have words. "It's so beautiful," *and so late,* she thought but didn't say. "I'll always love you, Roger," she said in a way that made him look at her strangely.

"Well, I'll always love you, too." He chuckled and kissed the top of her head. "Wait here." He stepped back into the bathroom. Bathtub water was running and after a while he walked out. "Go," he said, smiling. "Go look."

She slipped on her T-shirt, still too embarrassed to walk naked in front of him after all these years. There was a glow from the bathroom; he'd lit the candles around the tub.

"This is just lovely." She covered her mouth with both hands, still in Roger's spell.

"You relax," he said. "I thought this would be better than going out. We have our own little resort now."

She closed the bathroom door and moved the candles up onto the vanity—all she needed was to set her hair on fire. The warm water was heaven as she slipped into the tub—only it made her cry again. She did so in silence so he wouldn't hear, wouldn't know and wouldn't ask more questions. Damn it, what was wrong with her?

As she was using her cosmetics that someone had organized by function—eye shadow, mascara, moisturizer—it was weird to think someone had fingered all her things, giving more thought to them than she typically did.

She fixed her face, put on clothes that the "personal organizer" had sorted in "her" walk-in closet. Blouses, skirts and pants hung separately. Purses and shoes were all matched and sorted into cubbies by color and pattern. On one hand, it was pleasing to see everything so beautifully displayed, yet she felt violated in the way she had when someone had broken into her old apartment years ago and went through all her things, including her underwear, looking for valuables.

In the middle of the closet was an island of drawers devoted to her jewelry collection. She didn't even look.

Paula took in a few deep breaths as Heavenly would always

instruct her to do when she was upset. She checked the mirror—
the pink nose was a dead giveaway that she'd been crying. She
loaded up her cheeks with blush.

As she walked downstairs, the smell of garlic and rice was intoxicating.

They made love again late that night, this time in a very lazy way.
She didn't even remember falling asleep; the sun woke her early
to find that Roger was gone. She looked at the clock. It was six
thirty.

"Roger?" She searched him out. Stepping into the master bathroom, she grabbed one of the white terry robes and slipped it on.
"Roger?" She peeked in his closet and then walked upstairs to his
study. The room was dark. She then turned and walked into her
study. There was a Post-it note stuck to her computer keyboard.
"*P—Had to go in early today, see you later for dinner, love, R.*" He
never left for work this early.

She dashed back down to the bedroom, searching in her purse
for her cell phone, and punched his number. Of course it went to
voice mail. Going back up to her study, she fired up her laptop
and e-mailed him. "Why so early? I miss you already. Where are
you? Couldn't you stay?" After hitting the send key, she felt the
same old gnawing ache that traveled down to her fingertips in
waves of hurt. Only this time it felt worse. After six weeks of not
feeling it she'd forgotten how bad it was. "Shit, shit, shit." She
walked down the staircase into the kitchen in search of something to eat.

It felt like someone else's kitchen. She opened the refrigerator;
it was filled with wholesome food items that required more
thought and preparation than she was prepared to invest.

At least the coffee grinder and beans looked simple enough,
and after searching through yards of cabinetry she finally located
a coffeepot. It took several tries to figure out how to use the faucet and stove just to set a pot of water on to boil. Paula leaned

against the counter, crossing her arms and tucking her fingers into her elbows. It felt like Roger had deserted her in a stranger's house. He'd said nothing about having to leave early. As stupid as it was, she couldn't stop her feelings from being hurt.

While waiting for the water to boil, she remembered what Heavenly had said. Paula walked to open what had been the cellar door, only now it was a pantry, stocked with food she hadn't bought.

"Jesus," she said in mild shock, and shut the door to make it go away. Behind another door was a shiny washer/dryer still with tags. Finally a third new door led down to the cellar. Flipping on the light, she stepped halfway down; it smelled like fresh paint and new carpeting. The entire cellar had been drywalled and turned into a finished basement. It was empty.

She sprinted back up to the boiling water and ground a cup's worth of beans, pouring it all into the French press to steep. Then she bolted up all four flights of stairs to the attic. She stood there for a moment looking around. Roger had kept it locked so that she wouldn't go up there, but now there was no lock. Reaching up, she pulled the cord, and the stairs folded down. She climbed up and looked—it too was empty. She'd been half-hoping to find something, a stack of old newspapers, anything.

Before pouring her coffee, she stopped in the bedroom and slipped on jeans, a T-shirt and a cardigan. She paused by Roger's closet; it was mostly empty. Spotting his suitcases stacked against the wall, she wondered if he hadn't yet unpacked. She unzipped and looked. The suitcases were empty. She then rummaged through the drawers in his island. Except for underwear and socks, they were empty, too.

Stepping into the bathroom, she washed her face. Roger's toiletries were as scarce as his clothes. A can of his shaving cream on the sink reminded her she'd forgotten the two bags full of his shaving cream she'd bought at Maggie's store on her first day in Grand Marais. It was probably still dark in Minnesota. She pictured the sky beginning to lighten along the horizon as it would when she'd start walking with Fotis down the grassy path in the chilly pre-dawn hours to find Rick.

Something felt uncomfortable. Who was this personal organizer? Maybe she'd give this person a call. Paula rifled around Roger's closet, searching for a business card, an invoice, anything, but all she found were the typical receipts from the restaurants and bagel shops around Columbia. Walking up the stairs, two at a time, to his office, she flipped on the light and rummaged through his files.

"Well, this is weird." She headed downstairs, stopping to grab her purse from the bedroom.

Standing against the countertop, she poured her first cup of coffee and listened to her messages. Heavenly had called, saying that she and Tony wanted to have dinner that night—a welcome back dinner for Paula and Roger. Another message from Eleni said that Loukoumi had diarrhea since Paula had left but that Darryl checked him out, wormed him again and that not to worry, the puppy was now fine. She smiled thinking of them. Looking around the kitchen, she left the cup of coffee standing on the kitchen counter and headed out to McDonald's on Sixth Avenue to get coffee and an Egg McMuffin.

Paula called Roger again as she hovered with coffee and food in her hands, waiting for an elderly couple to gather their things and vacate a booth so she could sit. His phone immediately went to voice mail, this phantom husband of hers.

"Hi, call me," she said. "I'm thinking of inviting Tony and Celeste over for a welcome back dinner and to show off the house. If I don't hear from you by ten, I'm inviting them and shopping for food."

Roger called after a few minutes.

"What a great idea," he said. "I'll invite Jackson and Heather, too, and a few others. Call the caterer. Their card is up on the fridge—it's a magnet. Are you home enjoying the kitchen?"

"Yeah," she lied, looking around as if to tell everyone within earshot to keep it down.

"Who's talking?"

"It's just the radio."

"What radio?"

She ignored the question. "If the caterer can't on short notice, maybe they can recommend."

"Last night was amazing," Roger said. "You're amazing." His tone made her blush.

"How come you left?"

"Had to go in early."

"How early?"

"Early," he said. "Didn't want to wake you."

She wanted specifics but left it. The familiar muzzle of silence fell over her. *Don't ask or push. Don't be the pain-in-the-ass wife; turn the other cheek and let it be.*

"Let me know what happens with the caterer," he said. "Say, dinner for ten at eight tonight. I'll invite some of the Foundation people."

"Okay."

"I love you."

"Me too."

Paula ate quickly and then hurried back to the brownstone. The caterer's magnet was right where Roger had described. Luckily the caterer had a last-minute cancellation and was only too happy to recoup the lost work, plus the previous client's cancellation fee.

Paula phoned Heavenly, telling her about the dinner party. "So can you guys come?"

"Uhh . . . sure," Heavenly said.

"Well, you don't sound too excited about it."

"I was thinking a more casual dinner and not the Coronation. You know, pants with an elastic waist, braless, but for you, my darling"—Heavenly used one of her funny voices—"anything."

"I owe you."

"Bullshit."

"Yeah, yeah, yeah," Paula said. "I searched the place—nothing. Recognized some of his parents' antiques, but the junk's gone."

"Hmmm." Heavenly was thinking. "I'll call around, see what I can find. I'll ask Tony. Sometimes he hears stuff around the precinct."

"Thanks," Paula said. "Maybe you can pick up some sort of 'vibe' from him tonight, you know, that old-lady Sicilian village thing," Paula said, half-teasing, half grasping for answers.

"You miss it, don't you?"

"The junk?"

"No, genius—being out there. Your birds."

It came from out of the blue, catching Paula off guard. "What makes you ask that?"

"You know, that old-lady Sicilian village thing," Heavenly said. "I can . . . hear it."

Paula was quiet.

"I know you do, *miksa mou,*" Heavenly taunted her.

"Yeah, Heav, I do," she said, not wanting to sound ungrateful for their friendship. "More than you know."

The caterer arrived promptly at five and began with preparations. It felt like crashing someone else's party and Paula didn't know what to do with herself. She wasn't used to watching people work. Several times she'd offered to set out plates, silverware, anything, but the staff looked annoyed. Instead she slinked upstairs and paced, biding time by e-mailing Rick until Roger came home. She asked about Eleni, Fotis, the eagle and the new cases that had been admitted since she'd left. She asked about Maggie and Ephraim and Marvelline. Rick e-mailed Paula right back, having been up all night and day with a newly admitted eagle patient that had lead poisoning. The levels were so high they didn't even register on the lead analyzer. Rick was trying out a new method of detoxing another rehabilitator had recommended, and it was going to be another long night. She could picture it all so clearly, the smells, the sound of the analyzer when it was off the charts. She missed it. Heavenly was right.

Roger came home by six and Paula met him at the front door as if she were Fotis greeting her after a long day.

Swinging from Roger's index finger were dry-cleaner hangers covered with plastic. He kissed her and she followed him up to the master suite, leaning on the doorframe of his closet near the newly hung clothes, listening to the sound of shower water hitting the tiles. As he was drying off from the shower she remarked. "So, uh . . . what's happened to all of your clothes?"

He startled at the sound of her voice. "Oh." He chuckled. "These were at the dry cleaner's."

"I can see that, Roger. I'm talking about everything else." She felt like she was speaking to someone who could only read lips. "Did you forget them in France?"

He looked at his closet door and then glanced back at her, his face an open question mark.

"It's empty," she framed it for him. "Did the personal organizer ditch them?"

Paula gestured at the two pairs of pants and three hanging shirts. "When I left you had more than this. Remember? We went shopping last spring." Funny she should be scolding him for having too little of something; the irony was not lost on her.

"When the organizer called," he began, "she said so many of my pants were ratty and outdated she asked to toss them."

"Ratty?" Paula raised her voice. "They were new." Who was this personal organizer? Paula imagined the woman had put them in a resale shop or else had a husband that size who was walking around in Roger's clothes.

"I told her to toss whatever she thought," he said, holding up both hands in a *don't shoot* gesture. "I brought shorts and jeans to France," he said. "When I came home, this was what was left." It sounded plausible. Roger always sounded plausible, though now a bit nervous with Paula's cross-examination.

"She got rid of *everything*? Look." She twirled around in the empty closet, exaggerating to illustrate the empty space.

He shrugged in a way that said it was out of his hands.

"How come she didn't throw out any of mine?"

He shrugged again. "Maybe you have better taste."

She stared at him in disbelief, her face incredulous. "So now we have to go shopping to repurchase what we bought you last May," she said.

His face looked almost gray, as uncomfortable as she'd ever seen Roger look. "I don't have time now." He frowned, drying off his legs and arms from the shower, and then draping the towel around his waist.

"You need clothes, Roger." She scowled in a wifely way and her voice got louder. "You spend umpteen hundreds of thousands of dollars creating this palace; you can't go walking around in shorts and a T-shirt."

"I don't have time for this." He raised his voice along with his hands, urging her to calm down and lower her voice. "As soon as this photon project—"

Whatever. She turned into the bathroom, closed the door and stripped down, standing on the cold tile in the shower, trying to figure out how to turn it on.

The dinner went as planned, Roger entertaining the Foundation crowd as if he always stood poised in the living room this way. He was graceful and at ease, seamlessly moving around with an assurance that made her curious about the man who got so agitated if she moved one of his piles or questioned him about where something was. It was like a magical pill had cured whatever it was that had kept him stymied for so many years. And the more relaxed and comfortable he seemed, the more out of place she felt.

He turned on the gas fireplace insert in the living room with the flip of a switch and leaned against the marble mantel with a glass of wine, swirling it about as he laughed with a colleague. She couldn't look at him. A whole well of resentment rose from nowhere and she felt like she could hurl one of the vanilla-scented candles at him.

Paula looked at her watch. Where the hell were Tony and Celeste? Just as she felt ready to scream, the doorbell chimed. One of the caterers moved to answer it. "I'll get it," Paula sang, and raced from the room.

"Oh thank God you're here." She stepped out into the doorway and clutched them both.

"Jeez, party's that good, huh?" Tony said.

Paula laughed as she shifted to hug him tightly. "Thank God you're here," Paula said again.

"Jesus Christ, let go, Paula; I can't breathe," he joked.

Paula ushered them in, giving a tour of the house.

Celeste tapped her arm in the master suite and pointed. "Isn't that your couch?" she whispered.

"Yup. You don't have to whisper."

"Yeah, I know, but I feel like I should," Heavenly whispered back.

"This is fucking gorgeous, Paula," Tony said. Both he and Celeste stood ogling and not believing their eyes.

"Yeah, no meth labs, huh, Tone." Heavenly elbowed him. As they walked down from the third floor, both Paula and Celeste stopped to sit on the stairs.

"It's all very odd," Paula said.

Tony sat on the step below, looking at the creases in his hands. "You know, Paula, for all the years you've lived here, this is the first time I've ever been in this house."

"I'm so sorry, Tone." She leaned over, hugging him and kissing the side of his head. "You wouldn't have wanted to be; I swear."

"Yeah, Heav told me. Strange how out in the street people seem perfectly normal. But there's lotsa weird shit behind the walls of New York City. Behind any city for that matter."

The three of them sat for a while before making their way down to the dinner party. "So what's next for you and Roger?" Tony asked on the way downstairs.

Paula didn't answer.

Roger slept right through until morning. He drank and ate so much at the dinner party that it was more like he'd passed out, and she was relieved to wake and find him still there.

CHAPTER 20

For the next few days Paula wandered around Manhattan like a lost child. She couldn't settle into the brownstone and preferred a park bench or the McDonald's around the corner.

And while Roger was home every night for dinner, more often than not she woke in the morning to find herself alone. One night, she awakened to find him pulling on his pants to leave.

"You're going?" She yawned and sat up. He kissed her mouth before it was even closed and hurried off.

"I just got an idea; I'm going in while the lab is quiet."

"Oh, Roger, again?"

"Sorry, sweetie, I'll see you at lunch today. Sarbonne's? Noon?"

She nodded and yawned again but couldn't sleep after he left.

Later that evening they were rushing to get ready for a Friday dinner on the Island with some of his friends from the Foundation. She pressured him to commit to going shopping the next day for clothes.

"I don't have time," Roger dismissed. He walked back into the bathroom and lathered up his face with shaving cream in a hurried bid to get cleaned up and ready.

She stood in the doorway of the bathroom to watch. The words made sense, but he didn't. Back to the old state of confusion—the old eggbeater in the brain school of personal relationships. No one else but Roger made her feel like this, the one person she wanted.

"How come you don't work at home like you used to?"

He turned to her, his face covered with a white foam Santa's beard. She would have laughed had it not been for the seriousness of the moment.

"I thought I told you, new security protocol." He turned back to slice off part of Santa's beard. "None of us can work from home anymore." His voice echoed in the marble bathroom. "This photon project's crazy." He bent over and kissed her, leaving a drop of shaving cream on her cheek. She couldn't tell if he was acting guilty or not. "It'll be over soon."

"I'll say no more." She threw up her hands. "Soon you'll be leaving at the crack of dawn up to Columbia balls-ass naked," she said.

"You about ready?" The keys jingled in his hand. They still needed to catch a cab to Lexington to fetch his car from the garage.

"Yeah," she said halfheartedly.

Though Roger fell right asleep that night, Paula catnapped, keeping a watchful eye in case he got up to leave, determined to sneak out and follow him to see if he really was going uptown to Columbia. At one point he'd got up to go to the bathroom; she lay still, silent, holding her breath, listening for sounds of him preparing to leave. Instead he flopped back into bed, turned around and promptly fell asleep, snoring loudly. Reassured, she let herself surrender to sleep sometime after 2:00 am only to awaken and find him gone once again. "Shit, shit, shit." She threw her bathrobe onto the floor, cursing herself for having dropped her guard.

The next evening they went to a movie and afterward Paula sat guzzling cups of restaurant coffee as their friends sipped aperitifs.

"Careful, sweetie," Roger cautioned. "You'll be up all night."

Although her body was humming from the caffeine, she pretended to be asleep as Roger tossed and turned. He was having a restless night and she fully expected him to be up and out by midnight. She'd readied a pile of clothes—her clogs and purse were in the corner near her couch—primed for a quick exit. But Roger slept right through until morning.

She was up long before he was, a fresh pot of coffee sitting on the counter, the *Times* alongside it where Roger had taken to sitting in the morning.

"Morning, sweetie." He reached over to kiss her. Paula poured him a cup of coffee as he sat on the stool in front of the newspaper. She poured herself one and left it sitting on the counter.

"So tell me where you go off to in the wee hours of the morn?" she asked again.

He sipped the coffee, looking at the headline. "And why does this bear repeating?" he said without looking up. "It's a security violation to work online, I told you. I can't even gain access from home. So I go into the lab while the ideas are coming."

"Why not just jot them down on a notepad? Take it with you in the morning?"

He picked up the main section of the newspaper in a way that said, *Drop it.*

"Why not?"

He didn't answer and instead opened the first page, scanning the articles.

"Is it so top secret that if terrorists break in you'd have to wad up the paper and swallow it?" she said sarcastically.

He gave her a *stop busting my balls* look and turned the page, her cue that the conversation was over.

"You take the subway all the way uptown to Columbia in the middle of the night?"

"Cab."

"Must be tough to find a cab that time of night," she said. Maybe he'd met someone overseas. There'd been no overt signs such as unexplained fragrance, lipstick and whatnot. His underwear was as dingy and depressing as ever—you'd have thought the "personal organizer" would have culled them along with everything else. It was easy to picture someone else in his arms. Nothing would surprise her, and the idea didn't even elicit the usual scorch of jealousy.

"Okay, what?" He lowered the newspaper.

"What do you mean, 'What?'" she asked, lifting her hand.

"You have the strangest look on your face," he said.

"I was just wondering if you're having an affair," came flying out before she could squelch it.

He dropped back his head and sighed with relieved disgust. "Why do women always think their husbands are cheating?"

"Because, darling, statistics show that ninety-nine percent of the time they are."

The paper rustled as he set it aside and patted his thigh, motioning for her to come over and sit. "Now why would I go and do that when I have you?" She let him take her in his arms as she straddled his thigh. "Paula, I love you." He kissed her deeply and she responded. "There's no one else; there's never been."

She believed him about that but not much else. "I know."

"'I know'?" he said, laughing. "That's all you can say is 'I know'?"

She looked at him mysteriously; *mysterioudis,* they say in Greek.

"Anything else you want to ask while you're at it?" he asked in a sardonic way.

"Yeah." She paused and stood. "What happened to all of your stuff, Roger? Let's face it: for ten years you wouldn't let me throw out the garbage, much less allow 'organizers'"—she used her fingers as quotation marks—"to come in to touch and throw out your stuff."

His face hardened.

"Where is it? I'm curious," she continued. "It's like someone's lifted up the brownstone, turned it over and shaken everything out."

He laughed darkly at her imagery.

"It's not funny," she said.

"You have this way of putting things."

She rose and stepped away. Folding her arms, she felt a torrent of anger that took her by surprise. "It would have taken an army of cleaners weeks to have gone through everything with you." She fought to keep calm.

"Is that all you care about?" he asked quietly.

"You were in France until last weekend, Roger. Did you Skype with the personal organizer while underground in the collider?" She crossed her arms and studied his face like the eagle had studied hers that first day in the raptor ICU, and she could tell Roger didn't like it.

He squirmed under her scrutiny and stood. "What's happened to you?" he asked in the condescending tone she hadn't heard since she'd left. "You got what you wanted, you're still not happy."

It was more emotion than she'd ever seen from him.

"What more do you want from me?" he said, and left the room. She'd never seen him angry in such a naked, exposed way. But she didn't go running after him blubbering an apology like she might have months ago.

Moments later he came bounding downstairs with his keys jingling. The front door shut hard, though there was too much new weather stripping around it to give the satisfaction of a good slam.

CHAPTER 21

Paula felt surprisingly calm after Roger stormed out of the house. He'd never done it before and she was blasé, almost removed. She walked upstairs with a cup of coffee of which she hadn't yet taken a sip and headed toward her couch to watch the Sunday morning news shows; it wasn't even eight. Carrying her phone, she thought he might call to apologize.

She moved her pile of "hot pursuit" clothes onto the floor and sat, putting up her feet as she flipped on the TV. Her phone beeped. She knew it, a text: "Sorry for acting like a jerk. Lunch? 11 am? Make it up to you at Sarbonne's. Love, R." She texted back: "Of course." She smiled, not in victory but ready for answers.

Then something under the chair caught her attention. A crumpled piece of paper where he'd tossed his pants the night before. She tumbled off the couch and crawled over. It was a schedule for the Staten Island Ferry; early-morning departure times were marked with a pen.

Suddenly she remembered the property Roger owned on Staten Island. He never spoke of it; the only time she'd been there was just after they were married. A police officer phoned about a neighbor's complaint that a loose shutter was banging against the side of the house after a bad storm. Roger had been in France, so Paula had fielded the call, contacting the property management company who saw to it that Roger's Staten Island house met all the city codes. She'd taken the ferry and a cab to the address, watched as the shutter was reattached, and as far as she knew assumed that it was the end of the story.

She stood up, looking at the rumpled schedule and then in the mirror at herself, wearing the periwinkle silk nightshirt he'd brought her from France. Why would he go to Staten Island? Running up to his office with the ferry schedule in hand, she rummaged through files, his desk drawers, looking for property tax bills, something indicating he still owned the place. She came up empty except for a key ring with three keys, none of which she recognized.

She sat down at the desk, thinking. Trying to remember the street, anything, but it was so long ago and she hadn't paid much attention at the time.

"Tony," she said out loud, and phoned Heavenly.

"You killed him," Heavenly answered.

"Not yet. Is Tony there?"

"Yeah. But I'll warn you he hasn't had coffee."

"Neither have I."

"Hey, doll, what's up?" Tony said.

"Sorry for bugging you so early, but think you could find an address for me?"

"You got a name?"

"It's Roger."

She sprang into motion. Pulling off the nightshirt, she slipped into the ready pile of clothes she'd set on the floor. Grabbed her clogs, purse and phone and the piece of paper with the address Tony had found in the police database. Running downstairs, she locked the door and raced almost into the middle of the street to flag down a cab. The driver looked frightened.

"Ferry terminal, Battery Park."

It was a quick ride. She hurried through Battery Park toward the stainless-steel edifice and letters—Staten Island Ferry. As she walked up the incline, police with bomb-sniffing dogs were everywhere. Everyone entering the terminal was closely studied as they walked through the doors; yellow Labradors stood ready for duty and clusters of police stood watching.

Bright overhead letters indicated: Next Ferry: 6 minutes. Some people had just gotten off from work, dressed in their heath-care attire, others in uniforms and almost all checking their phone messages. The group was subdued, people alone with their thoughts and phones as they looked out to the water.

She stood, hands clasped, wondering. Last time she'd taken the ferry was to Roger's house. A vague recollection surfaced about it not being a long ride from St. George's Terminal and that she could see the harbor from the street.

The minutes counted down and then the doors opened. She followed the flow up the passenger ramp onto the ferry past thick, hoary braided ropes and chains that secured the ferry to the dock. The water was calm, the sky still hushed with morning colors. People sat around her, some slumped over with exhaustion, others leaning back to doze. It was a quiet time. A few young couples were still dressed in their Saturday night finery, falling asleep and leaning on each other for the thirty-minute ride. Police quickly walked through, checking everyone out before the ferry departed.

She felt the vessel pull away from the dock, and as it did, a million thoughts passed through her mind. Her heart started beating in her throat; she had a sick feeling. She kept flashing back to the crumpled ferry schedule just slightly under the chair. Pulling it out of her pocket, she looked at the times he had marked: midnight, 2:00 am, and 3:00 am. In his anger he must have thrown on his pants, letting the schedule slip out. How unlike Roger to be so careless.

Several cargo ships in the harbor were loaded with brightly colored containers. A barge steamed by, pushed by a tugboat. Hamilton Street. It rang a bell but also didn't. She'd get a cab there. The ferry ride was over after thirty minutes, the boat slowed and snugged up to the dock at St. George's Terminal. People were already huddled up to the doors, waiting for the final docking, eager to get out, get home and get to bed—to join their loved ones and lose the weariness of the night shift.

Once the doors opened, people surged in one motion. Paula

followed into a terminal that looked identical to the one in Manhattan. Her stomach fluttered. She didn't know which way to go, so she followed the crowd. They walked out to a long line of city busses parked by the curb. She had no idea what to do and doubled back into the terminal, asking a man sweeping the floor, "Excuse me, where can I catch a cab?" He pointed down a staircase without saying a word.

Paula raced down the stairs; a few cabs were parked by the curb. She made eye contact with the first driver.

"Hamilton Street." She gave him the address. He seemed displeased, probably too short of a ride to rack up any kind of fare. The cab drove around several one-way streets before turning down Hamilton. She looked at the address on the paper and then at the houses.

"Can't see no addresses, lady; can you?"

"No, but I know it's closer to the water," she said. "Keep going a bit."

He slowed as the street curved and started down a steep hill. The water was immediately visible.

"Here is good," she said. Looking at the red numbers on the meter, she gave him a ten. "Keep it. How hard is it to find my way back?"

He pointed toward the water. "Just follow down to the water, turn left on Richmond Terrace and go all the way; you'll see the signs. About an eight-minute walk."

"Thanks."

The houses were older but well kept, though nothing looked familiar except the harbor. She remembered the street being dumpier, but she also recalled Roger's conversation with someone at a dinner party about gentrification on Staten Island.

Paula spotted the address on Roger's house and stopped on the sidewalk to confirm. The house appeared to have new white siding, a new roof and no shutters. The lawn was tightly cropped, as if a crew had just finished raking and mowing. Knowing Roger, he'd probably contracted with a lawn-care service to keep from being in violation of city ordinances. Even still, bushes and weeds choked the foundation, too cluttered and unkempt looking compared with the surrounding houses. An eyesore the neighbors probably all wondered about.

Slowly, Paula walked up the front path, just shy of going up to the door. The windows were covered with cloth, not shades, blinds or drapes—just like he used to nail up old sheets to cover the windows in the brownstone.

She felt Roger's key ring in her jeans pocket and pulled it out. In her other hand she clutched the ferry schedule, the paper moist from her grip. She stuffed it back into her pocket.

A *New York Times* sat on the doorstep in a blue plastic bag. As she opened the screen door, the familiar smell of mold and mildew was overpowering. Like two months ago that tangy, pungent odor of the brownstone. She closed her eyes. "Oh no," she said as if praying. First she knocked and tried the doorbell but heard nothing inside.

Then she tried the first key. It didn't open. Neither did the second or third. "Shit." She backed away, let the screen door shut and stood thinking.

On the side of the house there was a door. She tried all three keys again, trying to peek inside past the cloth. As she worked her way around the whole house, each window was tightly sealed, offering no view inside.

Taking off her clog, she banged on the glass, trying to work up nerve enough to break it. Paula looked around again before hitting the glass harder. It cracked. When she hit it again, it finally broke, falling down inside somewhere. Knocking the rest of it out, she reached in near the doorknob and felt for a latch. She flipped the dead bolt and the door wiggled; she pushed, but it barely budged. The smell began to make her dizzy. She pulled off the pillowcase that had been nailed over the window and wrapped it around her hand. She knocked out the remaining glass, wondering if she could hoist herself up inside. Black plastic trash bags and boxes were in the way. She yanked them, pulling them outside, and as far as she could see there was a tangle of things up to the ceiling. She created a pile to stand on in front of the door, figuring if she could create a tall enough pile she could climb in.

Finally the pile was halfway up the door. Paula balanced on it, entering the broken window into a sea of trash. She fell, rolling through the bags, almost swimming through them. There was no way to stand or get a foothold in this ocean of stuff. Slowly she moved deeper into the house until she spotted a narrow path about six inches wide that led into the living room.

She passed through another room until she saw another narrow path, instantly spotting familiar objects from the brownstone. The rose-colored mohair couch she'd slept on for a decade turned up on its side, lined up with five or six other sofas. There were lamps, piles of journals, boxes of the mouse-eaten linen. As she climbed through tangles of boxes, broken chairs and furniture, barbeque grills and clothes, everything from the brownstone was there.

Then she saw it.

Roger's bed all set up. His bedroom re-created with stacks of astrophysics journals he'd used for a head- and footboard. Everything identically placed as it was in his old bedroom. Next to the bed was a freestanding metal clothes rack with all his clothes, everything he'd claimed the personal organizer had thrown out. The bedsheets looked fresh, his pillows crumpled into a familiar configuration of the way he slept.

The alarm clock sat on the table, a glass of water, the bottle with his blood pressure pills. Paula lifted the orange CVS bottle and looked; it had yesterday's date. Stacks of notepads scribbled with scientific equations and formulaic notes.

Her whole stomach and chest convulsed in one ache.

"Oh, Roger," she whispered. "Poor Roger." She began to hyperventilate and sat on the side of the bed, head hanging low, crushed with compassion. All the anger washed away in a second.

Poor, poor Roger. She thought of the brownstone. It was not his home either; it was not who he was or who he'd always been.

She phoned Heavenly.

"Where are you and how come you haven't answered your phone?" Celeste hollered.

"You wouldn't believe it. I-I found it. His stuff."

"On Staten Island?"

She nodded as if Heavenly could see. "He's got his bedroom here. He's been living here." Paula broke down and started to sob. "That's where he goes after I fall asleep; he comes here, Heav." She was hiccupping.

"Oh, *miksa,* I'm so sorry, honey. You want us to come get you?"

"No. We had a fight. I'm supposed to meet him for brunch. I'm gonna go."

She ended the call and sat there until she could no longer take the smell. Walking down the narrow path to the front door, she unlocked the dead bolt and yanked it open, crushing the boxes that were wedged behind it. She shut the door and left it unlocked.

Looking out at the blue of New York Harbor, Paula took several deep breaths to cleanse her lungs, though the smell was trapped in her clothes and nostrils.

Slowly she made her way back toward the dock. What the cab-driver called an eight-minute walk she stretched to twenty, pausing to sit on a bench and gain composure. She looked at her phone; there was plenty of time. Paula bunched up, grabbing her knees as she sobbed for Roger, for herself, for their life together, for everything she had ever hoped or thought it could be. For that young bride in her late thirties, so filled with hope and trust. She cried for that young woman and for what she had to go through to be the one she was today.

Slowly walking back to St. George's Terminal, she entered, walking past the police guards, the bomb-sniffing dogs. People glanced briefly at her. She wondered how she looked and whether she reeked of Roger's house.

Feeling sick, she headed to the bathroom. Mobs of teens were in there, fixing their hair, applying lipstick in the fingerprinted mirror, talking excitedly on the phone. Wet paper towels were on the floor. Paula found an open stall and bent over the toilet and vomited. The steel toilets had no seat, drops of urine, a discarded tampon applicator sitting on the back. She vomited again, her eyes becoming wet from the effort. She flushed, turned and tried to wedge her way between the girls who hadn't stopped talking, to the sink. She wet a paper towel under the faucet and wiped her eyes and mouth, trying to lose the smell of mildew.

It didn't take long for the ferry to load and leave. She'd found a seat and stared at the dirty glass windows, focusing on dried raindrops for the thirty minutes it took to land and dock. She was past thinking, feeling, and pulled the ferry schedule out of her pocket, glancing again at the pen marks Roger had made. As the vessel neared the pier, she studied the bulkheads, the antiquated system of docks and walkways that were still used in this maritime world she knew so little about.

People exited through the ferry doors. Paula followed them, figuring the breeze might help her feel less queasy. The wind blew a swatch of her hair in her eyes. As she reached to brush it away, the ferry schedule blew out of her hand and down into the water. She looked over the side, watching the floating paper as long as she could, until the crowd pushed her forward, forcing her up onto the dock.

Paula sat in Battery Park, not wanting to go back to the brownstone, waiting until it was time to meet Roger for brunch. She sat with her eyes closed, sporadically opening them to watch birds, pigeons, people pushing strollers and performance artists with painted faces.

She walked uptown and arrived at the restaurant a few minutes early. As usual Roger had already made a reservation. After being seated, Paula went to the ladies' room to wash her face with cold water. Her eyes were burning and her eyelids so swollen they wouldn't take makeup. She stared at her reflection in the mirror as if seeing someone else.

As she walked back to the table, Roger was there. He smiled when he saw her, but then his face shaded over once he saw she'd been crying.

He touched her hand. "I'm sorry for being such a prick."

He bent and kissed her on the cheek; she let him.

"I'm so sorry; please don't be so upset," he said.

But Paula couldn't speak.

"What's wrong?" he asked.

She motioned. "Ladies' room," was all she could eke out. She shouldered her purse.

A female attendant was now on duty. Inside the door was a "menstrual" couch, chairs with a table and lamp Paula had never noticed before. The woman attendant wore a gray uniform and smiled at her.

Paula stepped into a stall, latched the door and leaned against it, trying to gather her thoughts, her breath. Then she turned around and retched, though nothing came up but long strings of saliva. She propped herself up on the back wall, leaning over until she stopped shaking and trembling.

"You okay, miss?" the woman asked in a Dominican-accented voice, but Paula didn't answer.

She left the stall and stepped up to the sink. The woman handed her a paper cup with water.

With a trembling hand, Paula took a sip.

"Are you sure you're okay, miss?"

Paula didn't answer.

"Are you sick, miss?"

Paula shook her head.

"You want me to call someone?"

Paula shook her head no again.

The woman handed her a white hand towel; Paula held it under the cold water and then up to her eyes.

"Thank you." She took out her wallet and put a tip in the woman's basket.

Paula stepped out and saw Roger chatting with someone he knew at another table.

As she left the restaurant, she lifted her hand to hail a cab.

"La Guardia, please."

She took out her phone and called Eleni. "Mom?" She began to hiccup again, trying to hold it together.

"Paula *mou*, what's happened?"

"I'm coming home, Mom. I'll be back in Duluth as soon as I can catch a flight."

"Here's Rick; you can tell him."

"Hey, Paula."

"Hi. Oh God." She touched her chest. The sound of Rick's voice made her smile with relief. "It's so good to hear your voice."

"Yours too." He paused. "Everything okay?"

"I think so." She wiped her nose on her sleeve. "I'm coming back."

"Good," he answered quickly. "I was hoping you would."

"As soon as I can catch a flight."

"Text me your flight info. Eleni and I'll meet you in Duluth."

The cab dropped her off on the departure deck. She walked over to the Delta airline sales.

"One-way to Duluth, Minnesota."

"For today?"

Paula nodded and pulled out her wallet, handing over her debit card to the flight attendant. She couldn't stop tears from rolling out of her eyes in thick drops. The information was processed and the young man handed her a boarding pass.

"You got the last seat on the two pm flight," he explained. "Check-in time is at one fifteen pm, so you've got a little time. Change planes in Minneapolis. Will you be checking any bags, ma'am?"

"No." Paula looked down at her feet. "No bags to check."

ACKNOWLEDGMENTS

I'd like to thank Marge Gibson and the staff of Raptor Education Group, Inc., in Antigo, Wisconsin, who one snowy day in late December 2010 responded to a phone call from a stranger and granted us a full tour of her facility, as well as cooked and served us lunch. Marge introduced me to my first-ever eagle, owl, turkey vulture and many other raptors and other birds. Her generosity with this visit cannot be overstated nor can I thank her enough. The work they do at REGI is both unparalleled and amazing, and my heart and admiration go out to wildlife rehabilitators and rescuers everywhere. They are special beings who do special work. I would also like to thank Marlene Stringer, who is an amazing agent, for her levelheaded-sane interjection and sensitivity that are needed at times in the writing process. And also thanks to Stephanie Flanders, who is ever supportive and talented and whom I trust implicitly with my words and ideas. To my faithful "boots on the ground" beta readers, Nell Thalasinos and Karen McGovern, to whom I'm never ashamed or embarrassed to show anything, no matter how rough or bad. And to my family, who is always with me. And also to Ron Kuka, University of Wisconsin Creative Writing Program, for his unwavering support and encouragement through this process. And last, to all of the early Greek emigrants who left behind the land they loved in order to create a better life for the rest of us. Thank you for your sacrifice. Your steadfastness beats in the hearts of your grandchildren and will live on in all generations to come.